BLESSING
OF
LUNA

BLAISE RAMSAY

Black Rose Writing | Texas

ISBN: 978-1-68433-549-7
PUBLISHED BY BLACK ROSE WRITING
www.blackrosewriting.com

Printed in the United States of America
Suggested Retail Price (SRP) $19.95

Blessing of Luna is printed in Calluna

*As a planet-friendly publisher, Black Rose Writing does its best to eliminate unnecessary waste to reduce paper usage and energy costs, while never compromising the reading experience. As a result, the final word count vs. page count may not meet common expectations.

Cover illustration by Alisha Moore © 2018 Damonza

To the girl who thought she was a black cat.

I knew you could do it.

To Alisha Fisher, an amazing author and inspiration.

To my family for all those times I screamed, whined, moaned and complained. Thank you for putting up with me.

BLESSING
OF
LUNA

In the beginning, we were all that was
The darkness of the night lonely and quiet
How we longed to hear songs of praise
So, we gave a gift to our children
The ability to change into the beautiful hunters of the night
For centuries, we heard their songs of reverence
Reveled in their worship
But it was not to last
The dark one's jealousy burned with a fiery hate
His shadow descended upon our sons and daughters
The greed and jealousy of man drew him to them
His fangs piercing the veins of a mortal
Promising eternal beauty
Freedom from death
If man would do but one thing for him
Shed the blood of our children
Songs became screams of agony
Mothers begging for the lives of their pups
Fathers, husbands cursing the skies for the loss of their families
Their blood staining the earth
It broke our hearts to see them fall
The Night Father begged the Light for her aid
She reached out her hand, cursing the dark ones to fear the sun
Shadow melted to light with the arrival of the Paladins
Their origins unknown
But we were grateful
An uneasy peace began to reign
The dark one's bloodlust had been halted
It was not to last
The darkness was set free
Above the ashes of the bloodshed rose a daughter
Cursed by darkness
She was, yet was not our child
Wolf, yet not wolf
Yet, in her suffering
She sang our song of praise
So, my blessing, I gave to her

CHAPTER ONE

The morning was like any other in Montana during the cool shift from the end of the summer to fall. The forests got misty with the dampness of the rains holding themselves back due to the scorching summer sun responsible for raising the temperature to a sultry high 80s.

Jillian stood in the branches of a high pine tree, her advanced senses tuning into the cries of birds nesting in the trees and squirrels hustling to store food for the winter. Somewhere in the distance, soft calls of fishing loons joined in nature's musical ensemble, calming her mind from the raging torrent of memories. They always served as painful reminders of how it long it'd been since she heard the soft song of his soul.

The doubt and hopelessness got so strong, she finally stopped searching and settled down. She thought he had forgotten his promise to keep returning to her until peace could reign between the warring races.

Angry and frustrated, Jillian scaled down the tree, shifting mid-fall into her larger wolf form to go for a run in order to relieve some lingering stress.

The wind felt cool in her obsidian fur as she ran through the woods, her large paws padding amidst the wet leaves on the forest floor. Those still clinging to the trees above her rustled with each brisk fall breeze.

She slowed to a stop short of the winding road leading to the town of Big Timber.

Jill came to learn many of the inhabitants were her own kind, just living among humans as best they could in the shadow of the vampire coven hidden in the mountains.

It was ruled over by the very lord responsible for reigniting the flames of the Blood Wars by killing the man Jill loved countless times throughout the centuries.

She thought many times about seeing how strong the curse of immortality he asked the dark god to place on her was.

Dreams of charging into the mansion and killing every parasite she found until her fangs found the throat of the monster responsible for all of her pain played repeatedly in her mind.

Bones snapped, her muscles rippled, tendons stretched and popped back into place as she shifted back into her human form. The process would sound painful to someone who hadn't gotten to experience it firsthand. To Jill and her kind, the change was pure ecstasy.

Reaching into the hollow of a tree, Jill took the fresh change of clothing she packed in her backpack and covered her naked form. The idea of hiding her body was still a foreign concept to her despite how long she'd lived among humans.

To her people, the body was something to be appreciated, admired and respected. Being naked in front of each other or making out were both matters of needing companionship.

None of her kind forced themselves on one another. Courting and mating was something romantic. One might even say erotic and taken as slow as either party wished.

Humans. Jill thought to herself, laughing as she rolled her eyes. *Making everything complicated since the Neolithic times.*

She was jerked out of her thoughts when the roar of large truck engine rang out across the trees, drawing her attention to road. It was a moving van with a black truck chained to a trailer attached to the towing ball driving towards the city limits.

It made Jill curious because she'd seen more people leaving Big Timber in search of bigger city life with promises of rich employment. Not many moved into the smaller town where life had a rhythm and each day was similar to the one before.

Though she wasn't quite sure why, she decided to follow the large vehicle. She sprinted through the trees and back alleys until she came upon an old, abandoned Victorian house.

It lay resting at the base of a hill overlooking the town. The many attempts by the owner to find it a new tenant often ended in failure, leaving it empty.

Jill thought it was sad since she'd always seen it as quite beautiful to look at.

Its faded blue paint had begun chipping from the wood siding. A covered porch wrapped around the structure, ending just before the back door.

The whole house sat back in a small patch of trees connected to the main road by a long gravel driveway.

It was so large, she'd debated asking Gabriel and Kain to buy it to serve as a second living quarters for their packs in order to keep them closer to each other.

The large basement could easily be converted into a spare room. A yard big enough where the pups could run and play together lie separated by a chain-link fence into two sections.

The back side of the house just beyond the yard had a piece of land which could be converted into a garden. Plenty of room would remain to put a socializing area.

When the van ground to a stop in front of it, Jill hid herself in the thick brush on the side of the house and watched as the passenger side door opened to reveal an older man with ash gray hair.

He didn't look too bad for an older male. Almost attractive. If he were one of Jill's kind, he would most likely be an elder and a desire for most of the older females. Maybe even a few of the young ones as well, since it appeared he kept himself in shape.

The driver's side door opened with a loud creak, stinging Jill's sensitive ears. The gravel crunched as the driver dropped down the height of the truck.

At first Jill could only see the black leather work boots with chains held on studs that crawled around the heels covered by tattered jeans almost dragging the ground.

Trying to get a better view, she craned her neck only to duck back down behind the brush to avoid being seen.

A younger man with messy, dark hair wearing a tight black V-neck t-shirt, walked down the side of the truck to the trailer. The black jeans he wore hugged his gorgeous legs and ass in all the right places.

A black studded belt with a chain running from his hip to his mid-lower back ran through his belt loops. Black sunglasses shielded his eyes against the faint light of the sun peeking through the cloud cover.

He took off his sunglasses revealing two amethyst eyes so radiant; they hypnotized Jill and drew a heat of blush over her cheeks.

Moving closer, she was able to catch the faint hint of his scent on the wind. Her nostrils filled with the rich, dark mix of his scent. Jill's eyes closed as the intoxicating aroma teased her carnal senses.

Then she heard it. The soft melody of his soul captured her attention, making her heart stall. It was faint, but she could hear it as plain as if the moon herself were singing to her.

The blood in Jill's veins heated with overwhelming happiness, making fighting back the tears difficult as relief joined disbelief in her heart. *I found you. Thank Luna, finally I found you.*

Lucius Wolfe had been gone so long. Yet here he stood before her in a body more beautiful than any she had ever seen during all the years of searching for him.

Sneaking even closer, she scaled a pine to continue her surveillance; her heightened senses allowed her to see and hear what they were saying. She wanted to know more about this man so much she'd almost let her guard down. The temporary lapse in judgement nearly wound up with her accidentally getting seen.

"Unload the truck off of the trailer, Dame. I'll work on narrowing down the number of boxes and furniture so we have clothes to wear and a bed to sleep on." The older man grunted as he lifted a box, ready to take it into the old house.

"Got it, pops." The reply sent shivers up Jill's spine.

He lowered the ramps of the trailer and proceeded to unlatch the chains holding the wheels in place. "Damn, it's muggy and cold as hell out here. I thought it was summer."

Slipping a jacket over his broad shoulders, the man stopped to look around as if he felt someone watching him. When he didn't see anyone, he shrugged, jumping into the cab.

The truck's engine roared to life and started backing slowly off of the ramp.

As morning dwindled into late afternoon, Jill jumped from her hiding place behind the thick brush surrounding the house to the tall tree branches so she could continue watching.

Her curiosity became even more peaked when the twilight hours of the evening cast a magical array of light across the mountainsides.

The younger man came out with what looked like a camera to take pictures of the surrounding scenery. "What a view. I'd almost forgotten the majesty of this place. It has an otherworldly feeling to it at times like this." He said as he took in the breathtaking view, positioning his camera to get the perfect shots.

Jill was so enthralled by him she hadn't been careful to avoid stepping around the house onto a rather loud twig.

Damn.

The man's attention shifted to the direction of the noise. "Is someone there?"

Quickly, Jill used the hunger in her belly as an excuse to get away, deciding she would come back later.

Jillian returned later in the evening after her nightly hunt to find the light in the upstairs room still on. She scaled the tree closest to the side of the house where the window was.

As fate would have it, it was the young man's room. The tree provided the perfect venue for her to observe him and learn a bit more about his life.

He must've showered because his hair still dripped with remnants of water. Toned, sculpted pectoral and stomach muscles glistened from the moisture remaining after drying himself.

Everything about him was breathtaking. He was dressed in loose athletic shorts just low enough on his hips, Jill could see the dips where the bones began leading down into those perfect muscular legs. The tuft of hair leading down below his shorts made her body quiver.

He was different, yet similar in this body. Eyes the color of amethyst shone line jewels. His skin light with a hint of the sun's kiss. On his right shoulder was the tattoo of a tribal rose, his hair dark as the night sky when the moon chose to hide her face.

The muscles in his back were so developed, they would make any woman weak in the knees to be with him.

When the light went off, Jill used her sensitive hearing to tune into the softness of his breathing.

Easing to the edge of the branch, Jill tested the old windows held closed by a single, golden latch easily opened with something flat such as a knife blade or the claws of a lycan.

She extended her nail and slid it between the small crack in the window panes, opening the windows, landing silently on the wood floor.

Leaning over him, she breathed deeply through her nose, taking in the same scent of rich, dark musk mixed with subtle hints of cedar and pine. *It is you. It's been so long.*

Jill would have to wait until he woke up to see if he recognized her as he did with each rebirth. For this moment, none of it mattered to her. She'd waited for thousand years alone, watching history drift by like water over rocks. After all this time, she'd finally found the soul of the man she loved.

Curiosity drove Jill to look around his room to try to find some clue to what his name was in this new life.

The search was made difficult due to everything still being in boxes all labeled "Son's room."

One of them was open, revealing stacks of books and a photo of a woman. Her dark brown hair and soft smile made Jill happy and sad at the same time. She hadn't seen her come in with them.

Still nothing gave her his name.

What is your name, handsome? Jill thought to herself as she continued looking around. *Okay, this is frustrating.* She dropped to sit beside his bed.

The sounds of the morning birds made her curse the dawn. The light of day often served as a relief from the threats of the darkness for Jill and her people. However, this time, it was a source of frustration.

"We will meet again soon." Jill whispered and jumped out of the window into the breaking dawn.

As soon as the sun's rays came through his window, Damien jerked up in his bed, his breath heavy and quick as he looked around the room only to find he was still alone.

Nothing had been disturbed.

"Had to be a dream," he told himself aloud.

The cool breeze coming through his window confused him since he was certain he'd closed it the night before.

A knock on the door made him jump.

"C'mon Dame, don't want to miss your college orientation, do you?" Charlie, Damien's dad, and the new police chief called.

"Yeah. Give me a few," Damien replied, agitated. He got up from his bed, opening his drawers to pull out a pair of jeans and a black shirt.

A red plaid over shirt hung on his headboard. He took it and put it on, leaving it hanging open and rolling up the sleeves to his elbows.

The backpack with his sunglasses, wallet, cell phone, laptop and notebooks sat at the foot of his bed.

Damien moved fast to put his boots on and grabbed it, stopping by the box with the books and the photo of his foster mom, Sarah.

"Morning mom," he said with a sad smile as he put the photo on the night stand before racing down the stairs.

Damien got himself a cup of coffee and sat down at the table for breakfast.

"Busy day?" he asked, attempting to start a conversation.

"Honestly, I'm not too sure." Charlie spoke up from behind the paper he was reading, sipping his coffee.

Damien ran his hand through his hair, leaning back in the chair. "Do you still think about mom?"

The suddenness of the question caught Charlie off guard. "There isn't a day that goes by when I don't think about her," he replied. "I see her in my dreams as she was before she contracted her horrible sickness."

Damien hesitated in asking his next question, wondering if it may make him sound crazy. "Ever feel like she's still here?"

"Oh yeah. In my own dreams, I still see myself pushing her in her favorite backyard swing she used to love. It was before you came into our lives. She was never happier than the day we adopted you, Dame."

Charlie's eyes grew misty as he looked out the window at the old wooden swing hanging from the large tree shading the back yard. Their daughter, Bree, hadn't been too happy about their choice to bring Damien into their home. To Charlie, it was still one of the happiest moments since he finally had a son.

Damien's foster mom passed away from spinal meningitis when he turned sixteen. It was devastating to the family because it happened only a year after the accident, which led them to get Damien out of Big Timber as fast as they could. The pain was so great, Damien closed himself off from everyone, including his dad.

They weren't his real parents but, they loved him as if he were their own child. Their love and understanding helped in the healing of a wound inflicted by his biological mom.

The conversation died as many of them did. Charlie broke the silence by getting up to grab his jacket and truck keys. "We better get going. I'll need the truck for work. Mind asking Rob or Chelsea to bring you home? I should get a cruiser today so you can have the truck."

"Yeah, I can ask Rob for a lift. Thanks."

Robert McAllister, one of Damien's two remaining friends, still lived in Big Timber after Damien moved. Chelsea Masterson was the second. She was one of the most flirtatious girls in town and harbored a not so secret crush on Damien.

Following Sarah's death, Charlie brought Damien back so he could recover in familiar surroundings as suggested by the therapist.

When an opportunity opened for Charlie to become the new police chief, Charlie took the position despite Damien's many objections.

Damien jumped out of the passenger's side of the truck, closing the door after they arrived at the college. The front lawn bustled with new students joining the transfers to head for the auditorium.

"Dame."

Damien turned back around. "Yeah?"

"I love you, son. Things will get better, I promise."

Damien nodded. He wasn't reassured by his dad's words but he was grateful he was at least trying. The thought made Damien angry at himself. He'd detached from everything and just wasn't capable of being more receptive.

After Charlie pulled off, Damien turned to walk up to the auditorium. He paused to look around until his attention fell on a young woman with long raven hair sitting on the cement wall serving as a barrier between the grassy knoll and the sidewalk. His heart pounded behind his ribs at how beautiful she was. He kept staring as she rose from her sitting position to make her way towards the library.

She wore a black shirt cut so low he could almost see the tops of her breasts layered under a deep green shirt with the sleeves rolled up to her elbows. She wore low-riding black nylon pants, much like something a barista at a coffee shop would wear. The black leather boots came up her to calves and tied in the back with leather laces.

The way she walked was so lithe and graceful. The movement of her hips reminded him of a dancer.

Damien swallowed the knot in his throat so he could keep breathing. He couldn't help it, his jaw almost hit the ground. His head started to hurt, hitting him with a sudden wave of dizziness. His heart pounded hard.

What? What's going on? There was something oddly familiar about the woman. He couldn't understand where he'd seen her before.

Once the episode passed, he began to stand slowly when Chelsea ran into him at full speed. The impact threatened to take them both down, if not for Damien's quick thinking to grip the armrest of the bench.

"Damien!" Chelsea wrapped her arms around his neck. "It's so good to see you! How long has it been? Ten years?"

Chelsea was a bouncy blonde who only came up to Damien's chest. She'd once been a cheerleader when they were in high school.

Her crush on Damien had been common knowledge. She often bashed anyone who dared to try to ask him out with fierce gossip or rumors. Her deep blue eyes and large breasts made most of the football players in the school chase after her. The encounters wouldn't end well, and she'd often shoot them down in ways that made even Damien's masculinity ache.

"Yeah. It's good to see you again too, Chels." Damien replied, looking down then up again, hoping to see the raven haired woman. His eyes scanned every face to see if he could find her but she was gone "Where'd she go?"

Chelsea turned her head to follow Damien's gaze, her lips pursed in annoyance. "She? Dame, do you have a girlfriend?"

"What? No, it's not like that." He ignored the look of relief on her face, prying her arms from around his neck. "I just thought I saw someone I knew. I have no idea how, but she seemed familiar to me."

"Maybe she goes to school here. You might see her again or even have a class with her. Come on or we'll be late!" Chelsea took his hand and pulled so hard Damien stumbled forward.

Deep inside him, he hoped and wanted to see the raven-haired woman again.

Jillian stood behind a tree, ignoring the glances and cat calls of the passersby. A low growl escaped her throat.

She'd had him. So close to tempting him to come to her only to have his attention ripped away.

Another young man came up to stand next to her. From the looks of him, he was about to lay yet another corny pick up line on her.

Annoyed, Jill snapped at him, her voice low. She didn't bother to change her closed off posture or make eye contact. "Before you talk, I'm not interested."

The young man backed away from her. He ran as fast as he could, calling her a cold bitch over his shoulder. Had Jill wanted to, she could have caught up to him and beat the crap out of him.

She was frustrated, but at least she'd come to know the name of the target of her curiosity. Her only comfort from the disappointment of her failure.

Damien. Your name...is Damien. Her eyes glowed almost silver. *How appropriate.* She smiled a fanged smirk.

CHAPTER TWO

M an, do I hate orientations. They always act like we don't know anything about how school works. Like none of us have ever been in public school for twelve years. It's almost insulting." Rob said with an air of annoyance, while stretching his arms above his head. He'd run into Damien and Chelsea in the auditorium following the orientation.

Damien was too distracted by the woman he saw earlier to respond. She was almost too beautiful, flawless, like an angel one might see at the top of a Christmas tree or in a painting on the ceiling of the Sistine Chapel.

"Dame, you alright, bro?"

The snapping of Rob's fingers in Damien's face brought him back to reality. "Yeah, sorry Rob. I was just thinking about something."

Rob shrugged. "Nice to know you still space out on us, D. I swear man, where do you go in these crazy trances of yours?"

Damien ignored him. There was still a lot on his mind that he was trying to sort through. Everyone around him didn't seem to recognize him as the one they'd once slapped the label of town freak show on. However, he couldn't help the feeling he still didn't belong.

His friends and family loved him, but deep inside, there was still a void. Almost like he was missing a crucial part of himself. The sensation made him feel alone, even in a crowded room.

"Hey, mind if I get a lift home? My old man took the truck."

"Sure, bro. Want to get a burger like old times on the way?"

"Yeah, sounds good."

Once they made it back to Damien's house, Rob asked if he wanted to go hiking over the weekend like they used to in their scout days.

Damien agreed, looking forward to getting a few photographs for his portfolio. He'd taken up photography after his accident. The trauma made him realize collecting memories was more important than going to the skate park to see how many bones he could break.

"Cool! I'll bring my old man's poles. You still remember how to pier fish?"

How could I forget? Damien thought, remembering the times he and his father went pier fishing on the weekend for the family fish fry. His mom would fry and batter the fish and lay them on platters right next to his grandma's homemade Cajun hushpuppies.

He could still remember the sweet smell as it mixed with Cajun spices. The whole kitchen smelled of batter and peach cobbler. The memory was both comforting and upsetting.

"D, my bad man. We can do something else if it makes you feel more comfortable." Rob said, his voice tense as he waited for Damien to reply.

Damien chuckled. "It's fine, Rob. Yeah, I'd love to go. Saturday at the crack of dawn, as usual?"

"Stop off at old Bill's for sodas, bait and jerky? Hell, yeah." Rob held out his fist, earning him a fist bump.

Old Bill Hutchinson smoked his own jerky for his shop and smokehouse in his backyard in homemade smokers crafted from old kettle grills.

"Sounds good. See you Saturday."

"Yep, see ya then!"

It was after moonrise when Jillian arrived back at Damien's house. She watched as he paced his room without a shirt on, reading a book. His perfect hips swaying side to side with each step.

When the light went off, Jill snuck into Damien's bedroom through his window. Her heart stopped for a brief moment the instant the smell of him mingling with cologne and aftershave hit her nostrils.

Damien turned over, freezing Jill in her place when her icy green eyes were met with gorgeous amethyst pools half-drunk with sleep.

He blinked a couple of times before raising up to look her in the face. "You. It is you."

Jill didn't know what to do. She never expected him to actually catch her. Would he be mad at her? Think she was a creepy stalker?

Her heart beat raced, her hand brushing her dark hair away from her face. "Yes. It's me. It's nice to see you face to face, Damien."

"Who are you?" Damien asked, both curious and slightly annoyed. He'd begun feeling he'd only imagined this woman until now. "How often do you come by my house?"

Jill was dumbfounded, feeling a bit bad because she hadn't tried harder to meet him in person until this moment.

"I've come by almost every night since you moved here," She replied. Her words caught in her throat as she analyzed the features of his face.

"This isn't usually like me, I must admit. It just seemed like every time I tried to meet with you, something happened. This was the only time I knew of that we could be alone." She could feel the heat rolling over her cheeks.

For the first time in her immortal life, Jill felt like a teenager who'd gotten caught drinking or sneaking back into the house after curfew. She had no idea what to say.

"If we're being honest, this is creepy as hell. I wish you would have approached me before nearly giving me a heart attack. So, how about we start over? I'm Damien Pierce. What's your name?" Damien extended his hand to shake hers.

"Jillian. Jillian Styles. It's nice to formally meet you." She shook his hand, trying to hide the smallest hint of the shock she was feeling.

Lucius had never not recognized her in any of his reincarnations throughout the centuries. She wanted to find out why if she could in the future.

For now, she decided to be grateful the deception had ended and she was finally able to meet Damien without having to hide.

The rest of the night was spent with the two of them talking as if they were old friends. Unknown to Damien, Jill actually did know at least a part of him for most of her life.

She was so enthralled in the stories she was being told about the different reckless things Damien did in his young life, she nearly forgot she'd been concerned about meeting him.

As the night waned, Damien began getting tired. He passed out, leaving Jill alone to focus on the blazing question in her mind. *Why? Why did he not recognize me?*

She rose from her spot on the floor, heading towards the window. Her hand rested on the window pane as she turned to look at Damien over her shoulder.

I don't know what's going on, but honestly, I'm not sure I really care either. The beginnings of an emotion she didn't think she would be able to feel again grew inside of her. *Maybe it's time to let the ghosts of the past lay to rest.*

The next morning Damien woke up scanning his room. To his surprise, it didn't really bother him to learn Jill had come to his house almost every night. Something about her made him feel like he wasn't as alone as around normal people.

I know her. I don't know how, but...it's like I know her from somewhere. He scratched his head, grabbing a t-shirt and heading downstairs to breakfast.

Charlie sat at the table reading the daily paper when Damien arrived. "Well good morning, you're up early. That's not like you."

Damien finished getting his coffee. He knew he couldn't tell his dad about the beautiful woman who snuck in through his window. He did the only thing he could. He lied.

"Couldn't sleep anymore. Too many things running through my mind." Damien sat down at the table, taking a sip of his coffee. He was so exhausted he had to close his eyes against the dizziness of the fatigue.

"Something wrong?" Charlie inquired.

Damien rested his head against the heels of his palms on the table, his stomach full of rocks at the growing unease inside of him. It was obvious his father wasn't buying the lies.

"Alright. I won't pry. Just know I'm here if you want to talk about it. Otherwise, you're a grown man now. I'll respect your privacy." Charlie replied.

"Appreciate it." A feeling of guilt ached in Damien's chest. Once again he was deflecting his dad despite all he'd done for him. He leaned back in the chair to stare at the ceiling. "Sorry, dad. I know I'm messed up. I'm not sure how to go about fixing what's wrong with me."

Charlie's hand landed hard on his son's shoulder. "Don't worry about it. You've been through a lot. There's no reason to force anything. One day, you'll come around and we can talk like we used to. Until then, I'm not going anywhere. Why don't you go out with Chels today to get your mind off of things?"

Damien gave a short wave and nod of his chin to his father. "Okay. Have a good one."

"You too, Dame." Charlie grabbed his keys and jacket, closing the door.

Jill watched from one of the cast iron benches on the other side of the street, flustered as the one called Chelsea walked arm in arm with Damien.

She couldn't hold back a proud smirk at the look of disdain on Damien's face as Chelsea bounced around him. The look in her eyes flirting as she showed him each of the window displays in hopes of getting him to focus on her.

Following the night they spent talking, Jill made the decision not to really care if Damien truly was Lucius' reincarnation. She was going to pursue and eventually court him as her own.

The two of them went into a cafe for lunch, sitting down outside in the cool breeze of the day.

Jill waited until Chelsea left to go inside the cafe before she made her move.

Damien sat at the table reading. He read a lot from the many times Jill had watched him. She couldn't blame him. Books were a good escape from reality and had often been her own source of sanity throughout the centuries.

"Hi there," Jill said, sitting down.

She'd chosen to wear some of the most provocative clothing she could find, eventually settling on a light blue shirt with sleeves cut so they rested on her shoulders. Tight blue jeans and black boots with zippers on the side completed the outfit.

Damien lowered his book. "Jill. I was wondering when I was going to get to see you again. You look nice."

"Thanks. You don't look too bad yourself." Jill replied. She scooted her chair closer to him, putting one hand casually on his knee.

"What are you reading?" she asked, her voice smooth and seductive.

"It's a horror novel," Damien replied, swallowing hard as he tried to keep his mind focused. "I've read pretty much every title by this author. He's one of my favorites."

Jill chuckled at the internal struggle she could see going on inside of him. The trembling beneath her hand indicated he was interested. "Funny enough, he's one of mine too. The creepy clown and the dead animal books are two of my favorites."

"Really? Those are my favorites. The clown creeped the hell out of me but I got so into the story, I couldn't put the book down until I finished it. You like to read?" Damien's excitement flashed across his face, the tension leaving him the more he spoke.

"For a good part of my life, that's all there was to do. I never really got into the technology crowd until getting a cellphone became essential to my day job." Jill took out her phone, showing it to Damien. "Silly thing is still smarter than me."

Damien turned his head away, almost embarrassed at what he was about to ask. "So, your...your number? Could I have it?"

Of course. Jill thought to herself, her heart pounding with relief.

She held out her hand. "May I borrow one of your napkins on the table and a pen? I'll be happy to give you my number."

Once, the pen and napkin were placed in her hand, she wrote down her number. "Feel free to call or text anytime. For you, I'll answer even if I'm working." She handed them back, winking.

The scent of Chelsea on the wind signaled Jill to start cutting things short.

Jill ran her fingertips down Damien's jaw. "I look forward to hearing from you."

"Here, Dame!" Chelsea's voice rang out as she set down their drinks.

Damien tucked the napkin with Jill's number in his back pocket, his cheeks hot from the gentle touch of her nails. He looked up to see Chelsea's smiling wide.

"Wait. What?" Damien stood up, scanning the surrounding crowd for where Jill could have gone. He almost felt disappointed. The lingering feeling of her warm hand on his leg left him running his own along the path hers followed.

Jill stood on the opposite corner of the café, watching as Damien scanned around briefly for her only to sink back into his chair.

It hurt her to have to run from him, especially since it seemed as though he was getting comfortable the more they spoke but she didn't want to risk meeting Chelsea.

Oh well, he has my number. He'll call. She smirked to herself as her phone buzzed in her pocket.

"Well that was sooner than I expected." Jill took it out of her pocket, reading the text. It was indeed Damien asking where she had gone off to in such a hurry. She responded telling him not to worry. They would be seeing each other soon enough.

Damien's foot tapped in anticipation on the wood floor, his knee knocking against the bedside. He couldn't concentrate on the textbook sitting in his lap. His eyes kept glancing at the clock. 3am.

Disappointment started to manifest until Jill dropped onto the windowsill. He hurried to open the panes to let her in.

"I was beginning to wonder if you were going to come," Damien said, his voice betraying the fatigue he suffered.

"Sorry for being late. One of the clients from my job had me doing some early hour surveillance. You look exhausted. I can come back tomorrow or meet somewhere if you like instead."

Jill sat down on Damien's bedside, picking up the textbook off of the floor. "Doing some late night studying?

Damien stretched his arms above his head, his back popping against the uncomfortable way he was sitting. "Yeah. I have a couple of exams tomorrow for my summer classes. One right after the other. I took college classes before but damn I don't remember them being this demanding."

A chuckle left her throat as Jill turned the bedside lamp off. "Get some sleep tonight. Tomorrow is one of my days off so we can do something in the evening if you want."

"Jill."

"Yes?"

"I hope this doesn't sound weird but...have we met before? I can't shake the feeling I know you."

A knot formed in the base of Jill's throat. She wanted to answer him truthfully but knew she couldn't. It was too soon in their relationship to let him know the deeper, darker world he was getting into.

"I don't think so but it doesn't matter. We've met each other now. Have a good night, Damien. Good luck on those pesky tests." Jill teased.

Damien rolled his eyes. "Thanks."

After leaving, Jill stood outside of the house looking up at Damien's window. He needed to sleep to fulfill his obligations to his school, ending their night early.

Conflicting thoughts of logic met raging emotions as she weighed the options of pursuing or letting him go. Exposing him to her world would put him in severe danger.

I don't want this life for you but I can't help how I'm feeling. Dear Luna, am I doing the right thing?

The following morning, Damien's head hurt. The double life he was living was starting to wear on him mentally and physically. There were so many questions buzzing in his mind he wanted to ask Jill but he didn't want to seem rude.

She was beautiful. The kind of woman any man would give his left nut to be with. There was just something about her.

Something inhuman.

Just like him.

Despite his denial to the contrary, Damien found himself developing feelings for Jill. She felt right to be around. A comfortable presence who seemed to understand him.

He wanted to tell her what happened in his past. He wanted to share his secrets with her. Somehow he knew she wouldn't judge him.

Their exchange at the cafe was limited to brief small talk and then she'd run once Chelsea came back. The touch of her hand on his leg hadn't left him since the café like it had been imprinted on his skin.

Night after night, even sometimes during the day, Damien found himself wanting to see her.

What's wrong with me? I didn't even think I could feel things like this anymore. The feeling of aggravation rose in his chest as he rubbed his face, brushing his fingers up through his hair to try and get a grip on his raging feelings.

"D, hey!" Rob snapped his fingers in front of Damien's face. "You still having those headaches?"

"Yeah, they've been pretty much a constant. I hadn't been sleeping well either," Sarcastically, he added. "Think I'm being haunted or something."

Damien ran his hand down his face to the back of his neck. His double life seemed more insane the longer he'd even allowed himself to think about it. Something straight out of Supernatural.

There was no way he could hope to explain it to Rob or Chelsea. Hell, he didn't fully understand it himself.

Using Rob's love of the creepy and paranormal seemed like a good way to distract him from probing.

"Nah, you know me, D. I'm not one to put anything past the supernatural. Remember when we were kids? We debated on becoming a cryptozoology team. Investigating the mysteries unknown to humanity." Rob put his arm around Damien's neck, his other outstretched and moving across the sky. His voice slowing to match the pace and tone of Rod Sterling from the Twilight Zone.

Chelsea smacked Rob's arm. "Come on, Rob. You were the only one who wanted to go through with that nonsense. Damien and I wanted nothing to do with it." She turned her focus on Damien. "Tell us about this mystery woman you keep seeing?" Chelsea didn't have to try to hide the disgust in her voice.

"Mystery woman? Wow, D, you're seeing someone? Really?"

It was no mystery that Damien was attractive. However, he never really asked anyone out and was quick to shut down any woman who tried.

Damien sighed. He knew anything he said regarding Jill would make him look more like he needed a strait jacket.

"She's not really so much a mystery anymore. I learned her name when she sat with me while we were getting lunch Chels. It was only for about five minutes and then she disappeared when I looked away. Up until then, I'd only seen her around campus."

There was no way he was telling either of them the truth. Rob would probably make some dumb, "princess in the castle" joke which would make Damien have to slug him to protect his own pride.

"Dame was spaced out by her when I ran into him on campus. She vanished then too. I never saw her." Chelsea said as she filed her nails, the sharp tone of disappointment in her words.

"Damn, seems like you've got a stalker. Maybe a spirit from the sound of it." He leaned in close. "Hate to mention it bro, but do you think it could just be the old southern border overreacting? Maybe your woman-deprived imagination creating the perfect woman for your fantasies?"

"I'm pretty sure that's the furthest from what it is. Believe it or not, I don't honestly run to the idea of getting into a woman's pants, you pervert. There is such a thing as dating and getting to know the other person first." Damien wasn't the sleeping around type. His biological mother made sure of it when he was growing up before Charlie and Sarah saved him.

"Yeah Rob, Damien's not a man-whore. He's into girls with more class and dignity." Chelsea flipped her blonde hair, raising her nose in the air.

Damien and Rob looked at each other than back at her, both confused to learn Chelsea considered herself classy or dignified.

They'd known her since she was nine. If a guy looked good, Chelsea was flirting with him, often earning jeers from her classmates. Most of the time her escapades had been attempts at making Damien jealous. It never really worked.

"Hey, what if we go bowling? It'll get your mind off of your spirit woman and give us some time to catch up since you've been gone, Dame." Chelsea offered and leaned into Damien's chest, wrapping his arms around her.

"Yeah! Sounds fun! D, you in? I remember you used to bowl some killer games."

Damien ignored Chelsea's antics, looking around him. His mind ventured off into thoughts of where Jill could be.

A sharp elbow to his ribs brought his attention back to the moment. "Yeah, sure. I hadn't gotten to school you in a good game of bowling in a long time, Rob." Damien unlatched Chelsea to put Rob in a playful headlock.

The bowling alley was all decked out in its Halloween décor. A giant grim reaper with a dark, creepy voice stood sentry at the front, spooking the children and making them jump as they walked up to the sliding doors.

Their parents had to calm them down before they even entered. Some even ran into the parking lot forcing their parents to keep them from getting run over by the cars entering and leaving.

The walls had paint capable of glowing green when hit by the black-lights every hour accompanied by a Halloween dance tune.

Rubber bats hung from the ceiling and paper pumpkins decorated every table.

Chelsea jumped, squeaking when she went to get her ball and saw a rubber rat staring back at her, taking the opportunity to run into Damien's arms.

"Strike!" Damien pumped his fist in victory.

"Damn, D, I'll never figure out how you do that. It's creepy as hell. Almost like you're a pin whisperer or something." Rob's mouth was agape in amazement. "Alright, my turn. Watch and learn, sisters." He rolled the ball, knocking down all of the pins save for two on opposite sides of the box.

"Oof, vampire fangs. Those are never easy to recover from." Chelsea commented with a slight mocking chuckle. She took a sip of her soda and picked up another nacho to munch on.

Rob rolled his ball hard enough it managed to hit one of the pins, knocking it into the other earning him a spare. "Ha! Eat that, Chels. Your turn."

Chelsea stood up to bowl. She struggled as she tried to awkwardly roll the ball down the lane, only knocking down the center pins.

In order to avoid embarrassing her, Damien choked back his own laugh while Rob burst out laughing.

"Damn, I'm still no good! Next time we go to a movie or something. I suck at this." She stomped her foot.

The game went on with Damien scoring the highest as usual. They took a break from bowling to go sign up for the next laser tag session. Chelsea chose to sit it out, saying it was more of a guy thing.

"Your loss. Course if you shoot as well as you bowl, our team would lose anyway." Rob laughed, earning him a smack on the arm so hard, even Damien hissed through his teeth in pain.

Damien shook his head at his friends, enjoying his hamburger, fries and soda. They really hadn't changed much in the time he'd been gone. Rob was still his goofy, nerdy self and Chelsea still paraded around like a prima donna.

Not much had changed in Big Timber at all since he'd been gone.

Jill leaned against the bar, watching the three of them as they ate. Her nights together with Damien were doing well to help her form a bond of friendship with him but she still yearned for more.

However, it was becoming obvious that balancing the late hours with his school schedule were wearing Damien down.

Jill didn't know what to do in order to help. He'd texted her before they arrived, asking her if she wanted to go bowling. She'd refused because of the light of the full moon.

In order to address her needs as a lycan, she had to answer Luna's call. The late nights were affecting her as well since she worked during the day.

"Hey gorgeous, how about I buy you a beer?" *Here we go again. Another stubborn male thinking I'm remotely interested in entertaining him.* A quick glare at him sent him running, his tail between his legs back to his friends.

"That him?" The bartender, Alexander Kain asked while cleaning the cups and organizing bottles. He was a fellow lycan and one of Jill's oldest friends from the past.

"Yes. I'm sorry I was late Kain, how long has he been here?"

"I just got on shift. They were here when I arrived so it had to have been two hours at least. You sure about him? He looks more like a vampire." Kain replied.

"It's him. If I was honest though, I don't really care. I've come to love Damien as he is. You got my texts in regards to the late schedule I've been keeping lately," Jill replied, her voice indicating her fatigue. "It's really starting to wear on me. I'm having to meet the needs of the man I like while trying to keep the lycan in me satisfied. I know it's starting to hurt him too. He's having to handle summer classes and our late night talks. I want to be more than a friend but I don't want to push him too early."

"I can only imagine how frustrating this experience has been for you, Jillian. Usually we have to fight them off of us. Give it time. He'll come around. Maybe try courting him? It isn't any different for humans as it is for us."

Kain always seemed to know what advice to give at the right moment. Though she chose to remain a lone wolf, Jill liked having him around and valued him and his pack as close friends.

When Damien and Rob left for laser tag, Kain sent his adopted son in to fill for the last slot on the team. Clint worked at the same bowling alley as his father. It was his off day so he went in to keep an eye on them.

"Thanks, Kain. I have given thought to courting him but let's face it, he's from a different world." Jill replied, her voice downtrodden, her gaze directed at the floor.

"Don't stress out over it too much, old friend. Let things take their course. I'm sure it will work out for the two of you," Kain's tone made Jill think he might have been let down. "Are the vampires aware of him, yet?"

"Not to my knowledge but you know Demetrius as well as I do. He doesn't stay blind for long. He even has humans working for him to get into his good graces enough to be turned. I've been informed there are some of them serving as bleeders for the vampires now. Makes me sick to think about."

Demetrius Stone, the current vampire lord of Big Timber's ruling family, continued his crusade against the remaining lycans even after their arrival in the new world. His constant killing forced them to either become permanently human or hide in order to survive.

"Thank you for being my eyes when I can't be around, Kain."

"I'm still in your debt for getting as many of us out as you could after we were cornered. You know humans Jillian, they're afraid of their own mortality. They will do anything to stall death and aging as long as they can."

"It wasn't a problem, Kain. It was the least I could do to thank Pentacost for giving a mangy stray like me a home. We look out for our own since there are so few of us left." Jill replied, smiling.

She looked over to see Damien and Rob heading back to Chelsea to pack up and leave.

"It looks like they're done and leaving. I have somewhere I have to go so I'll be on my way. The vampires may have been dormant for a while but they are still hunting us so keep your senses strong."

"We will. Good luck, Jillian. May Luna always shine on your back and hear your song of praise."

"You as well, old friend. Tenebris watch over you and yours."

After the bowling alley, Jill took her spot in the tree overlooking Damien's bedroom. He'd gone through his routine of taking his shower, pacing his room with his nose deep in what appeared to Jill to be a textbook.

Damien always looked so adorable to her as he read. The expressions on his face changed depending on what he was reading. Sometimes he would actually talk to the book as though the characters or words could respond.

Well, now's as good a time as any. I hope he still wants to see me. Jill dropped onto the ledge, making Damien jump at her sudden appearance.

He opened the windows to let her in. "Christ, you about gave me another heart attack. A little forewarning would have been nice."

"Sorry. It looked like you were studying again so I didn't know whether or not you would want to see me." Jill dusted her jacket off, sitting on the bench in front of the window sill.

Damien set the textbook down on the bedside table. "Nah, just brushing up on some medical terms. I start my internship this semester. Wanted to make sure I knew what I was talking about when I met the physician in charge of signing the hours sheet. I didn't think you would come by. I know it's late."

A soft smile fell across his chiseled jaw as he averted his eyes to the floor. "I'm glad you did though."

A few moments of silence passed between the two of them as Jill tried to come up with some ways of making small talk. She was thankful Damien broke the silence.

"I was wondering," Jill couldn't help but chuckle at how cute Damien looked as he struggled to find the words. "If you aren't too busy, that is. I know you like books. Would you like to head to the book store sometime? I can't go this weekend since Rob and I are going to be heading out on a fishing trip..."

Jill softly placed her fingers on his lips. "I would love to. I wouldn't be able to do it this weekend either. A client of mine has me pulling a late night shift both nights. See you Monday for lunch? We can discuss our bookstore date then, how about that?"

"Sounds like a plan." Damien replied, relieved Jill helped him since he was almost tripping over his own words.

Neither one of them noticed how fast the time flew by. They talked about things like favorite foods they liked to eat, what they did and didn't like about Halloween and what their favorite music was.

"Wait, why don't you like the werewolf costumes? Some of them are pathetic, I admit but some are pretty good." Damien inquired, his curiosity peaked at the frustrated look on Jill's face.

"I don't think they're accurate. I mean, what would a human know about...those anyway?" Jill smacked her head with her fist, realizing what she said, regretting it the minute it left her mouth.

Damien tilted his head to the side, wondering what she could have meant. He glanced at the clock, sighing. Tomorrow was the day he was heading out with Rob he needed to get to sleep.

Jill rose up from her seat, turning for the window to prepare to leave. "I should go. I'm glad we were able to talk even for a short time."

Damien got up from his seat on the bed, his hand reaching out to grab Jill's wrist. "Wait."

The surprised look in Jill's eyes at the sudden action reminded Damien he'd acted without even realizing it.

"Jill, why don't you stay? At least until I pass out."

Her heart raced as she analyzed Damien's face. She couldn't believe he was asking her to stay with him.

Damien withdrew his hand, feeling suddenly embarrassed and upset with himself at what he'd just done. "Sorry. Too forward?"

"Not at all. I'll stay until you fall asleep but then I have to be going, okay." A flirting smirk snaked its way across her mouth.

Damien's heart leapt. "Really? That's great."

Jill took her jacket off. "Would it be alright if I hung this on the closet door? It's warm in here."

A quick nod gave her permission. She took her boots off while Damien made a place for her on the bed.

"I know it's not really what you would prefer but, I thought it would be better than the wood floor."

Without pulling back the comforter, Jill sat down, positioning herself against the headboard. "It's alright, Damien. I'm not staying the night. Just until you fall asleep."

"Right." Damien pulled back the comforter, laying on his side to face Jill. He was determined to talk to her about something he'd been curious about before she left. "Jill, what do you do for work? I know you've mentioned your clients and stake outs but what is it you actually do?"

"Let's just say I'm the one that's called in when someone wants to know someone else's dirty little secrets. I'm a private investigator."

"That sounds pretty cool. Bet you tend to make a lot of enemies."

Jill began involuntarily playing with Damien's hair. "Not really. I'm usually in and out after delivering the files to the DA's office. I do a lot of work for your dad's precinct."

A slight grin fell across her face at the look of realization on Damien's face.

"Damn. Small world," Damien replied. Jill smiled as he closed his eyes. It wasn't long until he was asleep.

Jill slid off of the bed, moving slowly to avoid waking him. She put her boots on and grabbed her jacket. *It is indeed a small world. At least for now. It's about to get much bigger and darker than you could imagine.*

Damien woke up the next morning to find he was alone. A thought occurred to him making him instantly agitated. He smacked his forehead, realizing he had forgotten to ask Jill why they could only see each other at night.

The alarm Damien set for himself went off, reading 6am. It was the day he and Rob were supposed to go to the pier and he was running behind.

One of the gym bags he used for his workouts was already packed with his camera, notebook, extra film and a battery. He grabbed it, ran out of the door, and down the stairs.

"Morning, D! I was fixing to come toss the mattress over to get your lazy ass outta the bed!" Damien thumped the back of Rob's head in a playful manner making him flinch.

"Sun's not up yet, I hadn't broken the rules. Now come on, we're taking my truck so we can pack up the poles and coolers."

Damien loaded one of the coolers with sodas, bottles of water and a few beers. He didn't usually drink too much but, he knew Rob could almost out drink a sailor in a drinking contest.

Rob jumped into the passenger's side and they headed out to Old Bill's smokehouse. By the time they arrived, the old man had already opened up the main part of the store.

"Well, hey guys! Haven't seen you in ages. How you been Damien? I heard bout your mom. Sad to lose such an amazing woman. She will be missed." William Hutchinson or "Old Bill" as he was known to the town, rung up the packages of jerky, bait and sodas Rob and Damien put in front of him as he spoke.

"I've been okay, Bill. Took some time to get to a level of comfortable coping. I think I'm finally starting to get a sense of control. Going back to school to finish my bio-chem degree."

"That's great! You were always studyin' somethin'. Never saw you without a book in front of your face. Glad your old man instilled in ya that brains are better than brawn." Old Bill let out a raspy, bellowing laugh at his own joke.

Rob took the bag and grabbed Damien by the arm. "I'd love to let you two ladies chatter the day away but I've got fish to catch and hiking to do."

Damien waved to Bill and headed out to the site they chose to spend the day. It had been their favorite spot since they were younger kids. Their dads would sit around and drink while their moms had coffee and talked.

Damien always loved to be outside. The freedom and openness of the woods relieved him of the stresses he was constantly under.

He was so captivated with nature around him, he didn't notice the large wolf in the trees. He about jumped out of his skin when he saw it. His fight-or-flight instincts kicking in until he looked deep into its eyes.

The fear inside of him melted away the longer their eyes met. The icy green orbs held a sense of familiarity.

Its fur was black as night. Not wiry at all like a normal wolf. It had a blue sheen like a raven's feathers when hit with the splotches of sunlight peeking through the leaves.

What surprised him the most was it didn't really seem to want to hurt him, only staring as though it were observing him.

"Well, doesn't seem like you want to eat me so, mind if I take a picture?" He had no idea why he was talking to the wolf as though it could understand him but it was so beautiful he wanted to try to catch a picture of it.

Slowly it walked down the steep ledge, stopping short in front of him. Soft whimpers escaped its throat as it sat down as if it were posing.

What is the deal with this thing? It's huge. I've never seen a wolf this big. Damien thought to himself, lining up his camera to take a photo when Rob called to him. He'd only turned away for a few seconds but when he turned back around the wolf vanished.

"Damn. It was so gorgeous too." The sudden appearance of Rob's arm around his neck brought about a slight jump. He had to stop himself from swinging. "Shit Rob! What the hell? I could have knocked your teeth out."

"Sorry dude. What're you doin' anyway?"

"Well I had a good photo opportunity of something I probably won't ever get to see again until you came along, you moron." Damien shoved him off, mad as hell at missing possibly the greatest photo of his career.

Rob chuckled. "Was it bigfoot?"

Damien rolled his eyes. *Always with the cryptos.* "No, it was a wolf. One of the largest I've ever seen with the most beautiful fur. It would have been perfect for my portfolio." He punched Rob's arm making him wince in pain.

"Sorry, man. Sounds like a tall tale to me but hey let's go fishing. Maybe the heat from the hike got to your head. Geesh, first it's women, now it's large wolves. Maybe you should drop the photography thing and go for being an author with all these daydreams you've been having."

Damien sighed in frustration. He knew what he saw wasn't a hallucination or a delusional fever dream. There was something striking about the wolf. It was almost like he knew it. Like he'd seen it before.

The catch they hauled in hadn't been bad for warmer weather. A few catfish, some sand bass and even a black bass the right size for cooking were put into the ice filled cooler to keep them fresh..

"Man, that was fun. We need to do this again. How about we give them to Bill? He does some killer smoked fish."

"Yeah." Damien was still upset about losing the photo of a lifetime and being told he was once again crazy enough to dream something up like large wolves. A sharp howl through the waning light of day reminded him that thankfully, this time he wasn't dreaming.

CHAPTER THREE

O n Monday, a week before school started, Damien met Jill for the first time during the day since they started seeing each other. Jill had the day off and Damien told Rob and Chelsea he would be busy, feeling bad that he once again had to lie to them about Jill.

They'd had to reschedule their lunch meeting the Monday following Damien's fishing trip when Jill sent him a text telling him something came up that required her attention at work. He was upset at first but soon forgot about his frustration when Jill sat in front of him in the bookstore café. Her dark hair tied up in a loose, messy bun at the top of her head. Her beauty still astounded him despite having seen her almost every night.

"Hey, sorry I'm late. Next round of coffee is on me as punishment." Jill replied, laughing as she scooted the chair back to sit down.

"It's okay. I'm just glad I'm finally getting to see you during the day. Which reminds me," Damien started, closing the book he was reading, setting it on the table. He leaned forward, his elbows resting on the tabletop. "Jill, I've been meaning to ask, why could you only meet me at night before? I know you work during the day and all but every job has their off days, right?"

Jill closed her eyes, taking in a deep breath to calm her anxiety. She knew he would ask this question, eventually. When it finally came, she suddenly found herself at a loss for words.

"Yes. That's true. In all honesty, Damien, I don't know how to answer that question. As I've said before, it always seemed like you were either busy with school or going out with your friends. After dark seemed to be the only time I could actually see you and spend time with you without getting interrupted. I know that's probably not the answer you're looking for but in the positive light, at least we're getting to meet in the day, now."

Damien couldn't help but feel as though Jill had inadvertently dodged his question but out of respect, he didn't pressure her to answer. "That's true. Guess I should count my blessings with this one but it still seems odd to me."

"In time, I will tell you more. For now, I just ask you to give me your trust."

The smell of espresso met the sweet aroma of pastries in the café as Jill talked to Damien about some of the few things she could remember without him knowing how old she was. The endless chatter of voices unnerved her senses, bringing about a feeling of unease since she hadn't really made it a point to get around big crowds.

When the conversation shifted to Damien, Jill had to cover her mouth to avoid bursting out laughing after he told her about all of the times he'd tried skateboarding and nearly broken something every time.

"I'm not kidding, I broke my hand just trying to stand on the damn thing. I thought Rob was going to crack a rib, he was laughing so hard. Chelsea pulled her mother hen routine, scolding Rob and racing over to me. I tried to tell the girl I was fine but, she didn't listen. She's always been like that," Damien chuckled as he spoke of his memory. "What about you, Jill? Do you have any friends around here? Maybe some you hang out with?"

"I guess technically you would call them friends. We don't really 'hang out' per se but there are rare times when we get together and socialize. Otherwise, I tend to like my peace and quiet. In case you haven't taken notice, I'm not really social." The harsh reality of almost always being alone since Lucius died came back to the forefront of Jill's memories.

Upon realizing the sudden downtrodden shift in Jill's mood, Damien took her hands in his. "At the very least, you do have one friend. I'm open to talking if you want to."

Jill felt her face heat at his touch. *A friend. At least I have one friend.* A gentle smile fell across her face.

Damien took their empty cups and threw them in the trashcan. He noticed that Jill appeared to be a bit stressed in the growing crowd.

"You want to go somewhere quieter? I'd like to share a special spot I like to go when I want to escape the world. Want to see it?" Damien asked as he held out his hand, eagerly awaiting Jill's answer.

Curious and elated that Damien was sharing another secret with her, Jill took his hand, letting him lead her out of the bookstore.

Damien led Jill to an old wooden bridge lying over a small river sourced in the mountains. Jill often used the woods around this place as her hunting grounds and was very familiar with it.

"I like to come here to think. It's quiet, isolated and calming. The sound of the river settles me down during those times I'm really stressed out." Damien rested his elbows on the old beams. The manner in which he spoke was as though he described a dreamscape.

Jill leaned her back against the beams, using her hands as supports. "I know this place. I come here too. It's a relief against the usual bustle of the town. It's amazing to me."

"What is?"

"How much we have in common. When I first saw you moving in, I must admit I had no idea what to expect. I came by your house night after night to see if I could learn more about you. It surprised me when you caught me. Scared me almost. I thought you would be angry and tell me never to get near you again. I never could have dreamed you would have actually given me a chance to talk so openly with you, Damien." Jill's heart fluttered like a bird behind her ribs as though she were starting to care for someone for the first time in centuries.

Damien stood up, turning around to lean against the wood. The frogs began to sing as the sun sank beneath the horizon. The air was cool, signaling the arrival of autumn to Montana.

They stood quietly for a while, just enjoying each other's company.

Curious, Damien asked, "I've never heard you talk about where you live. Do you have an apartment in town?"

Jill's jaw clenched, her hands gripping the wood so strongly, she nearly forgot to keep her lycan strength in control to avoid splintering it.

"I'm sorry, should I not have asked?"

"No, no. It's just," Jill didn't want to lie to him. She never really lived anywhere. Sometimes she would stay at the gym in her room, other times she spent the night in the woods as a wolf. "I stay with a friend most of the time. I have a room at his gym since I fight there a lot."

"You fight? What gym?"

"Solstice. The owner, Gabriel, is a friend of mine. Since I have good standing there, he lets me keep a room upstairs," Jill pushed her shoulders forward. "You're welcome to come visit sometime if you like. I like to watch movies and read after working out."

"Sure. I'd love to come by. My old man and I have driven by it a couple of times but I've never been. I tend to do my running in the morning before school." Damien replied, meeting her attempt at flirting with one of his own.

"Sounds good to me. I do most of my running at night." Jill giggled at her inside joke. "It's getting late though. We should probably be getting back. I happen to know college is in full session for you soon. If I can ask, what exams were you studying for over the summer?"

"Prelims and placement tests. A few of the courses allow us to see if we can test out of them. I grabbed as many as I could to lower the course load. Took some summer courses too. What can I say, I don't like a ton of downtime."

"I can understand that. I don't like too much down time either." Jill replied, hopping down from her spot she had taken on the wood rails during their talk.

They walked back down to where Damien parked his truck. He pulled open the passenger's side door to let Jill get inside, closing it for her before making his way to the other side.

"Where to?"

"The gym. I sent Gabriel a text to let him know I was coming."

Damien didn't understand why but he felt a hint of jealousy at the mention of Gabriel's name. "The friend you mentioned?"

"Yes. Don't worry, he's just a friend." Jill chuckled, finding the subtle hint of jealousy in Damien's voice cute.

Damien dropped his head to the steering wheel. "God, I didn't mean it like that."

"It's fine. Thanks for the lift." Another chuckle.

Without a word, once again feeling embarrassed, Damien started the truck. He backed up on the main road to head to the gym.

The last week of summer seemed to speed by as Damien spent the rest of his time catching up. Although he and Jill started texting each other more often, Damien chose to spend the time with his father and prepare for the upcoming school year.

Damien spent the night in his room doing his last-minute checks to make sure he had everything he would need for his classes including his laptop. He couldn't help but feel elated at the fact he was able to go back to school to finish his degree, grateful that his grades for the prelims and placement tests had been high enough to get out of a few courses.

Once he was sure he was finished, he turned on some soft music that had rain mixed into it and fell back on the bed, watching the fan blades while they spun casting shadows on the ceiling.

His mind went to Jill. He hadn't seen her since their talk at the bridge but he couldn't help but think about her. She was so beautiful, strong and independent. There was something about her drawing him towards her though he wasn't sure what it was.

The piercing sound of a wolf howling in the distance made Damien get up from his bed, walk over to the window and open the shutters. The moon was full with a burnt orange tint giving the night an almost supernatural air.

The fall moon. Damien thought, remembering reading somewhere it had another name. *The hunter's moon.*

The next morning, Damien didn't remember falling asleep. He'd been watching the moon and listening to the wolf howling until late into the night. The sound was comforting to him.

He rubbed his eyes with his thumb and forefinger to get the sleep out of them, his focus falling on his phone. *That's right! It's the first day of classes.*

"Morning." Damien said, practically running into the kitchen, excited about getting to start college.

"Wow, you're chipper. Have a nice dream or something?" Charlie chuckled, taking a drink of his coffee.

"Got some good sleep this time around. No idea what the change was, maybe it was the music. Did you see the first fall moon last night?" Damien asked.

"Sure did. Beauty, wasn't it? Night critters were happy to see her round and fat up there." Charlie chortled.

Damien stared curiously at the words his dad used to describe the moon. "You hear the wolves?"

"What? No, but there were plenty of bats and frogs singing."

"Oh. That's odd. Gotta be heading out for an early class, dad. If you beat me home, it's because I started my internship up at the hospital." Damien replied, still confused.

Unfortunately, he didn't have time to dig any deeper into why his dad hadn't heard the wolves since he was already running late.

"Alright, be safe out there. Make us proud."

Damien grabbed his sunglasses and leather jacket, accidentally slamming the door on his way out to find it pouring rain and cold.

Go figure. Damien thought, disturbed at his sudden change of luck. He hugged his jacket close, throwing his backpack over his shoulder to run to his truck and jump up into the cab. Charlie had started it to get it warmed up while Damien got ready.

The old man really did look out for him, he'd have to thank him when he got home.

The classes during the morning were always the hardest since Damien wasn't usually an early riser but he was glad when he got to meet Rob for lunch in the main building. It faced the main road cutting through the college and was the central hub for most of the college students' needs.

"You seem in high spirits today, bro. No monster wolves haunting your dreams last night?" Rob teased, taking a bite of a French fry.

Damien focused on his chicken wrap. "That's not funny. Speaking of wolves, I heard one howling last night at the fall moon."

"Yeah! Wasn't that cool? I didn't hear any wolves though. You sure you didn't imagine it?" Rob asked.

Rob hadn't heard the wolf either? Damien was sure he'd heard one. It was almost as though it was singing. The sound so comforting it put him to sleep.

"Hey, you start your internship today, right? Excited?" Rob asked.

"Hell yeah, I am. Been looking forward to it since the beginning of the summer," Damien replied. He'd been brushing up on his medical terms since summer began. He wasn't excited to get started. He was anxious. "Where's your internship?"

"Tech department of course. Looking forward to working with you, man. Gotta go though, shift starts in thirty. If you're heading out, I'll walk with ya."

Damien grabbed his trash and his backpack, the scrubs he'd need hung in his truck. "Sounds good. Let's go."

When Damien arrived at the hospital, he chose to park in the parking garage to avoid getting soaked by the rain since it'd chosen not to let up all afternoon.

Once through the double doors, he walked up to the nurses station where a rather young looking doctor stood talking to a cute blonde holding a clipboard.

Upon seeing Damien, the doctor walked up to him, holding out his hand. "You must be Damien Pierce. I'm Kyle Langston, one of the leading physicians. I'll be the one overseeing your training hours. Do you have any questions or are you ready to start learning some things around here?"

Damien shook the doctor's hand confidently. "Nice to meet you, sir. I'm excited to learn how things work."

Kyle laughed a hearty laugh, patting Damien on the back. "Don't worry, tonight's not going to be too hard. I'm just going to take you around and see where you are. That way I can see where I need to focus and where I can relax a bit on your training."

Kyle led Damien around the different aspects of the specimen labs, gauging what he knew through random questions and seeing where he still needed some help. He introduced Damien to Mackenzie Wilder, the lead lab technician.

"Mack here, is your first go to for any and all questions regarding lab work. She's pretty good at what she does so usually I don't have to get involved in anything. Mack, this is Damien Pierce."

Mackenzie reached out her hand. "Ah, so you're the new meat. Pleased to meet you. I've been expecting you. Dr. Langston mentioned we were getting some newbies around here. I'm grateful since I've heard you were quite the Brainiac."

Damien took Mackenzie's hand, slightly suspicious. She was lead lab tech and yet she didn't look much older than he was. Shaking off the feeling, he just smiled. "Nice to meet you. I promise to work hard."

"Damn straight you will or I'll be kicking your sexy ass all around this place." Damien stood baffled, the confused look on his face made Mackenzie laugh a surprisingly adorable laugh. "Don't worry about it, I haze all the new meat. Come on, I'll show you around."

The rest of the shift was spent with Mackenzie leading Damien around the labs. She showed him different machines, explaining how each type worked, where to find certain containers and charts that would need to be filled out daily.

At the end of the shift, Mack punched Damien in the arm, playfully. "Hey, not bad for your first day. Maybe I won't have to hold your hand as much as I thought. See you back here soon, Damien. Feel free to contact me if you need to. I'm a pretty good study buddy."

Damien nodded to her, shaking her hand. "Thanks Mack, I will. See you later." He replied, taking his backpack and heading out of the sliding doors.

Tired and hungry after the night at the hospital, Damien decided to try to run across the street to the burger joint built in the style of an eighties diner to get something quick to eat.

He was just about to go back across the street to his truck when he was suddenly grabbed by the arm and thrown into the brick wall of the alley next to the restaurant.

The impact was so hard it caused him to drop his food to the cold, wet ground. His head hit the bricks, dazing him for a few moments before he could figure out what was going on.

Two men dressed in all black suits looking like they belonged in some science fiction movie stood before him.

The feeling they gave him was different from the one he had when he was around Jill, Mack or Dr. Langston. His sense of danger rose to a level he'd never experienced before.

"Damien Pierce?" The taller of the two with a goatee and dreadlocked hair spoke in a smooth, deadly voice. It almost sounded sinister.

He wore sunglasses despite the rain and almost pitch black sky. The only source of light came from a few street lamps.

"Maybe. Who's asking?" Damien staggered as he got up from his knee, his back braced against the wall.

The shorter man with the shaved head slammed him in the face with what felt like a set of brass knuckles, bruising his cheek almost instantly. It felt like getting hit by a truck or kicked by a draft horse. His vision blurred to the point it made him nauseous.

"Wise guy's got balls. Got to give it to you for guts." He flicked his cigarette to the ground, stomping it out. "Nothing personal, but we're here to kill you."

"Kill me?" Damien had no idea why anyone would want him dead. His heart pounded hard enough to hurt his ribs. His mind ran through any option he might have to help him escape. A sense of helplessness quickly filled him with doubt that escape was even possible.

The taller of the two stepped forward and grabbed Damien by the collar of his jacket. He lifted and threw him halfway the length of the alley. He flew through the air until he landed hard on the gray lid of one of those heavy green dumpsters, knocking the wind out of him. The slick surface of the lid made him slide to the ground, landing on his side with a thud.

The memory of getting hit by the SUV ran through Damien's mind as he tried to catch a breath. His ribs ached with each attempt as he tried to lift himself up.

A sting in his leg made him look down to see blood pooling from the knee to the ground. His leg was broken.

Damien closed his eyes. His shoulder burned, feeling as if it had been fractured at the collarbone. His back hurt and his head felt like he might have a concussion. There was no way he could escape with the injuries he'd sustained.

The men walked down the alley towards Damien. Their steps slow like predators stalking prey they knew couldn't escape them. They seemed to relish the idea of finishing him off at their leisure.

Damien resigned himself to the thought he could actually die. There was no one outside since it was raining so trying to call out for help would be next to useless. He couldn't move or hope to fight them in his current state.

From the way he'd just been thrown, he doubted he could fight them, regardless.

"That's a good boy. Just surrender and we'll make this quick." The shorter man loaded a clip into his firearm. His gaze shot up just as someone jumped from a roof above the scene.

Jill's sudden arrival brought Damien's hope back to life. It was like she dropped out of nowhere, her long coat blowing as she landed from what had to have been at least six stories high.

Water splashed into Damien's face forcing him to shake it off to get the dirt-mixed rain out of his eyes. Jill positioned her body in such a way it could serve as a shield between Damien and the men.

She looked over her shoulder. "Damien, how badly are you hurt?" She asked, her voice low and holding a more threatening tone than it usually did.

It took Damien a moment to think. "My leg's broken, my back hurts. I'm pretty sure my collarbone is fractured and my head feels like it could explode. Otherwise, I think I'm okay."

A low growl escaped Jill's throat as she turned to kneel next to Damien with no fear of exposing her back to the men.

There was something different about her. Almost as though her whole persona changed in response to him being in danger.

Taking an old tarp off of a stack of mattresses, Jill started covering Damien, making him look at her in question. Her hand cupped his face so gently it made his heart flutter. Her thumb lightly brushed the bruise on his cheek. The look in her eyes was so filled with pain, it made him feel like he'd just swallowed rocks.

What's going on? Why is she looking at me like that? Damien thought, his own gaze meeting Jill's.

"No matter what you may hear, please do not uncover yourself, okay?"

Damien nodded. It almost seemed like she was afraid to do what she felt she had to.

Her smile was saddened. A deep longing lingered behind the words as she wrapped his knee with some material she tore from the inside of her coat.

After Jill covered him, Damien could only see the silhouette of her boots as she turned on her heel.

"You had no right to hurt him. You filthy, bloodsucking parasites had no right to touch him. I'm going to make sure you regret every injury you inflicted with interest."

The intensity in Jill's voice was unlike anything Damien ever heard. The voice he knew was soft, seductive and reassuring. This one was almost more of a low rasping growl than actual words.

Bloodsucking parasites? Sounds Damien never heard before followed the short exchanges accompanied by cursing from the two men.

Gun shots rang out as the men tried to defend themselves. Ripping, tearing, screams of pain and what sounded like a dog snarling and whimpering joined the gnashing of teeth as the fight went on.

Something metal bounced off of the concrete in front of Damien's face, making him scoot back to avoid getting hit by whatever it was.

The pungent copper smell of blood joined the scent of stale alcohol, trash and cigarette smoke until the screams of agony dissipated into the silent patter of rain on the concrete.

An eerie sense of quiet fell over the alley after the short battle.

Damien strained to hear any indication that Jill would be alive.

The sounds of footsteps made him stiffen. Fear gripped him as he thought he could have been wrong. His mind imagined Jill being killed.

The suddenness of Jill uncovering him made Damien jump, his eyes blurred as they tried to adjust to the brightness of the street lights behind her. The muscles in his body tensed as Jill proceeded to blindfold him using another strip of cloth.

"Jill, what's going on?" His voice shook with uncertainty as she covered his eyes.

She sighed, helping him stand to his feet. His weight supported by her body. "Forgive me. I'd hoped to introduce you to this a bit slower. For now, let me lead you. I'm taking you to the hospital."

Jill led Damien through the carnage of the fight to the black Mustang Gabriel lent to her on occasion. She helped him slide into the passenger's side and closed the door before walking around to the other side of the car.

After she closed the door, Jill started up the engine and shifted gears into reverse. Her foot landed firmly on the accelerator, halting the car before shifting into drive. The force of her foot back on the accelerator made the car tires screech in protest as they peeled out.

"Jill, what the hell is going on?!" Damien was almost yelling as he ripped the blindfold off. His wet clothes made him shiver against the cold of the brisk fall night adding to his already irate mood.

"Damien, take it easy. You've taken a lot of damage. Let's get your injuries looked at first and I give you my word I will tell you." Jill replied, her voice monotone as she reached to turn on the heat.

"Here, I thought you might need this so I brought one." She handed Damien a blanket which he quickly cocooned himself in.

He threw up his hands under the blanket, his frustration joining anger at the fact that Jill had been keeping so many secrets from him. He knew they hadn't really told each other everything but, he'd nearly just been killed!

Where the hell had she come from anyway? It's like she dropped from the sky or something. He wanted an explanation.

When they arrived at the hospital, Jill helped Damien into the emergency room where Dr. Langston stood as though he'd been waiting for them. He guided them to a room immediately and proceeded with his examination.

"Looks like a hairline fracture of your collarbone." Dr. Langston said, looking at the x-rays. His finger rested against his mouth, his elbow in his hand as he studied the images. "Your leg is definitely broken at the knee. We'll be sure to take care of that for you."

Damien fought hard not to blink at the bright light flashed into his eyes. "No dilation. That's a good sign but there is some evidence of a minor concussion. Good news is there's no significant damage to your back, just some bruising. What did you get yourself into Damien? You hadn't been gone an hour." Dr. Langston asked, his voice serious.

He glanced at Jill. The two seemed to understand what was going on between them. "Don't worry, I'll put in your medical leave for at least six weeks. Try to keep as much pressure off of your leg as possible. I'll prescribe some pain medication in case you need it."

Damien tightened his jaw, squeezing his eyes closed against the pain as Dr. Langston wrapped his shoulder, setting it into a sling. He knew he wouldn't need six weeks to recover. The wounds he usually got healed within a matter of days depending on the severity.

"Honestly, I don't know what I got myself into." Damien said, annoyed. He didn't want to freak the doctor out by telling him two grown men with the strength of the children of Hercules and Samson hurled him into a dumpster halfway down a dark alley. *God, what am I going to tell my dad, Rob or Chelsea?*

Jill stood next to the door, standing guard and watching.

"Well whatever you did, it looks utterly painful. There's definitely going to be some bruising and some soreness. Just take it easy and rest." Dr. Langston nodded to Jill. The two of them left the room into the hallway.

"It was the vampires, wasn't it?" Kyle spoke low enough to Jill so Damien couldn't hear. He'd chosen the examination room furthest away from the reception desk once he saw Jill walk in.

"Yes. Demetrius is aware of his existence now. They openly tried to kill him, Kyle. If I hadn't gotten the call from Mackenzie when I did, he would have been killed." Jill answered.

It was by sheer luck Mackenzie managed to get a hold of Jill after she saw the two vampires corner Damien in the alley.

"Looks like it's begun. We'll do what we can Jill, but most of us here are just trying to make a living. So far, Kain, Gabriel's pack and I have remained off the radar of Rayes. Be careful." Kyle's reply was sullen, his mouth down turned in a worried frown. His grip on his clipboard tightened to the point the plastic cracked.

Jill nodded to him. "Luna watch over you and yours, Kyle. Don't worry. I'll do what I can on my own."

"Luna watch over you, Jill."

Damien tapped his foot anxiously as they rode in silence. He hadn't even been on his internship for a day and already he needed to take medical leave. Jill hadn't offered up anything about what she and Dr. Langston talked about or the information she promised him about why he was attacked in the first place.

"Okay, seriously. What the hell, Jill?" His voice was more frustrated than he meant it to be but he still felt like she owed him an explanation.

"In time. For now, you should be resting. We're dropping by the gym so you have a safe place to stay for the night. I'll take you home in the morning." Jill tried keeping her own frustration at the situation under control.

"Solstice? Why there?" Damien replied, pissed at himself at the twinge of jealousy he was feeling.

"You'll see. I know you're mad. All I ask is for you try to control your temper. You can throw your fit at me later." Jill smirked at the look of defiance on Damien's face at her comment.

Jill looked at Damien in her peripheral, fighting back a giggle at how adorable he was as he sat fuming. It was a new side to him she hadn't seen before. Much different from the shy, sensitive guy she'd come to know.

Even injured he took her breath away. The rips in his shirt and jacket revealed his toned muscles. His bicep on the armrest almost seemed to beg her to reach out and touch it. To caress the soft hills and valleys of the rippling muscles along his arm.

From the mood he was in, Jill decided to keep her paws to herself. She knew for her kind, an argument like this often ended in some rough, hot make-up sex. It was something she looked forward to when she had him as hers. Apparently, he was an explosive firework when he wanted to be.

She decided to give Damien some of the information she promised him on the way to the gym. "The men who attacked you were vampires. Their Lord, Demetrius Stone wants you dead."

Damien whipped his head around to look at her. His eyes raised in a mocking array of confusion. He spoke half-chuckling. "Vampires? Like 'I vant to suck your blood', vampires?"

"Yes, though I've never heard them speak that way." Jill knew humans had come to mock vampires throughout the centuries in both literature and the movies.

Some of the changes were so laughable, Jill rolled her eyes at the idea that humans thought they understood anything about vampire culture.

"Come on Jill, there's no such thing. If there were, why in hell would they want me dead? What would I have that could possibly threaten a vampire? I've never even met one until you showed up."

"They fear the soul inside of you, Damien." Jill felt the sting of blame in his words. She couldn't deny the possibility of her interaction being the reason the vampires located him so quickly.

"Wait, what? The soul inside of me?" In all the time Damien knew Jill, she'd made him suspicious about the night visits. He never imagined it would link to something having to do with vampires.

A thought occurred to Damien as he directed his attention to the floorboard in front of him. His hands grew cold and clammy, his fists tightening into balls on his knees. "If those men were really vampires then what the hell are you to be able to kill them?" Damien asked, raising his eyes to look at her.

Jill kept her eyes on the road, staying silent. Her sensitive ears focusing on the rapid heartbeat in Damien's chest. Her greatest fears were quickly becoming realized despite her efforts to avoid exposing him to the darkness of their world.

Stopping in front of the gym, Jill sighed deeply, preparing herself for whatever Damien might say in response to what she was about to tell him.

"Listen to me carefully. The soul inside of you is known as the soul of a Purifier. To a vampire like Demetrius, it is a threat which must dealt with no matter what it costs him. Since they have become aware of your existence, you have to be very careful. Do not go out after sunset and never let anyone into your house neither you nor your dad don't know. Vampires can't enter anywhere they aren't invited."

Jill paused to get out of the car and made her way over to the passenger's side door, opening it to help Damien out before continuing.

"Nobles can enter without being welcomed but, it tends to injure them. They don't usually get involved personally in anything unless it's a social event calling for their presence. They also have humans working for them as well. You have to be skeptical of everyone, even the ones closest to you." Jill's eyes almost glowed, holding Damien's gaze.

"Jill!" Gabriel marched up to his car once they pulled up. His hair was dark and fell just to the middle of his neck. His body was built like a lean mixed martial arts fighter with well-developed muscles that bulged when he flexed them above his head. His shoulders were broad with a copper tone to his skin. Exotic with a slight accent, Gabriel was definitely someone a woman would drool over.

"Hello, Gabriel." Jill replied, exhausted from the night's events.

Damien felt the burn of jealousy when Gabriel wrapped his arms around her. His hands moved down to her lower back in the most sensual way Damien had ever seen. They came to lay flat, rubbing her ass as though he were her boyfriend.

Damien had to turn away, scoffing as Jill kissed Gabriel's cheek. Her hands resting on his hips.

Gabriel's attention turned to Damien, placing his hand on his own hip. His other one still holding Jill close to him. "So, this is him? I have to say, he looks more like a vampire." His laugh was mocking and deep. "You can do better in your choice, Jill. Maybe one of your own kind?"

Jill shoved him off. "Like you? Give me a break. You wouldn't fare any better than Kyle or Ray in the ring. My den still open?"

"Never doubted your skills, Jill. Just not sure this one's worth risking so much for. Seems like a real pussy to me." Gabriel replied, poking fun.

Damien growled. *Who was this guy?*

"Fang off, Gabriel. He's had a rough night. Now is my den still available or not?" Jill's apparent lack of patience made Gabriel raise his hands in surrender.

"It's still up there. I keep my promises. You keep your standing, you have a room. So far, with how you've been fighting, I don't see that going anywhere anytime soon."

"Good. Now if you don't mind, I have to get this poor thing off of his injured leg. Kyle's orders." Jill grabbed Damien's hand and pulled him into the gym. His eyes met the ferocity of Gabriel's as he went passed him.

When he stepped through the doors, there was a huge variety of workout equipment in the main room where some of the most ripped guys Damien had ever seen pounded the punching bags, sprinted on the treadmills and lifted weights.

Each one stopped to watch as Jill pulled him through the gym. Some with a look of disgust on their faces, others almost laughing at him.

Even the women seemed inhumanly strong in build. Most of them were attached to their choice of man. Neither one hesitating to hug, kiss and touch openly in the same manner Gabriel had Jill when she walked up to him.

Further through the halls, there was another large room containing a fight cage where two guys were going at each other in ways so violent it could get them sanctioned.

Wait, were those claws and... fangs?! Damien shook his head, blocking out the thought. *There's no way.*

"Jillian." The voice came from a man Damien recognized as Alexander Kain, the bartender from the bowling alley. He was shirtless and covered in sweat like he'd just gotten done with his own round of fighting.

"Kain. Just get finished wiping the floor with Scott's tail again?" Jillian asked, half chuckling as she spoke.

"As are most of my nights when I decide to come, to my greatest dismay. He's hell-bent on taking my place as alpha. Says I can't cut it anymore." Kain laughed, taking a drink of water from his water bottle. The gesture mocking his opponent's blatant accusations.

Alpha? Damien had so many questions he didn't know where he would even start. He'd known Alex for a while, sometimes exchanging words with him when he waited his turn to bowl.

To see him outside of work like this was confusing. It seemed like he knew Jill on a more personal level.

Kain briefly turned his attention to Damien. "Good to see you outside of work, Damien. Must say that was one sun's hell of a game you bowled the other night. You have some skill. Perhaps consider joining a league?" He turned his attention back to Jill after taking in Damien's current state. "I'm taking it those injuries are from a vampire attack? If so, he's lucky he got out alive. I hope you have a plan, Jillian. Have you considered turning him?"

Jill let go of Damien's wrist, getting in close to Kain's face. "That is never an option, Kain. Not as long as I can help it. You know damn well we live a cursed life. The vampires are growing in number while ours are falling faster than we can make pups."

"It was just a suggestion. I will honor your request, old friend. However, he might be safer if you did." Kain replied, hugging her. "I apologize if I angered you, Jillian. I just don't want to see you hurt. It ripped my heart apart to see my childhood friend hurting as badly as you were back then."

Jill returned his hug, reassuring him that she understood. Their touch was sensual in nature as well. From what Damien observed so far, to almost everyone in the gym, this public display of affection seemed as though it were normal.

Jill cocked her head. "Damien, what's wrong?"

He hadn't noticed how flustered he'd gotten. He turned his attention away, making both Jill and Kain chuckle.

"Better take him to your den, Jillian. I think he's a bit overwhelmed."
Kain walked off, ignoring the jeers Scott was giving him from the opening
of the men's locker room.

Jill led Damien up a flight of stairs into a long hallway toward a room with a
golden plate mounted on the door labeled with her name and the title of
"Cage Champion."

She hadn't even closed the door all the way before Damien backed
himself against the wall as far away from her as he could.

His heart pounded in his chest. His eyes widened with a mix of terror
and disbelief.

Sighing, Jill proceeded strip down to her panties and bra like Damien
wasn't in the room. Her body was beautiful. It was perfectly toned and built
like any one of the women he'd seen downstairs.

Damien felt his good knee get weak as Jill pulled out a pair of black
shorts with pink stripes down the side and a black spaghetti strap shirt.

Her long dark hair, she pulled up into a ponytail, stretching her arms
above her head. However, it was the array of different scars on Jill's
shoulders, back and hips that grabbed Damien's immediate attention. They
served as the proof of what she'd said about her fighting was true.

There were some he swore she couldn't have gotten from cage fighting.
They looked more angry. Almost like whatever inflicted them intentionally
tried to pull huge pieces of flesh off of her body.

Turning her attention to Damien, she sat down on the couch, crossing
her gorgeous long legs. "I can imagine your mind is swimming with any
number of questions. If it makes you more comfortable, you can sit on the
bed to prop your leg up and I'll stay over here on the couch to talk."

Damien couldn't move. He was too hypnotized by the Aphrodite sitting
before him almost naked. A mix of fear and sexual interest battled inside of
him as he fought not to stare.

Seeing he was paralyzed, Jill sighed, getting up to help him. She set up a
pillow to rest his leg on while still making it easy for him to sit or lay down
comfortably.

"Here. You need to get off of your leg until it heals. I'll stay away to give
you space. I gave you my word I would answer your questions and get you

home in the morning and I will." She gently led him to sit down on the bed, propping his leg up for him. "If you're worried about what your dad, Rob or Chelsea will say, I'm sure I can help with that too."

Damien had to work to pull his thoughts together in his mind to get a sense of clarity. "Okay, what the hell have I stepped into? Who were those men down there? Why did they touch you like that? And how the hell did you know I was thinking about what to tell everyone when I got back to my house?"

Jill's hand on his face made him stop. "Easy. You're going to have an anxiety attack at this rate. Maybe you should get some sleep. I'll answer what I can on our way to your house in the morning. Your mind will be fresh and you can quiz the sun's hell out of me."

"Sleep?! How the hell am I supposed to get any sleep after what I've just seen?! No way are you getting out of this, Jill!" Damien grew tired of all the damn secrecy.

He had no idea how he was going to get calmed down enough to sleep with the storm of confusion in his brain. Let alone in the presence of a woman with the ability to take on two armed vampires.

"Okay, I'll answer one question, then you're getting some rest, got it." Jill surrendered. The determined glare in Damien's eyes showed he wanted to get an answer.

Damien had so many he couldn't choose just one so he blurted out the first one that came to his mind. "Why did those men touch you like that?" The coy smile on Jill's face froze the rest of his words in his throat. "What?"

Smoothly she got into his face. Her thigh landed between his legs, pressing against his groin. A heat ran up his body as he felt her eyes searching his. Her thumb ran the length of his lips, flicking his lower lip in play.

"Why the sudden worry about who touches me or how? Are you jealous?"

A hard lump formed in Damien's throat. The deep tone of silken seduction in Jill's voice drove him into a desire he never thought he could feel again.

With as much effort as he could, he tore his eyes from her and quietly replied. "No, it's just...I've never seen it before between two people who aren't involved with each other. Are you sleeping with them?"

Jill burst out laughing. "That is such a human thought. No Damien, I'm not sleeping with any of them. For my kind, touch like that is normal. It promotes closeness and loyalty. It's never sexual unless we're courting or with our mates."

Jill's usually icy green eyes darkened with a primal lust. She leaned in so close her breath blew hot in his ear as she spoke. "Then it gets so hot no human could watch without getting embarrassed."

Damien couldn't help the rise of the goose bumps on his skin. The reaction completely contradictory to the growing heat in his groin. His heart continued to pound inside his chest like a drum.

Jill ended her flirting, pulling away from him. "Now, sleep. We'll talk more in the morning. I can see in those gorgeous eyes of yours you still don't understand. I promise you will." She smiled the soft smile Damien was used to, turning off the light. "If you need me, I'll be on the couch. You will be safe here, I promise."

Damien watched Jill as she walked over to the couch. Every movement so graceful and sensual he had to avert his eyes against the growing feeling of desire inside of him.

Stretching out to lay on her side, Jill had to fight back a smirk at the internal struggle her handsome roommate was going through. She rolled over to face the couch, wrapping up in a plush blanket with a body pillow.

Damien turned over to the side of his good arm, trying to avoid staring at Jill's back as his heart beat rapidly behind his ribs. The growing heat in his body made him clench his teeth against the memories trying to escape the recesses of his mind.

He fought sleep as long as he could before it eventually took him. The subtle hint of betrayal lingered at the fact Jill hadn't told him the danger he was in and it nearly killed him.

Jill waited until she heard him breathing deeply before she got up and walked over to the bed, scooting the chair up beside it.

The bruises Damien sustained had already started healing up and fading. It didn't surprise her. Lucius had been able to heal minor injuries like bruises almost overnight. No doubt the fracture and the break would be healed within a couple of days.

Jill couldn't help but feel horrible at the circumstances he'd undergone to get introduced to her world. She tried so hard to take things slow with him. "I'm sorry. I never intended for any of this. I know you must be so angry at me, probably a bit betrayed,"

Leaning down next to his ear, Jill continued. "Damien, you don't understand. I will do anything to keep you safe. Anything to have you as mine." A single tear fell from her eyes, landing on her knuckles on the edge of the bed.

CHAPTER FOUR

Damien couldn't focus the following day. He'd woken up in a strange place. The events from the night before hazy as he tried to sit up.

The moment he felt the sting in his leg, everything slammed into the forefront of his mind. The fracture in his shoulder had healed to a manageable level of discomfort. He took his arm out of the sling and unwrapped the tight bandages responsible for making sleep difficult.

He sighed. Healing this way happened since he got his first papercut in kindergarten. There was no blood and the cut healed right up in front of him as if he'd never gotten it in the first place. He'd looked around at his fellow classmates to see if anyone saw, grateful it went unnoticed.

The sudden onset of a purely disgusting smell almost made him gag. He sniffed his shirt to realize it was him. *Figures. What'd I expect to happen after getting thrown into a dumpster?* He wanted nothing more than to take a shower to get clean and clear his head.

An unwanted flinch ran through his body when the door suddenly opened to reveal Jill holding a plate of breakfast.

"Morning. I see your fracture healed up already. That's good." Jill set the plate down in front of him, backing off quickly once she saw he was still mad.

When Damien didn't reply, she continued. "Kain made it. He's pretty handy in the kitchen. He asks you to tell him how you like it."

Damien didn't look at her.

The fact remained, she hadn't told him about the very real danger he'd been in the moment they began talking. Instead she'd dodged his questions and ignited a fire of sexual arousal inside of him he hadn't been able to suppress.

"I'm...not hungry. Tell him I said thanks anyway." A loud growl from his stomach gave his apparent need for food away, making him curse under his breath.

"Damien, I know this is all new to you. I promised I would tell you what you wanted to know and I will but I wanted you to rest. Your mind was in a state of panic last night. I needed it to be fresh and open to hear what I was going to say." Jill took a fresh cup of coffee, sitting it down next to him. Her own mind preparing for the flood of questions he was likely to assault her with. "I suppose I should probably go with the obvious first question humans like to know. I believe it's 'what are you'?"

Damien didn't much appreciate her taunting tone but nodded.

Hesitantly, he took a bite of a pancake Kain made, surprised to find it pleasantly fluffy.

"Well to your kind I guess you would label us as..." She shuddered, making a blech sound with her tongue and mouth. "Werewolves, wolf-kind, loup-garoux, shape-shifter...I can go on. We prefer the term lycanthrope or lycan for short."

"Lycan? As in, capable of turning into a..." His memory went back to the large wolf he'd seen in the woods. Its behavior made more sense to him now that Jill told him. "That was you."

"Bingo and yes, I did want to eat you but not in the ways you were thinking." She gave a seductive smirk that made Damien avert his eyes, making her quietly laugh. "You can still have that photo if you want. I just wasn't keen on sticking around with Rob dropping in like that."

Shock began setting in the more Damien asked. "Kain...and Gabriel...are they?"

"Yes."

"This whole place...it's full of..."

"Yes. Anything else?"

Damien's head started spinning. *Vampires...and now werewolves...*

For all he knew, he was in a drug-induced coma somewhere. He rubbed his eye with the heel of his hand. "Oh, man. This isn't happening."

Jill got up to put some clothes on to go out in, once again not seeming to care he was in the room. "If there's nothing else then we need to go or you're going to miss your first class."

She tossed him a change of clothes she borrowed from Gabriel. "Gabriel says you can have them. You can't go to school in yours, they're too shredded. Feel free to take a shower."

"Jill, why do you do that?"

"Do what?"

"Strip down and get dressed like I'm not in the room. It makes me feel weird. Like I'm a peeping tom." Damien looked down at the floor in front of him, trying not to gawk at the beautiful woman getting undressed in front of him. She hadn't even put any pants on yet and was wearing high cut panties and a lace bra.

"Around here, this is normal. Both Gabriel and Kain have seen me naked multiple times. To us, it's not strange at all. The body is something to be appreciated and admired. A gift from our gods. Before you ask, no, we don't do it in front of humans. It's mostly lycans who use Gabriel's gym once the doors lock at night. Even so we keep it pretty contained in private areas." Jill smiled at the reaction she saw in the mirror.

Damien couldn't feel anymore jealous than he was. He couldn't explain why he was beyond unnerved knowing Gabriel and Kain had seen Jill naked on multiple occasions.

"You're so adorable when you're jealous. You're more than welcome to undress in here any time you want. I won't say a thing." Her eyes half-closed, winking at Damien as she spoke in the same seductive voice.

"No thanks. I'll keep my clothes on, if you don't mind. I would appreciate a shower though." Damien ignored the blunt way Jill flirted.

"Suit yourself." She opened the bathroom door, letting him close it. The lock clicking could be heard on the other side.

Damien turned on the shower, running some water through his hair while he waited. The more he thought about it, the more Jill's behavior started making more sense.

If she was what she truly said she was then it made sense as to why she was only comfortable coming to his house at night.

The unease around big crowds, the way she seemed uneasy when his friends were around, and of course there's her ironic hatred of the werewolf costumes on Halloween.

Christ, a werewolf. Vampires... Damien rested the heel if his palm against his forehead. *What the hell have I walked into?*

True to her word, Jill dropped Damien off at his house to get his truck so he could make it to college in time for his first class. They hadn't been easy to sit through for most of the day.

Damien's mind went from being angry at Jill and wanting to tell her off to wanting to ask the questions still buzzing around in his head.

All he'd gotten out of her on their drive back to his house was how she was able to jump off of a six-story building and avoided getting hurt when she landed.

Nothing he wanted to know would come out of his mouth. He'd been jealous when Kain and Gabriel had their hands on her and furious at the thought they'd seen her naked.

Christ what is wrong with me? I shouldn't be gawking at her like a hormonal kid during puberty. I should be cussing her out and telling her to leave me the hell alone for keeping so many damn secrets from me.

With his medical leave from his internship, Damien had nothing better to do but to head home after his classes to try to catch up on some of his reading. His leg had healed up to only a slight discomfort so he took the wrapping off, grateful he would be able to wear his jeans again. He'd chosen to hide the clothes Gabriel gave him as soon as he could.

His dad hadn't arrived home yet so Damien went into the kitchen to make himself a quick dinner.

After the meal was finished heating, he went into the den to watch some television in an attempt to get his mind off of what little he'd learned. He was still mad at her for not being forthcoming with him.

Damn. I must be losing my mind. It's not scientifically possible for someone to turn into an animal or to suck blood for that matter. He sighed as he lulled his head back, his arm dropped across his face.

Of course, it wasn't physically possible for someone to heal a paper cut in two minutes or a broken leg in a matter of days either. Not to mention getting hit by a car and not sustaining any severe lacerations or being killed. *Okay, so none of this was scientifically possible...*

Damien finished his dinner quickly, his mind still a blur of confusion.

Despite having a shower earlier that morning, he decided to stick to his routine. He turned on the shower, letting the water heat until the room filled with steam. He let his shorts fall into a pile before stepping into the water. His eyes closed as the hot water ran down his body.

An image of Jill in her bra and panties back at the gym flashed across his mind. The thought of her perfect body stretched out on her bed, wrapped tightly in her sheets or covered in sweat after a fight brought about a searing heat inside his body.

As if his hand were reacting on its own, Damien began rubbing his cock, feeling it had already begun hardening. His thumb rolled over the tip, feeling the warmth of the pre-cum the more aroused he became.

The idea of Gabriel touching Jill in her night clothes made Damien angry for reasons he just couldn't wrap his mind around. A low rumble started in the back of his throat the angrier he got at the thought Jill might move on from him.

A twinge of possessiveness unlike he'd ever felt before made Damien's muscles tighten as he imagined himself taking Jill as his own.

Despite his mind telling him to get a grip on himself, his breath grew heavy when his mind's eye drifted over Jill's long, sinewy body. Her gorgeous legs and hair so soft he wanted to bury his face so deep he'd be unable to breathe. He could feel his hands exploring every luscious curve, his fingers tracing every scar.

The carnal desire inside of him began to surface the more he let himself remember. Those gorgeous icy eyes so full of a hidden desire she tried so hard to hide. The sweetness of the seduction in her voice, the smell of her when she got close to him. It all drove Damien wild.

His eyes closed tightly as his own lust grew, his hand gripping his shaft. The hot water made him sweat despite the chills his feelings were sending through his body.

The orgasm was close, Damien could feel it. He leaned his forearm against the wall, biting down as he imagined sinking his teeth into Jill's soft skin as he made love to her. His butt cheeks tightened as the cum shot out from his shaft, his legs shaking from sheer pleasure.

What is wrong with me? He slammed his fist into the wall. He quickly washed his hair and body, turned off the water and dried off.

Damien put his shorts on, choking back a mixture of frustration, lust and overall guilt. He slid down the tile wall onto the floor, his head resting on the arm he set on his bent knee.

The fear of being hunted by vampires growing in his chest made his stomach churn with a bout of nausea. It nearly made him throw his guts up. Everything had been so crazy since he'd gotten back to Big Timber. He decided to take some time to try and get a grip on what was going on before it drove him mad.

After Damien hadn't answered any of her texts, Jill decided to drop by his house. His truck was in the driveway so she knew he had to be home.

Things hadn't ended on such a great note earlier in the day so she decided to stop to get Damien a cup of his favorite tea as an apology. She hoped he would give her the chance to explain.

When Jill didn't find Damien in his room, she thought he might have gone through with his nightly routine.

Treading on the side of caution she sat on the branch of the tree outside to wait, sipping the hot coffee she got for herself.

With each passing moment, Jill felt her heart sink. Damien still hadn't shown up. She began to get concerned despite the fact she couldn't smell any of the foreign scents that accompanied werewolves or the vampires controlling them. *Maybe he doesn't want to talk.*

Descending the tree, Jill made her way to the front door, ringing the doorbell. Damien answered, his hair a ruffled mess of stress.

"Hey, I wanted to drop by and give you this," Jill handed Damien the tea. "It's the one you told me was your favorite."

Still no response though he did take the tea.

"Damien, I'm so sorry. I never meant for any of this to happen. I tried so hard to take things slow," Jill found herself rambling. Something she had never done with anyone before.

The thought that Damien may chase her out of his life forever tore her apart. "You have every right to be angry but please, don't be afraid of me."

Jill had come to care for him so much, trying to take things slow and easing him into caring for her until Demetrius' men attacked him.

They gave her no choice. They could have killed him. She'd done all she could to shield him from the fight so it wouldn't terrify him.

At Gabriel's gym, she'd taken great care to avoid acting too strongly, allowing him to have his space aside from some light flirting.

When Damien stayed silent, only glaring at her, Jill decided it was time to tell him the truth. She took a deep breath and began.

"Damien, I know there's absolutely no way I could try to explain what's going on without it sounding like some child's nightmare or horror film gone terribly awry. I've waited for you for centuries." Her hand longed to reach out to touch his face, anything to get him to speak to her.

Damien couldn't take it any longer. The hurt in Jill's voice touched his heart. Deep down he knew she never intended for him to get hurt. He'd taken the time in his bathroom to come to grips with a few things, especially after what happened in his shower.

"Jill, no more secrets, okay. I'm guilty of holding some of my own back from you. I don't like the idea of almost getting killed for reasons I don't fully understand so you can come in if you come clean. I want to know everything about what's going on. In return, I'll share what I've been holding back, deal?" Damien replied, his voice more emotionless than she'd heard from him.

"Yes," Jill replied.

Damien led Jill into the living room where he offered her a place on the couch while he sat in his dad's chair. "Go ahead."

Jill sighed, heavily. "I'm not going to lie, some of this is going to sound unbelievable but you have my word that it is all truth,"

"For centuries, lycans and vampires have been at war, destroying each other for resources, territory and dominance. These feuds became known as the Blood Wars,

"The bloodshed got so bad that beings known only as Purifiers began walking the earth to try and keep some sense of balance to prevent the destruction of the natural order. No one knew where they came from or what powers they possessed. It was believed that they were paladins sent by heaven to keep some semblance of harmony,

"One night after a battle, I'd severely injured; beyond my natural ability to heal. I began to resign myself to death, enjoying the light of the moon for what I thought would be the last time."

Jill paused her story, her thoughts turned to the light of the moon on her back as she lay in the snow dyed red by her fallen brothers and sisters. The pain at seeing so many killed needlessly returned inside, turning into anger.

She had to compose herself to continue. "Lucius Wolf, the Purifier found me and nursed me back to health. He taught me that vampires and lycans weren't so different from one another. We both had similar needs and the instincts to survive in a world where we faced a common threat. Man, and his growing superstition. Lucius was wise and cared for both races so much I found myself falling in love with him. An uneasy truce was put into place with his help until the arrival of Demetrius Stone. The Vampire Lord believed lycans were no more than beasts and had no right to exist alongside vampires as equals. To him, we were slaves to either bow to his will or to be slaughtered like cattle,

"He called for Lucius to be killed. By the time I found him I barely recognized him anymore."

"What Demetrius didn't know was that Lucius made a vow to heaven. His soul would never find rest until there was some kind of peace between the races. I wanted to join him in his choice but Demetrius called upon the dark god to place a curse on me out of pure spite. I wasn't going to die but live so I could see the man I loved murdered over and over throughout the centuries,

"This was my life until one day, Lucius' soul disappeared. I tried and tried to hear the song it sang but when I couldn't find it I came here. I thought, maybe he'd moved on to the new world.

"For one-thousand years there was no trace of him. I almost gave up hope, thinking he forgot his promise. That he forgot me."

Jill paused, knowing she had just given Damien a buckshot blow of information at once, searching his wide-eyed stare for any sign he was going to say anything. Hopefully he didn't think she was crazy and kick her out. When he didn't respond, she continued.

"I'd thought you lost until I saw you the day you moved here, Damien. There was no mistaking your soul, no mistaking the song it sang. The vampires know who you are, they won't stop until they either turn or kill you. Knowing Demetrius, it'll be the latter. I won't let that happen again, not when I have the strength to stop it." Jill took a sip of her coffee, fighting to keep her strength in check to avoid shattering the mug.

"I must admit, that would have sounded like a fairy tale to me a couple of days ago. It still sounds a bit unbelievable but I'm sure from our time together, you've already seen I'm not exactly what people around here would call normal either. If I was honest with myself, I never really have been." Damien's response was relaxed despite his being angry and in self-denial only two hours ago.

The memories he'd long blocked still bothered him, almost torturing him like angry, wailing ghosts. Maybe he would find peace if he actually dared to share them with someone. Jill shared her past out of trust, it was only right that he extend the same trust.

Damien stared into the fire he'd started before Jill began telling her story. The room was warm and peaceful with the soft crackling of the wood and subtle smell of burning hickory. He inhaled deeply, slowly releasing the breath to relax his mind against the anxiety he could feel welling up inside of him.

"Charlie and Sarah aren't my real parents. My biological mom wasn't exactly what one could call parental material. I never met dear old dad. Apparently, he just knocked her up and then ran out on us. I'm not sure, nor do I really care to find out. What I do know is when I was very young, my mom did things to me. Things that, at the time, I didn't know were wrong. Anytime I would ask to go play with my friends, she would lock me in my room, yelling at me and saying things like I only wanted to get away from her like dad did. When it was time for me to start school, she freaked out saying I couldn't go because there were other girls who would take me away from her,

"It was only when one of the teachers reported the abuse to the town police that I was finally set free from that hell. Charlie and Sarah took me in as their own and despite my hesitation and anger at first, worked through the pain with me. I began seeing them as my only parents, locking away any memory of the other woman."

"Little did I know at the time, those memories were slowly destroying me. Things didn't get much better in school. We were cutting designs for Valentine's Day and I accidentally cut my finger. Before I could tell the teacher, it disappeared. It was the first time I knew I was different. The other kids had to go to the nurse for injuries like knee scrapes or cuts but not me."

Damien rubbed the bridge of his nose with his thumb and finger to keep his own anger suppressed. He'd kept it hidden deep within himself, denying its existence. Strangely enough, it felt good not to have to bear the pain on his own.

When he was sure he could, Damien continued his story. "All throughout school I did my best to hide being different until the day my dad couldn't take me to school so I decided to ride my new bike. I was so excited to show it off I guess I wasn't watching where I was going. A black car speeding down the street hit me, sending me up and over the hood. I landed on the pavement, expecting to be dead only to find I'd only been dazed,

"By the time the ambulances and police arrived, there wasn't anything severely wrong with me. They told my parents they couldn't explain it. When my mom and dad looked at me, I was afraid they might abandon me, thinking I was some sort of freak,

"At first, it seemed like I might have been right until my mom walked over to me and hugged me close to her. Things changed after that. The people in town started avoiding me. Some from the religious sect said I had been possessed by the devil. Even my own schoolmates distanced me. It's why I had to leave Big Timber. I lost my mom only a year after the accident. I hadn't been the same since."

Jill felt the sting of tears in her eyes at the pain she could feel radiating from Damien. Her own heart aching at knowing he'd suffered alone for so long.

"I never told anyone. I chose to close off and suffer in silence, thinking if I pretended things were fine, it would make the pain easier to deal with. It was never enough. I still don't feel right around normal people." Damien paused as Jill wrapped her arms around him in a comforting embrace. The warmth of her body calmed him against the angry ghosts of his past.

Jill fell to her knees before him, her hands taking his face. "I didn't know how bad things were for you. I know I've done nothing to prove the truth in my words I'm about to say but I would never abandon you, Damien. I'm a wolf. Loyalty to our loved ones is one of our strongest traits."

Damien couldn't stop himself, he wrapped his arms around Jill, pulling her tightly to him. All of the emotion he'd held back for a decade flowed forward into this one moment.

The guilt at what he'd done in the shower melted away, allowing the feelings that'd been budding inside of him to begin to sprout.

CHAPTER FIVE

T he morning following their soul-revealing talk, Damien stood by his window. He didn't have his first class until noon that day and was still on medical leave under orders from Dr. Langston. He leaned his forehead against his forearm on the wall, watching the rain falling in sheets once again outside his window. His mind a swirling mix of emotions he'd held back all surged forward all at once.

The more time they spent together, the more Damien couldn't deny it. He was developing feelings for Jill. He wanted her. Wanted to share his day-to-day life with her, to hold her and make her feel like everything would be okay.

Jill had played with fire by sharing a part of her world with him. She'd risked losing him just to do what he asked.

There was no doubt in his mind, Jill was dangerous. A force that existed outside the bounds of the realms of nature.

Something long hidden behind a veil of shadows surrounded by superstition and lore.

To add to the tension, rumbles of thunder could be heard rising above the trees and echoing across the mountains.

"I don't care, anymore. I don't care what you or how old you are, Jill. You've suffered alone for so long. I want to be there for you. At least then, you wouldn't have to hurt alone." Damien spoke out loud to himself in the emptiness of his room.

He knew what he wanted would come with a plethora of peril but he didn't care. Nothing was going to get in the way of being with the woman he'd come to love.

Damien pulled his truck up to the college, opened the door and grabbed his backpack to the building where his noon class was held.

He sat towards the back of the new lecture hall. It had been completed right before classes began. He could still smell the new wood and polish. The chairs were still stiff from needing to be broken in.

Damien checked the screen of the phone he pulled from his pocket.

Nothing. Not so much as a short response to any of the texts he sent following his speech to himself in his room earlier that morning.

Damn it. Damien thought to himself, disappointed. He dropped his phone to his lap, holding it in his hand.

His head lolled back to look at the wood paneled ceiling. The bright lights almost blinded him but he wasn't focusing on them.

The jeans and jacket he wore were soaked from the rain slightly chilling him. It wasn't enough to draw his mind away from the roving thoughts of raven hair and icy green eyes.

The micro-biology professor's monotone voice droned on about subjects Damien no longer saw as important as they were to him in the beginning of the year.

Yeah, right. He thought, sarcastically smiling to himself. *I wonder if the rules of natural selection and the roles of genetics in the preservation of species applies to lycans or vampires.*

The rest of the class seemed shamble by like a zombified snail. Damien tapped his foot, spinning his pen around his thumb. The phone in his lap grew heavier with its silence.

When the class finally ended, Damien quickly packed his books and headed for the door only to be stopped by Chelsea.

"Hey, Dame. It's been a while," she said, her voice more shy than usual. "I was wondering, if you aren't doing anything later tonight, would you like to go out?"

Damien sighed. "Not tonight, Chels. I want to catch up on some work I missed after being out of school."

"Oh. Okay, then," Chelsea replied. Her voice carrying a slight hint of dejection. "How about lunch?"

Damien smiled. He realized since everything had gone to hell, he hadn't really gotten a chance to go out much with his friends. "Sure."

A bright smile lit up Chelsea's face as she hugged Damien around the waist.

After they got their food, they chose to sit outside at one of the tables under the wooden gazebo since it was raining to enjoy lunch and talk before their next class.

"I'm so glad we finally got the fall weather but, this rain has been a nightmare. It was kind of weird this year. Almost like it couldn't make up its mind. The colors are always so pretty. I think this is my favorite season, don't you?" Chelsea chirped.

Damien wasn't paying attention. He was too focused on what had happened on the bridge with Jill and the night before. It was like they had shared a bonding moment so strong, nothing else mattered.

Chelsea smacked Damien's arm. "Damien, are you even listening to me?"

"What? To be honest, no. I'm sorry, Chels. I've had a lot on my mind lately." Damien replied, once again perturbed that he'd been hiding most of his secret life from everyone around him.

"What's with you? You've been spacing out more often than usual, you hardly ever talk to me and to top it off, we don't see you around much. It's almost like I don't know you anymore."

Damien took a drink of his iced tea. He could feel his temper flaring up inside of him. "I know. I'm sorry, okay. It's just things haven't exactly been...forget it."

"Damien, I want to help. You know how much I care for you. If something's bothering you, then talk to me about it." Chelsea rested her hand on Damien's arm.

"If I could tell you, I would. I just can't. You wouldn't believe me anyway." Damien replied, gently shoving her arm off.

They finished eating in silence, the air thick with tension.

Damien looked out at the grassy hill overlooking the river that ran through the campus.

The soft patter of the rain calmed him as he watched the ducks waddle down into the water. For once, he felt like he could actually settle down and enjoy the scenery. The nightmares melted away into afterthoughts. Dark dreams kept at bay by a sense of comfortable normalcy.

Damien noticed Chelsea fidgeting beside him, her hands teasing the ends of the sleeves of her purple sweater.

"What's wrong?" he asked.

"Damien, are you seeing someone? I watched you in class. You sighed a of couple times, staring at your phone and the walls as though you were daydreaming."

Damien sighed, a small smile rolling across his mouth. "It was that obvious, huh?"

"Yeah. It's been obvious since your outburst at the café. Do I know her?" Chelsea's voice sounded half-sarcastic mixed with a hint of disappointment.

"Not directly. I saw her at the orientation the day you ran into me, remember? After that, we kind of ran into each other at the café. We've been talking via text mostly ever since." Damien knew he hadn't told the whole truth but he hadn't completely lied either.

Without a word, Chelsea rose to her feet, her hands balled up at her sides.

"Chels?"

Chelsea didn't answer. As she started walking away, Damien thought he saw the glisten of a tear falling down her face. She also didn't seem to care that she was getting soaked by the rain either.

The last class of his day was in the science hall. It was one of the most isolated places at the campus. The hallway was long and narrow with cabinets, shelves and closets full of every kind of science equipment the students could want. Lab specimens were kept in the freezers and metal shelves sorted into species and body parts lining both sides of the halls.

The time went by with Damien not hearing half of what the professor said. He was still upset for hurting Chelsea's feelings only briefly before his mind turned towards thoughts of what Jill could be doing.

I bet she's doing something for a client. A sudden heat rushed in his groin as he thought of those icy green eyes and porcelain skin. He scooted closer to the desk to avoid being embarrassed by his sudden onset of male desire.

Relief came when Professor Hanson called the class.

Damien rushed to pack up his notebooks into his backpack and stepped out into the hall where he was met by a young woman with platinum blonde hair styled like an actress.

The blonde strands layered and curled in such a way, it seemed as though she'd taken hours to get it to fall to the side as it did.

She was highly attractive with her piercing red eyes and ruby lips. Her huge breasts struggled to stay behind the leather corset she wore. Her luscious, curvy body showed off her low riding leather pants and black leather knee-high boots.

Despite all of the woman's beauty, there was something about her that made Damien's neck hairs stand on end. He wanted to get away from her as quickly as he could.

"Hello Damien, it is the sweetest of pleasures to finally get to meet you. You're even more stunning in person." Her voice was as sensual as Jill's. Yet it was somehow darker, holding a slight accent Damien couldn't place.

The movements of her gorgeous hips were exaggerated as she walked right up to him, pressing her body against his. Her thigh met his groin as her hand ran down his side to rest on his hip.

Leaning her cheek in to rest on his chest, she sighed, the other she placed right next to her face.

"Do I know you?" Damien grew more uneasy as the hand on his chest moved down his side, pushing his shirt up so the woman could savor the muscles of his abdomen and chest.

The other moved down to his ass, squeezing it firmly enough to make Damien wince, hissing through his teeth.

"We haven't had the pleasure of meeting but I do know you, Damien. Your dog doesn't understand what a delicious treat she has."

The woman leaned in close to his face, her breath hot with a clear desire. Her perfume smelled like one of those very expensive name brands. A floral aroma hinted with vanilla wafted into his nose, shifting into a mellow hint of spice.

"What are you talking about? I don't have a dog."

Every nerve ending in his body told him he should try to get away from this woman. He could sense the same level of danger as the men in the alley. The encounter still left Damien with nightmares.

"Your lycan. The one you seem to be attracted to doesn't care about you, you know. She's only interested in her dead lover's soul you harbor inside your gorgeous body. I, on the other hand, couldn't care less and would give you whatever you could possibly want."

The woman's hand was cold as ice as her finger ran over his lips, playfully flicking his lower lip just as Jill had. "I don't care about the soul inside of you like that mongrel or my father does. You're so beautiful, who would care? Come with me. I promise you would enjoy the high life like a noble in our coven does. No one would question you or I would tear their heads from their bodies."

Damien closed his eyes, his jaw held tight. He didn't want to let himself think about the idea that Jill only wanted him for being an incarnation of Lucius. He wanted to get to her and find out which one of them she saw when they were together.

"I appreciate the offer but I need to go. I have a friend expecting me." He tried to get free of her only to have his wrists held firmly against the wall.

"Your dog, you mean? She can wait. I'm not done savoring my time with you." Damien jumped as her seductive voice became dark and demanding. She moved his hands behind his back, using one of hers to hold him in place as she took his jaw. "I wonder if you taste as good as you look."

The woman leaned in to kiss him. His heart beat thundered. He wanted to run but he couldn't get free from the strong hold she had on him. Her strength held his hands like shackles, her body pinned him firmly against the wall.

Just before their lips met, Damien heard the footsteps of someone sprinting down the hall. It wasn't until the woman was suddenly thrown from him that he became aware of Gabriel.

The sheer force of their collision sent the woman skidding down to the opposite end of the hallway, knocking over shelves and jogging freezers. She hissed at Gabriel as he placed himself between her and Damien.

"Damien, run! Run!" The desperation in Gabriel's voice made Damien get to his feet quickly. He grabbed his backpack and ran as fast as he could down the hall to the exit.

Damien stumbled out of the double doors of the building, his breath labored from running so fast.

The main quarter of the school was mostly deserted. The students finished with their classes for the day were most likely already back at their dorms to study or gone to get drunk at the local frat parties.

Damien looked around until his eyes fell on Kain leaning next to his car.

"Damien!" Kain yelled at him. "Hurry! Gabriel can't hold her off for long in his current state!"

Damien didn't fully understand what was going on but ran as fast as he could to Kain's car, got in and threw his backpack in the back seat.

Kain shifted gears, his foot slamming on the gas in reverse only to shift quickly back into drive as Gabriel shot out of the building, jumping into the back seat and slamming the door. He was covered in cuts. His shirt was ripped, his nose and head were bleeding from where he'd been hit.

"Kain, go! Go, go, go!" Gabriel yelled, patting the back of Damien's seat with the heel of his palm.

Kain slammed his foot back on the accelerator, the tires of his car screeched in protest as they peeled out of the college parking lot. All three of them grateful it was largely empty since none of them wanted to try and explain what was going on to campus security.

They arrived back at Solstice where Kain took Damien up to Jill's room. "I've called Jillian. She'll be here soon. Are you hurt?"

"No, but I'm fucking pissed as hell. What's going on, Kain? First, I nearly get killed by two vampires in a back alley, then I'm almost kissed by one I could have sworn had a huge crush on me. I'm pretty sure she wanted to take me in the damn hallway."

Kain leaned his hip against the wall, his arms crossed over his chest. "The vampire you encountered was Lilith Stone, the daughter of Demetrius

Stone. He's the ruling lord of the coven in the nearby mountains. You know the place if you think. It's the large mansion on the acreage just outside of town. Apparently, she's developed an interest in you. We just became aware of it. We think her intentions are to turn you into one of her kind and take you as her mate."

Kain took Damien's hand, seeing it had been cut on some of the shattered glass in the hall. "Here, I'll wrap that up for you. I can imagine it will heal on its own quickly."

"Great. That's just great. As if things weren't fucked up enough, now I've got a vampire super model on my ass."

"Damien, there's something you need to know. Demetrius is the one responsible for the first attempt on your life. He won't stop until he sees you dead. I'm sure Jillian has told you but I wanted to make sure you understood how much danger you are in," Kain's voice was surprisingly calm, despite the severity of his words. "There." Kain continued as he finished dressing Damien's cut hand.

"I know you're frustrated. Jillian shouldn't be much longer." Kain rose to his feet and turned to leave. He stopped briefly to talk over his shoulder. "Damien, she's taken with you. I don't think you understand just how much you mean to her."

Damien gave a slight nod. He knew what Jill told him at his house but what Lilith said in the hallway still bothered him. He had to know for sure if Jill's affection was directed at him.

Hours seemed to pass as Damien paced the floor, rubbing his hands across his face and scratching his head.

When Jill finally arrived, she sounded like she'd been sprinting. "Gods, I'm so sorry for making you wait. Are you hurt?"

"I'm fine, Jill. Today just hasn't been my day." Damien replied, trying to keep himself from sounding too angry.

"I tried to get home as soon as I could. Kain and Gabriel told me what happened." Jill said, trying to sound reassuring.

The room stayed silent for a while, the tension grew only thicker with each passing minute.

Damien sat down in the chair, his head against the knuckles of his thumbs, his elbows on his thighs. He tried to find the words he wanted to say before opening his mouth. Jill kept next to the makeshift work desk in the corner of her room.

Damien sighed as he leaned forward. His forearms resting on his knees. "Jill, I need to ask you something. I'm not sure how to go about it so I'm just going to be blunt."

"Go ahead."

"When we're together, do you see me as Damien or as Lucius?" Damien's voice was slightly strained, almost afraid of the answer.

Jill stood up and made her way over to Damien in the chair. She knelt down onto floor in front of him. Her hands rubbed his knees in slow, comforting circles. "Damien, I don't know what lies you were told but I can assure you they weren't true. Yes, it was Lucius' soul that called me to you but I soon realized I didn't care if you were him or not. When I first saw you, there was something about you that made me so curious. I had to get to know you more. The more time we spent together, the more I realized I was chasing a ghost. I'd forgotten what it meant to truly love someone."

Jill rose up, her hand slowly reaching for Damien's face, caressing his cheek. "To answer your question, I see you, Damien Pierce. The man who took my heart and soul the minute I gazed into your beautiful eyes."

Damien felt his heart beat hasten as Jill lay a soft kiss on his cheek, withdrawing and waiting for his response.

Without thinking, he reached his hand out to touch Jill's face, her skin softer than he imagined. His thumb ran the length of her cheekbone to her ear. She looked so human. No one would ever imagine she wasn't if they saw her this close.

It was as though he were seeing her for the first time. Her lips the color of strawberry, her icy green eyes so full of love and affection she harbored for him.

Damien rested his hand on the back of Jill's neck as he leaned forward. He brushed her raven hair away from her face, his heart pounded as his lips met hers in a gentle kiss.

The sensation was like nothing Damien ever felt before. He'd dreamed of kissing Jill, even debated on trying it during one of the nights they'd spoken. Something held him back.

He knew now what it was. He had to wait for this moment when he knew beyond any shadow of a doubt that Jill saw him for who he was.

Jill wrapped her arm around Damien's neck, her other hand reaching around him to rest on his lower back. She released his lips, backing away to look into his eyes.

"I've been wanting to do that for a while now." Damien said, slightly chuckling. His breath heavy.

"Me too." Jill replied. "It's late though and you've had a rather eventful night. Would you like to stay here? I can take you back to the college tomorrow to get your truck."

Damien hadn't noticed the time. He was too absorbed with the idea that not only had he kissed the woman who stole his own heart but a lycan. "Yeah. I should probably get to sleep. Let me shoot my dad a text to let him know I'm staying at a friend's house."

Jill took the same blanket she used the first night Damien stayed with her, putting it on the couch before getting her clothes to go change in the bathroom.

"What are you doing?"

"You told me it made you feel uncomfortable to see me get dressed so I was going to head to the bathroom."

Damien turned towards the wall. "I won't look, Jill. Do what you want. This is your room after all."

Jill smiled, not really caring if he used the mirror he had to have known was on the wall to watch. It didn't bother her to get dressed in front of him. To her, Damien was as natural to be around as any lycan.

After she finished, Jill went over to the couch to sleep for the night. A sudden warm, firm hand around her wrist stopped in her tracks.

"I'll sleep on the couch. You shouldn't have to give up your bed just because I'm here. It felt wrong to take it last time." Damien's voice was gentle as he spoke.

Jill looked towards the couch then back at Damien. "You know, I don't mind sharing the bed. You like to cocoon yourself so you can have the blankets. I'll lay on top of them and use the spare."

Damien let go of her to take off his shirt and set it on top of his backpack on the floor against the closet.

By the time he turned around, Jill was already curling up on the bed under the blanket. She looked so beautiful, her dark hair falling in waves over the pillow.

Damien flexed his hands, his knuckles turning white from how tight he closed them only to release the muscles again. He knew what he wanted to do but hesitated because he didn't know how Jill would react.

There were times when she was so strong. Like she didn't really need anyone. Others, she seemed reserved and shy.

Swallowing the uncertainty, Damien pulled the blanket back to slide in next to Jill. His arm draped around her waist as he maneuvered his body to fit into hers. The smell of her hair was pleasantly sweet. Like blueberries and vanilla with a hint of jasmine.

Damien fell asleep next to her. The once tortured ghosts that haunted him were laid to rest with each soft rise and fall of her chest.

CHAPTER SIX

The following morning, the clouds responsible for the rain the day before broke allowing the rays of the sun to shine in through the window of Jill's room. The light in his eyes made Damien raise his arm to try and block the piercing rays. He rubbed them as he rolled onto his back, a slight groan escaped him as he stretched his arms above his head. He rose up to find he was alone. The blanket they'd shared fell to his hips.

What time is it? Damien thought, reaching for the bedside table where he left his phone. It was already past 1:00 pm.

He got up out of the bed and looked around quickly. His shirt had been set down on the chair next to the desk in the corner. Damien took it and put it on quickly before he grabbed his backpack.

Out in the hall, it appeared vacant. No one seemed to be awake yet so Damien made sure to keep quiet as he descended the stairs.

Kain waited at the bottom of the stairs, drinking coffee and reading the paper. "Where are you off to in such a hurry?"

"I was going to ask Jill for the ride back to the college so I could get my truck. Do you know where she is?"

"Jillian went to the school with Gabriel early this morning to get your truck. She didn't want to wake you since the two of you had a late night. I promised her I would watch out for you just in case." Kain replied, calmly, folding the paper and setting it down on one of the workout benches.

"Kain, what am I doing? I'm not a werewolf or a vampire."

Kain winced. "Lycan, please. We don't appreciate that word."

Damien forgot what Jill said about lycans feeling insulted at being called werewolves. She never did tell him why.

"Sorry. I'm not a lycan either. I still don't get the full extent of what's going on."

"Damien, I know you have been led to believe you have to pretend to be something you clearly are not. You are not human. No more than anyone in this gym. You may not be able to transform or drink blood, this is true. However, how many humans do you know can take a hit by a vampire into a dumpster and suffer a broken leg only to have it heal completely in a few days," Kain asked, his gaze locked on Damien.

Damien looked down at the floor. His muscles tensed all throughout his body at the lycan's words.

"When was the last time you felt comfortable around them? Have you ever truly felt like you fit in man's world? You still feel like they're silently judging you. Like they're seeing you as some sort of outcast. You aren't a freak, Damien. You have been fighting against your true nature for years. Give it time. I know you will come to see us as family."

"Kain!" A call of challenge from Scott could be heard echoing through the gym along with his storming footsteps across the wood floor.

Kain rolled his eyes under his reading glasses as Scott screamed his name. "Think about what I've said. I know you feel in your heart I am right." Kain threw a towel over his shoulder.

Damien watched the lycan's back as he walked away. Kain was beyond wise, someone Damien quickly found himself looking up to.

After he left the gym, Damien decided to go for a run to think. He began to realize what Kain said fell in line with the realization he came to the night he'd imagined Jill in his shower. He'd never truthfully felt at home with normal people since his accident. Nothing had changed in the ten years he had been gone. It was as though the town had been suspended in time as if by some spell.

The phone in his pocket began to vibrate and ring. It made him stop in the middle of the country road just outside of town to answer it so he could keep listening to his music.

"Rob, what's up?" Damien asked, his breath labored from his run.

"Hey, D. Have you seen, Chels? She hasn't really been answering any of the calls or texts I've sent." Rob's voice sounded strained with concern.

"No. I haven't. We had lunch on the campus but then she left. She seemed pretty upset. I just thought she was mad at me." Damien's reply was laced with his own concern.

Even if he didn't feel the same for Chelsea as she did for him, he still saw her as a good friend.

"Damn. Hope she's okay."

"I'm betting she's fine, Rob. You know how she gets when she's pouting. She's probably with one of her girlfriends she's always chatting with online."

"Yeah, I bet you're right. Hey, you want to go see that new gory movie in the theater? Have some guy time?" Rob's mood appeared to have lightened.

"Sure. Just let me get back to my house. I'll see you around seven tonight, sound good?"

"Cool, see you then."

Damien hung up, taking a deep breath as he turned around to head back to the gym.

By the time Damien made it back, Jill was standing next to his truck with his backpack and keys in response to a quick text he'd sent her after he got off the phone with Rob.

"Enjoy your movie tonight, Damien. Just please remember what I told you about the vampires. Be careful and stay alert. Text or call after you get out to let me know everything is alright." Jill wrapped Damien in a firm hug, worried to leave him alone after dark.

Damien gently guided Jill's eyes to look up at him, kissing her lips. "Don't worry about me. I will be careful. I promise I'll call once the movie ends."

Jill nodded, hesitant to release him. She watched as he got in his truck and drove away.

Damien pulled up in the parking lot with thirty minutes left to meet Rob in front of the theater. He'd raced home to get cleaned up and dressed before heading back out, squeezing him for time.

Rob was leaning against the brick wall, his eyes locked on his phone when Damien ran up to him.

"Sorry I'm late. My girlfriend had to bring my truck." Damien froze the minute the words left his mouth.

"Girlfriend? Dude, no wonder Chelsea isn't talking. Who is it?" Rob asked, chuckling.

Damien figured there was no reason to hide the truth anymore. At least the part about Jill being his girlfriend. He hadn't even asked her yet.

"I'll tell you when we get into the theater, Rob. We have some catching up to do, that much is for sure." Damien replied, careful to watch his surroundings like he'd promised.

They bought their tickets and headed into the theater. Rob wanted popcorn so they stopped by the concession stand to get some. Damien settled on a bottle of water and nachos.

After they sat down, Rob didn't wait to bombard Damien with questions. "So, this girlfriend of yours? Why so secret? We've been friends for years." He asked, not hiding his excitement.

"Well, she's kind of an introvert. Doesn't really like to get around big crowds."

"Ah, one of those hiding types, huh? Can't say I relate but I can't blame her. People can get nuts. What's her name?" Rob spoke with a mouth full of popcorn.

"Jill…Jill Styles."

"Nice name. She hot? Wait," Rob paused as though he'd just had an epiphany. "Is this the 'spirit' chick? The one you kept seeing although Chels and I still hadn't seen her?"

"The very same. Sorry I lied, Rob. I just didn't want to make you two think I was more insane than I already sounded." Damien took a drink of his water, almost choking when Rob landed his hand hard on his back.

"Hey man, no problem. I get it. You did sound nuts for a while there but I'm glad it worked out. I'd like to meet her sometime but don't push it. If she's that introverted, I don't want to come off as too frontal. I'm an ultra-extrovert." Rob laughed.

Damien didn't respond, silently agreeing.

The lights dimmed signaling the start of the movie.

After the film ended, Damien walked with Rob to his car. He scanned the area to make sure he didn't see any suspicious people lurking about. His eye fell on a black BMW. The man leaning next to it smoked what looked like a vapor cigarette.

"Dang that movie was freaky! Now I know why I hate clowns! I'm so not sleeping tonight." Rob opened his car door, his voice held the slight edge of a tremble.

Damien's eyes stayed locked on the man. Something didn't seem right about him. The car had limo tints so dark he couldn't see into the windows. He was so focused he hadn't heard what Rob said.

"Uh-huh. Hey Rob, mind giving me a lift to my truck? I'm feeling lazy and don't want to walk all the way across the lot." Damien lied, still feeling suspicious.

"Sure, man. I got nowhere to be. Just heading home to game with some guild folks online. Hop in."

Damien got into the car, glad he was able to get his friend to give him a lift.

"Thanks, Rob." Damien said as he closed the door.

Rob stuck around until Damien was in his truck. He didn't move until Damien started his engine and began to pull out. They always looked after each other at school and tonight, Damien was more relieved than ever Rob had his back.

He pulled out of the lot to head back to his house.

The drive home was always interesting to Damien. His house lay just outside the town but the drive was the most enjoyable part.

Once you got past the city limits, there was nothing but woods. It was one thing Damien loved, especially when he went for a run down the trail.

He glanced in the rearview mirror to see what looked like a black car. His suspicions grew as it sped up, close enough to his truck, it could almost hit it only to whip around and speed back up.

Damien sighed in relief. *For a moment, I thought that might have been that same car.*

Only a few miles ahead, Damien saw what looked like a man standing in the middle of the road. He didn't want to hit him so he slammed on the brakes.

Before he had a chance to recover from the mild hint of whiplash, the man was next to his window. A wicked grin curled across the man's face as he stared at Damien.

He had the same pale complexion Lilith and the vampires in the alley had. His suit was a fine all black, tailored Italian and he wore the same black sunglasses despite it being pitch black.

A sharpened nail raked across the glass. The high pitch noise stinging Damien's ears. It stopped only to tap on the window.

Oh shit. Damien thought just before he felt his truck picked up and rolled down the steep ditch.

Once the rolling stopped, Damien kicked open the crumbled door. He only had a few scratches but felt dizzy and nauseated from hitting his head against the steering wheel.

He jumped down off of the truck, his knees giving way beneath him.

"So, you're the infamous Damien Pierce. It's a pleasure to finally meet you face to face," The man took a puff off of his vapor cigarette, blowing it out as he continued. "You don't really look like much to me. I don't see why Lilith is dead set on having you as her king."

Damien recognized the name Lilith as the one he met in the science hall. "And you are?" Damien used his truck to stand, slightly ticked that everyone around him seemed to know who or what he was but him.

Before he could even think about moving, the man was in his face. The distance between them closed in a matter of seconds. A billow of sickening smoke blew into Damien's face. He coughed as he turned his head.

"My name is Stoker Cromwell. I'm a vampire noble and you're moving in on my intended bride. Honestly, I don't know why everyone is making such a fuss. You should be flattered though. I'm going to be the one that crushes the life out of you."

"Somehow I don't think getting killed by someone is a reason to feel flattered. Look, Stoker, is it? I don't really have any interest in Lilith so she's all yours. I've honestly had about enough of everyone seeming to want to kill me lately." Damien replied, trying to fight the fear of his impending death staring him in the face.

It seemed like his encounters with the vampires were getting more frequent and every one of them either wanted him dead or to screw him.

Stoker grabbed Damien by the collar, shoving him hard against the crumbling body of his truck.

The sound of hissing brought Damien's attention to the exhaust line beside his ear. He knew from working with his dad on the engine a few times that the exhaust line gave off really hot gas and liquid.

"Okay, let's skip the bullshit shall we? I would like to end your pathetic life quickly and get back to my bride."

"That's going to be a problem. See, giving up and dying isn't really in my nature." Damien replied, using the knife he began carrying in his back pocket to puncture the hissing line.

"Shit!" Stoker screamed in pain as his face was suddenly sprayed with a mix of hot gas and liquid, forcing him to release Damien.

Damien took the opportunity to run as fast as he could through the woods. The woods around him seemed familiar. His house was only a few blocks away. Jill told him vampires couldn't enter his house unwelcome without being hurt.

"Pierce!" Stoker yelled into the woods.

The ache in his head made Damien stop to catch his breath. He still suffered from the whiplash of the crash. His head pounded in his temple but he couldn't give in to it or he would lose his life.

Stoker's black leather shoes could be heard crunching behind him. "That's it, Pierce. I was going to be merciful and end you quickly. Maybe drain you of every last drop of blood. Now, I'm going to tear you apart piece by piece. You will be begging me to end your life before I'm done."

Damien hid behind a wide pine, his breath labored. Swift thinking made him pull out his phone quickly to hit the speed dial for Jill.

"Damien? Why didn't you call me sooner? I've been worried."

"Jill, listen. I'm in trouble. I don't have a ton of time."

"What's wrong? Where are you?" Jill's voice was emotionless.

"I can't tell you the details. His name is Stoker Cromwell. He's wounded but, he's angry. I don't know how long I can dodge him. The woods only a few blocks away from my house. Please hurry." Damien hung up, the fear began to manifest despite his attempts to suppress it.

Just as the call ended, Stoker stood in Damien's face. His right eye, cheek and neck were badly burned. The bloodlust apparent in his angry scowl.

"Call your dog, did we? It doesn't matter. You won't be alive by the time she gets here. No one disrespects me like this and gets away with it." Stoker grabbed Damien by the throat and pinned him against the tree.

"Humans are such fragile creatures," he continued. "You think you have power. Blinded by thoughts that you are the dominant species. In reality, you are nothing but food for those of us higher up on the evolutionary chain."

Stoker slid his hand beneath Damien's jacket to his ribcage. "Don't believe me? Let me show you how weak you are."

A sharp pain accompanied the sudden snap of the bone as Damien's rib was broken as though it were a twig. The sudden onset made Damien sick to his stomach as he cried out in agony.

"See? I snapped your rib as though it were a pencil. You can have the best healing ability in the world. If your heart undergoes too much trauma, it will give out. Such is the fragility of humans." Stoker smirked.

Damien was hurled through the air, once again landing on his side. His hand went to his ribcage as he fought the urge to scream in pain.

Stoker picked up a thick branch off of the ground, using his foot to splinter the end into a sharp point. "I wonder how many times I can stab you before you die. The power of a Purifier has to be worth something. Rumor has it you healed a broken leg in two days. That's impressive. Almost like one of us."

Damien couldn't move. His side hurt like hell, his head pounded, and his stomach churned. His heart was beating so fast he felt like he was having a heart attack.

"Relax, Pierce. From the sound of your heartbeat, this won't last much longer." Stoker mocked. He walked over to Damien and used his foot to roll him onto his back.

Stoker raised the stick above his head, bringing it down with such force it went through Damien's side into the ground beneath him.

Damien screamed in pain.

"Don't worry, you won't die too quickly. I wanted to make sure I had time to drain you dry before your heart gives out. Your blood is definitely worth something from what I've seen tonight," Stoker's voice was lighter than it had been, almost as though he were actually impressed.

"I see why Demetrius finds you a threat. You can take some damage. Rest in peace knowing I actually complimented you. I don't ever do that," Stoker bent down over Damien, painfully yanking his head up to expose his throat. "Now why don't you be a good boy and lie still while I drain your blood."

Damien closed his eyes in preparation for the pain of Stoker's fangs when he suddenly heard the vampire grunt as he was hit by something. Something big.

His eyes opened to see Jill's huge black form standing on all fours above him, growling at Stoker. Relief filled his heart before the loss of blood took his consciousness from him.

Stoker kicked the debris away, dusting his suit. "So I was wrong. Looks like I got carried away with playing."

Jill bared her fangs, snarling with anger. When she arrived to find the wreckage of the truck, she followed Damien's scent through the woods.

The wound from the tree branch slammed through Damien's side caused his blood to flow in a steady stream to the ground. Time was short. The encounter would need to be ended quickly or he would die.

The lycan positioned herself protectively over Damien. She knew from her past encounters with Stoker, the vampire would use Damien as leverage to get a hand up in the fight.

"It's too bad really," Stoker took a handgun out of his pocket, loading the magazine with a clip Jill could see was full of silver. "Shame to waste all that good blood."

He pointed the gun at Jill. "Are you sure you want to risk so much for this human?"

Jill snapped at him. She crouched low to the ground, her body a shield between the vampire and Damien. She would make sure she was the only one hit with the bullets when Stoker emptied the clip.

She looked down at the handsome man beneath her. Her heart pounded like a kettle drum. She was determined to keep him alive. *I won't let him hurt you anymore. Please just hang on.*

Stoker laughed the whole time as every ring of the gun sent new stings of pain into her body. Jill could feel herself weakening but she couldn't move. If she did, Damien would be at Stoker's mercy.

Bang. Bang. Bang. The bullets rang out over and over until the click of an empty clip could be heard.

"Hm. Oh right, you're immortal. That's upsetting." Stoker got into Jill's personal space and proceeded to hit her over and over again.

Each strike made her whimper. Her legs trembled from the poison of the silver inside of her body. Her blood bubbled and steamed from the holes in her flesh. It fell to the ground in smoking droplets.

Luna, please let the sun rise soon. I'm losing strength mother, please. Help me protect the man I love.

Jill's prayer had been answered. The sun peaked over the hedges forcing Stoker to step back.

"Fine. I'll end this for now. You got off lucky, dog. Next time, he's not going to live though our encounter, I'll make sure of it." Stoker sprinted off, following the night to avoid being incinerated by the sun's light.

Jill's breath was labored when she shifted into her human form. She took the branch in her hands and pulled it from Damien's side. Her heart aching as he cried out in pain with each agonizing inch.

"Shh, it's okay. It's okay. It's out." She said as she ran her hand through Damien's hair.

Jill knew what she had to do. She could heal Damien but it would mean she would have to lick the wound. The curse that bound her to the world in her saliva would keep him from dying but doing so would bind her to him.

Taste was a part of a lycan pairing. The sharing of blood was as sacred as sex. It allowed mates, close friends and loved ones to speak to each other. To feel each other's pain. To see each other's past.

When Damien started shivering, she knew she didn't have a choice, she would lose him if she didn't act fast.

Using her grown claws, she tore his shirt open, lowering down to the wound. Her tongue took the sweetness of his blood into her mouth. Her eyes began to glow. The feelings of fear, pain, and confusion mixed with love, fullness and affection so strongly it almost overwhelmed her.

The flow of his blood through his veins was so clear it was she were looking at a CAT scan. She could hear the softness of his breath as it moved in and out of his lungs.

Jill pulled back, her breath heavy. Her fingers dug into the Earth, her teeth clenched as she tried to handle the bond forming between them.

Every memory he ever had slammed into her mind in a confusing whirlwind of images.

Part of him now belonged to her and she wasn't going to stop until she had all of him.

The gaping wound closed, leaving no trace.

Lifting him gently in her transformed jaws, Jill started walking back to Damien's house.

CHAPTER SEVEN

Jill barely made it to Damien's house, relieved his father wasn't there so she wouldn't have to answer any unwanted questions.

The silver burned inside of her. The effects of the new bond still manifested in her mind.

Her breathing was labored against the fatigue as she struggled to use what was left of her unnatural strength to drag Damien to the bathroom to get him out of his bloody clothing. She lay him down gently on the floor. The tile on the floor began to blur, a sign she was losing the battle with unconsciousness.

"Kain," Jill's words were hushed as her breathing became shallower. Sweat began falling from her brow. "I have to call Kain."

She pulled out her phone to dial Kain's number.

A brief silence on the other end indicated an answer. "Jillian, did you find him?"

"Kain, we're at Damien's house," Jill took a breath to keep talking. "Please hurry."

Before Jill lost consciousness, she made her way to Damien, laying her cheek on his chest. Greatly weakened against the poison of the silver inside her veins, she blacked out.

Outside, the rain began to fall, the thunder alerted the town to the arrival of yet another storm. In time winter would come to transform the angry rains to soft, comforting flurries of snow.

Jill opened her eyes to find she was staring into the lights of her room in the gym. She had no memory of how she got there but was grateful when Kain had gotten her message.

Damien lay beside her. His shirt had been removed. His ribs wrapped up from the shoulder down to his stomach.

"I am glad you're awake, Jillian." Kain's relieved voice broke through the haze of Jill's mind.

"Damien?"

Kain sat on the bed next to Jill. "He lost a rather large amount of blood but it appears he's going to be fine. His body is repairing itself perfectly. Worst case, he might just be tired as sun's hell for a few days. Whatever you did saved his life. You need to rest. I'll help you recover tonight at moonrise."

Jill forced herself to sit up. The anger at the situation still fresh in her mind. "It was Stoker. What am I going to do, Kain? The vampires are getting more aggressive."

"Don't worry about that now. You need to rest. I about burned my hand when I lifted you. You are full of silver." Kain held up his burned hand. The wounds were fading but still evident.

"I'm sorry, Kain. Tonight, we can go behind the gym. I don't want to do a full recovery in front of him just yet. He hasn't even seen me transform. I don't want to overwhelm him." Jill replied, concerned and tired.

"Jillian, you need to stop being so concerned with hiding who you are from him. I spoke to him briefly when you went to get his truck. He's more open than you think. From what he's been through, I think seeing you transform is going to be the last thing that bothers him. Show him and let him decide. I think you will find you're pleasantly surprised." Kain smirked, his eyes laced with certainty and hope.

"Okay. You've never steered me wrong, old friend. I'll see you tonight?"

"Of course. Sleep well." Kain replied, nodding. He closed the door behind him, leaving them alone.

True to his word, Kain met Jill in the evening at moonrise. Damien hadn't stirred all day. Dr. Langston dropped by from time to time to administer pain medicine as needed and to check the bandages.

Kyle insisted he was present at Jill's recovery as a physician so he stood next to Kain, watching. "It's amazing. Damien's healing ability is more than we could have ever imagined. His rib was almost completely rejoined and the muscle in his side gave no indication it was even punctured. In all my years in medicine, I've never seen this. Not even in our kind."

"Kyle, we don't understand the Purifiers. No one does. We can't hope to comprehend their power or what they're capable of. Damien's still asleep. I can only imagine what he would be able to do when he awakened," Kain replied, still calm despite Kyle's obvious excitement. He turned his attention to Jill. "Ready?"

Jill made an annoyed groan. No she wasn't ready. Full recoveries hurt like sun's hell and had to be done in human form which made it worse.

"Gods damn, these things sting!" Jill yelled. Her blood bubbled slightly where the silver poisoned it. If she hadn't been immortal, they would have killed her. Despite that, it didn't make the experience any less uncomfortable.

Kain nodded, a crooked smile formed across his face. "Good luck."

"Thanks." Jill replied, less than thrilled at what she was preparing to do.

Jill flexed every muscle in her body, her eyes softly glowing. Her back arched. She growled a wolf's growl, her fangs growing as her nails dug into the soft, wet soil.

The bullets slowly emerged from her flesh. Each dropped to the ground like hail stones during a storm. Her bones ached from where they'd splintered. Her blood was on fire from the sting of the toxins.

The moon's light through the clouds gave her just enough energy needed to heal the wounds left behind. The whole process left Jill so exhausted. She had her tongue hanging out of her mouth panting.

"That is never...a pleasant experience." Jill said, sitting on the ground while Kyle came over to check on her.

Kain shook his head. "I can imagine it isn't. It has been a while since I have had to do one."

"This is getting out of hand, Kain. We've been lucky so far but what happens when luck runs out?" Jill asked, slightly defeated.

Kain sighed. "Jillian, the easy thing for you to do is something I know you don't want to do. If your sun's hell-set on taking him as your own, then protecting him is a part of the deal. Yet another reason why we usually don't go after one of them and keep to our own kind. I know you are going to find a way."

"Kain, Jill's going to be okay. Are you doing alright?" Kyle asked.

"I'm fine, Kyle. Damien may need another look before you leave. Thank you for your concern." Kain replied, smiling.

Kyle walked back into the gym to go check on Damien before he left.

"See you inside, Jillian. I believe Gabriel is making dinner tonight. Should be interesting to say in the least." Kain joined Kyle, slightly chuckling at his own joke.

Jill knew Kain was right. She looked up at the waning gibbous in the cloudy sky. Half the face of her mother looked back at her.

Mother, I need help. I care for this man so much but I feel I can't protect him on my own. I've bound myself to him in the most sacred of ways. Please. I need a miracle.

Damien opened his eyes to see the ceiling fan blades spinning. The ball hung at the end of the longer chain clinking against its shorter neighbor. The soft whirr of the motor seemed distant as he tried to clear the fog from his eyes.

He had no idea how long he'd been out cold but his body ached from laying down.

As he tried to rise up, he felt so weak and drained he settled on rolling over to find Jill lying next to him. She had no blanket. The only cover was her athletic shorts and a sports tank-top. One would never think she was capable of taking on vampires with how she looked to him now. Vulnerable and tired.

"You really do care for her, don't you?"

Damien rolled over to stare straight into the intense gaze of Gabriel as he sat in the chair next to the bed, his arms across his chest.

"I do. I never thought I could care for anyone this much anymore," Damien replied.

Gabriel leaned forward to rest his elbows on his knees. The muscles in his arms combined with the fact that he was now face to face with Damien despite sitting reminded him of their obvious difference in size.

"You must really be special to her too if she's willing to go to such great lengths to protect you. Has she shown you, yet?" The annoyance in Gabriel's voice was evident.

"Shown me?" Damien replied, partially confused, and yet agitated at Gabriel's obvious attempts to size him up.

"By the way you've just responded, I'm guessing she hasn't. That's usually what breaks the deal when one of our kind tries to love a mortal," Gabriel leaned back, his arms crossed behind his head. "When she does, that's the ultimate test. I hope you pass it."

"Honestly, Gabriel, I can't tell if you're trying to help me or insult me. What I can tell you is based on what I've seen, I don't think seeing Jill becoming a giant wolf is going to be a deal breaker." Damien replied. He ignored the jealous alpha and got up to put his shirt on.

"To be honest, I have mixed feelings. I know she cares about you but at the same time, I don't like having to save your ass every other day. Jill means a lot to many of us in this gym. Ask Kain. Jill saved him from Rayes and his band of jolly wolf killers. It's getting upsetting to see her hurt so often." Gabriel stood up and headed towards the door.

He stopped and spoke over his shoulder without turning around. "Damien, look, as much as you may care for Jill, I think you should end this thing between the two of you. It may sound harsh but an alpha's first duty is to make calls to protect his pack. I've always considered Jill a part of my pack. That being the case, I'm asking you to think about what's best for both of you."

Damien couldn't respond. He just stood there baffled at the pain-filled intensity of Gabriel's words.

Kain came in with a plate of food shortly after Gabriel left. "Glad to hear you're awake. I took the liberty of making you something to eat since you have been unconscious for four days."

Damien avoided looking Kain in the face, angry at what Gabriel said.

Sighing, Kain sat down in the chair that Gabriel had. "Alright, what did Gabriel say?"

"I'm not even sure I should tell you." Damien replied, his sarcasm sharp and cutting.

"Damien, no one knows Gabriel Locke better than I do. He's stubborn, hot-tempered and doesn't always think before he speaks. What did he say?"

"He said I should end things with Jill. I wanted to think that somewhere there was a general concern but, it sounded like he was jealous."

"I see. Damien, do not concern yourself with what Gabriel said. He's worried. To Jillian, you are her world. It makes her nervous when she can't be next to you. Especially since the vampires are getting more aggressive. It scared her to death when she thought she might not have made it in time to save you from Stoker's wrath," Kain replied, sighing, almost saddened. "The wound Jillian healed, may I see it?"

Damien lay back down on the bed to let Kain guide his shirt up so he could feel under the wrapping where the branch had penetrated all the way through. The muscle had no indentions or indications it had been pierced, just as Kyle said.

"Amazing. The muscle isn't sore?" Kain asked, curious.

"No. I heal fast but something this severe usually leaves some soreness or a scar. Something." Damien didn't know how he'd healed so thoroughly.

Kain lowered his head. "I see. Damien, there really is no one else for Jillian anymore."

"What?"

Kain's disappointment was evident as he clasped his hands tightly, his forearms resting on his knees. His jaw tightening. "It is not my place to say but when Jillian wakes up, you should make it a point to ask her."

Kain left the room. The visit left Damien with more questions to ravage his mind than when Kain arrived.

A slight stir next to him alerted him to Jill waking up.

"Morning." Her voice was drained and tired. She stretched her body out all the way down to the tips of her toes, groaning at the action before sitting up.

Damien winced at the sight of the multiple scars on her back and hips. "Morning, Jill. Can I ask you something?"

"Sure," Jill scooted over to his side of the bed to let her legs hang over the side. "You're free to speak your mind anytime you want."

Damien sat down next to Jill on the bed, the mattress creaked under his weight.

"What is it, Damien? Are you still hurting?" Jill asked, concerned at how stand-offish he was acting.

Damien shook his head, taking in a deep breath to gather his thoughts. "I want to know. What exactly is going on between us? We've talked. Gone out a few times. You've saved my life on multiple occasions. I've hidden this double-life from Rob, Chelsea and my old man. What are we doing?"

"Damien, I can't decide for both of us. I never meant for you to get wrapped up in this war but you are now. I can't change that. I know now what it is for me but I won't force anything you aren't ready for. Whatever you decide to do, I won't stop you."

Damien looked over at her. Her beautiful hair covered her face, hiding her eyes. He could see she was expecting him to leave her. She gripped the bedside as though she were strangling it.

Swallowing the knot in his throat, Damien remembered when he called Jill his girlfriend in front of Rob and the declaration he made in his bedroom. He stood up from the bed only to fall to his haunches in front of Jill, his hand petting her face.

"Jill, I don't care what or how old you are. I don't care about the vampires. I want to be here for you. Until I met you, I felt so empty, alone and lost. I hung out with Rob and Chelsea but I still felt dead inside. When I saw you on campus, I didn't know what it was. I just knew I wanted to get to know you. Those nights we talked, I felt the loneliness leave me. I could actually laugh again without it feeling forced."

Jill's heart fluttered in her chest as though it were a hummingbird trapped in her ribcage. The man she had fallen for the moment she saw him knelt before her, pouring his heart and devotion out.

"I know it's not going to be easy but," Damien took her hands in his. "Will you be mine?"

Tears Jill could no longer hold back fell down her cheeks. She'd pined for him for so long, wanting to get to know his life and share hers. "Yes, Damien. I will."

Damien rose up to her, positioning his body between her legs on the edge of the bed. His lips met hers in a sweet embrace, his eyes closed as Jill's tongue ran the length of his lips. Her soft tip parted them, touching his teeth in an attempt to get him to open to her.

His strong hands gripped Jill's soft hair as he savored her kiss. His breath was heavy as one of his hands ran down her arms, her skin so soft he almost growled in anticipation but held back.

God, she was perfect. Beautiful, strong, independent and so loyal and caring. She'd tried her best to protect him against the darkness of her world. Listened to him when he revealed the secret he'd held onto for so long it almost destroyed his soul.

Jill raised her head, allowing Damien to kiss her neck, her fingers wrapped in his thick, dark hair, savoring its soft fullness.

Her hand explored the firm muscles of his shoulder and bicep as he ran his hand down her sides.

Damien pulled away. Their eyes met in a heated gaze. "Show me."

"Damien, I..."

"Show me, please. I want to know everything about you." Damien pleaded with her, his hand caressing the soft flesh of her neck.

Jill surrendered, sighing. "Okay."

CHAPTER EIGHT

That night, Jill led Damien to the woods behind the gym. Her heart pounded as the nervousness at what she was about to do became more and more real to her.

"Damien, if I do this, would you promise me you won't run. We don't usually reveal ourselves to humans. Not even when we marry them."

"Jill, I'm not exactly human either, remember?" Damien grinned, cupping Jill's face. "I'm not scared of you. I won't run."

Jill sighed. "You know I have to get naked for this."

Damien held up his hands in surrender. "This is natural for you. I'll behave."

Jill smiled. He was so adorable when he displayed his genuine smile. It almost alleviated all of the fear and uncertainty about what she was going to do.

She removed her clothes to a heap on the ground, leaving her naked before him. Closing her eyes, she reached inside of her soul for the beast she knew dwelled there, the huge black shape forming in her mind.

Damien watched as Jill's body began shifting and rippling. Her muscles distorted and popped to change from woman to wolf. Her mouth elongated, fangs growing as she fell forward. Her back arched as her spine elongated into that of her feral form. A pitch-black tail protruded from her tail bone, her legs shifting to the back legs of the wolf.

When the change was over, the same large, black wolf Damien met in the woods stood before him.

His eyes widened with both awe and surprise as he stood up to walk over to her, holding out his hand.

Jill lowered her head, nervously whimpering.

"I won't." Damien said as if he knew what she was thinking. "I won't run."

Jill closed her eyes, a soft whimper of relief came from her throat as his warm hand ran through her black fur.

Damien knelt before her. "You're beautiful, Jill. In any form. Rob would probably freak if he saw what I just did. Does it hurt?"

Jill shook her head. She stepped forward to lick Damien's face.

"I will admit, this is weird. Almost terrifying but almost getting killed by vampires does tend to numb a guy. You do realize, you are going to have to meet my dad and friends, eventually."

Jill let out a low groan that made Damien laugh. She pushed him over playfully. Her heart and mind filled with overwhelming relief he wasn't scared of her. No longer did she have to hide from Damien. He knew all of her and the best part was, he loved it.

The morning following her revealing her true nature to Damien, Jill was kick-boxing one of the bags in the boxing room.

Damien had gone to college, leaving Jill to spend her day off working out and chatting with Clint all day.

She paused when she saw Holt walk in with his beta, Cade.

"This can't be good." Clint said as if he were able to read Jill's mind.

"What's Holt doing here?"

"I don't know but from the look on his face, I'd say it isn't good." Clint replied just as his father came in.

"Jillian, Gabriel has requested your presence. It is very important." Kain's authoritative tone held no room for argument.

He rarely used it but when he did, it was something very urgent.

Jill followed Kain into the meeting room Gabriel usually only opened to alphas and betas.

She was neither.

The meeting room as it was called had a large ovular table where Gabriel held elder meets which usually consisted only of Kain, his beta, Chase, Gabriel and his beta, Dolph. Now it housed all three packs' leaders and their betas.

"Holt, my old friend." Kain hugged the alpha, shaking Cade's hand. The tension between the two apparent in the strength in which they grasped their hands. "What is it that drives you from your clan? You remember Jillian Styles?"

Holt was much like his other brethren. Slightly shorter than Kain, Holt sported a head of pitch black hair with ashen highlights and eyes as dark as the night sky. He was built stockier, his muscles and stomach a bit wider than Kain's because of his size.

Nonetheless, to many of the females of his pack, Holt was a true desire and very easy on the eyes.

His beta, Cade was a hard-bodied soldier. He was a few inches taller than Kain, built like a bodyguard with longer red hair so dark it was almost black with a red overlay. His body was covered in scars from his years of war. Both human and lycan. His light eyes almost shined out from the darker shadows under his eyes.

If it weren't for the fact that his skin was a more copper tone, he could have been mistaken for a vampire.

"Of course, who could forget the legend herself? It is good to see you again, Jillian."

Jill lowered her eyes out of respect. "It is an honor to see you again as well, my alpha."

Holt let out his signature, boisterous laugh. "Now, now, there's no need for such formality. You are welcome here," he turned his attention back to Kain. "The news I bring isn't good, old friend. I wish I had better. Thanks to Cade, I've been kept up to speed with most of the news of what's been going on but I'm still missing a few pieces."

Holt's accent was heavy as he spoke. A mix of Germanic and Polish since his ancestors moved to the States, Holt often had to focus to make sure he was understood when he spoke. "Let me start this gathering by saying how elated I am to see all of you again. It has been too many moons since we've seen each other. I just wish my tidings were more of the glad sort,

"We have news of one of the rogue packs, led by Lune's brother, Nathaniel has gotten into an encounter with Rayes. The exchange didn't end well and Nathaniel is demanding we help him in getting payback. Lune doesn't desire to get involved but unfortunately it's not going over well,

"Gabriel, we know you have had dealings with Nathaniel. We came to ask you to talk to him on our behalf. The boy has a hot head and is already challenging me for my position as alpha. He's gaining support from my own pack. All of us here know what will happen if he takes over. He'll get them all killed with his recklessness."

"That kid never could keep it in his pants as far as fighting went. I'm surprised he's even allowed to run a pack at all." Dolph's disdain was thick. He'd once encountered Nathaniel and gotten a scar across his face for it from the alpha's beta, Vincent.

Gabriel silenced Dolph with a glare. "I'll talk to him, Holt, but I'm not sure it would do any good. As much as I hate to admit, Dolph is right. He didn't listen then, why would he listen now?"

"Because if he has all three alphas represented here standing against him, it would bring the supporters who are drawn to him back. They're doing it out of fear. There are more of us dying or forgetting every day. I guess they'd rather go down fighting than just waiting to die by the vampires' hands or traps."

Jill was well aware the lycans numbers were dropping. They all knew it. With the growing number of vampires it wasn't making it easy for the lycans who were just trying to survive.

"Holt, we can't live in fear. That's what the vampires want. If we get scared, we become easy to target. So far none of the lycans here in Big Timber except Gabriel, myself or Jillian have had an encounter with a vampire. Most of us manage to live normal lives. Nathaniel is just stirring the coals to get more troops. We will stand with you. The last thing we need to do is something reckless and charge the coven head long." Kain replied, keeping his cool demeanor. He handled most of the situations brought to him the same. This was just another one.

"Good. I'm glad I have the support of the ruling clans of Big Timber. Another thing is..." Holt closed his eyes, rubbing them with his finger and thumb as if he didn't want to say what he was about to. "Lilith killed her father."

Gasps filled the room, each leader looking at the other.

Jill's eyes were probably the widest. The lord responsible for killing Lucius and threatening Damien, the most feared vampire in the United States had been killed by his own daughter?

"It's true. She killed her father in his sleep and taken up leadership of the coven. We don't know the full extent as to why yet. Howling has it she's planning something. Something big." Disbelief showed in Holt's eyes the more he spoke.

Chase, Kain's beta, stood up, leaning his hands against the edge of the table. Chase was a younger lycan but still formidable. He kept his platinum hair military cut in honor of his father and was built like a surfer.

"Sun's hell! What are we going to do about it?"

"Nothing yet. We don't know what it is. We just know she's moving and trying to get the coven ready. She could even be preparing to make more vampires, we just don't know. We'll keep you in the loop but I suggest, as the packs closer to the fire, you keep your noses to the breeze." Holt concluded what he said, sitting down.

"Actually, I do have some news that needs to be addressed considering the danger it clearly poses." Cade spoke up. Something the man known as the "Silent soldier" never did.

Kain glared at Cade, almost appearing to know where he was going.

"What of this mortal the vampires are so interested in? If my intel is correct, he is the bearer of the soul of a Purifier. I have been told many of you have had to save him on multiple occasions. Are you not concerned with the threat that poses to us?"

"Enough Cade. That is none of your concern. I knew it would come up which is why I asked Jillian in here." Kain's voice held an almost threatening tone.

"What mortal?" Holt asked.

"My apologies, Holt. I wasn't going to mention him. His name is Damien and he's...my boyfriend." Jill replied, somewhat annoyed at Cade's call-out.

"Is what Cade says true? A Purifier? After so many centuries?"

Kain took over the conversation. "He's still asleep, Holt. It's too soon. Leave it alone out of respect."

"Alright, if that's all, then we can adjourn. Holt, Cade, feel free to stay here. You can travel back home tomorrow. Extend my invitation to Nathaniel and Vincent. Tell him he can have a go at Kain in the cage, that'll have him jumping." Gabriel added, ending the fight he could see going on between Kain and Cade.

Jill turned to leave, her phone buzzed with a text from Damien.

"Jill, hold up a minute." Gabriel called out, exerting his own authority as alpha.

"What is it, Gabriel?"

"I spoke with Damien about this relationship between the two of you. I know you like him. Kain told me you showed him your other form but are you sure this is wise? He's a human. I'm not too keen on the members of my pack getting killed for a mortal. Purifier or not."

"Fang off, Gabriel. You know as well as I do the vampires don't care. To them he's a threat, plain and simple. Purifiers were mortal. They could be killed just like any lycan. I'm not letting go of him, no matter what you say." Jill turned her back on him, leaving the room.

The doors slammed behind her.

CHAPTER NINE

D amien sat down in front of his laptop, opening it up to look at some of the photos he had taken over the years. Memories from different periods of his life illuminated the screen all at once.

His mom, Sarah laughed as she was pushed on the wooden swing his father had hung in the large tree that overshadowed their backyard. The early mornings on Christmas day when he would sneak into the living room to tear open his presents before his parents woke up only to be caught by his sister, Bree. She would blackmail him to do something for her to keep her from telling their parents. Memories of him and Bree in their Halloween costumes at the age of six. It all reminded him of how simple life used to be compared to now.

Bree left home after their mom died, to find work in marketing and journalism. Damien rarely ever spoke to his sister. They usually always fought and she made it clear she never wanted him there in the first place.

Damien continued scrolling through the photos, each carrying a mix of both joy and sadness at the happiness their family used to have before his accident.

The full moon had just begun to peak over the trees. It made Damien wonder if Jill was out in the form of the beautiful wolf whose photo he still wanted to add to his album. He'd meant to get it when he first saw Jill transform but once again, he didn't have his camera.

Pushing his rolling chair away from his desk, Damien looked up at the ceiling. His head rested on his arms crossed behind it.

A knock on his door caught Damien's attention. "Come in." he said, his voice muffled by the pen in his mouth.

Charlie opened the door, dressed in his police uniform. Grant Callahan, his deputy came in with him.

"Dad, what's going on?" Damien inquired, his brow raised in curiosity and slight aggravation.

"Dame, Chelsea's missing. Her parents haven't seen her for almost a month now, none of her girlfriends have seen her and neither has Rob." Charlie paused to run his hand over the back of his neck.

"Your point?" Damien replied, angry at the accusation he could hear hidden in his dad's voice.

"A witness says you're the last one who saw her."

Damien turned in his chair, dropping his hands in his lap. "Are you kidding with this? I didn't see her after she left at the college, that's it. I went to class with Professor Hanson and then sent you a text, remember?"

"I remember but I have to ask, where were you in the time after you left class to when you sent me that text?"

"This is unbelievable. Are you actually interrogating me? I was with my girlfriend. Ask Alexander Kain from the bowling alley, he saw us."

"Wait, you have a girlfriend? When were you going to tell me?" Charlie inquired, taking on a more dad-like demeanor than a cop.

"I was going to tell you at Christmas. I hadn't seen Chelsea since the college. Can I stop being treated like a suspect now?" Damien replied, sarcastically throwing up his hands.

"I believe him, Charlie. Damien's never been one to lie. We can go ask Alex next, he's usually pretty honest."

Charlie rose from the bed. "I'm sorry, Damien. I was just doing my job. Take care and if you do see Chelsea, please tell me."

"I will, thanks for the heads up. You could have just asked without Callahan here."

Charlie smiled. "I know. I will next time, I promise."

The morning following the "interrogation," Damien was in a really foul mood. He felt humiliated for being questioned in front of the sheriff's deputy without so much as a warning.

"I was just saying, maybe you could give me the courtesy of a heads up the next time you decide to come into my room in full uniform with Callahan and start questioning me like I'm some sort of kidnapping lunatic?" Damien was almost yelling at his dad across the kitchen.

"Damien, I told you I was doing my job. Now show some respect. You still live under my roof. I don't care how old you are, you will show me some mutual respect." Charlie replied, angry yet trying to keep his voice down. He knew he should have approached Damien before he brought Grant into it but he needed to know.

"Respect goes both ways, I'm a grown ass man, not a child. You know what? Forget it. I have finals coming up next month and a term paper to write." Damien grabbed his jacket and backpack, opening the door and letting it slam behind him.

The weather had gotten colder as fall began to transition into winter. The clouds heavy with snow held back in waiting for the biting December winds.

Damien hugged his coat around his body, stepping to the side of the old tar road upon hearing the engine of a car.

To his surprise, as it slowed next to him, he recognized it as Kain's car.

Kain rolled down the window. "You look cold, Damien. Get in. I have somewhere we can go."

Damien got in, thankful to be out of the cold and in the warmth of the heater. "Thanks, Kain."

Kain smiled, watching Damien in his peripheral as he drove off.

The drive was silent. Damien spent his time looking out of the window, watching the trees as they rushed by. The way he spoke to his father bothered him but it upset him that he'd been treated like a criminal. Chelsea was his friend, he'd never do anything to hurt her.

When they turned off the main road to a small gravel country road, Damien turned to ask. "Where are we going?"

"You will see." Kain only smiled, refusing to avert his eyes from the rocky road.

They pulled up to a rustic log cabin that looked like it could have been built during the age of the Civil war, sitting back into the side of a hill, hidden by the line of trees from the main road.

Kain turned off the engine and got out of the car, followed closely by Damien.

"What is this place?" Damien asked, his awe at the old house apparent on his face.

"This is my home. I'm not here too often because of the demands of being an alpha and the full-time job at the bowling alley but it serves its purpose."

A sharp howl rang out in the trees. The sudden sound made Damien tense out of the memory of his encounter with Stoker.

Kain chuckled. "It's okay. That's Clint. This is my pack's territory." He unlocked the door to let them inside.

Damien closed the door behind him, taking his jacket off and setting his backpack down.

"Make yourself at home. I will get the fire started and make tea and coffee." Kain said, making his way into the kitchen.

Damien looked around, taking in every detail. The cabin looked like one of those hunting lodges he and his dad would stay in on their camping trips. The brick fireplace served as the only source of heat in the living room. The sofa and chair had leather bases with fabric cushions decorated with native patterns.

Even the stairs were crafted from wood and creaked under foot when Damien walked up into a short hallway with a long runner rug on the floor. From what he could see, there were three bedrooms and two bathrooms.

All in all, the place felt really old but still modern.

Damien went back downstairs to the living room to find Kain putting wood into the maw of the fireplace.

"I trust you enjoyed the short tour?" Kain asked, smiling at the look of sheer awe on Damien's face.

"You live here? For how long?" Damien asked, sitting down on the sofa, taking the old tin cup of tea Kain gave him.

"I've lived here since I left Europe during the Blood Wars. Things were chaotic at first but then settled down, thankfully." Kain replied, sitting in the lounge chair, his own cup of coffee in his hand.

"How long? This place looks old."

"Damien, let's just say I was here long enough to see the Confederate soldiers surrender to the Union under President Lincoln." Kain replied, taking a drink.

Damien felt light-headed. Kain was even older than he thought.

"Grant and Charlie came to see me last night at the bowling alley. Something about a friend of yours missing?" Kain said in an attempt to distract Damien from his questions.

"Yeah. Chelsea. Dad interrogated me in my room with Callahan present. I told him I was with Jill and to ask you if he didn't believe me. Sorry about that, Kain. It pissed me off."

Kain laughed. "It's alright. I've seen a few things in my day, Damien. I'm more concerned about you. What in Luna's name were you doing out on the road in the cold?"

Damien sighed. "Dad and I had a fight this morning about what happened. I yelled at him and stormed out. I'm beginning to feel like a stranger in my own room and it's getting worse."

"Take it easy. You're adjusting to some serious changes, Damien. It's no surprise you're stressed. Change can be hard and sometimes leads us to do and say things we normally wouldn't to those we love." The fire flickered in the lycan's eyes, almost like he was reliving a memory.

A knock on the door brought a smile to Kain's face as he rose from his chair. He opened the door to find Jill shivering slightly in the cold.

"I was wondering when you would get here, Jillian." Kain said as though he were waiting for Jill to take Damien off of his hands.

"Jill!" Damien stood up, excited.

"I know, Kain. I'm late. I got your text in the middle of a meeting." Turning to Damien. "I heard you and Charlie fought. Is everything okay?"

"Chelsea's missing, Jillian. There's been no sign of her in almost a month. Charlie and Grant came to see me at work as well." Kain interjected, pouring Jill a cup of coffee.

"Chelsea Masterson? Her parents were in my office today. They wanted me to investigate what happened. Do you think it was them?" Jill asked in her more stern voice.

"One can't be sure but it can't be ruled out." Kain replied, tossing another log on the crackling fire.

The renewed flame heated the room, filling it with the smell of burnt hickory. The crackling the only source of noise in the now silent room.

"Why would they care about Chelsea and not Rob? It doesn't make sense." Damien added. The silence broken by his curiosity as to why Rob hadn't been targeted if it was the vampires that took Chelsea.

"Who knows but we have to look at every possibility, Damien." The threatening tone in Kain's voice demanded the attention of everyone in the room.

Another knock at Kain's door came in the late hours of the night.

"I will get it." Kain said, making his way to the door. Jill sat on the couch with Damien, who had begun to fall asleep in her lap.

Gabriel walked in, unshaking despite the cold. "Thanks, Kain."

Kain closed the door while Gabriel walked into the living room, a scowl falling across his face.

"You brought him here? Kain have you given a thought to the threat he poses to us?"

"Gabriel, calm yourself. Need I remind you, you are in another alpha's territory. Honor our laws and respect my authority." Kain warned, his hand on Gabriel's chest halting his fellow lycan's advance. "He is here as my guest."

"Right. Apologies, old friend. I'm still uptight from the unfortunate company I got today at the gym." Gabriel dropped onto the floor next to the fire.

"I take it Nathaniel made his presence known without so much as a warning?"

"As usual. Gods, that kid is never pleasant to be around." Gabriel said, smacking the heel of his palm to his forehead.

Kain smirked. "No, he's not. Hopefully Chase behaved himself. I know those two don't really get along too well."

"You're telling me. I thought I was going to have to throw them in the ring to cool their heads. The good news is I managed to force him into backing off of Holt. Needless to say he was a bit let down when you didn't show. He really wanted a chance at taking you on in the cage." Gabriel replied, half-chuckling.

"Nathaniel aside Gabriel, we need to talk about what Holt said. Jillian can't keep protecting Damien on her own. Like it or not, the vampires will come for him."

Jill ran her hand through Damien's dark hair, smiling at the soft sigh she heard coming from him. "I won't ask the packs to help. I got him into this, I need to take responsibility."

Kain and Gabriel looked at each other then back at Jill.

"It's true. If I had stayed away the vampires wouldn't have gotten curious so quickly. I just...I can't help who I love."

Kain knelt before Jill, placing his hand on her knee. "Jillian, it wouldn't have mattered. Demetrius would have figured it out, eventually. We can't help what has happened but we can focus on what will come. You were in the meeting with Holt, you know Lilith is planning something. We need to focus on devising a plan."

"As much as I hate to admit it, Kain's right, Jill. Closing ranks around Damien right now seems to be the best course of action. If he is what you say, then he's a threat to them and a hope to us. I'm sorry I've been such a pussy." Gabriel admitted, surprising both Jill and Kain.

Kain stood up from the floor. "It's settled then. We direct our efforts and energy to protecting him and his family. We all know the vampires will use them as leverage. Chelsea's already missing. I don't want to risk Charlie and Rob's safety. For now, Jillian when was the last time you hunted?"

"It's been a few moons but I'll be okay. I'm more worried about, Damien." Jill caressed Damien's face, relieved he was sleeping so peacefully after the trauma he'd suffered from his run-in with Stoker.

"He will be safe here. We need to hunt. I can carry him to the guest room. Gabriel, go stand guard outside, I will be there in a minute. Jillian, grab Damien's backpack and come with me." Kain hoisted Damien up effortlessly, making his way up the stairs to the second bedroom.

Jill came in with Damien's backpack, setting it on the floor. His jacket, she hung on a hook in the closet.

"I will leave you to say good night. Come join us when you're ready." Kain said, closing the door.

Jill sat down next to Damien on the bed, her smile both happy and sad that she had gotten him into such trouble.

"I'm sorry, Damien. I truly never intended for any of this to happen. I'll see you in the morning." She said, kissing his cheek before joining Kain and Gabriel to go hunt beneath the light of the moon.

CHAPTER TEN

D amien woke up the next morning in a cold sweat. His night had been plagued with nightmares in the wee hours of the morning.

He dreamt he was standing on what appeared to be solid ground only to find himself falling through water.

As hard as he tried, he couldn't swim back to the surface. His lungs felt heavy as he tried to catch his breath, sinking further into a black abyss.

A low, dark and almost sinister chuckle could be heard echoing through the void. Two angry, glowing red eyes appeared in the gloom, staring straight at Damien although they were piercing into his soul.

It scared him so bad he jerked awake to find he was still in Kain's cabin. Only he'd been moved to one of the bedrooms.

What the hell was that? Damien thought to himself, getting up from the bed.

Quietly, he opened the door, walked out into the hall and down the creaking stairs.

Kain lay on the couch asleep in front of the fire. Gabriel was in a sleeping bag in front of the fireplace.

Gabriel? When did he get here? Damien shook his head. He must have passed out earlier than he thought.

The sudden wrapping of arms around him nearly made Damien whirl around and swing only to find Jill standing there.

"Sorry, I didn't mean to scare you so bad. What has you so jumpy?" Jill asked, partially chuckling. She had barely dodged Damien's swing.

"God, Jill. I had a weird nightmare. Guess it scared me worse than I thought." Damien replied, his breath heavy. His heart pounded against his ribcage.

"It's okay. Hungry? Kain made breakfast when we got home from our hunt this morning. Guess he didn't want you to go hungry." Jill led Damien into the kitchen, getting him a plate while he sat down at the table.

"Jill, I need to tell you something. I want you to come home with me for Christmas."

Jill set a plate in front of Damien, taking the chair across from him. "Hmm. On one condition."

Damien swallowed the bite he was eating. "Okay, shoot."

"You have to come to the First Moon event with me."

"A what event?"

"First Moon. It's when the alphas of the surrounding packs welcome the pups who have just learned to transform officially as members. I've already bugged Kain and Gabriel about it. They're okay with you going. Deal?" Jill held out her hand.

"Um, okay. You swear you'll come to Christmas, I'll go to this...First Moon thing."

They shook hands with Jill stealing a kiss. "Good. Now eat up. I want you to meet some other lycans in town."

Jill and Damien snuck out of the cabin after breakfast down to a bright, cherry red Charger.

"Woah. Whose car is this?" Damien asked, his hand running over the sleek paint like a kid who just got a really expensive toy.

"Mine. Gabriel has a friend in the auto business. He managed to negotiate a good price and bought it for me. Apparently he got mad at me for constantly borrowing his Mustang."

"It's...nice." Damien wondered just how much the car could have cost and how in the world Gabriel could afford it. From what he knew, Gabriel ran a gym. There's no way he could afford something like this, could he?

"Want to drive?"

"What?"

Jill dangled the keys in his face. "You wrecked your truck. Would you like to drive?"

"Hell yes, I'd love to drive. By the way, it was Stoker who did the wrecking, not me. Thanks." Damien replied, getting in the driver's side.

Jill laughed jumping into the passenger's side.

Their first stop was the coffee shop where Damien got his London Fog tea almost every morning before class.

Betsy McClain, the older cashier stood at her usual post while her daughter, Rayna, made coffee like a champion.

"Jillian, my how beautiful you are, dear. What can we do for you?" Betsy's voice was raspy but her smile always made Damien's day. From what he could tell, the old woman smoked like a chimney in London.

"Betsy, Rayna, can you make it to tonight's First Moon?" Jill let her fangs cross her coy smirk as though she were sending a silent signal.

"Oh, heavens yes, wouldn't miss it! Damien, welcome, my boy! You want your usual?" Damien's eyes met Rayna's as she smiled, her fangs slightly showing him what Jill was asking of them. Betsy did the same though hers were more aged.

When they walked out, Damien was dumbfounded. He never even realized that Betsy and Rayna were different. They acted so...normal.

"Who else? I would have never suspected Betsy or Rayna."

"Many more, Damien. Spence, Kyle, a few of your professors. How else did you think Gabriel knew you were in the science hall when Lilith attacked you? Professor Hanson is a lycan elder. He's been at that school since it opened."

The school in question opened in the fifties and was much smaller then. It would mean Hanson was well over fifty.

Christ, Damien didn't know anything about these people either.

Jill took him all over town, introducing him to multiple people he knew. Some from his childhood turned out to be lycans.

"So, they weren't looking at me because they thought I was a freak, they were looking at me because you asked them to protect me." Damien had been wrong. So wrong.

"Yes. Most of the population here save for about twenty-five percent of them are lycans. We all work together to protect each other. When you came back, I sent out a chain howl to tell them. Even when we're not in wolf form, we can understand the call."

The sun sank below the horizon line, announcing the hour of twilight.

"We need to head to the woods' edge. You probably know it. It's off an old trail now closed to the public. From there we walk to Holt's camp and then to the sacred site. This is much like the equivalent of a human birthday, Damien. I probably should warn you that some of the pups can be kind of...intuitive. They may ask some strange questions. When you meet an elder or one of the chain of command, lower your eyes. It's a sign of respect to them. Gabriel and Kain usually don't do it at the gym because not only lycans use the gym during the day. I'll tell you more the closer we get."

The drive out to the wood's edge was so long Jill had advised Damien to get some rest since he would need it when they got there.

"We're here." Jill ran her hand through Damien's hair to wake him.

The hike from the wood's edge to the encampment reminded Damien of the hikes he and Rob often went on. When he got tired, Jill sat with him to let him catch his breath only to help him up to continue.

What Damien saw once they finally arrived at the encampment was unlike anything he'd ever seen. Kids that appeared human ran around with what looked to him like puppies. They seemed to be arguing over a toy as if they spoke the same language.

A large gray wolf bared its fangs at them, barking. They stopped in their tracks and lowered their heads in submission. When they saw Damien, they began eyeing him curiously.

Jill picked one of them up and whispered in his ear. The little one chuckled and ran off towards a large brown wolf who was sleeping next to the fire. She looked up at Damien, her orange eyes watching him.

"Damien! Welcome to my pack. Nice to finally get to meet you. I've heard so much about you." Holt's voice was full of excitement to see he was there. He embraced Damien, almost crushing him.

Remembering what Jill said about lowering his eyes, Damien spoke to Holt. "Thank you, sir."

Holt let out a hearty laugh. "No need for formalities, my friend. Anyone that is the mate of Jillian Styles lowers his eyes to no one. The legendary lycan has all of our respect, it is an honor to have you here."

"Mate? Wait, I'm not..." A hard hit on his back made him choke on his own breath.

"No need to be shy. We all know what's going on. Jill's clearly courting you, it's no secret." Holt continued patting Damien's back, his arm going around his neck.

"My alpha, Damien is my boyfriend, not my mate. I wasn't going to tell him I was courting him until Christmas." Jill addressed Holt, a hint of embarrassment in the form of a blush fell across her face.

"Whoops, guess I gave it away. Sorry about that. Congratulations, Mr. Pierce, you've successfully done what most of us couldn't." Holt released Damien, walking away still laughing.

Jill helped Damien back to his feet. "Apologies for that. Holt is a bit forward."

Damien didn't say anything. Not only could he still not breathe from the hard hits Holt administered, he was shocked to learn that Jill had apparently been courting him. Whatever that meant.

"Friends! Sons of Tenebris, daughters of Luna, we have two very special individuals among us. Jillian Styles, the lycan of legend has graced us with her presence. She brings with her, her mate, Damien Pierce. You will show them honor, you will show them respect and dignity or you will answer to the alphas among you. Alexander Kain, Gabriel Locke or myself." Howls joined claps and hollers as the lycans acknowledged Holt's speech.

Jill shook her head, taking Damien's hand. "We have some time, would you like to see one of my favorite places? Don't worry about what Holt said."

"Uh, sure. Jill, what does courting mean? To a lycan. I know to humans, it's dating but what is it to you?" Damien asked, a bit nervous as to what her answer would be.

"It's almost the same. Only for us, it's when we're intending to take the one we're courting as our mate. I really wasn't going to say anything until Christmas. Holt just beat me to it."

Damien wasn't sure what he thought. He loved Jill, that much he knew but all of this was still a bit overwhelming to him.

"Damien, courting doesn't mean immediate commitment. Like humans, lycans take our time courting each other. We don't date multiple individuals. Most of the time, we court who we want to mate with." Jill said, trying to ease the tension she could see in Damien's eyes.

They walked in silence, both thinking about what their future together might be.

CHAPTER ELEVEN

J ill led Damien to a place so beautiful, it took his breath away. Weeping willows shielded a small pond from one side while the other was a rock ledge covered in vine flowers and brush kissed with the wisps of winter frost.

A waterfall cascaded over the rocks turning into a soft mist before churning water so clear you could almost see to the bottom. Small hints of steam rose up from the surface.

The smell of the flowers mixed with the soft hint of the winter chill and the leaves and bark of the weeping willow. It was a relaxing scent that eased the tension in Damien's body as he looked around.

He nearly lost his footing when his eyes fell back on Jill.

She had stripped down to her underwear and bra and stepped into the water up to her waist. Her raven hair fell in silken waves down her porcelain back, the scars a faded pink against it.

The light of the moon pulled the blue highlights out of her hair, illuminating her icy green eyes.

Christ, she was perfect. Damien stood frozen at her beauty. his head fighting the heated need nagging his groin.

Jill turned to meet Damien's gaze, smiling at the look of wonder she saw in his eyes. She held out her hand, inviting him to join her. "Well, are you going to stand there like a handsome statue or are you going to join me? This spring is warm for most of the year. It feels good on your skin."

Damien hurriedly stripped down to his underwear, joining Jill to find it was almost like a hot spring only a bit cooler. The gentle warmth of the water relaxed his frayed nerves and eased his tense muscles.

Jill felt so full of love as her cheek met his chest, savoring the beat of his heart. Her hand rested on his pectoral muscle to feel the rise and fall of each breath. The other rested upon his hip, feeling the indention of the bone against the muscle. The soft murmur of his blood as it moved through his veins relieved her to know he was still alive. The easy beat of his heart comforted her, bringing forth a sigh as she closed her eyes.

Damien raised her face to embrace her mouth with his, savoring the feeling of desire that radiated from her kiss. All doubt melted into nothing as his tongue explored her sweet recesses. His hand traveled down her side to her lower back, his fingers flattened over her tailbone.

Gently he pushed to bring her into his body as far as he could. His other hand caressed her face and neck. Their bodies fit so perfectly into each other it was if they were made to be together.

Damien didn't know how but it was like he'd been waiting for Jill.

The pain, the loneliness, the awkward feeling of not belonging all disappeared in this moment when he allowed himself to truly be with her. No longer did he want to hold back his feelings. She'd shown him her world, opened herself to him willingly despite the slight fear of what he would think or do when she did.

Damien lifted Jill's legs over his hips, the water helped him handle her weight even further as his hand held the soft cheek of her rear end. His thumb savored the smooth skin of her thigh.

Jill's fingers tangled through the strands of Damien's hair. The feeling of his muscles as they tightened and relaxed under her hand excited her. His lips felt gentle against the skin of her neck, sending shivers down her spine.

The smell of him filled her nostrils, intoxicating her and raising her desire further. She had to be careful to keep control to avoid hurting him. Her hands ran over every dip and rise of the muscles of his arms.

Damien's mouth on her collarbone made it hard for Jill not to grip his arm so hard it could bruise.

Damien grasped Jill's hair, his fingers savoring the soft, raven strands that possessed his dreams almost every night after he first saw her on the college campus.

The feeling of needing to know her burned inside of him until he caught her in his room on their first night together. Then it wasn't a matter of needing. He wanted to know her.

Everything felt right with Jill. She filled the holes in his heart he didn't think anyone would ever be able to heal. She understood him on a level no one, not even his parents, could.

When their eyes met, they were dazed and full of the hidden desires they both knew existed for each other. A deep desire neither one of them could fight much longer lingered between them.

Damien rested his forehead against Jill's, his eyes closing. "I love you." He said, his hand stroking the soft skin of Jill's face.

"I love you too." Jill smiled, her mouth once again meeting his in a sweet embrace.

They held each other close for what seemed like hours, their kisses warm and deep, the heat of their bodies mixed with the heat of the water.

A soft howl rose across the wind, grabbing Jill's attention.

"That was Kain. We better go."

Damien kissed her lips one last time, upset that he had to let her go. He wanted to make love to her.

Damn. He thought as he watched Jill get out of the water, shaking before getting dressed.

A thought came to him as he put his own clothes on, having to go commando since he didn't have a change of underwear. He didn't really care since he knew what Jill was getting for Christmas and it wasn't going to be courting.

When they got back, Kain met them at the camp. He wasn't wearing any clothing since he'd just shifted back to human form after calling Jill. Damien turned his eyes away, embarrassed since the idea of being naked in front of a stranger was still new to him. Jill wrapped her arms around Kain's waist.

"You almost missed us leaving. I am glad you heard my call." Jill kissed Kain's cheek.

"I wouldn't miss this, Kain." She turned back to look at Damien. "Ready to see your first, First Moon?"

Damien didn't know what to expect. He was still trying to get over how open the lycans were with their sensual touching. It made him jealous to see Kain's hands on Jill's lower back.

"Well, ready is a bit strong but I am curious." Damien replied, pulling Jill away from Kain, his hand going around her waist.

Jill chuckled at Damien's sudden display of possession. "That's a start."

As they walked away from him, Damien couldn't help but see the look of heartache on Kain's face.

"Wait, Jill. I'll meet you there. I want to talk to Kain."

Jill nodded, confused. Shifting into her wolf form, she joined the others already walking behind Holt, Cade and Gabriel.

Damien walked up to Kain, careful to avoid looking into his eyes. "Kain...I'm..."

"She chose you. There's nothing to be sorry for. You make her happier than I have ever seen her. I will always love Jillian but I know now I could never give her what she needed. You complete her, Damien. That is what is important."

"Still."

"Don't. You're a good man. I can accept defeat from someone with such a strong heart and will. Just treat her right and give her strong pups." Kain choked on a chuckle at the look on Damien's face.

"Oh, they are coming. All lycan females want pups. It's just a matter of time." He patted Damien's shoulder. "Come on, I will show you where you're going."

Damien's mouth stayed agape the whole way. He wasn't even thinking about having pups, yet. He'd just decided when he was going to have sex with Jill the first time. Lycan or not, if she wanted pups, she was going to have to wait.

"We are here." Kain's voice served to help Damien return to the moment.

The place they arrived at was a wide-open circle of trees.

The moon shone like a spotlight over a large stone that overlooked a smaller circle formed from a barrier of smaller rocks. It had been cleared of debris almost as if it were sacred.

"I have to go. As an alpha, I have to be present for the changing. Jillian's coming your way." Kain shifted into a beautiful sandy coated wolf much larger than Jill in size.

In her own wolf form, she lowered her head to her alpha, whimpering in submission to his position. Damien could swear he saw Kain smile before he walked off.

Jill snuggled up close to Damien's side, her muzzle meeting his stomach. She closed her eyes as his hands ran through her obsidian fur, the sensation pleasing her to the point of joyful whimpering.

Holt stood above the packs in wolf form as the different pups of both species, human and lycan shifted in front of the alphas. Kain and Gabriel stood on either side of Holt, each greeting the pups of their packs with playful nuzzles.

Damien couldn't believe what he was seeing. The children he saw earlier shifted clumsily into wolves in front of his eyes. The pups shifted into human form, each jumping for joy to try and please their leaders.

It continued until each one had met the alpha of their pack, lowering their eyes and showing their allegiance.

Once the last pup was inducted into its pack, Jill took Damien over to a mother who had newborn pups nursing.

"We can give birth either way. It depends on how we are when we're ready to have them. Some of us have them like this, others as human babies." She handed the small ball of fuzz to Damien. It looked like a regular puppy to him only slightly bigger, yawning as it snuggled into his chest.

"We aren't so different, Damien. Luna has just blessed us with the ability to change into the lords of the night. We still have our children and love them just as any human would. We aren't the monsters we're made out to be." Jill knelt down, petting each pup. They squeaked and wiggled at her touch.

Damien looked down at the little whimpering fuzz ball asleep against his chest.

"Seems she likes you." Jill said, smiling, her cheek coming to rest on Damien's shoulder.

"She?"

"Yes, that's a little girl. The mother told me she had four girls and three boys." Jill took the pup from Damien and gave her back to her mother.

"You can have that many?" Damien asked, sort of worried at the idea.

116

"Sometimes but it's rare nowadays. Most of us only have two or three. Lately, we haven't been able to keep them alive. Having more is beneficial and increases their chances to reach the age to change. Our kind is dying, Damien. The vampires are killing us faster than we can produce. Most of those pups you saw won't make it to even a year old."

The sad tone in Jill's voice tore at Damien's heart. Her kind were in trouble and he didn't know how to help though he wanted to.

Damien didn't really speak much on the way back to Holt's camp. Jill walked beside him in her wolf form, Kain on his other side.

After they arrived back at the encampment, Damien spent time with Jill, Holt and Kain for the rest of the night. Each one taught him about lycan culture, explaining how they were different from vampires while the mothers all put their little ones to bed before sun rise.

The more he learned the more he realized how wrong the stories and lore were. Humanity made them out to be snarling monsters looking to kill when they wanted. They confused the lycans with werewolves.

When Jill came up to Damien, he was about out cold from being so exhausted. "Come with me. Holt says he has a tent we can stay in for the night."

Jill led Damien to a large tent near the base of a tree. On the outside, it looked like a nomad's living quarters with meat and fish hanging from poles set to dry in the sun. The door was a flap that could be zipped like a modern tent but inside it was larger than he expected, as if it were a one-room house.

Jill undressed, crawling underneath one of the thick blankets on the floor.

Damien lay on the blanket next to her in his jeans. "You know, as amazing as this all is, I have to admit, I'm a bit overwhelmed."

Jill turned over, reaching out to pet Damien's face. "Take it slow and handle what you can. I know you've been through a lot lately. This would be too much for me too if I were in your shoes."

Damien raised up to rest his head in his hand. "I have to be getting back tomorrow. I'm sure Dad's worried since Chelsea's been missing for so long."

Jill sighed. "I know. Just let me have tonight beside you."

Damien smiled. He got up to get behind her, using his own blanket to cover up and falling asleep to the sounds of the night.

CHAPTER TWELVE

The following morning was bitterly cold. The bite of the wind whistled through the trees, muffling out the sound of the morning animals as they began their daily search for food.

The sun was well into the sky, casting the different colors of the fabrics of the tent across the floor.

Damien woke up in the soft fur bed he fell asleep in, not realizing where he was at first. He hadn't gotten the chance to take a detailed look since he was so tired the night before.

The floors were adorned with decorative rugs depicting all kinds of different patterns. One in particular was a deep red with golden patterns that had what looked like tribal wolves woven into what appeared to be flower petals.

The walls had different furs hanging from wooden poles, all from all varieties of animals. In the corner was a small area someone could make coffee and enjoy a good book.

All together it was very homey.

Jill was already awake, letting Damien sleep after the late night they'd had. As his vision became clearer, he began remembering the events of the previous night. Damien remembered how close he was to making love with her only to be suddenly ripped away. Honestly, it seemed like a pattern in their history together. They rarely were alone when they wanted to be.

He'd seen the lycan children weaving in and out of the tents. Their mothers talked in both wolf and human form like they were speaking the same language.

Damien's heart ached at the pain in Jill's voice when she spoke of the situation her people were in. She'd mentioned the odds of the little pup he'd held living to reach a year old were slim to none.

Jill walked in with some breakfast, sitting down on the ground in front of Damien. "Good morning. I hope you rested well."

"It was okay. Thank you for breakfast." Damien replied, his voice sullen.

"What's wrong?"

"Nothing. Just needing some coffee is all." Damien lied to avoid worrying Jill. From the raised brow on her face he was pretty sure she didn't believe him.

Jill kissed his cheek. "Try to eat. I'll take you home after you've had time to get some food."

She got up to go meet Holt and Kain about trying to get Damien some clean clothes. Much to Damien's dismay, he might have to settle for wearing Gabriel's again.

When they pulled up to the house, Damien hesitated, staring out of the window towards the wooden door he'd gone through so many times. Only now it was almost intimidating. He still had no idea how he was going to explain Jill or where he'd been.

Sighing, he got out to head up the wooden stairs leading to the door.

Jill stayed in the car. She knew this was already hard enough for Damien. Her kind didn't reveal themselves to strangers too often unless the situation called for it.

"Damien!" Charlie hugged his son close to him. "Where have you been?"

"Sorry, dad. I know it's been a while. I've been staying with Kain. Where he lives doesn't have the best cell phone service. I did text you though." A sense of guilt filled Damien for keeping his father in the dark but he thought it would keep him safe.

Charlie patted his son's shoulder. "Right. You did but still, I'm going to give Alex a piece of my mind the next time I see him."

Oh man. Damien thought. Once again his dad was going to go after poor Kain for something he did.

"Leave Kain alone, pops. I was the one who stormed out. I shouldn't have spoken to you like that. It was wrong." Damien scratched his head, nervously before continuing. "I was going to wait until Christmas for this but since she's here, I want you to meet my girlfriend."

Charlie's eyes grew wide with anticipation as Damien walked them back outside where Jill stood leaning against her car. "Dame. She's beautiful."

Jill shook slightly. A small knot of nervousness formed in her stomach. She'd been uneasy at the thought of introducing herself to Damien's father. She'd been alone for so long, she'd almost forgotten how to act casually around humans.

"I'm Charlie Pierce," Charlie extended his hand. "It's a pleasure to meet you, Miss?"

"Jillian. Jillian Styles." She shook his outstretched hand.

"Well Jillian, I have no idea how my son managed to get such a gorgeous woman but I'm glad he did."

Damien playfully shoved his dad. "Jill is the one I've been seeing all this time. She was the one who picked me up after the accident with the truck."

"I was going to ask how that happened, Dame. The truck was in bad shape. I'm glad Jill was there to help you," Charlie's jovial mood turned severe. "I know you told me you fell asleep at the wheel but there were indentions on the step rails resembling human hands. A man from what our crime scene unit could tell."

Damien looked over to Jill, silently asking her for help.

"I saw those indentions, Charlie. Rocks roll down those hills all the time. The side of the ditch Damien drove into was full of them. Maybe they were responsible?" Jill answered as though she'd rehearsed the line.

No telling how many times she'd had to make up excuses for vampire attacks throughout her life.

"That could be. No reason to think about it now I suppose. I'm just glad Damien found someone to care for him. His mother and I tried everything we could think of." Charlie took Jill's hands in his, revealing them to be rough and cracked from the trials he'd had to face in his life.

"Take care of him, Jill. I am so thankful for you. Would you like to come in? I'd love to learn more about my son's girlfriend."

"Sure. If you don't mind though, I'd like to change clothes." Damien chimed in, catching a devious chuckle coming from the gorgeous woman beside him.

Charlie and Jill sat in the living room drinking hot coffee after Charlie built a fire to heat the room against the cold outside.

"They say we're about ready to get our first snow of the season. I can't wait! It'd be nice to enjoy the decorations covered in white powder. Of course, it's one of my busiest times of year since so many people tend to get stuck," Charlie laughed at his own story. He often got called out to get folks out of their cars after being buried in snow. "I know I shouldn't be laughing but some things you just can't help. How about you, Jillian? Do you live close?"

Jill didn't really have a place she called home. She was mostly nomadic unless she was spending time at Gabriel's gym or staying with Kain. On rare occasions she had been known to stay with Holt.

"You could say that. I work as a private investigator. Sometimes for your office. When I'm not working I tend to spend my time at Solstice to kick box. The owner there is a personal friend."

Damien came downstairs, freshly showered and happy to be in his own clothes, settling on a black t-shirt and jeans.

Jill's heart fluttered in her chest when his scent hit her nose. That rich, spicy, dark musk she spent so many moons pining for brought about an overwhelming heat inside of her.

"What'd I miss?" Damien sat next to Jill on the couch, throwing his arm around her shoulder.

Jill smiled, leaning her head against his chest. Her hand came to rest on his leg, rubbing the muscle underneath his jeans.

"Nothing much. Jill just told me what she did as a job and where she liked to work out. Dame, I'm afraid we're going to have to cancel our camping trip. The town needs me here." Charlie leaned forward, the look on his face serious, his mouth and eyes flattening into a thin line.

"Why? What's going on?" Damien asked, feeling both relieved that he didn't have to go and concerned about the look on his father's face.

"There have been some strange things going on around here lately. Livestock have gone missing from some of the local farms. A few people too. We hadn't found anything to point us to the problem yet but I want you to be careful." Charlie took a drink of his coffee.

"How many?" Damien asked, the feeling of unease and nausea settling in his stomach.

Jill paid close attention as the two men exchanged words. The hair on the back of her neck stood on end as she fought not bare her fangs. A low growl rose in the back of her throat.

"So far not many people. Just mostly animals. We did find a few carcasses torn all to hell. Maybe a wolf, coyote or something got to them but until we know what's going on, be very careful."

Jill got deathly still. Her gaze was so intense it would burn the wall if it could. She stood up suddenly, her fists clenched at her sides.

Once again her kind had been indirectly accused of the carnage plaguing the town when she knew exactly who was responsible.

"I have to go. It was a pleasure to meet you, Mr. Pierce." She said as she grabbed her jacket and keys, heading back out to her car.

Damien got up quickly and followed closely on her heels until they reached the door.

"Jill, what's going on?" When she didn't stop, he reached out to grab her wrist. "Don't you dare close me out. Tell me what's bothering you."

Jill took a deep breath, releasing it slowly to calm herself. She turned around, reminding herself that nothing happening was Damien's fault.

Gently she placed her hand on his face, softly rubbing it. "I'm sorry, Damien. I have to leave you for now. I have to tell Kain, Gabriel and Holt what's going on. Stay here with your dad. Don't go outside after dark and don't let anyone into your house you don't know. By now, I know you can tell what a vampire looks like."

Placing her hand on the back of his neck, she guided him down so she could kiss him. Pain and fear filled her at the thought of leaving him alone but she had to get the news to the alphas.

The vampires were moving faster than they initially anticipated. They needed to act.

She stood in the open door of her car, staring up at Damien on the porch, fighting a battle inside. Her people were being threatened. She had to be sure they were taken care of. Damien was her lover. He was still human and vulnerable to attack. It was hard to choose.

Jill got into the car and started, mouthing "I love you" to Damien on before driving off.

The sun was hidden behind thick clouds that looked like they offered the promise of snow later in the evening. The wind definitely was cold enough to support the frost. It whistled like an angry banshee heralding the coming of the chaos and war.

Jill got out of her car, the cold wind biting against her coat as she pulled it up to shield her cheeks.

She walked up to Gabriel's gym, meeting Scott at the door. "Scott, I need to speak to Gabriel and Kain, now. It is the utmost importance."

Scott didn't say anything as he led Jill to where Gabriel and Kain were sparring against each other in a room with mats covering the floor designed for such exercises.

Upon seeing her, they stopped. Their breathing heavy from their work out. Their hard bodies covered in fresh sweat. Their hair dripping small beads onto the floor.

"Jillian, how are you? I take it things went well with Charlie?" Kain wiped his face with a towel, getting a drink of water from his water bottle.

"They went fine, Kain." Jill's voice held the sternness she often had when she was fighting.

Both alphas looked at each other.

"Doesn't seem like it. What's got you so worked up?" Gabriel wiped his face, putting the towel around his neck, shaking the sweat from his dark hair.

"Charlie mentioned some disappearing livestock and mangled corpses from the farms outside of town. A few people have gone missing too and they're blaming wolves. We all know what happens when humans become paranoid about things like this. We often end up as the poor souls to get hunted and killed for it. It appears Lilith has started making her move but, it wasn't what we thought. So far Charlie and the local police have been able to keep it quiet. If it escalates, there'll be no way they can keep it hidden."

Gabriel landed his fist into the nearest punching bag, a deep growl rolling up from his throat as his fangs extended. "Damned parasites. Why can't they just let us live in peace?"

"My guess is their end goal is to attack us openly. Lilith riles up the town and makes them panic. The humans go on some witch hunt forcing us to stop hunting which will have devastating results on our pups. It seems the ruling nobles of the coven don't like having to share space with us." Kain's arms crossed his chest as he propped his hip against the wall.

He continued. "Either way, they have started moving so we have to move. Staying still could get us killed."

"Okay. Kain, tonight, send out a howling call. Let Holt know that in seven moons, we convene at his camp. We're going to need some help. Alone we can't stand against the coven, not all of us can fight. I don't expect those around here who are just trying to live their lives to give them up. It wouldn't be fair to them. Gods damn it all!" Gabriel punched the punching bag again only this time it was hard enough to send it flying into a mirror, cracking it.

"Jillian, stay close to Damien. Lilith still wants him, there's no doubt in my mind. She'll even kill him to keep you from having him if she can." Kain advised Jill, earning him a hug around the waist.

"Thank you. I'll stay in howling's touch Kain, I promise."

"I know." Kain kissed her forehead. "Luna watch over you, Jillian."

"And you, old friend."

Damien sat on his couch, his foot tapping nervously against the floor as he thought back to the look on Jill's face. He wanted to go with her, to support her through whatever it was she felt she needed to run off to Kain and Gabriel for.

"Dame!" Charlie's voice from upstairs drew his attention.

"Yeah."

"Take the trash, out will you? I have to finish putting this desk together." Charlie had chosen to set up an office in one of the spare rooms so he could bring work home with him if he needed to.

The moon was in full view. The trashcans were outside and Damien promised Jill he wouldn't go out after dark.

"Well, shit." He said. Heading into the kitchen he packed up the trash and recyclables to take out to the cans.

Careful to pay attention to everything around him, Damien made his way out to the trash cans at the end of the back of the house.

He'd gotten finished putting the recyclables in the can when he felt a hard hit against the back of his head. He hit the ground, dazed.

As he fought to stay conscious, he heard voices talking above him.

"Finally. Bind his hands and put him in the trunk. Make sure he's blindfolded and gagged. We don't want him calling for help in case there are any dogs around." One of the voices spoke, his accent thick with either a Russian or German undertone. It was unclear which it was.

The only thing Damien remembered before the darkness took him was the blindfold over his eyes and the sting of ropes as they harshly bound his hands. His shoulders aching in protest.

CHAPTER THIRTEEN

"Jill!" Clint sprinted up as Jill walked out of the gym. The noise drew the attention of Kain and Gabriel who stood in the entrance of the building.

"Clint, what is it?" Jill asked, placing her hand on Clint's back.

"I'm sorry. I'm so sorry. I screwed up. Sun's hell, there were four of them. I couldn't do anything." Clint rambled off apology after apology as he spoke, each one more grief stricken than the last.

To the human world, Clint would look like he was still a kid. Due to his lack of experience, he still was in the lycan world as well.

Kain adopted him after he found him freezing and close to starving to death next to the body of his older brother.

Jill's stomach churned in knots as she tried to make out what Clint was trying to say. He had been put in charge of watching over Damien until she could finish talking to Kain and Gabriel, sending out a howling call if anything went wrong.

The fact he was here meant something was horribly wrong.

"Clint, why are you not with Damien? What happened?" Her voice slightly scared Clint as his eyes searched his father's for some sign of an upcoming repercussion.

"Jill, I'm sorry. They took him. I couldn't stop them. Rayes was there. For the likes of me he's more than a match. There were three others with him. I didn't recognize two of them but Jack Nantucket, the old farm hand was one of them. Gods, I'm so sorry." Clint smacked his head with the heels of his hands.

He knew he messed up but Rayes was one of the vampire elite, he would have torn someone as inexperienced as Clint up in a minute.

Kain walked up to his adopted son, patting his back.

Wide-eyed, Jill fell to her knees, her hands tensed in front of her as she let out a scream to the skies that became a half howl. Her fists met the cement hard enough to splinter it as she fell forward, her nose meeting the remains of the shattered concrete in front of her.

"Jillian, we will save him. I promise you." Kain knelt in a shallow puddle of water next to her. "They waited. Damn them, they waited."

"Bloodsuckers must have been scouting the house for weeks. For them to send Rayes, Lilith must have been beyond pissed at having to wait. Stubborn stuck-up brat." Gabriel slammed his fist into his hand.

Jill growled as she struggled to get free of Kain's hold on her.

Kain took Jill's face in his hands, his thumb brushing the furious tears from her eyes. "We'll save him, sweetheart. I swear on Luna's name. We will get to him before they change him."

Jill dropped her eyes. No one swore on either deities' name unless they knew their word wasn't going to be broken.

To do so would get them punished by the deity on whose name they swore. Jill knew this and immediately she felt guilty for even making her friend get to that point. Especially if it was Kain.

"They still have to get to the coven in the mountains. There's only one lycan I know capable of getting us in and out of that place without getting killed," Gabriel spoke up. By the tone in his voice, he seemed hesitant to mention who he was talking about. "Lune can get us in but I don't know how bad things will be once he does. This whole thing is a damned suicide mission no matter how we shake our tail at it."

"Whatever we have to do, Gabriel. We have to save him." Kain replied, holding a now still Jill against his chest. She gripped his white t-shirt firmly, as if he were her only anchor to sanity.

Damien woke up to find himself unable to see. His mouth was gagged and his hands were bound behind his back.

A huge bump of the moving car made him hit his head against the lid of the trunk, disturbing an already upset condition and reminding him of what happened.

He'd gotten finished taking the trash and recyclables out for his father only to be ambushed. Then he was hit so hard it dazed him, making him black out. Now he was in the trunk of a car heading to only God knew where.

His heart pounded in his chest as he struggled to get the ropes around his wrists loose enough so he could try to reach his phone in his back pocket, surprised it had been left.

The car jolted to a stop followed by the sound of the creaking of what he could only imagine was an automatic gate.

Damien had been hit so hard it kept him out cold the whole time. His breath stalled in his chest as time ran out for him to try and think of a way to get out of this mess.

When the trunk opened, he was yanked out and dropped on his feet with a thud.

"Glad you're awake. I would have hated to have to carry your worthless carcass all the way to the catacombs," The speaker's voice was the same one who ordered him bound and gagged. "Get moving or I'll break your leg so I have an excuse to drag you."

A hard shove forced Damien forward, stumbling.

The sound of crunching gravel gave way to the softness of what Damien realized could only be grass.

From the coolness of the breeze around him to the calling of the night birds, Damien could tell it was either the wee hours of the morning or late evening.

"Take him to the catacombs and lock him up. I'll go inform Lilith that we got her little pet."

Great, Lilith again. Not looking forward to another encounter with her. Damien thought to himself, remembering his encounter with the vampire bitch in the science hall.

The terrain seemed pretty normal despite the elevation. The air was so thin Damien had trouble breathing as he tried to keep the pace his captors set. Then the terrain suddenly changed. They began descending into what felt like the ground.

Hopelessness set in the further he went. He wondered how Jill would be able to find him in whatever hell he was being dragged down into.

The air around Damien grew cold, musty and stagnant. The horrible smell of rot and decay filled his nostrils as he was led the catacombs his captors.

Distracted by his thoughts, he tripped, landing him against the wall. They felt like brick or maybe stone. The surface cold and wet from the ground water seeping in through the cracks from all of the rain.

The feeling of the walls and the dankness of the air reminded Damien of the old mazes under the Vatican in Italy he'd read about in European History. He was pretty sure he never got thrown into a box and put into the cargo hold of a plane. Why were there walls like this under the ground?

"We're here." A deep southern accent, Damien recognized as belonging to Jack Nantucket, a farm hand that worked on one of the cattle farms outside of the town. Jack had been one of the earliest cases of missing persons reported by his wife, Nancy.

Guess it was no longer a mystery as to what happened to him. The thought terrified Damien even more.

The bonds and blindfold were removed before he was shoved harshly forward.

A thick, wooden prison door resembling those in the English prisons during the Dark Ages was slammed in his face. He looked around the room to find an old, rickety bed covered with a dusty old mattress in the corner of the room.

The dripping of water and the musty smell nearly made him gag.

Except for the small rectangular opening in the door, there were no windows.

"Don't worry, you won't be here long." Jack smiled a new twisted and demented smile, revealing two sharp fangs. From the look in his eyes, Damien couldn't help but feel like he wanted to eat him.

"Back off before you get your head ripped off, newborn," The heavy accent from before returned making Jack back off. He opened the door, grabbing Damien's arm and yanking him out. "Lilith wants you in her chambers. You smell like dog so she'll probably make you get cleaned up and changed into new clothes before meeting her."

Lune sat with Holt, Kain, Jill and Gabriel around a fire as he told them about the coven's mansion high in the hills.

On the outside of the mansion, it resembled an old English castle the noble class resided in. The whole structure consumed massive amounts of land. The interior was lined with elongated hallways and different sections where the nobles would be able to cavort with whom ever they wished and not be disturbed.

Tall ramparts and a massive front lawn where the vampires could entertain social events to bolster their standing in the human world lie just in front of the house.

Lune began. "It's a horrible place. Beautiful only in elegant décor. That beauty is only outer walls deep. The outer perimeter is gated. The gate patrolled by hired human muscle during the day and werewolf and vampire slaves at night," Lune took a drink of the water he'd brought with him to the meeting.

"Below the mansion are catacombs. At the end a prison resembling those of the ancient days in England and Romania. The only way in besides jumping the fence, is a single automated gate where guests have to buzz in. It's isolated so even if you got stuck there and howled for help, there wouldn't be any guarantee anyone would be able to get there in time. The high elevation makes it hard to breathe. Not too damaging to a vampire but to their servants, it's harsh."

"Where would Lilith keep Damien? She has a crush on him and has threatened to turn him. Is there any way for us to get to him before that happens?" Kain asked, his eyes closed and directed at the ground. His voice was strangely calm. A feature common to his character.

Lune sighed, leaning back against the log serving as a makeshift bench where Holt sat with Gabriel. "It would depend. Most vampires won't turn anyone during the day so that would be the best chance to get him back. The only problem is, she's a jealous bitch with as little patience as a two-year-old. There's a chance she might skip turning him and kill him. Odds are she knows even if she turns him, there's no guarantee he would be with her."

Jill's anger rose within her the more she thought about Damien being locked up. "Lune, please. Help us. You're the only one to ever get into that hellish place." Jill clenched her fists so tightly, her nails began to draw blood.

"You truly love this man? Enough to risk the lives of your fellow lycans to get to him?" Lune replied.

"I do not ask for the sacrifice of those here. I'll go alone. I love Damien more than anyone I've ever met. He's the only thing in this world I can't live without. For him, I would face the fangs of the dark god." Her brilliant green eyes met Lune's.

Lune rose, smirking. "Good, because you may live to meet those fangs if you go through with this plan. It's nothing short of suicide. Not even I got out of there without a reminder of how utterly insane it is," Lune revealed a jagged scar across his chest. "However, I will go with you. It has been centuries since I have seen any action. I just hope your love for this man is as strong as you say. You may have to be ready to be the one to end his life."

CHAPTER FOURTEEN

D amien sat on the bed in Lilith's chamber, tapping his leg. He'd been forced to take a shower and get changed into a black silk, button-down shirt and pants. Clothing he would otherwise never wear out of feeling it was too high class.

He felt like one of those rich playboys who spent most of their time at strip clubs to see how many women they could score and take them home to their beds.

His heart sank as he thought about Jill. He rested his elbows on his knees, his head in his hands. *She's coming. I know she is.*

His chest tightened with growing anxiety and fear at the thought that he wouldn't be able to see her again. Kiss her soft lips or hold her warm body against his or hear her sweet voice say his name. He regretted his decision to wait until Christmas to have sex with her. Now, he may never get the chance.

I can't just sit here. He thought, getting up to go and test the doors. The shadows underneath the cracks made him aware of the guards placed there. *Okay, not getting out this way.*

His next idea took him to the window. At first glance it looked like a normal sliding window; easily unlocked. The problems were the werewolves and the guards patrolling the outer perimeter.

Escape seemed impossible. Even if he somehow managed to slip out through the window, he didn't know where he was or how to get back to Big Timber. The situation seemed hopeless.

Damien decided if he was forced to become a vampire he wouldn't stop begging Jill until she ended his life. He wouldn't be able to exist without his soul. His heart frozen in his chest only to be forced to steal the life force from another to live.

The thought of it made him sick to his stomach.

Even if he didn't come to hate her, there was no way he would allow himself to touch her. He would feel as though he were defiling her. He would be the very thing responsible for her pain.

Damien watched as the sun fell below the horizon heralding the hour of twilight. An hour of magic when the sky was painted a mix of the heated oranges of the day and the cool purples and pinks of the night.

These moments were often seen as times to take a good photo. This time it was filled with stress and anxiety.

All Damien could do was wait to see what Lilith might do to him when she finally arrived. Every footstep he heard outside of the door made his heart race with fear since Jill hadn't arrived.

Lilith came in as if on cue followed by one of the house servants carrying a tray of wine that looked as though it would cost Damien his life's savings. Two glass cups with gold accents accompanied the bottle on the tray.

The vampire's eyes lit up with underlying lust when she saw him.

"Still so breathtaking. Welcome Damien. It is a pleasure to have you in my home finally. I do apologize for the tactics I had to use to get you here. It was the only time we could find when you were away from your dog long enough for us to get a hold of you. I do hope you're hungry."

Damien's stomach growled. He hadn't eaten anything since he was dragged all the way out into the wilderness the night before. His lack of trust in Lilith not to poison or drug him with anything made him deny her offer.

"No thanks." He rose off of the bed to get as far away from the vampire as he could. He was careful to keep his eyes away from her as his back pressed against the nearest corner.

Lilith's laugh was surprisingly sensual despite her dark nature. "Oh, come now. You think I would go through the trouble of having Rayes bring you here if all I was going to do was poison you? Oh no, for you precious, I plan on enjoying every moment of your company. Come, sit back down."

"I'd rather not. After nearly being killed three times, stalked, hunted and having my head bashed in, I'm fine staying on my own side of the room. Oh and I'm pretty sure you almost raped me, so no. I'm staying here." Damien didn't try to hide annoyance and sarcasm.

"Damien, it was my father who tried to have you killed. As for Stoker, I can assure you, he was severely punished for his little stunt with your truck. Rayes was a bit anxious. I will let him know I disapprove of how you were treated."

Lilith smiled seductively, rubbing her pale fingers over the blood red sheets of the bed. "As far as that pitiful excuse of a school, I wouldn't have taken you in such a crude place. You deserve to be taken in sheets so soft, they tickle the senses of your already gorgeous body," Lilith said motioning for him to take a seat next to her. "I'm willing to forgive our little incident at the college. Come sit down and enjoy some of this delicious wine with me."

She sniffed the wine, taking a drink and licking her lips. "I give you my own word that you will be taken the greatest of care of. That dog of yours doesn't know how to give you what you deserve as I do. I've told you before. She only cares for the soul you carry."

Damien glared at her, his eyes rolling at the toxic words she'd just spouted.

Lilith rose up from the bed in a single smooth motion. "I know what is hiding behind those beautiful jeweled eyes of yours," Lilith said, flipping her platinum bangs out of her face before continuing.

"From the smell of you, I can tell you hadn't even had sex with her yet. So tell me something, why is that? If you were Lucius instead of Damien, do you think she would have waited? I don't think so. What exactly do you think you mean to her? If you didn't have Lucius' soul inside of you, she would never care you existed. She would have given herself to..."

Lilith spat the name out in contempt. "Alexander Kain."

Damien's heart skipped a beat, his blood cold. He knew Jill and Kain had history but he didn't know she'd once loved him and entertained the idea of becoming his mate.

"I don't believe you." Damien spoke low through clenched teeth. His fists balled up as he fought the overwhelming rise of betrayal and hurt.

Lilith rose from the bed, closing the distance between them in only a few short seconds. She pressed her breasts into his chest, placing her pelvis snug against his.

Taking Damien's jaw in her hands, she leaned in close enough she could have kissed him if she wanted. Her eyes half-closed under dark eye shadow as lust darkened her red eyes.

"Why else would she just happen to be in the exact same place just as he was about to get killed by Rayes? What makes you think she's not still in love with him? That she's only entertaining you until you die so she can be with him? Stay with me, Damien. I would give you everything you could ever want. Everything a human heart lusts for would be yours in an instant. I would even welcome your father into my coven. He would never be changed unless you or he asked."

Pain set his heart on fire, the blood rushed from his head as Damien tried to shake away the thought that Jill wasn't coming for him. He'd given her everything he'd never given to anyone else; opened his heart so deep to her. It would devastate him to learn she was just using him.

"No." Damien shook the negative thoughts away as he held on to every time Jill looked at him with sadness, her eyes full of longing that he would accept her love for him every time he saw her. Her willingness to take things slow and get to know him.

The night she listened to him as he struggled to tell her the secret he'd held onto. No one who doesn't love someone would do what Jill had done.

"Excuse me?"

"I said no. Jill's done nothing but proven her love to me. Unlike you who constantly threatens to make me something I don't want to be. If I had the ability to choose who I would put my trust in, it wouldn't be you, Lilith."

Lilith's eyes flashed red as she dragged Damien over to her bed and threw him down, locking his hands above his head with one of hers. The other tore the shirt open as though it were paper.

"It doesn't really matter. I've been kind long enough. After I meet tonight with some of the elders from my cousin's coven, I will be sinking my fangs into your throat whether you want it or not. Then we'll see how much your dog loves you. Maybe she'll be merciful and end your life."

Damien tried to struggle against Lilith's hold, knowing full well it was futile. He flinched when her hand went between his legs, rubbing him.

"Maybe I'll enjoy you first. Might be fun to feel the warmth of your body against mine. I hear your blood is quite rich to the taste. Either way, cherish your last few hours of being human, Damien Pierce. Soon you will belong to me." She licked her ruby, red lips, bending down to kiss the side of his neck.

Her lips were cold when they met his. Her tongue forced its way into his mouth so she could taste every part of him she could reach.

"So sexy. I can't wait to bind you to me for all of time."

Lilith pulled away, ending her forceful kiss. The hold on his hands released.

Before Damien had the time to get up from the bed, she was gone. The door locked from the outside behind her.

He walked over to the window, furiously trying to get the feeling of Lilith's kiss off of his lips. It had been forced, demanding and bitter with no love behind it at all.

To her, he was just a possession. Something she could do what she wanted when she wanted. His heart ached as the anxiety welled up inside of him to the point of making him dizzy. *Jill. Please. Please hurry.*

I'm coming, Damien. I can hear you. Just stay strong. Jill ran as fast as her four legs could carry her. Her chest heaved with each stride as she pushed her body beyond its natural ability to get to her lover. His blood inside of her allowed her to hear his desperate cry for help. The fear he felt burned in her chest.

Kain, Lune, Gabriel and Holt all followed closely behind her. Their hard panting served as reassurance that they supported her decision to infiltrate the coven despite how dangerous it was for them.

She knew they would have to make it before dawn or they would be too late. Lilith wouldn't wait past the night to turn Damien. In her mind, she'd waited too long and would most likely be infuriated once she'd learned he would never give himself to her even if she turned him.

When they arrived at the mansion, Lune took the lead. Shifting quickly and scaling the outer fence via a large oak that had a single branch overhanging the bars. Kain went with Holt around the back of the mansion while Gabriel and Jill went with Lune from the front.

"I can smell him. He's in the room on the second floor, first left from the front entrance." Jill channeled her anger so she could get to Damien, fighting the urge not to pull anything reckless though she knew she couldn't be killed.

His emotions and thoughts were a whirlwind that almost dizzied Jill too much to run. He'd gone from overwhelming fear to hurt, back to anxiety and helplessness.

It angered her to think about all that had been done to him to cause him to suffer such a variety of emotions.

"At least his location is easier than it could be. Kain and Holt will take out the security in the back. Once we get their signal, we can move in. Be careful, that room is Lilith's. Odds are it'll be guarded not only from the outside but from the inside doors as well. She wouldn't risk him being taken so easily," Lune ducked back down.

A werewolf began sniffing the air, its red eyes glanced towards the brush only to be pushed by the vampire holding its leash.

Jill's nails raked strips off of the bark of the tree. "If I have to face the bitch, I will. She's hurt him for the last time."

"Don't get overly cocky. The vampires may live the high life but they've proven themselves formidable. After all, their numbers are still increasing because they prey on the weakness of human fear." Lune warned, kneeling on one knee.

The arrival of a black limo made them hide deeper in the brush. It stopped in front of the main entrance. The driver got out to open one of the doors in the back. A tall, beautiful woman adorned in a black sequined dress with a mink fur around her neck got out of the back. Her features were rounded, her black hair done up in a tight bun at the top of her head giving her the look of a red carpet celebrity.

She looked around before walking through the double doors of the mansion, greeted by Lilith.

Lune's eyes widened in visible surprise. "That's Desdemona Cardoza."

"Who?" Jill asked, confused. She hadn't made it a point to learn vampire nobility.

"She's Lilith's aunt, Demetrius' sister-in-law. The matriarch of their sister coven in the nearby city of Great Falls. Her son Anthony, is no laughing matter. He's recognized as the Don of that city and rules it with an iron grip. He will kill anyone who dares stand against him without hesitation. She must be here to question Lilith's murder of her father. This could get ugly, really fast. The Cardozas rarely ever leave Great Falls."

For once in centuries, Jill felt the shiver of fear run up her spine. "We have to hurry. We have to get Damien out now, Lune."

A soft bark from Kain signaled Lune, Gabriel and Jill to make their move.

Gabriel broke the neck of the werewolf that crossed in front of Lilith's window, dragging the body away while Lune took down the vampire guarding the corner of the house, crushing the vampire's head in his jaws like a grape.

Jill easily scaled the ivy-lined trellis of the wall to perch in the window. Peeking in, her heart fell through her chest to the ground.

Damien lay on the bed in clothes she knew he would never be caught dead in. The look on his face was nothing short of sheer hopelessness and defeat.

Seeing Lilith wasn't anywhere in sight, Jill tapped the glass with her nail.

Damien looked up to see her, practically running to her. "Jill! Thank God." He put his hand on the glass, leaning his forehead against it. Relief replaced the anxiety inside of him when he saw her.

Jill put her hand on the glass, smiling in her own relief. She had gotten to him on time. "Get back, babe. I'm getting you out of there."

Damien stepped back as Jill prepared to shatter the glass to get to him. He didn't want to linger a moment longer knowing what was in store for him if he stayed.

Kain and Holt sprinted around the house. Jill tuned into them talking.

"We have to go. Now or we won't be leaving alive." Holt was breathing heavily, sweat covering his brow as he bent over to catch a breath. "I know you saw who came in that limo."

"We did. Jill almost has him." Lune replied.

Well no time for subtlety. Jill slammed her elbow into the glass, tearing the window from the frame of the house. The noise was bound to attract some unwanted attention. "Come on, quickly. Jump. Lune is below me, he'll catch you. We have to go, now."

Damien jumped to get caught by Lune before hitting the ground. "Jill. Jill, come on."

Jill was just about to jump down when Lilith came storming into the room, throwing the doors open hard enough they bounced off of the walls, rattling the foundations.

"You filthy bitch!" Lilith hissed as she charged at Jill.

"Get him out of here!" Jill yelled to Lune.

"Jill! Come with us!" Damien called out to her, afraid to leave her behind. "Kain! Take him!"

Kain grabbed Damien and the four of them took off, running as fast as they could. Scaling the fence, sprinting at full speed. They were pursued by some of the werewolves guarding the house.

Jill stood face to face with Lilith, making sure she kept her body between the window and the angry vampire.

"You will never and I mean ever touch him again, Lilith. Do you hear me? You think killing your father will make you half the lord he was?"

"Silence, dog! My father lost his ferocity in dealing with you filthy beasts! Every single one of you deserves to be wiped from existence. Under my rule I'll make sure that happens! Your lover may have died at my father's hand but he was a fool to leave you alive. He should have killed you as well!"

A dark and demented smile curved across Lilith's fangs. "Maybe I'll make you watch as I sink my fangs into Damien's throat. How would it feel to know the cycle will end and your precious Lucius will be in the arms of a vampire? Doesn't that piss you off?"

Jill bared her fangs, growling as she lunged at Lilith with such great speed the vampire didn't have time to move. Her claws raked down Lilith's face making her scream in agony as the sting of pure silver burned into her skin.

Lilith's hand trembled as she reached up to her face, taking the black blood from her cheek and looking down at it in her hands. "You...you disgusting...filthy dog!" She yelled, lunging toward Jill only to miss as she effortlessly jumped backwards out of the window. "You're dead! You hear me! I'll find a way to end your life, Jillian Styles! You can't run from me forever!"

After scaling the fence Jill shifted into her wolf form, sprinting through the waning night towards Gabriel's call in the woods.

Damien paced beside the car as Gabriel let out another howl, perking his ears to try and hear a reply.

"She should be back by now. What if she's hurt? Kain, I have to go back." Kain's hand on his shoulder kept Damien where he was. He lowered his head.

"She's coming. I just heard her call. From the sound of it, she's alright. Be patient."

Damien's mind wandered back to what Lilith said as he stared at Kain. The lycan alpha was definitely a match for Jill's affection. His dirty blonde hair, tall size and well-defined musculature would be a match for any male. Combined with the inhuman beauty of his people, Kain was, to Damien, more appealing than he was.

"Kain. Lilith told me you and Jill..."

"We didn't. Not once. The most we ever did was make out for the sake of companionship. It never went further."

"Then what's your history? Lilith said Jill wouldn't care about me if I didn't have Lucius' soul. She would have given herself to you. Is that true?"

Kain sighed. "My father, Pentacost saved Jillian as a puppy. Her pack was nearly destroyed by the vampires. Her mother held out as long as she could but took her last surviving pup and ran. She lay dying beside a brook when my father found her. She begged him to take her. I was about a century younger than Jillian so I guess you could technically say we grew up together since our years aren't the same as yours,"

Kain looked up at him. "Damien, whatever Lilith said to you, most of it wasn't true. I do love Jillian, more than anyone in this world but she's chosen you. I will give my life to protect you for her sake."

Jill came up through the woods. Her fangs and jaws wet with blood from fighting with some of the werewolves in the forest.

A huge bite taken from her left shoulder made her limp, her breathing heavy from fatigue.

Damien ran up to her without hesitation, his arms wrapping around her thick neck. Her huge paw rested on his shoulder in a half hug.

"I knew you would come."

She shifted back into her human form, her breathing heavy as she tried to heal the wounds inflicted on her.

Kain reached in through the window of Gabriel's back seat to pull out a backpack containing a spare set of clothes. He tossed it to her.

"Thank you, Kain." Jill got dressed quickly. "The wound in my shoulder is something I won't be able to heal completely. It'll scar, that much I know for certain."

"At least you are safe, Jillian. Want to tell me why Lilith was screaming?" Kain smiled, his own relief evident in his voice.

"I nailed her in the face. Silver nails and all, it'll most likely leave one sun's hell of a blemish. We all know how much she loves her face." Jill let out a slight chuckle. She was one of the few lycans left with claws made of pure silver. Yet another dying trait in the lycan race.

"Ouch." Gabriel snickered.

Lune was less than thrilled. "This is not the time for laughing. She was just paid a huge insult and now she knows there are at least three alphas in Big Timber. Luckily for us, Desdemona really couldn't care less about Lilith. The Cardozas rarely ever get involved personally but, that doesn't mean we shouldn't keep our guard up."

Holt patted his friend's shoulder, his eyes meeting the other two alphas in front of him. "Stay alert. War is coming. It's just a matter of time. I'm going to be calling in as many of the neighboring packs who are willing to help as possible to join our meeting. I won't force those who don't want to fight to do so. Don't draw any attention, the humans are already spooked as it is. Damien, you're a part of us now, we're going to need help in the human world as well."

"You're kidding, right? I've already proven I'm not strong enough to handle avoiding getting kidnapped. Jill got hurt because of me." Damien cursed under his breath. His own weakness pissed him off. Not only had he gotten Jill hurt again.

Now Lilith was beyond furious and this Desdemona character knew about the three alphas. All of this, in his opinion was his fault for not finding one single excuse to stay inside to keep out of trouble.

"Let Charlie know it's not the wolves doing the killing. If you need to, have Jill or Kain explain things. Whatever it takes to avoid a panic. You have to do this or our families are going to suffer even more than they are. We won't be able to hunt out of fear of being trapped or killed which will starve our pups and pregnant mothers." Holt replied.

Damien thought back to the pup he'd held in his arms. That little ball of fuzz wouldn't harm a fly, let alone a full-grown person. The thought of her starving made him angry.

"I don't know what I can do, but I'll try."

CHAPTER FIFTEEN

The sun was just rising when Jill and Damien arrived back at his house. Damien hadn't spoken the whole ride home. His mind was a swirling torrent of thoughts and concerns over everything that had happened. He'd turned down Jill's offer to drive, choosing to stare out the window as he thought about Kain's history with Jill.

When Jill had asked him what was wrong, he just shook his head. He knew she didn't believe him.

Charlie wasn't home yet so Damien took his spare key out of the old mailbox and unlocked the door, flipping on a light so they wouldn't run into any unwanted surprises.

"Damien, what's wrong? You've been quiet since we left the mountains." Her warm hand cupped his face, her thumb running along his cheekbone.

"Nothing's wrong. Just...thinking." Damien replied, taking her hand from his face.

"You can't lie to me, Damien. I can feel what you feel. Please, open your heart to me. I want to help."

Damien didn't reply. He just walked up the stairs to his room and sat down on the edge of the bed. Jill followed him, sitting next to him. She took off her jacket to reveal her sleeveless tank top. The gaping scar on her shoulder exposed to him. The wound had been deep enough, it left a jagged groove indicating where the flesh was torn from the muscle.

"Christ, Jill. That looks bad." Damien turned away, disgusted. He'd once again been the reason Jill was injured.

Jill looked down at her shoulder. "I can cover it if it displeases you."

Damien shot up from the bed, his shoulders tensed. His hands rigid. "Displeases me? Damn it, Jill, it's not that! It pisses me off that once again you've had to go through so much to save my worthless ass. Because of me, Kain, Gabriel, Holt and Lune are all in danger now too! I could have gotten them killed!"

"I wasn't going to let her turn you, Damien. I couldn't handle it. It would shatter my soul to pieces." Her arms wrapped around her, gripping her shoulders at the thought that she couldn't have made it on time. Knowing Damien, he would have begged her to kill him with her own fangs.

"How did this start, Jill? What went so wrong it has the two of your races tearing each other's throats out?"

Jill rose to go stand next to the window, looking out over the expanse of the landscape as she tried to picture the past. "I only know the stories Pentacost told me when I was old enough to hear them. The exact event was lost many centuries ago."

"Tell me." Damien came up behind her, his hands rubbing her shoulder against the pain he could hear in her voice.

Jill reached up behind her. Her hand petting the soft flesh of Damien's cheek. The light tickle of his facial hair teasing her skin as he bent down to kiss her jaw. She closed her eyes, sighing.

"Centuries ago, before the songs of the children of the night were heard, Luna rose into the sky greeted by the brothers Tenebris, the night father and Barghast, the shadowed one. In the beginning, it was only the gods in the heavens. Everything else was dark and empty. Tenebris and Luna were lonely and longed to have children of their own. As millennia passed, they began falling in love with one another. Tenebris, eventually proposed to Luna. This angered Barghast for he was in love with her as well. His jealousy burned the blazing red of his eyes. He threatened his brother, swearing if he went through with his marriage to Luna, he would forever hunt and kill any children they had,"

Jill felt a pain in her chest, the memories of countless innocent lives lost as a result of jealousy burned with anger inside of her. Damien put his arms around her, holding her to provide support.

"Despite this, Luna married Tenebris. Their love gave birth to the wolves. The rulers of the night. To Luna it wasn't enough, she wanted more. She asked Tenebris to help her bless us with the ability to change. To live among man. As his own gift, Tenebris gave us inhuman beauty and the ability to stand on two legs with power beyond any force in nature. For centuries they loved their children but,"

Damien sat down on the windowsill to allow Jill to snuggle into him. She lay between his legs, her cheek against his chest. The soft beat of his heart helped to ease the tension working its way into her soul.

"Barghast's rage soon fell upon us. His soul poisoned to the point he began to feed on the blood of man,"

"In order to carry out his threats, Barghast's fangs found the veins of man's greed and fear, giving birth to the first vampire. He bade him to hunt down the children of Luna and Tenebris, killing all he saw."

Damien ran his hand through Jill's soft hair. His sense of amazement overwhelming him. It was as though he could see the events Jill was describing in his mind's eye. "What about the werewolves? Did Barghast have something to do with them?"

"Yes. His shadow fell on one of my kind, dementing the beauty Luna and Tenebris created. His curse had been fulfilled. The Blood Wars had begun. Tenebris feared the genocide of his children so much he called upon Luna's sister, Solaris to aid in our protection,"

"Solaris answered his cries and reached out her hand to drive the shadows away, damning them only to live in the darkness or die in the sun's light."

"Jill, I still don't understand the Purifiers? I mean, it's the reason I'm being hunted, right?" Damien asked, eager to learn why he had become public enemy number one on the vampire's most wanted list.

Jill looked up at him, her eyes sullen. Her fingertip tracing the muscle of his chest under his t-shirt. "I'm sorry, I don't know. We don't know their origins. We only know they tried to protect man's world from being wiped out by our war. I only met one in my entire life on this planet. According to legend they can live just as long as one of us, if not longer."

"How long can a lycan live?" Damien asked, curiously.

Jill closed her eyes, a low growl formed in her throat. "Damien, in our early history we could live for centuries if we weren't killed by man or slaughtered by vampires. Many of us long to live out the lives of a normal human to get back into Luna's loving embrace and out of the chaos. Many are forgetting, ignoring the call of our mother. Others are giving their lives in last-ditch efforts to take some of the vampires down. Our world is a world of fear and unease. It's not for the faint of heart."

Damien brushed his knuckle over her cheek. "I'm sorry. I shouldn't have pressured you into telling me."

Jill took his wrist in her hand, softly kissing it. Hearing the soft murmur of the streams of his blood as it drifted peacefully in his veins gave her peace. His pulse was calm. His heartbeat gentle and comforting. "It's okay. You deserve to know why you're being hunted. I just wish I knew more."

Damien had been curious about the Purifiers but so far no one could answer any of his questions. All he knew was there was something about him the vampires saw as a threat big enough to want him dead.

Lilith's words came forward in Damien's mind despite his best efforts to suppress them. His heart hurt so bad he needed to know so he could move past the feeling of betrayal nagging in the back of his mind.

"Jill, I have to know. If I didn't have Lucius' soul inside of me, would you have given me a second look? Would you even know I existed or cared to know?" The words tasted bitter as Damien said them. He wanted to trust Jill's love for him but his uncertainty couldn't be ignored.

Jill's lips met Damien's in a loving kiss. It wasn't demanding or possessive like Lilith's had been. Her hands tangled in his hair, holding him in place as she savored the taste of him. She positioned her hips so they relaxed against his, her stomach flat against his own. Her breasts conveniently pressed against his chest.

She pulled away, staying close to his face. "Damien, I told you. I'm not going to chase ghosts anymore. You took my breath away the minute I saw you. My heart fluttered like a hummingbird's wings when I saw these gorgeous jeweled eyes of yours. I knew I wanted to be with you the rest of your natural life. I didn't mind taking things slow as long as I could eventually have you to myself. You may have Lucius' soul but you have made it your own. Its unique song is more beautiful than any I've ever heard,"

Jill ran her hands down Damien's sides, positioning them so she could begin guiding his shirt up.

"It's your voice that I hear, your heart that I feel, your pain that fills me when you're under stress. Your blood that flows through me."

Damien pulled away from her, his brow furrowing in confusion. "My blood?"

"When you were hurt by Stoker, I had to do something truly desperate to save your life. I think it's time I told you," Jill took a deep breath, knowing what she was about to tell him would sound strange to anyone that wasn't a lycan or hadn't seen it done before.

"I've tasted your blood, Damien. You were dying. The only thing I could do to close the wound was use the curse inside of me. To my kind, the sharing of blood is as sacred as sex. It gives us the ability to talk to each other, even if we're miles away. It's how I heard you when you begged me to hurry to rescue you." Jill sighed, her fear of him rejecting her inched forward in her mind.

Strange? Strange didn't even begin to describe the way Damien felt about what he'd just been told. Didn't vampires drink blood?

"I know what you're thinking and no. It's not the same. For us, it's a bond. All of our memories, our feelings become one when we share it. Vampires drink blood to stay alive, maintain their power and create more of their kind."

"Wait, so because you healed the wound in my side, now you can tell what I'm feeling. What I'm thinking?" Damien asked.

"No, it's not like mind-reading. Only lycans bound together by the gods can read each other's minds. It is rare. Think of our bond as more of a telephone. You don't have my blood in you so you can't hear me but I can hear you. I can't talk to you. It's an unbreakable bond that keeps us together even if we leave each other." Jill said, her concern intensifying the more she felt the growing unease in Damien.

"Okay. That doesn't make any sense to me and quite frankly, creeps me the hell out." Damien replied, slightly disturbed. Internally he was debating on how to process what he'd just learned.

Jill scooted away from him on the other side of the sill. "Do you want me to leave?" She sat on her knees waiting for his reply.

"No Jill, I don't." Damien scooted over to her, his hand reaching out to stroke her face. He smiled at her wide-eyed look.

"It's just something else I'm learning about you. It's strange but I want to make it work between us, Jill." He wanted to know as much as she was willing to let him. "Speaking of which, is turning from a human into a lycan painful when they're bitten or something?"

"Kain or Holt would know more since they've both done it. From what they've told me it's excruciating. The body's white blood cells try to fight the change, putting the heart under extreme duress. If one survives the initial change, shifting from one form to the other is actually very pleasurable. You've witnessed it before. You can actually get to a point where you can easily slide from one form to another with little effort,"

Jill leaned in close to Damien's face, her hand cupping his neck. Her thumb ran softly over his cheekbone. "I won't ever turn you. It's your mortality that makes you beautiful and free, Damien. This life is cursed. It's not one I would wish on you."

Damien hadn't thought about asking her to turn him, he was just curious as to how it worked.

Jill placed a gentle kiss on Damien's eye before getting up. "The elders wish your presence at the meeting tomorrow. I suggest you sleep most of the day and take it easy tonight. Some of these alphas you've never met before. They can be stubborn in their old ways. Your mind is going to need to be fresh."

She walked over to the bed to lay down, her own mind worn from telling the dark and blood littered history of her people.

Damien sat down next to her. There was still so much he didn't understand. The vampires feared him but what was his role in all of this? No one could give him any answers and from what Jill said, no one knew.

CHAPTER SIXTEEN

The evening found Damien in a state of unrest. His mind was running wild with everything Jill told him regarding her history.

His dreams shifted from different scenes of the story. The Purifiers, battlefields littered with the dead and dying, screams of mothers as they pleaded for the lives of their children. The pain he felt threatened to tear his soul to shreds.

Eventually his mind settled on a single scene.

He stood in what appeared to be a clearing in a ring of trees. It was burned to cinders leaving nothing more than the crippling black bones of trees that desperately tried to hold on to their roots. In the distance were huge structures resembling giant stones set in a circle. Animals ran in all directions around him, nearly hitting him as they tried to escape from what was about to transpire.

From the colors of the sky it was the hour of twilight, only less beautiful in light of the flames raging in the distance.

The sky was masked in blackness from falling particles of ash. A thick miasma poisoned the air, making it hard to breathe.

The moon began to rise in the east following the setting of the sun, stained red as if it were a harvest moon. Only the color seemed to drip from the surface. It sounded to Damien as though she was crying. Her soft face stained with blood.

From the west rose Tenebris. His ears straight up in the air. His sculpted chest heaved forward. A long white tail flowed behind him. He stood on two muscular legs that bulged with power. His elongated feet crushed the earth beneath him. His fur was as white as snow, flowing as though it was created by sheets made of wind.

The god's eyes were a crystal blue illuminated by the light of the stars in the sky. The heavens radiated with a power so great it could make the earth itself quiver in reverence. He stood as a mighty titan upon the ground poised for the battle to come. He was beyond beautiful to Damien's eyes. So much it overwhelmed him.

The wolf god let out a howl of challenge across the sky.

Suddenly, Damien felt the earth under his feet splinter and crack. It was if it were struggling to give way to whatever was trying to burst from its bowels. He had to step back with each fractured piece as it tore away like a scab from a wound. The severity of the quakes made it hard to stay standing.

From the east, a giant creature resembling a giant flying fox stood on the same types of legs that Tenebris possessed. It had a tail and face that reminded Damien of a wolf. Its eyes burned the colors of ember flames. Its fangs bared in a rage so powerful Damien could feel the hate burning in his chest as it eyed its opponent. Its wings were massive, leathery structures protruding from its arms. They extended down the lengths of its sides to thighs so muscular, a body builder paled in comparison.

The thick fur was as black as night, smoking with the ashes of the flames. The mane around its neck behaved as if it were only wisps of shadow as it flowed with the soft breeze of the evening.

Barghast, the Shadowed One made his appearance, answering his brother's call of challenge with his own loud roar.

With another roar, Tenebris ran towards his brother, lunging at him with nails made of pure silver.

When they hit each other, it sounded like a crack of thunder so loud and real, it ripped Damien out of his dream.

He sweated profusely, saturating the bed beneath him. His chest heaved to keep up with the terror instilled within him from the pure power of the two beasts he'd just seen. He could still smell the burning cinders of the forest, hear the roars the two titans let out as they challenged each other.

Jill was still asleep beside him, curled up in the blanket they both shared. The look on her face content despite the story she'd told before they both lay down to get some sleep.

Damien got up to go to the bathroom to splash some water on his face. His head hurting with each flash of memory.

The dream felt so real. His legs remembered the shaking of the ground. He could feel the rage in Barghast's eyes as he glanced at him just before Tenebris smashed into him.

Unable to go back to sleep, Damien sat on the edge of the bed. Jill's cool hand against his heated skin made him jump away. The panic forced his breaths to come out in short and shallow bursts.

"I'm sorry. I didn't mean to scare you. What's wrong? You're as pale as a ghost." Jill rubbed the sleep from her eyes, trying to hide her concern. Damien's body seemed to be trembling. "Damien?"

Damien wanted to answer her but, he didn't know how. He felt as if his very soul was on fire. It felt as though Barghast had burned a reminder into him that he was in way over his head. Almost to the point of drowning.

"I... nothing. It was just a dream I had." Damien replied, his voice trembling the same as his body. He did his best to sit back down, trying to calm down.

Jill moved to sit next to him, leaning a cheek against his bare shoulder. "Okay, I won't push you to talk. Just promise you won't hide your heart from me."

"I won't. It was just a nightmare." He tried to smile to show Jill he was okay. The lie he was telling didn't do much to reassure either of them.

It wasn't just a nightmare and Damien knew it. He'd seen the dark god's eyes before. He'd heard his laugh. He just couldn't remember where.

The following night was the night of the meeting of the elders. The lycans all waited in anticipation to learn which alphas would be gracing them with their presence.

Kain stood next to Gabriel as though he were protecting him while they waited. Dolph and Chase took their places next to their alphas.

Holt and Cade had gone to the town's station to pick up the new arrivals in Holt's truck.

Damien sat next to a fire with Jill who was playing with the pups. Answering questions in regards to how old she was, if she ever killed anyone and how lonely it was to be by herself for so many centuries. The smile on her beautiful face a dim mask to try and hide the years of pain she'd endured.

A sense of protection rose up in Damien's chest as he watched her. She was so strong and beautiful yet the scar on her shoulder reminded him she could still be hurt. Immortal or not.

He was so angry at himself for his own mortality. He should be her shield against the world as her boyfriend, not make her protect him whenever he got in too deep.

The flames of his dream burned inside of him, making him wince at the pain. He tried to hide it to avoid worrying Jill.

"You have seen something." Kain's soft voice took Damien by surprise with his sudden arrival.

The alpha was always capable of relaxing him for some reason and seemed to always know when he needed his advice.

When their eyes met, Kain could see the sweat on Damien's brow. "I can tell from your eyes you have seen something. Care to tell me what it was?"

"It was a nightmare, Kain. That's all." Damien replied, frustrated.

Kain didn't appear convinced. He sat down next to Damien. His arm rested on his bent knee, his other leg extended in front of him. "Damien, one does not shake or start sweating from just a nightmare. Something you saw is affecting you. Tell me."

Damien acquiesced. "Fine. I don't want to say anything in front of Jill. Can we speak somewhere?"

Kain nodded, standing back up and offering Damien a hand to help him to his feet.

He led them to the tent Holt kept for him when he chose to visit, offering Damien a seat so he could make them some hot tea to warm them against the cold night.

Sitting down across from him, Kain asked Damien again. "So, what was it? What did you see?"

Damien's body burned with the flames. His jaw tightened as he wrestled with how to tell Kain what was happening. His eyes squeezed closed. "I don't even know. Jill told me the story of the gods before laying down. I guess I must have fallen asleep. I'm not sure when but I found myself standing in a burned meadow. All around me the forest was burning or burnt. I could feel the heat of the flames, smell the cinders of the wood. Even the animals as they brushed by me gave off a breeze I still remember."

Damien felt the burn intensifying as he recalled the dream.

"There were two colossal beasts. The first one looked like a giant bipedal wolf. His fur was pure white. His eyes glowed a blue so light it reminded me of the stars at night. He let out a roar, like a lion, not a wolf. It shook everything around him like he was challenging something. Something he didn't want in his territory. For some reason, I knew he him. I was seeing the Night Father in his full lycan form."

Damien's chest ignited in a searing pain as he neared the part in his dream where Barghast appeared. It felt like his body was being ripped apart from the inside. His heart beat quickly behind his ribs, making them hurt.

The look in the devil's eyes was still fresh in his mind.

"The other one was terrifying. He looked like a mix between a bat and a wolf. His fur black as coal. His eyes burned with a hate so strong I felt it trying to borrow its way inside of me. He had giant, leather wings and thick horns coming from his brow. He rose from fire and ash, angry and tormented. His roar sounded like the screams of a thousand souls. The Shadowed One. I don't know how I knew him. Tenebris began to run towards him,"

"When they clashed, it sounded like a loud crack of thunder. Just before I woke up, Barghast's eyes fell on me like he saw me. Kain, I can still feel the flames his hate burned into me. It felt so real."

Kain got Damien some water. Damien's tongue felt like sandpaper in his mouth form the heat inside of him. He took the water and hastily drank it dry.

"It was no dream. It was a vision, that is why it was so real. Barghast is aware of you now, Damien. He sees you as a threat and he won't stop until he gets his way." Kain didn't appear to be shaken in the least.

"What should I do?"

"Nothing, just keep your guard up and be aware of anything that feels like a sign to you. Tenebris' appearance of challenge means he knows you as well and is prepared to defend you. Congratulations. You are now in our gods' eyes. This has never happened before in our history."

Kain smiled at Damien, extending his hand. "You have my friendship and my loyalty."

Damien's breath stalled. The look in Kain's eyes was one of pure respect unlike any he'd ever given him in their time together. He took his hand, letting him help him up.

"Damien, listen to me. Up until now, you have been asleep. Your abilities as a Purifier have been dormant inside of you. The gods' appearance means that you have begun to awaken."

"How do you know all of this?" Damien inquired, his sense of caution coming forth with the sudden change in Kain's attention to him.

"In time you will know. For now, be careful and stay alert." A soft howl alerted Kain to Holt's return. "We better go. The others are here."

Holt returned later in the evening with two other alphas and their betas. To Damien's surprise one of them was a woman. He'd never seen a woman alpha before.

With a nod, Holt led the alphas and their betas, Lune, Damien and Jill to his tent. He posted a guard outside to keep away any prying ears or eyes. They all sat in a circle in human form so Damien could understand what they were saying.

"Welcome friends. I know it has been a while since a few of us have seen each other. My heart sings that you were able to make it." Holt opened the introductions. "Jill, I'm sure you know Yuna, Galeck and their betas, Harou and Channon."

"Yes, it is my honor to meet you in the flesh though I have heard of your exploits in aiding us in time of need." Jill lowered her eyes out of respect at each of the alphas. "This is Damien. He's my lover and the keeper of the soul of a Purifier."

Gasps could be heard from the new alphas and betas. Their eyes locked on him as if studying him.

"So, you are the one we have heard so much about. We welcome you, great one. It is an honor to be graced with your presence again after so long." Yuna's voice held an eastern accent as she spoke, her head bowing to Damien in reverence. "To you, lycan of legend, please do not feel you need to lower your eyes. We have heard the tales of all you have done over the years. It is we who should yield to you."

In a gruff voice that sounded like a lumberjack from the old country, Galeck spoke. "I am Galeck of the western packs of the Rockies. This is my beta, Channon. It is an honor to be in the presence of both of you. We agree with Yuna. Please, do not feel either of you have to lower your eyes for it is we that respect you and will yield as well."

Damien didn't know how to take all of the respect he was getting. Until now he'd gotten looks of only disgust and disdain from the people of Big Timber.

"I know we're all aware of why we're here. The vampires of Big Timber have begun moving against us. Demetrius Stone is dead, killed by his own daughter. Lilith has declared open war. She is threatening to kill Jillian and take her lover for her own. We need as many of you who are able to come aid us." Holt's voice was full of dire need.

Yuna took a deep breath. The look on her face calm as she took the time to think. "We will help you. In times as dark as these, it would be foolish for us not to stand together. Our numbers are falling. Our pups dying. My pack will offer every available soldier we can."

"We as well. The mountains have been our safe haven but, it has been harder and harder for us to find food for our young. I cannot tell everyone here how many I have had to bury in the past few years. It has to stop or we won't last another century." Galeck replied, downtrodden. From the look in his eyes, he'd buried more than his fair share of pups and loved ones.

Damien looked around at the depressed mood that fell on each leaders' face. The wicked grin Barghast gave him started to make more sense the more he heard.

A vibration from in his pocket alerted both Damien and Jill to his phone. Rob sent him a text telling him he needed to see him immediately.

Worried it might have to do with vampires, Damien stood up. "Forgive me but I have something I need to attend to."

The elders all looked at each other than back at him. Kain's eyes held him the strongest.

"My lover's needs come before my own. Forgive me but I must go with him." Jill was unsure as to the reason why Damien suddenly had to leave. She rose with him. Her loyalty to him unshaken even if it meant angering the elders.

"Of course, a lover's loyalty is to be unquestioned." Yuna addressed Jill for the other alphas as the two of them turned to leave.

Kain walked out with them, pulling Jill close to him. "I will catch you up when you come home, Jillian. Be safe." His eyes met Damien's as he held Jill's hips. "Remember what I said. Be mindful of what is going on around you, Damien."

Damien nodded, the understanding between the two of them almost confused Jill as he walked away with her on his heels.

Rob paced outside of his house, his face distorted in confusion when Damien walked up.

"Rob, what's going on? Why the sudden text?"

Rob was more frustrated than Damien had ever seen him since they'd been friends. Usually he was laid back and didn't let anything get to him.

"What hell, D?! Where have you been?! People have been going missing left and right. Then you just up and vanish?! Chelsea was gone for months!" Rob exclaimed.

"Rob, will you calm the fuck down? I hadn't seen Chels since the college, I told you that. She got upset at me and then left. I've already been questioned by my dad and Callahan. Her parents won't even talk to me anymore." Damien kept his reserve despite the lingering feelings of frustration at being treated like a criminal. His mood wasn't made any better with Rob's accusations being added on.

Jill walked up behind Damien, getting the attention of Rob who eyed her with a look of intense annoyance and frustration. "Let me guess, Jill, right?"

"Got a problem, Rob?" Damien put his hand on Jill's hip, pushing her slightly behind him.

"Problem? Hell, yeah, I've got a problem. Chelsea came to see me last night. There was something way off, D. She was pale with circles so dark under her eyes, it looked like she was dead. She told me some crazy shit about someone named 'Jill'. Said she was a witch or something, casting a spell on you."

Damien's eyes widened. Chelsea had openly lied about Jill. What was worse and slightly more terrifying was the description he'd used.

"Rob, do you know how crazy you sound? Jill didn't do anything to me. I fell in love with her. She's my girlfriend, not a siren."

"Dunno, D. No one saw her during the whole time you were 'falling in love with her'. Seems weird to me." Rob crossed his arms over his chest. His overall posture showed the amount of distrust he'd been holding onto until he was able to see Jill in person.

"Rob, I'm sorry I haven't been around but there are things going on that you don't understand. If Chelsea comes back, don't talk to her. She's not the same. I'll try to explain better. For now I need you to trust me. Jill's not the villain here."

"Sorry for flipping out, man. Just scared the shit out of me with all this talk of wolves ripping people up." Rob replied, taking in a deep breath. "I still don't trust her though."

Jill winced. The paranoia was setting in among the humans. She worried about the fate of her people.

Damien hadn't said a word on their way back to Gabriel's gym. He'd been wondering about what happened to Chelsea and how. It hurt him to think she had been turned and no one knew what happened.

Jill sat silent, letting Damien drive her car as she wrestled with her own thoughts.

When they arrived back to Solstice, they walked upstairs to Jill's room, speaking only after Damien closed the door behind them.

"Chelsea's a vampire now, isn't she?

"Yes."

"Jill, what're you going to do? She's my friend. One of the only ones that ever stood by me after what happened."

"Damien, I'll do what needs to be done to protect you and the packs. If it means killing Chelsea, then so be it." Jill's voice was emotionless, unwavering as she changed into her black clothes and coat.

"Wait, you would just kill her? Jill, you can't."

"What would you have me do, Damien? Let her kill my people just because she can?"

"What if I can reach her? Let me talk to her." Damien pleaded with Jill. He could see she was angry but Chelsea was his friend.

"Damien, she could kill you without batting an eyelash or worse, turn you. She's already proven she doesn't care. Did you hear what she said to

Rob? She's not the same woman you knew. She would kill you just to spite me. Do you really want to take that risk?"

"What I want, Jill is to believe not all vampires are manipulative war mongers. What if there are some who want peace too? All I'm asking for is a chance to talk to her."

Jill could feel the emotions going through Damien's body growing stronger. "I can't take that chance. Damien, I can't lose you. Even if it means hurting you. I'm sorry but my people are in danger. Please, trust me."

Damien wrestled with himself. He wanted to try and make things right with Chelsea. He'd hurt her feelings. He couldn't help but feel somewhat responsible for her changed state.

"I do trust you, Jill. I need you to trust me. I won't let you hurt Chelsea, I have to try to reason with her."

"I'm sorry, Damien. It's not you I don't trust." With her last words, Jill left the room.

CHAPTER SEVENTEEN

D amien opened door only to come face to face with Scott and Cade.
"Sorry Damien, we can't let you leave. Jill asked us to make sure you didn't go anywhere until she gets back." Scott didn't sound sorry and Cade seemed to be enjoying Damien's house arrest.

"You're kidding me, right? Where is Jill?"

"She went hunting." Cade said, emotionlessly.

"Let me go, Scott. I have to find someone."

"No. Quite frankly, I'm glad she's finally put you on a leash. I was tired of rescuing your stupid ass every five minutes."

"Step aside, both of you." Kain stepped between Cade and Scott. "Let him go. I will accompany him."

Scott scoffed at his alpha.

"Did you say something, Scott?" Kain's eyes met Scott's, forcing him to back down the longer he stared.

"No, my alpha." Scott said, lowering his eyes.

"I didn't think so."

"Kain, I need to find Chelsea. Please. I want to try to reason with her." Damien interrupted the lycans, desperate to reach Chelsea before Jill found her.

"Damien, there are some souls that cannot be saved. Especially when they are already gone." Kain forced Cade aside, his voice calm despite his frustration.

"I have to try. Please."

"Very well." Kain surrendered, leading Damien down to his car.

Jill returned to find Damien gone. She'd left Scott and Cade in hopes that she could speak with Damien about what happened.

"Kain went with him. I had no choice, Jill. As much as I hate him, he's still my alpha."

"Did they say where they went?" Jill replied, clenching her gloved hands against her sides.

"Damien wanted to find that Chelsea girl who went missing. Kain said he'd take him back to his house."

Jill thanked Scott, heading back down to her car to Damien's house.

When Jill arrived at, Kain was standing by his car waiting for her.

"Kain, where is he?"

"Jillian, I understand you are worried. You love him but he is doing what he was sent here to do. The Purifiers were keepers of peace between the races. You cannot interfere with that." Kain replied, calmly.

"Where is he?"

"I don't know. He took off on the motorcycle Charlie got him. He asked me not to follow. I honored his request."

"You don't know or you won't say? I know you, Kain."

"Jillian, I do not know. Now, go back to the gym and work off some of your anger. Your emotions are clouding your judgement. He will be fine. He's going through some changes and may need some time to think. This incident with Chelsea hit him pretty hard."

Jill took a deep breath. She thought about Damien's words when she left. He'd asked her to trust him and that's what she would do. No matter how worried about him she was.

Instead of going back to the gym, Jill went for a walk in the town to enjoy the decorations and hear some of the bustle of the holidays. The music had always been some of her favorite genre.

Getting around crowds used to make Jill nervous but after she met Damien, she began to appreciate interaction with people. Many of them were either lycans that recognized her as one of their own or those that had long forgotten how to change.

The cold snow coated the ground, crunching beneath her boots as she walked down the street. Damien still hadn't come back or answered any of her texts or calls. Gods, she hoped he wasn't angry at her. She would never forgive herself for overreacting like she did.

Jill looked up at one of the wreaths that adorned an old-fashioned lamp post, her heart breaking as she longed to see him. She couldn't feel his emotions as though he'd found a way to hide himself from her. Wherever he had gone, Jill couldn't hear his voice or the soft song of his soul. It was if he'd disappeared.

Damien, do you not know how much this hurts? I can't feel your emotions. I can't hear your soul anymore. Where have you gone?

Jill hugged her coat around her against the cold and ache in her heart. She longed for him to be beside her. She'd felt his emotions, heard his voice in her mind. Now it was empty. Like half of her was missing.

"Sucks, doesn't it?"

Jill's eyes opened to find the very cause of her pain standing in front of her. Chelsea had her hands in her pockets. Her blonde hair golden from the immortal beauty she'd cursed herself with. Her eyes darkened with not only layer upon layer of dark purple eye shadow but the dark circles characteristic of a vampire.

"You. You knew he would react this way. Don't you dare tell me you didn't. Which parasite did you beg to change you?" Jill's anger was beyond her control the moment Chelsea appeared.

Chelsea's smile was dark and sadistic. "Doesn't matter who changed me, bitch. Did you think I would let a slut like you take what should have been mine years ago? Where is he by the way? I haven't seen him in weeks."

"What do you care? You don't know anything about him. He would have never opened his heart to you and you know it."

As if she knew what was going on, Chelsea chuckled. "Oh that's too funny. He's severed your connection, hasn't he? Impressive. He's even more powerful than she said."

"How do you know about him?"

"Doesn't really matter, does it? I've known Damien since he was nine. I stood by him when the town thought he was nothing but a monster. Where were you? Why didn't you come to his rescue then?"

The vampire's toxic words stung like salt in an open wound. Jill hadn't been around when Damien was a child. If she had she would have protected him from those who dared call him an outcast. She would have watched over him until he was old enough for her to court.

"I don't have to explain myself to a newborn bloodsucker like you. You think you know, Damien? If you would have taken the time to get to know him instead of constantly throwing yourself at him, maybe he would have actually opened up to you." Jill replied, smirking.

"Don't you dare assume you know how I felt. I tried to get him to open up to me. He just never would. Maybe with you gone, he'll finally wake up and get his head on straight." Chelsea hissed her reply. A small amount of spittle shot from her fangs.

"Chelsea, I won't face you here. Vampire or not, this is still your home, or it was. Would you really risk hurting these people?" Jill replied, trying to keep calm. Even though she hated her, Chelsea was still Damien's friend.

"I would have cared, dog. Except for the fact that I hate you too much to give a damn about these people. Don't fight if you so choose but I'll tear you apart. Maybe deliver your head to Lilith as a gift."

Jill growled, her fangs extending beyond her lips. She knew she'd have to draw the vampire out of the town to avoid drawing too much attention.

The ground splintered as she took off at top speed into the woods with Chelsea hot on her heels.

"Chelsea, we don't have to fight. It isn't right to Damien to make him have to choose. He still sees you as a friend. He ran because of you." Jill circled the vampire, careful to keep her back from being exposed.

"I didn't send him away, bitch! If he ran, then it was on you. You should have been a better girlfriend to him." Chelsea yelled at Jill, her fangs bared as she hissed at her.

Jill jumped forward, shifting mid-air as she prepared to meet Chelsea head on. If she didn't, then she could have been seriously injured.

Jill stop!

Hearing his voice in her mind, Jill's ears perked up. She froze. Her fangs just above Chelsea's face.

Whimpering she turned to see Damien walking into the clearing. He was still so beautiful. Untouched by all the time they hadn't seen each other.

Jill ran up to him. Her muzzle met his stomach as she rubbed against him, whimpering in happiness. His emotions filled her. The feeling of his voice in her mind elated her as she tried not to push him over.

I know. I missed you too. Damien stroked the soft fur, reassuring her she wasn't dreaming.

"Damien? Where have you been?" Chelsea asked, the voice of the woman she once was piercing through the darkness.

"I stayed at Kain's for a while. He gave me a spare key to go whenever I wanted. I knew if I disappeared Chelsea, you would come looking for me. You were always playing mother hen when we were kids." Damien replied, still petting Jill's head.

Jill's eyes met Damien's, almost misty in apology for what she did.

It's okay. You were looking out for me. I get it. Don't do it again. Damien shoved Jill's head, playfully.

"Don't touch her!" Chelsea yelled. Her body began rippling with her anger. Two large gray wings protruded from the back of her jacket, now tattered and torn from the emergence of her new leathery wings. Her fangs extended larger than her mouth could handle. Her fingers elongated with her nails turning into a tint of gray.

Jill stepped in between Chelsea and Damien.

No, Jill, let me talk to her. Damien walked around the wolf, determined to try to reach his friend.

The large wolf heard him, staying close in case she needed to interfere.

Chelsea looked nothing like herself. The image of Barghast ran through Damien's mind as he stared at her demented form.

"Chels, it doesn't have to be this way. Please. This isn't you."

"Step aside, Damien. I don't want to hurt you." Chelsea's voice was almost a high-pitched hiss. "Please. Move. I have no war against you."

"No. I won't let you hurt Jill anymore. What happened to you, Chels? The young woman I grew up with would never do anything like this. She wouldn't lie to her friends or try to kill over jealousy." Damien replied, keeping his body between Jill and Chelsea.

"She doesn't love you, Damien. She can't. She only cares about her filthy pack. She forced you to run away for weeks. Are you going to say that's okay?"

"I wouldn't Chels, except for the fact Jill didn't force me to do anything? I chose to stay low for a while. I needed some time and space to think. I worried sick over you. So did Rob. When I heard you were turned, I lost it. I felt like part of it was my fault. Chelsea, I'm sorry I hurt your feelings but I fell in love with Jill. I knew if I disappeared, you would eventually come looking for me. Please, you don't have to do this."

"Oh, but I think I do." Chelsea's grinned "I never wanted this, Damien. I wanted you to love me but you never even saw it inside yourself to give me a chance." Her wings flexed as she pushed herself skyward, preparing for a forward dive.

Damien held his ground, his hand behind him kept Jill where she stood. *Stay there, Jill. Please. Trust me.*

Jill whimpered as she watched the vampire getting closer. She almost jumped over him when the sound of a splintering log drew her attention to the wolf that flew through the sky above them. He landed just in time to take Chelsea's wrists in his clawed hands. His feet dug into the ground as he took the brunt of the speed of the plummeting vampire.

The sandy fur identified him as Kain. Only he stood on two muscular legs instead of four. His jeans were only ripped and he wore a red, plaid jacket with Sherpa inlays tied around his waist.

The image of Tenebris taking on Barghast ran through Damien's mind as he watched Kain hold Chelsea back. His experience clearly dwarfing her as she fought to try to push the large lycan back.

"Alexander Kain. I've heard of you. Damn you for interfering!"

Kain almost smiled as he threw her back, skidding across the ground. He readied himself in a stance mirroring that of a martial artist.

"Fine. I'll retreat for now. I know I'm not strong enough to handle the likes of you. Not in your true form. I won't forget this, Damien! I'll see you dead before I see you in bed with her!" Chelsea lunged skyward to fly back to the coven.

Kain turned around, allowing himself to shift back into human form as he walked forward. "Are you hurt, Damien?"

"No," Damien replied, upset. "What was that? I've never seen them take that shape before?"

Kain untied the fur-lined jacket from around his waist, putting it on. "Only high-ranking vampires can grow wings and talons like that. The nobles can go further into a form almost rivaling the dark god himself? Whoever it was that changed her was strong."

Damien took off his jacket to cover Jill after she shifted back into her human form. "Jill, I'm sorry. It was the only thing I could think of to get Chelsea to come out of hiding."

Damien's words were cut short by Jill kissing him. Her arms pulled him firmly into her, her fingers tangling in his hair.

"Damien, why did you run? Why didn't you tell me?"

"He had to stay silent, Jillian. It was the only way to draw out Chelsea to see if she had been turned. I didn't know of his plan until he contacted me right after I saw you. He called me in to either handle Chelsea or to keep you back. Now that we know she can't be reasoned with, we won't need to do anything like this again." Kain replied for Damien.

"Jill, I'm sorry, I really am. I needed some time." Damien caressed Jill's face, his thumb brushing the lone tear that fell down her face.

Jill didn't speak. She only held Damien close to her, content that she could feel his emotions and hear his soul again.

CHAPTER EIGHTEEN

Two days passed following the encounter with Chelsea. The first heavy snow of winter replaced the flurries that fell at the end of fall, sticking to the roads and cars.

Damien stood watching the new white sheets join those already frozen to the ground. He'd woken up later than usual considering finals were over, deciding to catch up from the late nights he'd pulled to get his schoolwork wrapped up.

For breakfast, he settled on the all American bacon, eggs and toast with a cup of hot coffee. He retired to the living room, sitting next to the fireplace to stay warm. Charlie left him a text letting him know he'd been snowed in at the station so he couldn't get home until the snow plows cleared the road.

The news relieved Damien because he'd made plans of his own and didn't want to risk Charlie barging in and interrupting them.

Rocks settled in his stomach from the thoughts running through his mind. He'd sent Jill a text asking her if she could come over, that his dad had been snowed in. Jill replied she would be at his house around the early afternoon meaning Damien had little time to make sure everything was perfect.

A knock came at his window around one in the afternoon.

"Hey." Jill said happily, shaking the snow off before jumping down to his floor.

"No car today, huh? Can't blame you." Damien replied, smiling.

"Nope, chose to run. Too dangerous to drive. Besides, I love a nice fresh powder beneath my paws. It's better than the burrs. Those hurt to get out."

Damien shrugged, glad he didn't have to pull burrs from his paws. He'd had to pull them from his jeans and boot laces. That alone was miserable. "Have you eaten? I have some extra from breakfast. I woke up late so I didn't make lunch."

"No, I hunted before coming. Actually nailed a deer today."

"Oh. Well, okay. I'm not too sure how to reply to that."

Jill chuckled, making her way over to Damien to give him a kiss. "Next time I'll bring you the antlers. I hear rumor your dad likes to hunt for trophies."

Damien held up his hands. "No thanks. I wouldn't know how to explain where I got them. Dad barely bought the whole truck in the ditch thing. Besides, that's cheating. Hunters usually like to score their own bucks."

Jill sat down on Damien's bed, thankful to be out of the cold despite her thick fur.

Damien sat next to her, his nervousness reminding him of the arrangement he'd made for them that afternoon. "Jill, I love you. I didn't think I could love anyone like this anymore. I want to be with you."

Jill smiled, putting her finger to his mouth. "Shh. Don't speak."

Her lips met Damien's in a soft kiss. Her hands drifted over the muscles in his arms under the sweatshirt he was wearing, back up his shoulders.

Damien nipped Jill's lower lip, begging her to let him in to taste her mouth. Her tongue wrestled his at the opening of his mouth as he deepened their kiss. The sweet smell of jasmine hung thick in the air around Jill's hair and body. The taste of mint from the gum she'd been chewing flooded his mouth, exciting him.

His hand kept a firm grip on her neck. His thumb traced the length of her collarbone as his lips traveled down to the groove in her neck where her throat met her shoulder. The heat in his body intensified the more he imagined making love with her.

Jill let her hands venture under Damien's sweatshirt. Her fingers savoring every shallow hill and valley of the gorgeously developed muscles of his abs. She'd seen him shirtless before but feeling them ignited new and exciting sensations inside of her. She was beginning to see him as a mate.

Without thinking, she began to slowly push his shirt up, hoping he would let her remove it. Damien raised his arms above his head, letting Jill take off his sweatshirt. She dropped it to the ground, returning to fondling the beautiful man in her arms.

She let her mouth venture down his throat. The gentle patter of his heart as it heated his blood titillated her senses. Jill had to remember to stay in control. She didn't want to risk hurting him despite her strong desire.

One slip of her fangs piercing his skin could change him on accident.

The breath in his lungs was more precious to her than even needing to hunt. She would do anything to protect him. To keep him human as long as she could.

Jill let her tongue roll over the flesh of Damien's shoulder, his skin hot despite the cold outside. She rested her hand on his face, her thumb teasing his lips as she kissed his jaw up to his ear. He smelled so good. Dark and natural as though he were a lycan.

Damien pushed the jacket Jill was wearing down. Happy to find she let him remove it to the floor next to his shirt. His hands drifted over her shoulders as he peppered her porcelain skin with soft kisses.

He pulled Jill down onto the bed. They sat on their knees as Damien undid the latch on her bra, pulling it off to reveal her breasts to be even more beautiful than they had been in his dreams. The soft pink nipples enticed him to tease them until they turned red.

Jill's hands held Damien's hips as he teased her breasts with his mouth. Her thumbs pushed down on his belt loops so strongly she felt one rip.

Damien looked up at her.

"Uh...sorry, about that." She replied, red with embarrassment.

Damien just smiled returning to her breasts, his hand holding her butt while the other rolled the round nub between his thumb and pointer finger.

Jill gritted her teeth as the heat between her legs rose. Damien's tongue was so warm on her skin, she had to fight the wolf inside of her. A low growl rumbled in the back of her throat.

She pushed Damien back to lay on the bed, her eyes meeting those beautiful amethyst jewels she dreamed of every moment they were apart. Her hair fell like a satin curtain around them.

Damien guided Jill's hair over one shoulder, pulling her back down to kiss him. Her hands tickled his chest moving slowly down his body until she gripped his hips.

He gritted his teeth, hissing in pain through them at how firm she held him. He didn't want to ruin this moment by scaring her away so he kept quiet. There would probably be a bruise in the morning but he didn't really care. He wanted Jill, to hold her. He wanted inside of her.

Damien felt the erection behind his zipper struggle against his jeans as his desire turned into lust. He rolled them over, surprising Jill with his sudden movements.

"May I have you, Jill? I want you so bad." Damien asked, barely able to hold back his desires.

"Damien, if we make love, according to lycan law at least, we're mates. I don't want you to bind yourself to me if you aren't ready."

Damien kissed her, a hint of longing in the kiss. "Then we're mates. I can't be without you. It terrifies me to imagine a life without you, Jill. I couldn't live in a world like that. I would rather you killed me."

Jill smiled, petting his face. "I can't be without you, either, Damien. Even as an immortal, a life without you would be hell."

Damien's heart raced in his chest. He'd long wanted to have sex with Jill but wanted to make sure she was ready so he'd waited.

He kissed her as his hands pushed her pants down, revealing her favorite high cut panties she liked to wear.

Jill kicked off her boots to let Damien finish taking her pants off, leaving her in her panties beneath him.

She gasped slightly as he slid his hand in her panties, his thumb finding the bundle of nerves between her wet folds. He rotated it in smooth circles to heighten her pleasure.

Her nails dug into Damien's back as she restrained herself to avoid accidentally hurting him. His hand ran the length of her arching back, his thumbs tracing each flexing muscle in Jill's side. His fingers explored every small groove in her back until he reached her hips.

The pleasure in her body made her muscles tremble in anticipation as Damien used his unoccupied hand to unbutton and unzip his jeans. He smiled Jill's favorite crooked smile as he pushed them down. His underwear followed shortly after, leaving him naked above her.

Jill's heart pounded at how beautiful and well-built he was. His body rivaling that of any lycan male she'd known. There was an ornate Celtic cross tattoo that lay across the skin of his hip, perfectly accentuating the deep-v of the muscles. Jill hadn't noticed it before.

Damien removed Jill's panties, kissing her deeply. She felt his tip at the opening of her sex. She gasped as he slid into her. His lips placing reassuring kisses on her neck as he made love to her.

Jill ran her nails down Damien's back, relishing the hard muscles as they flexed with each movement he made. Luna, he felt so good. Reaching every part of her in need of his attention. She clenched her fangs as she felt herself reaching her climax.

The heat of Damien's body drove her primal senses wild as he thrust into her. Damien's own low growl escaped his throat as he felt his own climax drawing near. Jill was tighter than he thought she would be. He actually had to work to get into her.

The sounds Jill was making made Damien's eyes roll into the back of his head with pleasure. His balls tightened as he came close to filling the woman he loved. Finally he was claiming her as his.

"Damien!" Jill called out his name as her orgasm rippled through her body. Her muscles squeezing him pushed him just enough, his own orgasm rocked through his body. He pushed into her as far as he could filling her with as much of him as he was able.

The muscles in his arms trembled as he struggled to hold himself up. He pulled out of her to sit beside her on the bed, panting in an attempt to catch a breath.

Jill's chest heaved as she tried to catch her own breath. She rolled onto her stomach, panting to try to cool down from the intense heat.

"When did you get your tattoo?"

"I got it for my eighteenth birthday. It's on my hip because I thought my dad would have killed me since I didn't ask first. To be honest, I don't think he knows even now that I have it. You know cops and tattoos. You have one, you're a gang affiliate." Damien chuckled at his own joke.

Jill heaved out a labored laugh. "It's beautiful. Very nice ink work. You felt amazing."

"Thanks. I'd like to think I'm somewhat good at sex despite this being my first time."

"Really? You could have fooled me."

"Nope. First time. No experience."

Jill snuggled into Damien's chest. "Well, it was wonderful."

Damien guided her face up to look at him, kissing her lips. "It won't be the last time, Jill. That much I can promise you."

CHAPTER NINETEEN

"D ame! I'm home!" the sound of Charlie's voice brought Damien's attention to his return.

Damien got up to find that Jill left him a note letting him know she'd gone out hunting. He felt sore in his hips from where she held onto him during their love making. He looked in the mirror to find that one of them had actually gotten bruised.

Damn. I'll have to hide that or she'll never touch me again. Damien thought to himself as he put on his underwear, jeans and sweatshirt. *When the hell did I fall asleep?*

His phone vibrated on his bedside. The screen lit up showing Rob's name.

Oh boy. Damien thought answering it.

"Dude, Chelsea came by again last night. What the hell is going on, D? She told me if I wanted to know what all the drama was about, I should 'ask Damien about it'. What'd your girlfriend do? I want to stay friends, D but I can't if you don't tell me what's going on."

"Rob, I'll try to explain things as soon as I can but for now, don't talk to Chelsea. She isn't the same girl we grew up with, okay. She'll say whatever she can to poison you against me and get you to accept an offer you probably wouldn't want to and regret almost immediately. We've been friends for a long time. I'm asking you to trust me."

"D, since you've met this Jill chick, you haven't been the same. The hell she did to your mind, bro!? What's your problem all of a sudden?!"

Damien squeezed the phone, his teeth clenched tightly. "My problem is for years I've tried to pretend I was something I wasn't! I just drifted through life like no one looked at me like I was some sort of circus freak! I actually thought the accident was my fault! That I was the one messed up and everyone had the right to look at me like they did!"

"Wow, I'm sorry, D. I might not understand the full extent of what it is that's going on but I'll be careful the next time Chels shows up." Rob replied.

"No, Rob. Don't talk to her, don't let her into your house. As she is, she won't hesitate to kill you or your family. She threatened to kill me to keep me away from Jill." Damien replied, his voice low and stern.

"No way! Dude, she's had like a major crush on you forever!"

"Rob, just trust me. Don't let her in and don't talk to her." Damien hung up the phone, putting back on the desk.

After the rather disturbing phone call with Rob, Damien made his way downstairs to find his father in the living room.

"Morning, dad. Glad you finally made it back from the station. Everything go okay?" He asked, his mood sullen.

"Yeah, it went fine. Electricity stayed on so we managed to keep warm. You do okay here?"

Damien took his coffee and sat down only to have to get back up to answer a rather desperate knock on his door. He opened it to stare into the eyes of Chase. He appeared out of breath and slightly upset.

"Chase? I don't think I've ever had you at my house. What's wrong?"

Chase took a moment to calm down. "Damien, my alpha sent me. I need you to come with me, now. Something happened while Jill was hunting."

"Is she hurt?" Damien replied, inviting Chase in so he could get his boots and jacket.

"No but, she's not okay either. Hurry."

Damien grabbed his keys, wallet and phone. "Dad, I'm going out. See you later."

"Okay, be careful!"

Damien followed Chase to the wood's edge, parking his motorcycle next to Holt's truck before hitching a ride on the wolf to Holt's camp.

Kain met him at the entrance. "I am glad you're here. She needs to see you."

"Where is she?" Damien replied, nervous.

Kain nodded his head towards the direction of the tent belonging to Leah, Holt's mate.

Leah hugged Damien upon seeing him. "Damien, thank Luna. She's in my tent, it was awful. I've never seen her so upset."

Damien walked through the flap to find Jill kneeling facing the wall. "Jill? Are you okay?"

Jill rose slowly from where she was kneeling, turning around to reveal a small bundle of blankets in her arms.

Damien felt his heart shatter. The blankets were in the shape of a small body.

"This is what they do. They kill without remorse. I rescued her from werewolves, nursed her wounded leg and thought she would be okay. She passed away just as you walked up." Jill choked back on the emotions in her heart. The hope dwindled in her eyes as she held the pup close before putting it down on the floor.

When Jill rose back up, Damien wrapped his arms around her, pulling her into him and petting her hair. He rested his finger under her chin, guiding her eyes to meet his own.

"I'm so sorry, Jill." Pain filled his eyes as he lowered his lips to hers, tasting the cold of the night along with the sorrow flooding her heart.

Jill held onto his jacket so tightly, she thought she would rip it. "Damien, I'm not sure my heart can take much more. I'm losing hope."

"Jill, you have to hope. It's all that's left. My mom used to say when you've hit rock bottom there's only one way to go. I would say we're at the bottom, wouldn't you? Lilith won't get away with this. I won't let her." Damien answered, determined to make Lilith pay for what she'd done.

Jill smiled, kissing him. "I have something I want to show you. Come with me." Jill took his hand, leading him through the encampment. A large tent on the outer perimeter had been put up just so they had a place to stay when they visited.

The inside of the tent was more ornate than the others, almost as if it were built as a small temple to honor a deity. The carpets a mix of rich royal blues and purples with golden hems and tassels.

The bed was more like something one would see in a hotel. It was much larger with silk sheets and a comforter that was deep red. The pillows adorned with silken cases.

"Wow, Jill. Why all the over the top décor?" Damien asked, a bit overwhelmed.

Jill zipped the door closed and began to undress. "This is from Yuna and Galeck. They insisted the keeper of the Purifier's soul should be treated as someone next to royalty."

"I'm not sure I'm okay with this. I don't want any special treatment. I'm not even sure what a Purifier is or what I'm supposed to do as one." Damien replied.

"Yuna is very traditional. She insisted on doing this for Gabriel too but he refused."

"Gabriel? Why him?" Damien asked, curious.

Jill looked away, cursing herself for saying what she did. "He'll tell you when he's ready. He doesn't really like to talk about it."

Damien was curious but, he wasn't going to pry. He and Gabriel weren't exactly on the best grounds for friendship.

"Jill, what happened? You left me a note to tell me you went hunting and then Chase shows up at my door. I can only imagine it has something to do with the pup."

"Kain assigned Chase as your night watch last night. You've had a lycan on you since the incident with Lilith. As for the pup, werewolves attacked her mother without any reason. There were four of them. She never had a chance. I managed to kill them and thought the pup would be okay but she died. I'm pretty sure it was from a broken heart." Jill ran her thumb over her eyes to hide her tears.

"Anyway, I'm glad you came, Damien. I wasn't doing so well this morning. I nearly called you but I didn't want to wake you. Is your hip okay? I know I was a little rough."

"It's...fine." Damien lied to avoid worrying Jill since she'd already had so much on her plate. "Rob called me this morning."

"What'd he say?"

"Chelsea dropped by his house again last night. Some of the things she said. I just can't believe she would do this. I never would have seen this coming." Damien dropped his head in his hand in disbelief, his other one propped on his hip.

"Damien, that's what happens. Sometimes the change brings out the worst in people. It's one reason why we never turn anyone unless we know for certain their souls are pure. Most vampires are less careful. They turn people on a whim. I did tell you, didn't I? This life, this world. It's not for the faint of heart." Jill replied, wrapping her arms around Damien's waist, her cheek rested on his back against his jacket.

Damien took Jill's hands in his. The worry for his father and Rob's safety grew stronger as he thought about Chelsea.

If the vampires had gotten to Chelsea so easily without anyone knowing then what could stop them from getting to his dad or Rob?

Everything began spinning out of control so quickly, Damien couldn't help but think it was because he came back to Big Timber.

"It's all my fault. If only I would have gone after her at the college that day. Maybe I could have saved her." Damien said, his grip on Jill's hands firm with frustration.

"Damien, if you had gone after her then whoever was responsible for turning her would have either killed you or taken you to Lilith. This isn't your fault. This is what they do. It's always been this way."

Damien pulled away, turning around. "Are you hearing yourself? You're doing exactly what you're accusing them of doing. I've learned so much about the lycans. However, lately, I've had a nagging inside of me to try and find out if the vampires are just as sick of losing loved ones as you are."

The words Kain told Jill ran across her mind. *Purifiers were the peacekeepers between the two races. He's doing what he was sent here to do. You cannot interfere with that.*

"I hope you're right, Damien. I really do. I need to sleep though. I hadn't gotten much since the incident with the pup." Jill replied, hopeful that there were peaceful vampires in the world.

"Okay. I'm going to go talk with Kain."

"Damien."

"Yeah?"

"Will you stay here tonight?"

Damien smiled, nodding before heading out of the tent.

CHAPTER TWENTY

D amien waited until he was sure Jill was asleep before taking out his phone. He knew she would be angry at what he was about to do but he needed to try to reach Chelsea without Jill around.

He opened his contact list to scroll down to Chelsea's cell phone number. *God please let her still have the same number.* Damien sent the text asking her to meet him.

A reply came shortly after agreeing to meet him alone at a place known to the townsfolk as the Lookout.

"You are going then?"

Damien looked over to see Kain leaning against a tree.

"I have to. I need to know if she's really gone."

"You realize this could be a trap. It is cloudy outside, Damien. Vampires aren't as affected during overcast days. What is there to stop Chelsea from harming you?" Kain asked, a sense of concern laced his voice.

"Nothing. She won't trap me, Kain. I don't know how I know, I just do." Damien put his phone in his pocket, walking towards his bike with Kain on his heels.

"I won't stop you, Damien but I will tell you I don't like this. We wouldn't be able to help you."

"You won't need to. Just make sure Jill isn't too angry when I get back." Damien retorted, getting on his motorcycle. The engine roared to life and he headed out onto the main road towards the Lookout.

Damien sat on his bike looking out at the mountain range in front of him. The view always took his breath away. The woods spread out as a green sea. In the distance the clock tower at the top of the town hall peaked just over the canopy. A hawk's call could be heard ringing out across the landscape.

The sudden chill up his spine alerted him to the vampire who had once been his friend. Chelsea rested her hands on Damien's shoulder, her cheek leaned against his arm.

"It's messed up isn't it? We're supposed to be going for college degrees, getting jobs, falling in love, and getting married." She purred, kissing his shoulder.

"Chelsea, you don't have to obey the vampires. You can choose to stay who you were."

"Damien, that time is over. I like being with the coven. Becoming a vampire opened my eyes to just how pathetic humans are. Look at me, Dame. I'll be beautiful forever while you age and die. I have power that I never would have gotten as a human. You are so much more powerful than even you know, Damien. Come with me. Let Lilith change you and stay as handsome as you are now."

"Right, and have my heart and blood frozen inside of me in return. I don't think so. Chelsea, this isn't you. I refuse to believe that you've become nothing more than a heartless monster."

"Then you're in denial. Tell me Damien, why did you choose that dog? You never even knew her until that day at the school. What makes her so special to you?" Chelsea spat, pinning Damien against his motorcycle.

"Jill completes me, Chelsea. You always talked about soul mates and meeting the 'one', remember? When our eyes met, I just knew. I knew Jill was my soul mate."

"And yet here you are. Unchanged. Dying with each second while she remains young. Please, Damien. You're a temporary thing for her. Once you're gone, she'll run to Kain and you know it."

"Is that Lilith talking or you?" Damien replied.

"It doesn't matter. She won't get the chance to change you." Chelsea's eyes darkened with the shadows of the vampire.

Damien found himself held tightly against his motorcycle, his back aching from how far it was being forced to bend.

"I told you. I will see you dead before I see you with her."

Just as Chelsea was about to sink her teeth into Damien's throat, a single ray of sunshine pierced through the clouds, burning her so badly she jerked back almost shrieking in pain.

Damien took the opportunity to start up his motorcycle to head back to Holt's camp. His heart hurt from the realization that Chelsea was gone. His once gentle friend was replaced by a vindictive, jealous vampire.

Jill woke to find she was still alone. The moon had risen well into the sky, yet Damien was nowhere in sight. She got up and got dressed, heading out into the main section of the camp to meet Kain.

"Kain, did Damien stay?" Jill asked, nervous.

"He did. He's in my tent, Jillian. I told him to sleep there tonight."

"What? Why? Let me see him, Kain."

Kain didn't move, his hand on Jill's shoulder kept her in place. "Jillian, he needs to rest. He's developing quickly and adjusting to changes not even he understands. I recognize you are worried. You love him but you need to give him time. Let him sleep tonight. You can see him in the morning."

Jill was upset but knew that Kain always had her best interest at heart. She worried about Damien but loved him enough to give him the time he needed.

Instead of going back to sleep, she decided to go hunting to relieve some of the stress.

Damien woke up at the crack of dawn to find most of the lycans, even Kain still asleep.

He walked down to the small pool with the waterfall to splash some of the water in his face. The cold morning breeze made him shiver despite how warm he felt from the thick blankets.

"Good morning." Holt said, cheerfully.

"I've never known you to be an early riser." Gabriel joked, resting his elbow on Holt's shoulder.

"Morning Holt. Gabriel. What's up?" Damien replied, shaking the excess water off of his face.

Holt handed Damien a thick jacket. "Nothing. I hope you liked the gift Galeck and Yuna gave you."

Damien didn't say anything. He wasn't really one for over the top décor.

Upon seeing the look on Damien's face, Holt let out a boisterous laugh while Gabriel choked back his own.

"Don't worry, we know how you feel. Yuna likes to overdo some things since she's a bit better off in the human world. We tried to tell her you'd react this way but, she didn't listen." Gabriel said, his voice cracking.

Damien felt overwhelmed the minute he'd seen the inside of his tent. He didn't have the heart to tell either alpha he'd spent the night in Kain's tent.

"Holt, I want to ask something of you."

"You are free to ask anything of me. Well, as long as it doesn't put the pack in danger. What can I do for you?" Holt replied, still trying to stop laughing.

Damien could see Gabriel nodding his own silent agreement.

"The vampires are targeting my friends and family. Chelsea's visited Rob twice trying to turn him against me. I'm concerned about their safety. I know you already have so much to handle with the war coming up but I'm asking for your aid in protecting them. I couldn't live with myself if either one of them were hurt without even telling them what was going on."

Holt looked at Gabriel as though they were trying to come up with a plan.

"Spence can watch over Charlie. He's already in the station. I believe Leah is already there as well. It would be when he was at home that would be the problem." Gabriel offered. Spence was a member of his pack and already worked at the station.

Holt's mate, Leah was the secretary at the station so Charlie would be safe with the two lycans during the day.

"I can watch over Charlie. It would allow me to repay an old debt. Besides, I gave you my loyalty and trust, Damien." Kain walked up behind the three of them, shocking Damien at how tired he looked.

His dirty blonde hair was a mess. His usually bright green eyes had become darkened by the deep purple circles shadowing them. A haze seemed to cloud the irises of the alpha. The darkness familiar to Damien the longer he stared.

"Kain, you look tired. What happened?" He asked, his eyes wide with worry.

"Nothing for you to concern yourself with, my friend. I will watch your father when he's at home. It's the least I can do." Kain replied, patting Damien's shoulder. He gave him a tired smile before stretching and heading to his own tent.

"Now if you don't mind, I am getting some sleep. Call on me only if you need, Gabriel. Otherwise, I will throw the nearest rabbit I have at your big head."

Gabriel tilted his head, holding up his hands in surrender. His eyes closed. "No problem. I shouldn't need anything today, Kain. No one will bug you. I think they want to live longer than that."

Kain waved him off, walking away. His shirt was torn and tattered like he'd been in a fight, thin lines of blood flowed down his back.

Damien hadn't remembered seeing them before, his curiosity peaked at what it was that Kain could be hiding. "Gabriel." Damien asked only to be cut off.

"Don't ask. In time, you'll come to learn more. It's best you don't ask him about it. He'll tell you when he's ready, if at all." Gabriel replied.

Damien felt saddened. He'd looked up to Kain as a mentor since he'd been introduced to a side of him he didn't know from the few exchanges they'd had at the bowling alley.

"Anyway, I'm impressed, Damien. You seem like you're almost glowing with a confidence I've never seen in you before. It's really something." Holt tried to lighten the mood, nearly breaking Damien's shoulder. The pat on his back so hard it almost knocked him forward a few times.

"Thanks, Holt." Damien said through clenched teeth as he rubbed his shoulder where Holt had been patting him, trying to get the stinging to stop.

When Damien returned to their tent, Jill was still asleep. He walked over to her, sitting down beside her.

"Good morning." Jill's voice was tired but more beautiful than the singing of birds as they woke with the rising sun.

"Morning. I'm so sorry for waking you but I have to get home. My dad is off today and wanted to spend some time with me. I promised him we'd get the tree up for Christmas. Jill, I have to tell him what's going on. Even if he doesn't believe me, I have to tell him something."

Jill sighed, stretching out under the soft, silk blankets. "I knew this was coming. I guess as long as we can make him understand that we aren't the ones ripping sheep to shreds, it's worth it. Do Holt and Gabriel know?"

"Yes. I spoke to them before coming to you. They're going to help watch over my dad and Rob," Damien replied. He couldn't help but think about how bad a shape Kain was in. "Jill, I saw Kain this morning. He looked really roughed up. Do you know what's going on?"

Jill lowered her eyes, giving him the answer he was looking for. "I only know what he told me. It's not my place to tell you. All I can say is, in our world, there are a few of us more in touch with the gods than others."

Damien's heart froze for a brief second as he recalled how Barghast looked at him in his dream. How at times he still felt as though his body were engulfed in flames. How Kain had known it wasn't a dream but a vision. Could it be that Kain had the same encounters?

Once Jill had gotten dressed, she took Damien's hand. "Come on, your dad is waiting to see you. Don't worry about Kain. He's a wise old wolf and cunning as sun's hell. He'll be fine."

He wanted to believe her but Damien's growing concern for his friend wouldn't let go of him as he stood up to go with her.

Damien's heart pounded behind his ribs as he leaned his forehead against his hand on the glass. He had no idea how he was going to make anything he was going to say sound any less insane than it did to him.

How on Earth was he going to make his dad and Rob understand that everything they thought was nothing more than myth and made-up Hollywood drama was actually real and going on beneath their feet?

He'd told his dad that his injuries from his encounter with the first two vampires were because he slipped off of the steps in front of the hospital. He was lucky his dad actually believed him.

"Breathe, Damien. I'm here with you. We'll make them understand. Charlie is your father, he's already proven he's willing to stand by you after you were hit, remember? I'll be right by your side." Jill reassured him by rubbing his arm to get him to calm down.

When they got into the house, Charlie's laugh could be heard from the living room. Another voice Damien recognized as belonging to Rob responded to his dad.

From what Damien could tell, it appeared as though they were telling stories about when he, Rob and Chelsea used to run around the house. Most of the time it was from Chelsea thinking she had cooties. Those were easier days before all of the madness.

"Well, speak of the devil!" Charlie said, boisterously laughing. "I see you brought Jill with you. Welcome back! Thanks for texting me last night, Dame."

"Yeah, sure dad. I've come home to keep my word for that father-son time you asked for. Still want to put the tree up?" Damien replied, a bit vexed at his dad's choice of words when they walked in.

"Of course. I'll go get it out of the shed." Charlie kissed Jill's hand.

Damien sat down next to Rob. "Hey, Rob. Still mad?"

Rob smiled, punching him in the arm hard enough to make him wince. "There, now we're even. C'mon bro, you know guys never talk about their problems. They just punch each other and move on."

Putting up the Christmas tree was relaxing as Jill sat with Rob enjoying some of Charlie's hot cider while Damien helped his father.

"So, did he really paint the entire bathroom?" Jill asked. She couldn't help but chuckle. Charlie told her about how he'd caught Damien in his underwear painting the bathroom with his mom's makeup.

Damien got so embarrassed, he rubbed his eyes with his thumb and forefinger. *Great, now that's all she'll see the next time we're having sex. Thanks, old man.* He thought, grinding his teeth. His head lowered.

"Sure did. It was the funniest thing. He was only seven. We hadn't even had him a year. It was adorable because he said it was supposed to be a thank you for saving his life. We just couldn't get mad at him after that. Sarah just melted."

Jill snuggled into Damien's chest. "That's sweet. You have a very big heart, babe. It's beautiful."

Wanting to change the subject to avoid further embarrassment to his pride, Damien cleared his throat. "Rob, Dad, there's something you need to know."

Rob and Charlie looked at each other than back at him.

"Okay, what is it, D?" Rob spoke up first.

Just as Damien was about to go on, a knock on the door took his and Jill's attention.

Charlie started to get up only to have Jill stop him.

"I'll get it. Stay here. Damien, don't let them get up." Charlie looked at his son, confusion radiating in his eyes at how serious Jill suddenly got.

Jill opened the door to meet Kain. He looked more rested than Damien said he had earlier that morning. Less tattered and more like himself. "I'm sorry I'm late, Jillian. I'm Charlie's personal watch. I got here as soon as I could."

"It's okay, Damien. It's Kain." Jill called over her shoulder as she let him in.

"Good grief, it's cold." Kain shivered so Jill led him into the warm living room, letting him sit by the fire.

"Alexander Kain. You haven't changed a bit. Maybe matured a little but I'm glad to see you again." Charlie shook Kain's hand. "Still working at the bowling alley?"

"Yes, though my time there is a bit less nowadays. It's good to see you, Charlie. I take it Spence is still doing what he can to help you at the station?"

Damien got confused. His dad knew Kain? How in the world had he not wondered why Kain still looked the same though he'd been gone ten years?

Kain noticed how Damien was staring at him. "Oh, I'm sorry, Damien. Yes, I know your father very well. I was younger then, but Charlie came in quite often when Clint was going through his phase of rebellion. It was a time we became very acquainted with one another."

Damien didn't reply. It wouldn't make sense to him no matter how much Kain tried to explain it. He was just happy to see Kain seemed to be feeling better than he was earlier when he'd been worried sick about him.

"Anyway, dad, Rob, there's something I have to tell you. I can't explain it in any way that doesn't sound crazy so here it goes. I know who's been responsible for the disappearances. It's not wolves." Damien said, knowing he probably sounded crazy.

The sudden ring of Kain's phone once again diverted everyone's attention.

Good God, I give up. It's almost as though I'm not even supposed to say anything. Damien thought, dropping his head into his hand.

The look of terror in Kain's eyes combined with the fact that he was slowly rising from his seat on the floor had Jill hurriedly standing.

"We have to go." Kain thanked Charlie for his hospitality, grabbing his coat and walking towards the front door.

"Alex, what is it?" Charlie grabbed his shoulder. "I'm the police chief. I need to know what's going on?"

Kain's reply was short. "Fire at Gabriel's gym. It could collapse at any moment."

Charlie grabbed his keys, not bothering to ask permission. "Get in the cruiser, I'll give you a ride. Dame, you ride with Jill and Rob."

Jill took out her keys, handing them to Damien before jumping into the passenger's side. Rob sat in the back as they follow his dad's cruiser. Its sirens blaring down the snow-covered streets.

CHAPTER TWENTY-ONE

T he ambulances and paramedics were already on the scene by the time the group arrived.

Gabriel, Dolph, Ray and Scott were all being seen by the EMTs while Holt stood with Cade. Both were scowling. The flames of revenge burning in their eyes.

Kain ran up with Charlie, Jill and Damien. "Holt, what in the name of Tenebris happened here?"

"It was some of their goons. Humans seeking to be turned that set this place ablaze. They will pay for this Kain." Holt clenched his fists at his sides as he fought to hide the fangs grinding against his teeth.

Kain's eyes scanned the landscape. He appeared worried. Chase, his beta was nowhere to be seen. "Chase?"

Cade and Holt shook their heads.

"He...he didn't make it, old friend." Holt said, putting his hand on Kain's shoulder. "I'm sorry."

Damien's heart sank as he watched his friend lower his head, the pride that defined him shattered in a single moment.

"I see. Knowing Chase, he gave his life to get everyone out safely."

"Oh, Kain." Jill wrapped her arms around Kain's waist, hugging him close to her to offer some comfort. "I'm so sorry."

Kain smiled at her, kissing her forehead before walking away to be alone.

Concerned himself, Damien followed Kain into the woods behind the burning gym. The alpha had fallen to his knees on the cold ground.

"Kain, I'm sorry about Chase."

Kain looked over his shoulder. "It is nothing for you to be sorry for. Casualties are a part of war. It's our existence." Kain rose to his feet, his posture straightening back up to the strong figure Damien had begun seeing as a mentor. "But that is not all you wanted to say, is it?"

Damien never understood how Kain seemed to know what he was thinking.

He took a deep breath. "No. This morning. I was worried about you."

Kain's hand on his shoulder made Damien raise his eyes to meet Kain's own. "You were worried about me?"

Damien nodded his head. "I know it's none of my business, Kain."

"Give it time. Mature a bit more and I give you my word I will tell you. You have a strong heart and soul, Damien. As a lycan you would be an amazing alpha. Watch over Jillian for both of us."

Kain stepped around Damien to head back to the others, stopping briefly. "Thank you for your concern, my friend."

Kain and Damien arrived back at the site of the flames to see Holt trying to comfort Gabriel as he knelt before his gym. One of the homes for his pack, as it collapsed in the snow.

Rob ran up to Damien, struggling to catch his breath. His eyes wide in surprise. "Is it true? God, D, tell me it's not real. Tell me she's lying?"

Damien got the hint. Jill told Rob and his father what was going on while he was away comforting Kain. "I wish I could say it was a lie but, it's not. It's true."

"So, Chelsea...Chelsea is really a...?"

"Afraid so."

Rob stared at Kain who stood behind Damien as if he was ready to protect him. "And... Alex, Jill, Gabriel and Holt? All werewolves?"

Kain winced, a growl rumbling in his throat.

"Lycans, Rob. They don't really appreciate being called werewolves. I know. I didn't understand there was a difference at first either." Damien responded.

Rob started backing up from Kain. Jumping away from Jill as she walked up beside him.

"Rob, they aren't monsters. Nothing you think you know about them is true. I've spent time with them."

"D, dude, I'm sorry. This is just too much. I swear I won't tell anyone but I can't get mixed up in this. My parents would freak if I called them to tell them my best friend was dating a...lycan." Rob said, his voice shaking with nervousness.

Damien's heart broke. His best friend from childhood. The one who talked about chasing around cryptids for a living, ended their friendship when he actually met one.

Rob turned and walked away, his shoulders slumped forward.

Damien stared at his father, wondering if he would react the same way Rob did. His body burned as the pain hit him at the realization that his father may abandon him over a technicality after all they'd been through.

Damien tightened his jaw against the burning flames inside of him, his hands rolling into fists at his sides. "Dad, I can understand if you don't want to ever see me again but I'm in love with Jill. I can't be without her."

"Dame, nothing's changed. Your mother and I knew you were different after your accident. It scared us so bad, we nearly walked away. Then you looked at us with the same eyes you're giving me now," Charlie took his son in a hug. "You were our child. Just as confused about what happened as we were. You're still my son, Dame. I may not understand what's going on, but I will stand by my son. I'll try to help in any way I can."

Damien had to fight back his emotions as he hugged his dad closely to him. He didn't know what to say so he just stood there.

"Thank you, Charlie." Kain said, sighing.

"Alex, you sly dog. You should have just told me."

Kain chuckled. "Would you have believed me?"

"Hell no, but it beats the alternative. Now tell me what I can do."

"For now, old friend, just keep the townspeople calm. Keep them out of the surrounding woods. Make sure they don't let anyone they don't know in their homes. We'll end this as soon as we can but we don't yet know what our enemies fully intend to do."

Charlie nodded. "I'm pretty sure as police chief, I can find some way of justifying a curfew. Now get out of here. We'll wrap it up. I'm sure you don't want any unsolicited questions." He snickered, waving the group off.

CHAPTER TWENTY-TWO

The events at Gabriel's gym the night before lingered. Holt had called all of them to come back with him to his tent so they could talk.

The air in the room was thick with sadness and despair as each of them tried to offer comfort to each other. Jill leaned her cheek against Damien's chest while he petted and kissed her hair.

Gabriel sat next to Kain, trying to offer comfort to his friend where he could. Silence lingered until Holt walked in accompanied by Nathaniel and Vincent.

"So, this him? The Purifier? What a pussy." Nathaniel smirked at Damien.

Damien got up on the floor to get in the alpha's face. He'd been called a pussy way too many times and wasn't about to let a complete stranger talk down to him.

To prevent a fight, Jill stepped between the two men. "Watch what you say, Nathaniel. Keep in mind, more than one of us here has wiped the cage floor with your sorry ass more than once."

Nathaniel's angry eyes met Kain's as he growled at Jill. "Whatever. Personally, to me, you're just another dumb bitch who needs to be put in her place. He's just another human."

The lycan's words were cut short when Kain slammed his fist into his jaw so fast, he stumbled to keep from falling.

"I have had enough of your tongue, Nathaniel. The next time you open your mouth it better be useful or you will be the one put in his place. You are only here because we need the extra body. If you are not going to serve a purpose then leave. I will not hear you disrespect Damien or his mate again, is that clear?"

"Fine. Whatever, Kain." Nathaniel snapped, rubbing the blood from his lip.

Jill's gentle hand on Damien's chest guided him to sit back down as well. "Easy. As you are, you don't stand a chance against another lycan. Let Kain, Gabriel or me deal with him. He hates Kain and would do anything to start a fight with him."

Damien honored Jill's request and backed off.

Usually jocks like Nathaniel didn't bother him, he could hold his own in a brawl. However, against a lycan, he knew he stood no chance and it angered him.

Holt sat down in the circle. "Yuna and Galeck's reinforcements arrived this morning. They are formidable but even with their help, we are still outnumbered. Unfortunately, we've exhausted our allies so this is all we have. The females with pup or mothers that have them have been moved into the mountains. The soldiers have chosen to stay. We have but one option; to end things quickly."

"Lilith. We have to take her down." Lune spoke up from his spot in the corner. "We take down the queen, the rest will fall apart. By their nature, vampires focus more on getting underlings to do their fighting for them. I got word that Desdemona refuses to get involved. She's come here to make sure the coven doesn't collapse and to rebuild after Lilith's war is over."

"I will worry about, Lilith. She's hurt Damien more times than I choose to forgive." Jill replied, pissed. She was the best choice. She couldn't be killed and Lilith would be the strongest vampire on the battlefield. Her true power had yet to be revealed. "Then's there's Rayes and Stoker."

"Holt will handle Rayes. He has history with the bloodsucker for killing his brother," Kain supplied. "That means I will handle Stoker. He is a coward when faced with an opponent of equal or greater skill. It is unlikely he will not put up much of a fight."

With most of the power players covered by the more experienced lycans, the field would be more even than initially anticipated.

Damien didn't like the idea of doing nothing but he didn't know what he could do. His phone vibrated in his pocket showing his father on the screen. He stood up to go take the call, excusing himself.

When he didn't return for a while, Jill began getting nervous.

Kain watched the tent door until Damien walked back in, the color of his face gone. He leaned into Jill's ear, telling her his dad had called. He had to get home but she shouldn't worry.

Lune's eyes met Jill's as Damien grabbed his coat to head out to his motorcycle. A look towards Kain had both Lune and Jill rising to go follow him. The clear look of stress on his face combined with the suddenness of his departure raised some red flags.

Damien pulled up to his house, shutting off his motorcycle.

Taking off his helmet, he clenched his teeth in frustration. His chest felt heavy as he unlocked the front door to his house, sighing at the fact he'd lied to Jill.

Hesitantly he pushed the door open. He set his jacket and keys down on the table in the foyer. His head lowered as he walked into the living room.

"So obedient when you don't have your little hound on your heels, aren't you?" Stoker sat in Charlie's favorite chair by the fireplace. His chin resting against his clasped hands. His legs were crossed, sitting like the vampire nobility he represented.

"I did what you wanted. I came alone. Where's my dad?" Damien tried to hide the trembling in his muscles as Stoker rose from the chair.

"He's in the basement. Oh, and don't worry, he's still human. You and I have a lot of catching up to do, don't we? The night is young. I'll have all the time I need to make up for the insult you've shown me." Stoker's hand landed hard across Damien's face, knocking him to the floor.

Damien shook his head against the dizziness, raising up to his hands and knees only to have Stoker slam his head to the floor.

"Only this time, you won't be healing from any of your wounds. Of that you can be assured." Stoker spoke low and angry.

Despite their clear difference in power, Damien had to chuckle. He could hear the small pops and smell the putrid scent of burning flesh.

"Find something about your imminent death funny, Pierce?"

"Not really. Just the fact that you seem on fire. I'm taking it my dad didn't invite you in?"

Stoker grabbed Damien by the throat, raising him off of the ground. "Oh, it stings. It stings like hell but it's worth paying you back for burning my face. Those wounds took me killing a couple of humans to heal."

Stoker dropped Damien back to the floor, crushing his knee under his foot. Damien fought hard to avoid giving Stoker the satisfaction of hearing him cry out in pain. He hissed through his teeth, the pain excruciating.

"Impressive. A human would have wailed in pain from having their knee crushed."

Damien rolled over to his side, sarcastically speaking. "Wow Stoker, that's twice you've complemented me. One may start to wonder if you're actually beginning to like me."

Stoker growled, kicking Damien in the ribs. "Let's get something straight, I hate you, Pierce." He grabbed him by his collar, dragging him into the kitchen.

"You've taken everything from me. You about got me thrown out of my own coven." He threw Damien against the oven and put his foot on Damien's hurt knee to keep him in place.

Damien tried to breathe against the agony in his knee. "Last I checked, I'm not the one who ran headfirst into your fist. Oh and the tree branch you tried to skewer me with, that was on you too."

Stoker rested his hands on the island. "You actually think you're funny, don't you?" He rummaged through the drawer of knives Charlie used. "These will do." Stoker said as put two large steak knives in his pocket.

Seeing the knives, Damien felt a knot in his gut. "Yeah, well, you know. Imminent death and all, might as well enjoy some humor."

Taking a hold of Damien, Stoker pulled him out behind the house. In one fluid motion, he hurled him out into the yard.

Damien landed with a sickening crunch against the fallen branches and leaves. A groan rose in his throat as he rolled over onto his back on the ground. The pain in his knee killing him.

Stoker stood over him, glaring. "It's apparent to me that you need to be reminded of just how weak you are, Pierce. Your dog was a fool not to turn you. Who knows? You may have stood a chance against me if she had."

"You're a real dick, you know that Cromwell? Bit of a pussy too."

Stoker smirked, seizing Damien and forcing him to his feet. He shoved him so hard against the faded blue siding of the house, it caved and splintered.

Damien's nerves were on such high alert he felt nauseated.

Stoker raised one of his arms above his head. "So I've been told but really it doesn't mean much coming from someone who hides in a pack of wolves for safety."

The sudden sharp cold of metal through his hand made Damien yell out in pain. The warmth of his blood trickled down his bare arm making him shiver against the cold of the wind.

Stoker took Damien's jaw in his hand. "That cry of pain is so much better than the arrogance. Let me hear it again, won't you?"

He repeated the action with Damien's other hand, ramming the knife through the flesh and bone to the handle.

Damien's breath grew heavy as his blood dripped down his arms.

"There, see. Is it so hard to respect someone more powerful than you? After all, you're still only human. You're weak and vulnerable. I was wondering how long you were going to hide behind Kain's shadow. He seems fond of you. Maybe I'll send him an eye in the mail."

Stoker ran his sharpened nail down Damien's shirt, tearing the fabric. "Now where shall I put the next hole?"

Damien's heart raced fast enough to make him dizzy. Jill didn't know what was going on, neither did Kain. He could get killed and neither one of them would know.

Stoker leaned into Damien's ear, speaking through clenched teeth. His anger apparent in his words. "Let's see, I could pierce your heart and end this quickly. However, I think that would be too merciful. I want you to feel the agony as I tear your limbs off for what you did to me in our last meeting."

Stoker's nail traveled down to Damien's stomach stopping at his lower abdomen. "Here. It should paralyze you long enough for me to torture and drain you before your heart gives out."

White sparks flew across Damien's eyes as the sharp pain of Stoker's hand pierced his lower stomach. It had gone so deep, he could feel the vampire's nails against his spine. His eyes bulged out of his skull, his breath caught in his lungs from the agony.

Memories ran through his mind all at once. He thought of Jill. Her beautiful body, hot with sweat after they made love. The gentle smile on her face unhindered by the fatigue in her eyes.

The thought that this may be the end of his life made Damien angry and saddened he hadn't taken her sooner. Then he thought of Kain. He didn't know why but it felt like he had a deep connection with the lycan alpha. Much deeper than anyone, even Damien knew.

He dropped his head, gasping. His knees shaking to hold him up to avoid slicing his flesh worse from the knives.

"You see, Pierce. You really are weak. Parading strength behind your little mongrel. Had you taken the offer of immorality, you wouldn't be hurting like this. I commend you on being silent but I know this hurts. There's no reason not to show it." Stoker grinned a wicked grin as he pulled his hand from Damien's stomach.

Damien coughed against the pain, his vision blurring. His strength began to fail. His body grew cold from blood loss. *Jill...I'm...I'm so sorry.*

Stoker guided his head up. "Good. Stay silent. I'll take your blood in peace."

Lune leapt over the brush behind the house. He growled as he threw his full weight into Stoker, sending the vampire flying into the wooden shed behind the house. The front of the small building shattered into pieces.

Jill came around the side of the house after Lune. "Damien!" Her heart stopped at the sight that met her eyes. "Luna, no. Oh please, no. No, no, no."

She pulled the knives out of Damien's hands, using her body to hold him as she lowered onto her knees, pulling him close to her. "No! Damien, please! Don't leave me!"

Lune positioned himself between Jill and Stoker who stood up out of the splinters of wood. His black blood dripped from the wound in the side of his head.

"Lune Maxwell. You pathetic excuse of an outcast abomination. How dare you lay your filthy claws on me." Stoker snarled as he dusted himself off. "He's dying. Let me have his blood. It's of no use to you or your pack of dogs anymore."

Lune ignored Stoker. Baring his teeth, holding his ground.

Kain arrived shortly after with Gabriel who joined Lune in wolf form.

"Alexander Kain, Gabriel Locke. Two of the most famous dogs in the Blood Wars. It is never a pleasure." Stoker spat, pissed. His face distorting into a deep scowl.

"Jillian, Damien's dying. You cannot heal him this time. Either change him or let him die." Kain's eyes burned with rage when he looked at Stoker.

Jill clenched her teeth as she held her lover in her arms. She'd tried to let him stay as close to human as possible. She'd fought to protect his innocence, his purity but, she knew she couldn't be without him.

Damien coughed against the pain in his stomach, choking as his lungs filled with blood.

Jill cupped his face, guiding him to look at her. The once vibrant jewels in his eyes had begun to darken. The light of the soul she had come to love was leaving.

"Damien, I can't let you go. Without you, I might as well be dead. But it has to be your choice. I can't make you do this."

Jill's eyes filled with tears reminding Damien of all of the times she'd watched him nearly get killed. Those frozen green orbs so full of love always had an underlying sense of fear. Fear he would reject her affection. Fear he would run. Now, there was the fear of losing him.

He wasn't afraid of dying, he was afraid of never being able to see her again. To never be able to make love to her or hear her say his name when they woke up together. With the last of his strength, Damien put his bloodied hand on Jill's on his stomach.

A gentle smile told Jill what she needed to know. Her heart ached with the knowledge she was having to curse the man she loved to a life of constant chaos. Softly petting his hair, she guided his head up.

"Bare your throat to me, my love. Your new life will be hard. The change will hurt at first but at least you will be safe. We can make this beautiful." Jill's fangs sank into the place where Damien's throat met his shoulder. His flesh tender under the force of her fangs.

The sweet, dark taste of his blood once again entered her mouth.

Flames joined shocks of electricity inside Damien as Jill's saliva met his blood. Her curse flooded into him, burning his veins as his body fought to heal itself against the change. It hurt so bad he started thrashing, crying out in pain.

Jill held him firmly against her. Her hand rubbing his neck to try to calm him against the pain.

Kain jumped up, running into the house only to return with a blanket which he wrapped firmly around Damien to help against the thrashing.

"Shit." Stoker cursed as he tried to get past Lune only to get grabbed and thrown back into the remains of the shed.

"Gabriel, go help Charlie. This bastard is going to pay for this." Kain rose from Damien, shifting into his full lycan form. He roared in challenge against Stoker.

"Fine, change him. It won't fix anything. You're all still outnumbered. Next, we meet, killing you will be more of a pleasure." Stoker fled in the face of his new opponents.

Kain hurried to help Jill, hoisting Damien up into his arms. He spoke to Jill in her mind. They'd shared blood in order to keep in contact with each other. *"He's going to hurt, Jillian. His body is trying to heal itself against the change."*

Jill tried to hold strong against the pain of hearing her lover scream in agony. "I can feel it, Kain. I can feel everything. What have I done?"

"You saved him. He would have died, Jillian. You could not have healed him this time. We will get him to Holt's camp, he has some medicine that will help with the pain. Come on. He's going to need you. He'll be strong enough to protect himself now, Jillian. On your feet!"

Jill stood up, shifting into her wolf form to go with Kain back to Holt's camp. Her heart torn to pieces that Damien was in so much pain. She had cursed him to a life she'd long sworn she never would.

Back at the camp, Kyle went into Jill's tent with his doctor's bag. "I didn't believe it until I got here. You actually turned him. Holt came to get me because Damien is a different case. His body heals itself against almost any trauma it goes through. I just hope his heart can handle the stress of the war going on inside of him."

Jill rose from Damien's bedside, getting out of Kyle's way. "He's burning up. I may be able to give him something to relax him but it's only temporary. I'm not sure, Kain. This is a strange case. He may not be able to handle it. Are you prepared to end it if it gets too bad?"

Kain looked at Jill who dropped her head, her eyes drowning in tears. She hadn't thought about Damien healing himself against the change to such a degree. She didn't think her mistake could have cost him his life anyway.

"If it comes to that Kyle, I'll disconnect his heart myself. Just do what you can. I know this is a strange case. To my knowledge, a Purifier has never been changed."

Jill left the tent, she couldn't take his screams anymore. Her soul was already shattering. Her heart was ripped apart at each throb of pain she felt Damien was going through.

Kain came out shortly after. "He's calm now. Kyle gave him some morphine and a muscle relaxant."

Jill threw herself into his arms. "What have I done, Kain? He's in more pain now than when he was dying. At least it would have ended for him. I've done nothing but ruin his life with everything I've done."

"Jillian. He chose to change. He wants to be with you more than anything. He's strong. He will make it through. You have to stay with him. Touch him. He will come back to you. I can tell he's going to be a strong lycan. Maybe even stronger than Gabriel or I. His heart and soul are unlike any human I have ever seen. Go to him."

"Kain, are you doing okay? You've been drained lately. More so than usual." Jill asked, concerned. She knew the burden Kain endured as the last of his family line.

"I am okay, Jillian. My strength will hold. I was actually thinking about finding a plump pheasant. I am fond of them and it is the peak of their season. Stay with Damien, he will need your strength to get through this." Kain walked off, leaving Jill.

She hadn't believed him.

CHAPTER TWENTY-THREE

A soft falling snow covered the camp, forcing most of the remaining lycans who hadn't retreated to the mountains into their tents to huddle around fires to stay warm. Kain chose to stay with Damien and Jill.

Jill stroked his soft sandy fur as he whimpered to try to comfort him while his natural healing ability did its best to close fresh gashes.

Damien was still unconscious. He had been for days; showing no sign he could hear anything going on around him.

Kyle came in to make sure to check on him from day to day, giving him more morphine if it seemed like his pain flared up again. "Still no change. His heartbeat is weak but, he's still alive. He doesn't seem to be in any pain either. Jill let me handle Kain. He looks bad this time. You stay with Damien. I think you're the only that will be able to get him back." He genuinely looked worried that Damien wouldn't come out of his coma at all.

Jill had just laid down next to Damien on their bed when Lune came in with Gabriel and Holt.

"Still nothing?" Holt asked, concerned.

Jill shook her head, her hand caressing Damien's chest to feel the soft rise and fall of each breath. "I don't understand. Kyle says there's nothing wrong. He's not in pain or anything but he won't wake up."

Kain shifted back into his human form and politely pushed Kyle off of him. He put on the jeans he'd brought with him and made his way over to

Gabriel's side. "Gabriel, why don't you take Jillian with you to check on the females in the mountains? You can see if they need anything."

Gabriel nodded, seeming to understand Kain's intentions. "We'll see if things are going well in town as well. I hadn't heard any more in regards to Charlie's efforts. It may be helpful for us to check on the situation there while things seem quiet."

Kain nodded to him, requesting that Holt keep everyone out of the tent so he could do what he needed to do. Holt nodded, walking out with Gabriel and posting guards at the tent opening.

Kneeling down next to Damien's bedside, Kain put his hand on his friend's forehead, the other on his heart. "Damien, I know you can hear me. I know something is wrong. I'm going to try to help you but I need you to open your mind to me."

Damien's eyes twitched giving Kain the signal he needed.

Closing his eyes, Kain used his connection to the gods to enter into Damien's mind. He was one of the few lycans more closely in tune with the wills of the gods. He knew the dark god better than anyone in the lycan race. His family had long been cursed to bear a burden far heavier than even the highest noble.

When he arrived, he found Damien's mind in a state of disarray. Red fibers reminding Kain of tendons that connected muscle tissue to bone hung loosely like threads of a spider web.

The empty space was dark save for the nebulous sea of stars above him. He stood in awe at the scene around him, his breath taken at the majesty of the design. He'd never witnessed anything like this in the mind's eye of any lycan he'd had to save in the past in the same way.

Something about Damien was more than he or any of the lycans knew or could probably even comprehend.

Kain had to focus to get his attention back on the matter at hand. He'd come to save his friend from whatever these tortured vines were that seared his flesh the moment he touched them.

"Kain." Damien's voice sounded weak as it echoed in the void.

"Damien, where are you?"

"I don't know. I can't move. I'm so tired."

Kain weaved through the vines, taking in the subtle wisps of the voices he could hear throughout the tangled jungle.

Only the heavy beating of wings alerted Kain to the presence behind him. His chest grew heavy, his eyes closed as the dark god made himself known.

The scene changed to a darkened abyss void of light, the once majestic light above Kain's head became covered by darkened, angry clouds.

"Alexander Kain. My brother's pet bloodline. What business do you have here?" Barghast's dark voice echoed in the space around them.

Kain turned to meet the dark god's eyes. "I think you need to ask what business you have here? This body belongs to a Purifier. You have no reason or right to enter it."

"I have plenty of a reason to be here, Alexander Kain. Watch how you address your god. A forsaken child like you has no right to speak to me so disrespectfully. The Purifier is in a deep sleep. He will rot in his own mind, posing no threat to me or the plans I may have for my brother's children." Barghast smiled a wide-fanged grin, moving his huge clawed hand.

Kain suddenly felt himself restrained by the very tendrils he'd been trying to avoid. The feeling equal to being stung by a jellyfish, searing his flesh like a hot iron. He felt his strength suddenly ripped from him, forcing him to his knees. The very blood in his veins felt as though it were being drawn out of his body.

"I had no plans to torture you, Kain but since you've once again become a thorn in my side, I suppose I can make an exception." Barghast smiled as he got into Kain's space, taking his jaw in his claws.

Ignoring Barghast's presence, Kain drew on his will to call out to his friend. He needed help or both of them were going to die.

"Damien! You have to wake up! Don't let him take control!"

"Kain." Damien stirred, hearing Kain's call to him but felt so tired he couldn't get his body to respond.

Barghast's hand landed across Kain's face. "Damn you, Kain. Why is it you always see fit to interfere with my plans?" With a strong beat of his wings, he took off into the darkness in an attempt to keep Damien from waking up.

"Damien, wake up. Jillian needs you. Please. Don't let Barghast hold you prisoner. This is your mind. He has no power here if you don't let him have it. He will kill us both if you don't wake up." Kain felt his strength dropping. The dark god's power draining him of his life the longer he was held prisoner.

Damien opened his eyes to find himself ensnared with the red fibers. His determination to get free reignited as he thought about his lover being left alone in the world. He felt a strange feeling of warmth rise up inside of him only to manifest in a radiant light.

Markings of blue in the likeness of ancient runes covered his body, incinerating the fibers. With an angry roar, the dark god was driven out of his mind, freeing both him and Kain.

Kain dropped to the ground, shaking against the weakness. A warm light illuminated the gloom, transforming the plane back to the glorious sea of stars.

"I'm sorry, Kain. He got in when my mind was weak. I couldn't fight him. Thank you for coming to get me." Damien smiled, helping Kain to his feet.

"You are welcome. I am just glad I made it in time." Kain replied, winded.

When Jill arrived back at the tent, her heart jumped out of her chest. Damien was sitting up in bed with Kain on the floor beside him. The two of them talking and laughing.

"Damien!" Jill threw herself into Damien's arms, gripping him tightly around his chest. "Oh, thank Luna! I'm so sorry!"

Damien held Jill close, her beauty radiating even more vibrantly in his newly changed eyes. The sound of her voice made him think about how the angels of heaven sounded.

The strong smell of jasmine and pine permeated her skin, exhilarating him. He almost couldn't control himself. His desire for her blistered inside of him.

His lips met hers in a sweet embrace. His hand ventured down her back. The other tangled in her plush, raven hair.

"I'll leave you two to catch up." Kain said, slightly chuckling. "It is good to have you back, Damien."

"It's good to be back. Thank you again, Kain."

The following morning, Damien woke up feeling surprisingly well. The sun peeked over the horizon turning the clear sky a blushing pink against the fading blues and grays of the night.

He'd made love to Jill multiple times during the night, each time more passionate than the last. Her body craved his after being deprived of his love for so long.

No one else was awake so he made his way down to the pool he and Jill nearly made love in the night of the First Moon event.

A pup made its way down to the pool drawing Damien's attention. "Well hello there. Where's your mom?"

The pup's mother came shortly after. "I'm sorry, my lord. He ran off. I was trying to get him before he got all of the way down here. I know we're supposed to be in the mountains but he forgot his favorite stuffed toy. It has been a nightmare to try and get him to sleep without it."

"It's okay. You don't have to address me so formally." Damien picked the pup up, laughing as he tickled his stomach. "Come on, let's get your toy so your mom can get back to the warmth of the caves."

Damien walked with the pup and his mother to the camp.

Kain met him at the opening, surprising Damien to see his friend was slightly bowing to him. "Good morning."

"Kain, what's with the bowing? You know I don't want any special treatment." Damien said rolling his eyes, giving the pup to his mother.

"Something I forgot to mention to you after our encounter was a part of your power awoke inside of you. It was what set us free from the dark god's hold. It is my duty to serve you."

The way the lycan mother addressed Damien suddenly made more sense to him. Holt and Kain must have mentioned to the pack that they were to treat him differently since a part of his soul awoke during his encounter with Barghast.

"Kain, I don't remember what happened. I just felt a warmth inside of me as I thought about Jill. I don't remember much after that. I don't want anyone treating me like I'm some sort of deity or royalty. I just want to stay me, okay."

Kain nodded. "As you wish. I respect that humility in you. I would gladly follow you as an alpha if you so choose to take the title one day."

"Oh please, Kain. This newborn, an alpha? He's barely a lycan. I bet he hasn't turned once yet."

"For the gods' sake." Kain smacked his head with the heel of his hand as Nathaniel walked over to him with Vincent and Kaden from his pack.

"So, pussy boy, how about we go a few rounds once you get a pair between your legs? I'd love to shove Kain's little pet's face into the ground to show just how pathetic you are."

Damien rolled his own eyes. He'd dealt with assholes like Nathaniel in high school. They didn't bother him then either.

"Look, I don't know what your problem is. Quite frankly, I don't really give a damn. I've dealt with jocks like you before. Whatever macho issues you may have, you can deal with on your own time. As far as 'going a few rounds', I'll pass. I have better things to spend my time on." Damien replied, turning his back on Nathaniel.

He heard Kain snicker as he started to walk away only to have his shoulder grabbed.

"Don't you dare turn your back on me, newborn. I don't appreciate being disrespected by someone who barely can call themselves a lycan. Let alone someone who hides behind Kain and Gabriel because he doesn't have the balls to stand up against me himself. Either you face me in five days or I'll be sure to make your life hell until you do."

Damien shoved Nathaniel off of him only to get in his face.

Kain placed his body between the two lycans. "That's enough, Nathaniel. Damien refused your challenge honorably. I told you the next time you opened your mouth, it better be useful or I would put you in your place, personally."

"Fang off, Kain. This is between me and your little man crush. If he can't handle his own against me, then he can't handle it on the battlefield."

A fire burned inside of Damien, making him angry. As much as he hated to admit it, he knew Nathaniel was right. If he didn't stand up now, then he couldn't let himself step on the battlefield and hope to be useful against a vampire.

"You know what, asshole. I'll accept your challenge." Damien said, getting back into Nathaniel's face.

Kain smiled in respect for Damien's choice. "Very well. The rules of combat stand. Nathaniel, since you have disrespected the honor of what it means to be an alpha, your title will be what is at stake."

"Fine. If I win, Damien has to hit his knees and surrender to my authority as an alpha and join my pack," Nathaniel replied, an arrogant smile curving on his lips. He thumped Damien's forehead with a flick of his finger. "Got that? Once I plant your face in the dirt, I want to see your belly in submission. No more hiding behind Kain." He shoved past Damien, laughing.

"That guy really pisses me off. The hell is his problem?" Damien asked Kain, still upset.

"Nathaniel is Lune's younger brother. He is an arrogant pup. He did not have to fight to earn his title. He took it in a hostile takeover of Sombra's pack after he passed away. Perhaps if he learned more from Sombra he would not be the way he is. I will train you myself, starting tomorrow. He is right, you need to change. I can teach you how. You will need to hunt as well. Meet me by the pool at sunrise. I suggest you rest up, you will need your strength." Kain walked back to his own tent, zipping the door closed behind him.

"Damien, you've been acting strangely since this morning. Is there something wrong?" Jill rested her cheek against Damien's back. Her fingers tickled his skin as they ran down his shoulder, following the path to his hip.

"Nathaniel challenged me to a fight. As much as I hate to admit, it has me nervous. Kain says he's going to start training me but Jill, what if I can't do this? They all have such high expectations of me as a Purifier. Kain actually bowed to me." Damien couldn't help the nervous feeling welling up inside of him.

All of a sudden it seemed like everyone's expectations of him reached new heights. He was terrified of letting them down.

Jill kissed his shoulder, letting her hands run down his back and sides around to his stomach. "Don't worry about any of that. We aren't expecting you to fight this war alone. If Kain is training you, then Nathaniel won't be a problem either. He's one of the strongest lycan fighters we have. For now," Jill spoke low and hot in his ear as her desire for his attention grew. "Let me enjoy your company. Let me pleasure you."

Damien felt chills go down his spine as her hands slid up the front of his muscle shirt. Her nails lightly tickling the muscles of his abs up to his chest. He raised his arms, letting Jill take his shirt off, raising up on her knees behind him so she could plant kisses on his neck and shoulders.

"Come up here with me. I want to get between those gorgeous legs of yours." Jill backed up on her hands and knees, her finger beckoning Damien to join her on their bed. Her back arched and eyes half-closed in a seductive fashion. Her hair fell across her face, down her shoulders.

She wore only her underwear, licking her lips as she enticed her lover.

Damien rubbed his face. Jill's favorite crooked smile curled along his lips as he crawled up to her.

After leaning up against the makeshift headboard made of pillows, Jill nestled between his legs, resting against his bare chest. His hand felt warm as ran across her cheek, down her neck. Their lips met in a loving kiss.

"You're so beautiful. I honestly don't know what I did to earn someone so beautiful and strong."

"You existed. That's enough for me," Jill reached up to pet Damien's face, her eyes dreamy as she stared into his. "Your eyes are like jewels. I don't think I've ever seen eyes as deep purple as yours. It's like Tenebris made you for me."

Damien ran his hand up under her shirt, silently begging her to take it off. She obliged, granting him access to remove her bra before kissing her shoulder. His fingertips slid down her arms in sweet appreciation of her beauty.

Jill craned her neck, her pleasure soaring as his hands ran over her skin. The feeling of his lips on her neck and breasts made her heart beat harder. Her breath grew heavy with heated passion.

Everything she had done to win his love led up to these glorious moments when all else happening around them faded into the background. His love seeped into her with each touch; each gentle kiss on her body.

It wasn't long before Damien had Jill on her back, their clothes laying in piles on the floor. The late winter afternoon brought about a snow chilling the wind. It drove them under the blankets of their bed as a shield. Their arms and legs entangled.

Jill let out a soft gasp as she felt Damien slide into her from behind, the suddenness of his entry didn't allow her body time to adjust around him. He went so deep into her she felt the sting of pain in her hips, making her wince. She unconsciously tried to get away from him only to have him hold her firmly against his hard body.

Damien's finger rubbing her tender flesh made Jill's pleasure surge. Her body longed to give him all he wanted to take with each thrust into her tender opening. She was so wet. His rich, deep, sexual scent intoxicated her to the point she became drunk on his love.

Damien held Jill's hip firmly to keep her still. His other hand held her throat, turning her head so he could plant loving kisses on her jaw.

Jill's nails dug into Damien's thigh the closer she got to her orgasm. Small gasps and whimpers escaped through clenched teeth with each profound thrust.

He rolled them over so Jill was on her stomach, his body pressed against her while making love to her as if it were the first time.

Jill had to bite down on the pillow to avoid crying out against the pleasure flooding her body. Her nails dug into her lover's arm as he took her.

The sudden arrival of her orgasm made Jill's muscles pulse around him, taking him deeper into her. His own orgasm made him dig his teeth into her shoulder, his hand holding her hip so tightly he knew it would bruise but he couldn't stop himself. He wanted her to take all of him into her womb.

When he finally released her, Jill stretched out her back to loosen her muscles against the strain. She felt slightly nauseated at having to handle everything Damien had to give her.

"Sex is always so hot with you, babe." Damien kissed her neck, his tongue lapping up the sweat on her shoulder. "I have to admit you surprised me. I had no idea you were able to get so aggressive when making love." Jill snickered, out of breath.

She wanted more. More of his attention, more affection, more love making. "Would you lie on your stomach for me?"

Damien lay down next to her, smiling as he crossed his arms to rest his chin on them.

Jill lay down on top of him. The curve of her stomach met his back, fitting her pelvis in the curve just above his butt. Her feet caressed his calves and thighs. She let her hand stroke her lover's throat, softly kissing his jaw before moving up to his ear to nip it.

It was more than she could have ever imagined. The love she felt for Damien was deeper than it ever had been with Lucius.

To her, everything they had been through was worth this one moment. She was going to savor it, savor him until he had to leave her to meet Kain.

CHAPTER TWENTY-FOUR

The next morning found Damien up and out of bed before the sun rose above the horizon. It was the day he was leaving with Kain to start training with him in preparation of his upcoming fight with Nathaniel.

Even though it wasn't something Damien looked forward to, he knew it was the only way he was going to get the overly narcissistic alpha off his case.

Since he woke up from his encounter with Barghast in his mind, everyone in the camp had been referring to him as "my lord" and bowing. It made him feel strange, afraid he may let them down in the end.

Damien made his way down to the pool that Kain asked him to meet only to find he was alone.

"Kain?" He started looking around.

"I'm here." Kain came out from behind a large boulder that served as a barrier to the pool. His mid-length dirty blonde hair was a disheveled mess. His shoulders marred with new gashes resembling claw marks.

The usual purple circles under his eyes were so dark, his emerald green eyes were almost lost in their darkness.

"Kain! What in God's name happened?" Damien asked, running to Kain's side to help support him.

"It's alright. It looks worse than it feels. Are you ready to begin your training?" Kain held his hand up to stop Damien, walking as though nothing was wrong. He held onto his usual pride and confidence despite how much pain he had to have been in.

"Kain, we don't have to do this. You look like you're not feeling well."

Stopping mid-footfall, Kain spoke over his shoulder. "Damien, trust me. I will be fine. There is no way in sun's hell I'm letting you forfeit to someone like Nathaniel. Now come with me."

The rest of the walk went in silence. Damien spent most of the time staring at his friend's back. It was covered with a mix of old healed scars and new fresh gashes down the length of his back. Some even wrapped around his hips.

It was the same on his chest and arms. Whatever it was doing this, it was obviously trying to kill him.

Kain led Damien through the forest until they reached an open meadow. The grass was as soft as bamboo sheets; green and fresh like it had just been watered by the spring rains.

A fading mist weaved in and out of the grass, dissipating with the rising sun. The air was brisk and cool in contrast with the winter back at the camp. It smelled like fresh lavender and jasmine. The sun shone warm above them.

It felt like it was a different world.

Lying far in the background was a ring of mountains. The horizon masked them purple and pink with the sun peeking over the ridges.

"Kain, what is this place?" Damien asked in awe, taking in the landscape.

His eyes came to fall upon a large circle of stones shaped liked large ovals. Carved into each of them were different symbols, almost like the runes that Rob showed him in some of the PC games he played.

"This is one of the oldest temples to our gods built when we arrived here. With the arrival of man, we had to flee from this place since they built a settlement so close by. Surprisingly, they haven't found it. It is believed that as if by some power or magic, it's hidden from the eyes of man. The perfect place to train a new lycan," Kain took the remains of his shirt off, hanging it on the branch of a nearby tree. "Damien, tell me something. Why have you not tried to change yet?"

"I'm not sure I can. I haven't felt any different since Jill bit me," Damien replied, his fists clenched tightly against his sides. His chest tightened as the nervousness at what he was about to say filled him. "To be honest, I think I'm afraid to. I'm not sure why."

"Fear and uncertainty," Kain lowered his head, slightly sighing and half-chuckling. Damien's eyes met Kain's. "That's all I heard."

Kain took a thin piece of tattered material out of his pocket, making his way over to Damien. "Tie this around your eyes. If fear is what is blinding you to your true potential, then it is that fear we must eliminate first. To a human, darkness is the most terrifying entity so it is darkness that you need to face."

Hesitant but trusting Kain, Damien tied the makeshift blindfold around his head, instantly blinding him from the beauty around him. Chills ran up his spine as uncertainty met uneasy anticipation at what Kain's intentions were.

"Now that your eyes have been taken out of the picture, it is time for you to see the world the way we do. Lycans rarely rely on sight since we hunt in such darkened conditions and often have to see our prey even before it is visible." Kain laid his hands on Damien's shoulders, gently guiding them down.

"Relax your mind and body. Feel everything around you. The breeze, the grass, the rustling of the leaves. Hear the sounds of the birds, the padding of deer hooves in the distance. Then will you understand what it feels like to see the world. Only blinded can you truly see the beauty of Gaia."

Damien tried hard to focus as he was being instructed, his body tensing as he tried to force his new senses to adapt.

Disappointment leaked its way into his mind, making him feel as though he was failing just as he feared he would.

"I...I can't do this. I knew I couldn't meet everyone's expectations. I let them down. I let you down, Kain."

"Stop trying to resist. Your whole life you have been led to believe you needed to pretend to be something you are not. Stop trying to be human. You are not one. You never were. Up to this point, I have been easing you into this but it is time I was honest. I will break you, Damien."

A short gasp escaped Damien's throat, his heart beating faster as he fought hard to keep a hold on his trust that Kain wasn't going to hurt him. "Break me?"

"Yes. I will break you but I will rebuild you into something stronger. I am not as patient as Jillian when it comes to training someone. There is a reason why Gabriel reacted the way he did when I told you I was going to train you. You won't be going back to Jillian until you are trained."

At the end of the day, Damien was on his knees, exhausted and upset at his repeated failures.

"I can't do this, dammit!" He slammed his fists into the ground, grinding his teeth at the fact he wouldn't be able to get back to his mate's side because he couldn't get his head on straight.

Kain knelt down beside him, his hand resting on his shoulder. "Easy. You are much stronger than you think you are. I promise you, by the time this is over, you will come to realize it yourself."

The full moon rose above them, signaling the arrival of the night. The soft breeze whispered through the trees. Owls hooted in the distance while loons called gently from the lakes.

"I have to hunt now."

Damien's head shot up, surprised. "You're leaving me here?"

"Of course. I told you, did I not? What better way to train your instincts than being forced to use them. If you get tired, sleep in the center of the stones. You will be safe there. I will return in the morning."

Kain shifted into his wolf form, shaking his muscles against the discomfort of the gashes.

Damien was in awe at the large sandy haired wolf standing before him. He felt strange inside. Like something was trying to get out.

It wasn't until his eyes met Kain's in his full wolf form that he felt a burn in his chest. It was different from the burn inflicted on him by the dark god. This one felt comfortable. As if it was meant to be there.

Kain lifted his head, howling to the moon. The sound echoed against the trees and the range of mountains around them. The aura surrounding him filled with a primal power.

Kain's eyes once again met Damien's, almost smiling. He turned and sprinted off towards the woods.

Alone, Damien wandered through the woods in search of something he could have for dinner. His stomach was so empty it hurt, making him feel nauseous. The headache he'd developed after Kain left him began throbbing behind his skull. The burn he felt earlier still nagged him inside.

He was so dazed, he lost his footing, sliding down a steep incline. Rolling across broken branches, sharp rocks, wet leaves and dirt, Damien landed in a small brook.

Tired and hungry, he felt content just lying there. His spirit felt weakened. His hope crumbled that he would ever come to understand anything about himself.

Barely able to stand, he forced himself to his hands and knees, crawling out of the water only to fall to his stomach.

Jill. I'm sorry. I failed you. I failed Kain. I failed everyone.

Damien closed his eyes, furious. His thoughts turned to Jill. Her warm body snuggling alone in their bed back at the camp. How worried she must be. How he longed to be next to her, making love to her, kissing her soft lips. The heat of her body as her pleasure rose beneath his fingers and lips.

A soft howl rose above the wind's shrieking wails. The sound familiar and comforting. *I love you. Come back to me soon.* It was Jill's howl.

Determination overtook uncertainty as Damien forced himself to his feet, ignoring the pangs of hunger and exhaustion to make it back to the circle of stones Kain told him to rest in.

Damien only barely made it back when the sun began to rise behind him. The first night a horrible reminder of just how little he knew about his new abilities.

He fell to the ground, curling up to try and catch some sleep before Kain came back. Jill's words on the wind served as his only comfort against the cold of his wet clothes and broken spirit.

The smell of something cooking woke Damien up from his exhausting, restless sleep.

Kain sat by a newly lit fire with a small black pot hanging on a makeshift spit while fish roasted on a grill grate. It smelled wonderful. Damien's stomach growled so loud, Kain turned around.

"Well good morning. From the looks of you, I'd say the first night didn't go so well." He let out a slight chuckle.

"Yeah, yeah. Laugh it up. You make this look so easy," Damien sat down across from his friend, his eyes locked on the dancing flames in front of him. "Kain, I don't know if I can do this. Last night, I didn't feel anything but a slight burn inside after I stared into your eyes."

"That's a start. The wolf inside of you must be something if you can't see him yet. Usually most of us are able to change as soon as the pain disappears." Kain handed him a bowl of the stew he was cooking and two roasted fish.

Curious, Damien broached the subject he'd long been curious about since Jill mentioned it. "Kain, have you ever changed anyone?"

Kain stopped what he was doing. His eyes locked on the flames and the bubbling stew in the pot. "Yes."

"Where are they?"

Kain closed his eyes, sighing. "I...had to kill them."

"I'm...sorry. May I ask why?" Damien took a sip of the stew, amazed at how good it was. Jill hadn't been lying. Kain could cook amazingly well. It took he had not to gulp it down in a single swallow.

"In the middle of the change, they turned into a werewolf and tried to kill me. It's not a pleasant feeling, Damien. It's why most of us don't turn someone unless we know they won't become monsters. Kyle was worried that you may become a werewolf after you didn't wake up for so long," Kain took his own bite of fish, offering Damien some water. "I told him I would end you myself if that became the case, knowing Jillian couldn't do it. For now, my friend, eat and regain your strength. We will begin again when you are ready."

Damien watched as Kain rose to his feet. There was something about him that demanded respect. Something powerful Damien couldn't wrap his head around.

After breakfast, Kain had Damien once again blindfolded. Only this time, he made Damien remove his shirt so he could feel everything around him.

Kain coached Damien through how his body needed to feel. How he needed to relax and realize that the darkness held no fear.

Slowing his breathing, Damien remembered Jill's howl. He understood the words she said over the wind.

The burn inside of him expanded to his muscles as his mind's eye took a large shape. Its eyes the piercing amethyst color of his own. It was just within reach but still so far away.

The hours passed by, changing the golden rays of the sun into the pale silver and grays of the night.

"The moon rises, Damien. It is time for me to leave you. You did well. Your senses are developing nicely. Try to make tonight easier. I will return in the morning." Kain began tying the jacket he usually wore around his waist.

Instead of the feral wolf of the first night, Damien now locked eyes with the same image he'd seen when he'd encountered Chelsea.

Kain stood on muscular legs bent at the knees. His thighs and calves bulged with hard muscle. Torn and tattered jeans hung off of his knees. His chest bare and sculpted. The faded crest of what looked like a medieval wolf holding a shield engraved on his left hip.

Damien was awestruck by the beast above him. He was the spitting image of Tenebris from the vision he'd had when Barghast fought his brother in the burning meadow.

The huge lycan howled. Only this time, it was almost like a song. Soft and melodious despite the ferocity of the beast it came from.

Kain sprinted away as graceful as a marathon runner into the woods.

Great, how badly can I mess tonight up? I'm not even sure what I'm supposed to do. Damien thought, mentally preparing himself for the no-doubt horrible night to come.

Damien went back to the fire to sit down and watch the flickering flames. His mind focused on the huge shape he saw in the training with Kain earlier. *That's what I can do.*

Blindfolding himself, Damien sat in the meditation pose Kain taught him to relax his mind and become more aware of the landscape around him.

At first his body tried to force his instincts to adjust, bringing about a sense of frustration. His chest tightened as his desire to give in almost took control. Damien took the blindfold off, cursing under his breath. *Why can't I figure out something that should be so natural to me? What the hell is wrong with me?*

Looking up at the moon, Damien had to choke back the uneasy sensation nagging at him. What if he couldn't ever change? He'd let everyone he knew and come to care about down. They'd be in danger. Jill would be in danger if he couldn't pull himself together.

Jill. Damien laid down on his back, his eyes locked on the glowing orb in the sky. A sense of warmth falling over him as he felt his mind being pulled into sleep.

CHAPTER TWENTY-FIVE

D amien opened his eyes to see a woman staring down at him. She was beautiful. Her hair strands of pure silver light flowed down her back to rest upon the ground all around them. Her skin was so white, it would make even the snow blush with envy.

Her long, slender fingers comforted him as they ran through his dark hair. Their touch felt cold, like the soft kisses of snowflakes on his cheeks on a dark, December night.

"Who are you?" His eyes grew wide as he found he was speaking without moving his mouth. His voice almost an echo in the nebulous space around them.

The woman smiled, leaning down and kissing him softly on the forehead. *"Do you truly not recognize me, my son?"*

Damien didn't understand. He hadn't remembered ever seeing this woman in his life. *"I'm sorry. I don't."*

The woman ran her fingers over the muscles of his chest up to his neck where Jill bit him. The marks had long healed yet glowed a bright silver sending a wave of warmth through Damien's body.

Realization hit him as to who she was. He was staring in the face of Luna, the Night Mother herself. *"Luna. You're... Luna."*

Luna let out a silken chuckle. *"Yes. I am."*

Damien sat up quickly, scooting away from Luna as far as he could. His eyes bulged with shock at the beautiful goddess in front of him.

Her dress was a soft blue, barely concealing her slender, naked form. Her silver hair falling the length of her height as she stood, dragging the ground in soft ripples like a river of stars.

Wisps of cloud drifted from her body as she moved, reminding Damien of the steam that happened when warm breath met the cold of winter.

The space around them was foreign yet so familiar to Damien. His eyes looked up to see the vast sea of stars and nebulous clouds. He'd been here before but he didn't know when or how.

"I can see in your eyes that you are confused, my child. You do not need to be afraid. I come on behalf of one we both love. One who will soon need your help as badly as you have needed theirs."

Luna walked over to Damien, her feet bare and light as she stepped forward. She knelt before him, her hand reaching out to cup his face, caressing it as she spoke. *"You have such a beautiful creature inside of you, Damien Pierce. I long to hear his song of praise. Will you set him free and let me hear it? I will bless it to sound so much more beautiful than any of my children. Its power will be the ability to give hope in the darkness when all other hope is gone. Please, my child. Will you let your mother hear her son's voice?"*

Damien looked away, overwhelmed at the promise Luna just gave him. He'd only seen a shape, not a full form and had no idea how to release it.

"I don't know how. I'm not even sure I can," Damien got on his hands and knees before Luna, his fists propped up on his knuckles as he lowered his head. *"Please, mother. Can you help me?"*

Luna rose to her feet, smiling as her size began increasing to that of the titans in Greek mythology. Her mortal body deteriorated to match the sea of stars around her. Her eyes glowed a radiant royal purple.

Damien felt himself rising up off the ground. His eyes meeting Luna's as her light surrounded him.

The muscles in his body began burning. Not with pain but with the utmost of pleasure.

Unlike most lycans, Damien's bones didn't snap or twist in to place. They merely adjusted just as water moved around stones blocking its path.

214

His tendons didn't pop or snap but moved out of the way until his newly formed flesh and bone shifted from man to wolf.

His cries of sudden shock melted into a howl so silken it sounded like the comfortable combination of wind blowing through a Native American flute and the loon of the night.

As Luna promised, she smiled at the sound. Her voice gentle as she spoke. *"Your song is so beautiful, Damien. I hope to hear it more in the very near future. Now wake up, my son. The day arises. My child will be waiting for you."*

Damien jerked awake, taking a deep breath of the fresh morning air.

Had it been a dream? No, his chest felt hot as though it had been seared with a poker. His lungs burning when he tried to breathe. He knew this feeling. It was the rage that he saw in the dark god's eyes the first time Damien had seen him. He must have been angry that Luna interfered.

"Glad you finally woke up. I was beginning to worry." Kain's gentle voice came through the burn. He made them breakfast, waiting until Damien chose to wake up.

"I had a dream. I saw Luna. I felt her touch me," Damien's mind went hazy as he tried to remember the details of his dream. His body felt strange. A craving filled him as he tried to sit up. His hand went to his face as he vaguely remembered what happened. "She..."

"What? What happened?" Kain's usually relaxed demeanor appeared stressed. When their eyes met, Kain's eyes widened. Damien's eyes had a different feeling about them. As if something inside had been set free and waited to be revealed. "So, you are truly, finally awakening. It is an honor to witness this."

Damien shook his head, not sure what anything Kain said meant. "I have no idea what you're talking about, Kain. Lay off the formality. I'm still the same guy."

Kain scoffed, handing Damien a plate of food. "Of that I have no doubt. However, I have a feeling tonight will be much different than any we have seen from you since this all started. Tonight, you will hunt with me. Tomorrow I teach you to fight."

The moon rose, bringing with her angry clouds ready to burst. Low rumbles of thunder made Damien flinch slightly as he thought about the dark god's fire.

Kain's hand on his back helped Damien relax back into focusing on the area around him.

"Ready? Tonight, you show me the wolf behind the man. Do not be hesitant. To our people, the change is even more natural than staying in the human form we have to take. Remember, the wolf in us was our first form until we were given the ability to turn into man." Kain walked around Damien to stand in front of him.

Damien watched as Kain's muscles grew tight all over his body. His fangs growing from his mouth as his jaw extended into the muzzle of the sandy haired wolf.

He fell forward onto his fingertips. His back legs bent like a marathon runner whose eyes were trained on the finish line; focused intensely on their goal.

It amazed Damien how easily the change happened for Kain despite how painful it appeared due to the scars that marred his copper skin.

The large tawny wolf raised his head to howl to the moon as her face disappeared behind the dark clouds. The rain beginning to fall echoed in the woods around them, the wind blew in strong gusts across the soft grass.

Kain made it look so easy. Damien had witnessed him shift walking forward after Chelsea ran. He'd seen Kain rise from his feral form to his human form like it was nothing to him.

Damien closed his eyes, trying to remember the events of the dream. Luna helped him free the wolf inside of him. He thought of Jill, her words over the wind the first night he suffered so badly just to try and make it through. He thought about how many times she'd looked at him with eyes so full of pain and worry as she placed herself up as a sacrifice to protect him. Her soft smile as she looked up at him after they made love, the deep gash in her shoulder she'd gotten after she'd saved him from Lilith.

I want to protect that smile. I don't want her to hurt anymore, not if I can actually do something. I want the power to help her. I need the power to be what she needs me to be!

A whimper escaped Kain's throat as Damien fell forward, his body rippling like the surface of the water after a rock had been dropped into it. His back arched as he threw his head back.

A slight roar escaped his throat as his arms and legs became the legs of a large wolf. His jaw extended with less effort than any lycan Kain had ever seen.

The tips of Damien's tail and legs were dark like his hair in his human skin. The white fur as pure as snow flowing like ocean waves in the wind.

Damien raised his head and howled. Kain lowered his gaze, turning to lead Damien towards the woods to teach him to hunt.

At first Damien had trouble walking on all fours, slightly stumbling as he tried to walk forward. He soon swallowed his uncertainty and let his instincts take over, clumsily following his friend.

Kain stopped to allow Damien to walk shoulder to shoulder with him. The sandy alpha almost yielding in respect to his companion. His ears perked suddenly as if he were trying to focus on the sound of potential prey through the rain and thunder filled woods.

A deer with her fawn were heading into their den for the night to seek shelter from the rain. The buck stayed outside to chew on some of the pine needles and bark of the trees.

Kain lowered his head, his body getting close to the ground to stalk the buck. Damien followed suit, his body almost acting on its own as the two wolves closed in on their prey. A light bark from Kain told Damien to go around the other side to cut off the buck's escape. The heart inside Damien's chest was racing, his blood heated from excitement as they got closer.

Kain jumped first landing on the back of the deer, struggling to sink his teeth in the tough hide despite how large he was.

As if drawn by some unknown force, Damien jumped at the buck's throat, his fangs finding its jugular, holding on tightly until it eventually grew too weak to struggle and fell.

A slight sting on his front leg left a thin line of blood where the buck's antler had cut him. It healed almost immediately as with most of his smaller wounds.

Nodding, Kain took the buck in his mouth, pulling it back towards their camp site between the stones. Damien's first night's hunt had actually gone pretty well and for once, it felt natural.

Back at the site, Kain set up a shelter made out of some thick branches and vines he used as ropes. He sat beside a fire he set and began preparing the different parts of the buck for their next meals for the last few days.

"You did surprisingly well for your first hunt. Your wolf form is one of the most unique I have seen in my many years of life. That howl alone is not of this world. I should have realized ahead of time that you were struggling because your situation was different. For my failure, I apologize, my friend." Kain looked over at his friend, his emerald green eyes full of concern.

Damien stared blankly into the flames, the taste of the buck still lingering in his mouth. "It's fine, Kain. Not like you know what goes on when a Purifier is bitten by a lycan. I don't know what happened. I just thought of Jill. I wanted to be strong enough to protect her and it happened. I felt like I was kicked out of my own body; looking through the eyes of something else. It scared me but felt good."

"That sounds about right for the first time. Your devotion to Jillian is beyond astounding to me. It's giving you strength unlike any I have witnessed. It continues to intrigue me, I must admit. For now though, get something to eat and then get some rest. I will teach you to fight wisely in battle and then we will return home so you can face Nathaniel. I have a feeling he's bitten off too large a bite of the buck this time and is going to finally choke on it."

The two of them laughed together at the idea of Nathaniel having his tail handed to him.

Damien didn't know when sleep took him but sometime during the night, a loud clap of thunder startled him out of his dreams.

Kain was still awake, stoking the fire. The only shield against the cool air was his plaid Sherpa jacket he often wore after he transformed and a pair of tattered blue jeans. No words would come out as Damien stared at the alpha who seemed oblivious to the fact he was awake.

"You should be resting, Damien. First time changes can be taxing on the mind and body."

I should have known. Kain doesn't miss anything. Damien thought as he sat up. "Thunder woke me up. Why are you still awake? Isn't it somewhere around three or four in the morning?"

Kain smiled, closing his eyes as he lowered his head. "You have such a big heart. I'm fine. Just woke up myself."

Damien rolled his eyes, knowing Kain hadn't gone to sleep. He wasn't a very good liar.

The scars on his body looked so angry. The edges jagged as though whatever made them meant to inflict the most damage it could without killing him.

"Kain, I want to know. Those scars, the gashes. Why you sometimes look like you're so tired you could drop at any moment. What are they from? Are you fighting someone?"

Kain didn't look at Damien. "You aren't ready, Damien. As strong as you have become in these three short days alone, you aren't ready to understand. At this time, I just ask that you trust me. There is so much more about this world that you will learn in time. Go back to sleep."

"You should too, you know. Don't want to kick your ass because you're too tired to stand on your own feet. That would be cheating. Especially against an apparently, old man like you." Damien joked, laying back down.

Kain burst out laughing. The sound made Damien smile. He was finally able to reach Kain on a more personal level.

"Is that right? So, I'm an old man, am I? We are going to have to see about that. I will get some rest. I give you my word."

The warmth of the blankets and the crackling of the fire helped Damien drift back off to sleep. His mind still focused on finding out Kain's secret he was trying so hard to hide.

The following morning found the two men up at the crack of dawn.

Despite the fact that Kain had been up so late, Damien still found himself on his back time and time again.

"Okay. I take it back. I take it all back." Damien panted as he rolled onto his hands and knees to get up to receive some more punishment from the very alpha he'd insulted the night before. *I was wrong. Damn I was so wrong. I'm eating so much crow right now.*

Kain chuckled, his hand running through his dirty-blonde hair. "So, what was that about me being an old man that would be, what was it, 'too tired to stand' on my own feet?"

"Yeah, yeah. I already took it all back. What else do you want? Blood?" Damien regretted his words as soon as Kain round-house kicked him across the face. The force sending him skidding across the ground. Damn the man could kick.

"Shit, Kain. I don't think Clydesdales can kick this hard." Damien rubbed his cheek with his hand, looking at his palm as though he might be bleeding.

"The problem is you aren't anticipating anything. You should read every movement of your opponent's body and predict what he is planning on doing before he even thinks about it. The body tells on itself before it acts. Learning to read these indications is key to staying on top in battle." Kain threw another punch at Damien only to miss him. "Good. Let your instincts guide you and you either won't get hit or you can lessen a blow. Now. Again!" Kain threw his kick. This time faking Damien out and throwing his elbow into Damien's chest.

Damien bent over. His lungs burning as he tried to catch his breath. "Okay... that was so low..."

"Anticipate, Damien. Read. Only then will you be victorious in battle and in hunting."

The rest of the afternoon went by with Damien being kicked around over and over again. As he tried to get up from having his legs taken out from under him, Kain stood over him. The look in his eyes intense.

"I'm not letting you sleep until I see a change in how you're fighting. Nathaniel will try every dirty trick in the book. You have to be ready or do you want to be his pack bitch for the rest of your days?"

Oh, hell no he didn't. Damien felt a sense of unbridled determination flood his body. There was no way in hell he was going to show his belly to someone as low on the pole as Nathaniel.

A sudden jolt inside had him dodging almost every hit Kain was throwing at him. *What's going on? It's like I can see what he's going to do before he does it.*

"Very good." Kain held back his last hit. "You are ready. Tomorrow we go back so you can face Nathaniel. I am very honored to have been able to teach you." Kain bowed to Damien, earning one in return.

"Thank you, Kain. You've done so much for me. I don't know if I can ever return the favor." Damien lowered his head towards the alpha in respect.

A pat on his shoulder had him looking back up. "You don't need to. You are my friend, Damien. My best friend. I would gladly do it all again. Get a late evening nap. We will hunt tonight and take it back to the camp in the morning. No doubt Holt may need some more supplies."

Napping sounded really appealing so Damien curled up on his makeshift sleeping bag and fell asleep. *Jill. I'm coming back to you. Just a few more hours.*

CHAPTER TWENTY-SIX

T he following morning Kain and Damien made their way back to the camp in their wolf forms.

Almost immediately, Damien found himself getting slightly uncomfortable at the looks on each of the faces of the lycans in the camp. Gasps erupted across the small crowd joining whispers Damien could barely hear. He shook his head whimpering until his eyes landed on the one woman he'd longed to see since he'd been gone.

Jill walked through the crowd, her beauty radiating from her with such intensity, Damien felt his breath ripped out of his lungs. It was as though he'd never seen her before. Her beautiful green eyes lit up as she walked up to him. All time seemed frozen. Every movement exaggerated in his eyes as he admired her beauty. She stopped in front of him, falling to her knees.

"You're so handsome," Her arms wrapped around his neck, her cheek resting against his shoulder. The softness of his fur brought about a heat of desire inside of her. The powerful scent of pine and male musk infiltrated her nose. She leaned back to look into his eyes, her own full with sweet seduction. "I'm happy to see you."

Damien whimpered as he nuzzled into her, his huge paw on her back. His heart filled with joy at finally getting to feel his mate's warmth once again next to him.

The pain and disappointment he'd suffered melted away in this moment when her soft, raven hair met his cheek. His arms wrapped firmly around her, not wanting to let her go. *Finally. Finally I have her in my arms again.*

"Kain's back!" A young pup in his human form was soon joined by multiple others as they ran over to Kain, weaving in and out of his legs. He struggled not to trip while dragging a pack of supplies to Holt.

Jill covered her mouth against a snicker as Kain whimpered after nearly face planting from a pup under his front leg. She turned her attention towards her mate. "Come my love, I yearn for your affection. May I have some of your time?"

Damien's heart raced. A nervous lump forming in his throat at the saucy, frozen green bedroom eyes he was staring into.

His body grew hot as he watched Jill sashay her hips back into their tent. She stopped only briefly, looking over her shoulder as she pulled one of the spaghetti straps of her shirt down, disappearing behind the cloth door.

Once inside, Damien stretched his arms and legs out against the stiffness. His hand on his shoulder while he rotated it.

Jill sat in nothing but her shirt on the edge of the bed, her hands sitting on the edge between her spread legs. Her eyes roamed over her lover's body, savoring every defined muscle as it grew tight and loose with his movements.

The sweat glistened off of his perfect skin, now toned a light copper from the change. His hair dark as the night sky clung to his skin from the sweat yet still beckoned to have her fingers grip it tight while they made hot love.

Unable to contain her desire any longer, Jill held out her hands to beckon her lover forward.

Damien smiled, walking over to stand between her legs. Jill hugged Damien's thigh, her other hand running slowly up his abdominal muscles to his chest. The tattoo of the cross on his hip seemed to plead for attention. Briefly she leaned down to softly lick it, causing his skin to tingle under her tongue. She sighed as she pressed her cheek against his stomach, caressing his leg and butt cheek, savoring the toned muscles she felt under her fingers.

"You have such a nice ass, babe." She looked up, curious as to what his reaction would be. Usually he was shy in regards to such open flirting but this time he seemed almost content.

A slight crooked grin curled over his lips. His eyes cocky at the look she was giving him. This sudden change of behavior combined with the aggressive way he made love, thrilled Jill to her core. It made him even more appealing.

The light scratching of her nails over the skin of his stomach made Damien shiver against the warmth of her cheek.

Jill lay back on the bed, her hunger for him growing beyond her ability to control. Her hands ran up his bare arms.

The heat of his body made Jill arch her back, moaning. She wanted him and she wanted him now. "Make love with me."

Damien crawled up on the bed, careful to scoot Jill up with the strength of his forearm between her legs until her head rested on the ornate pillows. He lowered his mouth to Jill's, kissing her while his hand ran down her side to her thigh to guide her leg up to his hip.

The tip of his erection had just found her swollen, wet opening throbbing with need only to be interrupted by a searing pain in his chest.

Damien clenched his teeth, hissing through them. His hand gripped his chest. His heart raced in his ribcage.

The very bones of his ribs felt like they were on fire. He struggled to hide the discomfort from Jill, attempting not to worry her. He got up from the bed, trying to catch any amount of air into his lungs that he could.

"Are you okay?" Worried, Jill got up off of the bed to go to Damien's side.

"Fine, sweetheart. I'm just...needing some fresh air." Damien got dressed before he left the tent, not giving Jill a chance to respond.

He hated himself that he was so close to taking her after being apart only to have to suddenly stop. He needed to find Kain to tell him what had happened.

Damien looked around at the camp. Each lycan still had some kind of strange look on their face.

He found Kain talking to Holt in regards to the reasons as to why the females had come back from the mountain caves.

"Glad you made it back in one piece, Damien. Not everyone who trains with Alexander Kain comes back in such good condition. Sun's hell, some of them don't come back at all." Holt laughed, his thick accent making it hard for Damien to understand some of the things he said.

Right, if you only knew, Holt. He was right about training with Kain. It had been sun's hell. *I don't think I've landed on my ass so many times in my damn life.*

"I'm not that bad, Holt. Stop scaring the boy." Kain chuckled as he took a drink of whatever hot beverage was in the metal cup he had.

"Kain, I need to talk to you." Damien turned to Holt. "Holt, weren't the females supposed to be in the caves? What are they all doing here?"

"You."

"Huh?"

Kain gagged on the drink. It was if he recognized the lack of wording Holt used so he clarified the alpha's rather vague statement. "What Holt means is you give them hope that the war will soon end. They want to remain close."

"Is that why they're looking at me like that?"

Kain nodded. "Yes. They have never seen a white lycan. The only other one is the Night Father himself. It gives them hope that they may get the peace they have longed and prayed for."

Damien stumbled back. This was all going too fast. Just a short time ago he was going to school for a bachelor's degree and trying not to get killed by vampires. Now he was some sort of symbol of hope?

"You were wanting to speak with me? Is it something you would like to talk about in private?" Kain spoke, appearing to sense his friend's nervousness.

Damien shook his head, trying to focus. "Yes."

"Holt, would you excuse us for a moment, please?"

Holt nodded to Kain, making his way back to his tent, instructing lycans as he went.

"Now what is it, Damien?"

Damien didn't know how to start. "I felt the pain again. It hurt so bad this time I got nauseous."

"It is the dark god. He knows the hope you are bringing back to us. It's making him angry. Do not let him dissuade you. It is what he feeds on."

"What if I fail, Kain? I mean, it hadn't been a few months and now I'm some kind of symbol? I barely just learned how to change into a wolf. What if I can't handle all of the pressure?"

"Shouldn't be a 'what if' from a pussy like you," Nathaniel's arrogant voice pierced through Damien's ears. He rolled his eyes as the narcissistic alpha stopped in front of them. "Well, well, well, if it isn't the newborn and his man crush. Hope I didn't interrupt you girls but if my memory serves, I have a nose to plant into the ground," Nathaniel shoved Damien in the chest. "I'm surprised you even bothered to show back up."

Just as Kain was about to speak, Damien held out his hand to stop him. "That's enough. I've had it with your stuck-up attitude. Someone needs to put you in your place, Nathaniel. You want me, here I am."

Nathaniel burst out laughing. "So that's how it is? You're gone with this washed up has-been for five short days and now you think you're strong enough to handle me?" Nathaniel got into Damien's face. His bare chest bowed up. "You're nothing but a newborn. A pussy who thinks he's got balls now that he has his baby fangs. If Jill hadn't saved your ass as much as she did, you'd be a dead man. I'll wipe the floor with you and then shame Kain for failing in your training."

Kain stood silent, smirking. Almost anticipating the outcome.

Kain stood in the middle of the ring while lycans of all ages and kinds gathered on the outskirts. Damien stood face to face with Nathaniel in a circle of trees. Some jeered at Nathaniel while others took bets on how long it would be before Damien started begging for mercy.

Damien had to silence the crowd in his mind or he wouldn't be able to focus. He knew Nathaniel was much more experienced. He looked at Kain. The pride in the alpha's stance reassured him of his teacher's faith in him.

"Alright, you both remember what's at stake for this fight?" His eyes met Nathaniel who scoffed at him. "Nathaniel, if you lose, then you are henceforth banished with your beta and will forfeit the alpha title to Damien," Kain looked at Damien, his eyes full of trust. "Damien, if you lose then you will join Nathaniel's pack and submit to his authority as alpha."

A shutter ran through Damien's body. Surrendering to Nathaniel was one thing but shaming Kain was completely different. *I won't lose. I can't lose.* He took a deep breath, taking the stance Kain taught him.

Nathaniel smirked, lunging at Damien with impressive speed.

Damien didn't move, keeping his eyes closed. He felt the forest around him, the soft bite of the cold breeze as the day turned to evening. The sounds of the lycans around him cheering and booing the fighter they supported.

If I fall here, I would have let them all down. They're counting on me. Jill, Kain, they're counting on me. Gabriel, my dad, Rob. Damien opened his eyes just in time to side-step Nathaniel's punch. His body completely relaxed as he effortlessly dodged the lycan's blows.

"What the hell?!" He tried lunging again with the same result. He began panting. His teeth clenched in anger. "There's no way you can be this good this fast! Kain's a nobody!" Again and again he swung and kicked only to miss.

Eventually Damien grabbed Nathaniel's fist, gripping it tightly in his hand. "He's not a nobody, Nathaniel. If he was, you wouldn't be trying so hard to dishonor him. Your problem is you're hiding all of your uncertainty and low self-esteem behind a false sense of power and confidence."

Damien borrowed Kain's legendary round-house kick, his heel finding its mark against Nathaniel's jaw. The force sent the alpha skidding on his heels across the ring. He lunged at Nathaniel, taking him into a submission hold to the ground.

"When this is over, you will apologize to Kain for disgracing his name and to Jill for demeaning her like you did. Got it?"

"Fuck you!" Nathaniel gasped as Damien tightened his hold. He struggled to free himself, each attempt proved useless. "Fine! I forfeit!"

Damien let Nathaniel go, rising to his feet. The defeated alpha huffed and puffed on the ground on his knees.

"Well done. Very well done." Kain patted Damien's shoulder. "I have nothing more I can teach you. You are now an alpha in your own right. Congratulations."

Me? An alpha? Damien's eyes widened in surprise. "Kain, I don't want the title. I'm not ready. Actually," Damien's words were cut off as Kain walked over to Nathaniel, towering above him.

"The rules stand, Nathaniel. You are hereby stripped of your alpha title and sentenced to be banished with your beta to the mountains."

Nathaniel clenched his teeth, growling through them and glaring at Lune who stood up against a tree shaking his head.

"Wait!" Damien's voice rang out, silencing the crowd.

Kain turned to watch as Damien made his way over to the kneeling lycan.

He reached out his hand. "No. It's not right. I don't want the title."

"What?"

"I don't want the title. What I do want is your help. We already have too many enemies as it is. We don't need to fight amongst ourselves," Nathaniel looked at Damien's hand. "Will you help us?"

Damien saw Nathaniel's eyes soften as he took his hand. "Yeah."

Kain nodded. His grin as wide as Damien had ever seen it. "A wise choice. For a newborn." Kain chuckled, earning a playful shove from Damien.

"This from a 'has-been'?" Damien smirked thinking he got the better of the older alpha until he once again found himself flat on his back. *Okay...still...so wrong...*

The fight left Damien's muscles sore on so many levels. When Jill offered to give him a back rub in the hot springs, he never knew existed just a short hike up the mountains he was quick to agree.

"Ow." Damien cringed as Jill massaged his shoulders, trying to get the knots out of them.

"You are such a big baby sometimes. That was amazing by the way. You fought so beautifully and gave Nathaniel mercy when he clearly didn't deserve it." Jill rested her cheek against Damien's shoulder. "You really are so amazing, babe. You continue to astound and baffle me. You have such a pure heart and soul."

"I'm not special, Jill. Everyone expects so much out of me. I don't have a clue what I'm doing or what I'm supposed to do."

Jill's hand running down his chest to his stomach combined with her warm tongue licking his neck froze the words in Damien's throat.

"You aren't alone. You have the respect of every alpha in the packs present. Our people love you. Our pups adore you. Why is it so wrong for them to see you as a symbol of hope?"

Damien hadn't thought about it the way Jill described. The Purifiers were supposed to be symbols of hope according to what she told him.

Jill's hot breath in his ear sent trembling chills down his spine. "My love, I'm with pup."

Water flew in Jill's face as Damien shot up out of it. His eyes wide, his chest heaving with anxiety.

Jill shook her head trying to get the water out of her face. "I was late so I had Kyle take a test. It came back positive. Damien, I'm pregnant."

Silence lingered between them for what seemed like hours.

Jill watched as Damien paced the floor of their tent, his hand running over his face multiple times. "Damien...are you angry?"

Damien stopped pacing. His hand ran the length of his face prior to glancing over at Jill. His heart felt like a rock in his chest capable of falling through his body to the ground. She was looking at the floor as she did when she felt he would reject her.

To comfort her, he dropped to his knees in front of her. Using his finger and thumb on her chin, he raised her head. "No Jill. I'm not angry. I'm actually really excited. It's just I don't know the first thing about being a father; let alone to pups." It still felt weird to call them that. His thoughts shifted to the upcoming war and the probabilities Jill had given him about pup mortality.

Jill had been elected to take on Lilith. Now, there was no way he was letting her fight. Not when she was carrying his children.

The sudden wrapping of Jill's arms around his waist brought Damien's attention to the beautiful woman in front of him.

"I'm so glad."

A squeak escaped Jill's throat as Damien quickly lifted her onto his hips. The thin material of her athletic shorts barely a shield against the hard length behind his own shorts.

His lips met hers in passionate love. "Jill, I want you. Nothing is going to stop me from taking you this time."

Jill's ice green eyes turned into the half-closed bedroom eyes Damien came to love. "As you wish, my alpha."

Damien couldn't stop the feral side of him that wanted to make love to her so badly he almost tore her shorts and panties to pieces as he pulled them off. Holding Jill up with one hand he pulled his own shorts and underwear down to his knees freeing his full erection from its prison.

Jill licked her lips as her mate's tip pressed against her slick folds. Her hands gripped the sheets in anticipation.

"Someone needed me, didn't she?" That crooked grin that Jill loved so much fell across her lover's face. He pulled her towards him until her lower back sat on the edge of the bed. His body was hot against her skin as he pressed into her. She clenched her teeth as the small, swollen opening struggled to take his full girth.

As he thrust into Jill, Damien let his thumbs caress the soft skin of her thighs, his face buried between her throat and collarbone.

She felt so hot inside. The velvet walls squeezed around him, taking every inch of him that they could. It was pure ecstasy. He decided to take his time, savoring every thrust of his cock. His hands fondled her breasts, making her nipples harden and turn to a bright red.

Sweat glistened on her hard stomach, now full with his children. Her raven hair spread out above her. *Damn it, she's so beautiful. She's mine.*

Damien leaned over, his breath hot in his lover's ear. "You're mine. All mine."

Jill turned her head to the side to allow him access to her neck. As he peppered it with kisses. His fangs brushed against her porcelain skin.

Her voice labored, just above a whisper as she said his name. "Damien..."

Her nails dug into the muscles in his shoulder blades, making him growl with primal excitement. Not much longer and he would bury himself so deeply into her warmth she would never want him to leave.

Making love to Jill never felt awkward, it felt natural. As though her body were made for him as he was for her.

Jill's screams as her orgasm hit her excited Damien. Her nails dug into his shoulder blade and back making him eager. He bit down on her shoulder, his fangs tasting her soft flesh as he pushed one more thrust into her. His own orgasm sending his warmth as far as he could go inside of her.

When Damien released his hold on Jill's shoulder, her flesh was bruised. "I'm sorry, Jill."

Laboring, Jill giggled. "It's okay. I have longed for your fangs to find my flesh more often while making love." Jill kissed Damien, gently nipping his lip. "Just so you know though, now that you've bitten, it's free game."

Damien swallowed hard, wondering just how much trouble he'd unanticipatedly gotten himself into.

CHAPTER TWENTY-SEVEN

A hazy mist ghosted its way through the camp, a cold breeze signaling the sign of the coming of the winter storms. Damien shivered as he stepped out of the warmth of his tent. Wrapping his jacket tight around himself, he walked down to the stream to get some water.

Kain stopped him. "Good morning. Would you mind bringing me back some water so I can make breakfast? The pups are practically begging for flapjacks this morning. Woke me up at the crack of dawn." He slightly laughed, handing Damien the black pot he usually used to make stew.

"Sure. I can do that." Damien took a second to think before he asked what he wanted to since the fight with Nathaniel the day before. "Kain. May I ask you something?"

Kain's head tilted to the side. A pup ran around his legs, begging him to pick it up. "Of course. Anything." He fell to his haunches, picking the pup up before rising back to his feet.

"You still don't have a beta, do you?"

"No, I hadn't chosen one yet. Why?"

Damien ran his hand through his hair down his neck, looking at the ground. "I'm not ready to be an alpha. I don't know the first thing about leading a pack. I want to learn more. Would you be willing to take me under your wing as your beta until I'm ready?"

Kain stood silent, his eyes widened in surprise. The pup snuggling into his chest had begun falling asleep in the warmth and comfort of his jacket. "I would be glad to. It would be an honor."

"Thanks. I'll be back soon."

The pot almost finished filling with water when Damien closed his eyes, taking a deep breath as the familiar scent filled his nostrils.

He rose to his feet, turning his attention to the vampire that had made herself known despite the sun rising.

"Hello, Dame." Chelsea stood in the shadows of the rocks to stay out of the sun's light.

"Chels. I'm surprised to see you again. What do you want?" Damien's sense of caution made him leery. He kept his back from being exposed to avoid a surprise attack.

Surprisingly, the look on Chelsea's face was downtrodden. "I just wanted to see you again. I'm sorry for what I did the last time we saw each other. I still see you as a friend, Dame. I don't understand why you wouldn't give us a chance to be together. You know how much I still care about you. I know you do."

"Chels, I've told you this so many times since we were kids, okay. I wasn't ready for a relationship. I had too many things I had to deal with. You remember how long it took me to even say anything to you and Rob the first time you came up to me? I was messed up." Damien's chest tightened as he thought about his encounter with Barghast.

The memories of how many times he was nearly killed only to be saved by Jill. The pain at Rob's abandonment. He was still trying to cope with all of it and now he'd had his own kid on the way.

"Chels, it doesn't matter what you may say. Nothing excuses you from what you've done. Why in the hell would you sink so low to become the jealous monster you are? I never would have expected this from you."

Chelsea sighed. "I lied, Damien. I never wanted this. After I left you on the campus, I spent most of the night sobbing into my sheets. I was hurting so bad because I loved you so much I just didn't understand why you were so against us even trying,"

She paused. Damien could see she was trying to hold back her tears. "I went for a walk that night and sat down on a bench under the trees near the shopping center. That's when he showed up. He sat down and was so kind to me. He asked why I was so upset. I mentioned I was having guy trouble so he asked me to go on."

Despite her pale complexion, Damien thought he saw a hint of shame. "He offered to take me to a hotel so I went with him. I was so upset Damien. I know I shouldn't have gone but, I was hurting so bad! The thought of someone actually caring about the pain that you would turn me away despite all those times I stood up for you against the evil things people would say made me feel better inside!"

More tears broke free of their cold prison sending jolts of pain through Damien's heart to learn she had been hurting so badly.

"I didn't know what was going on. We were having sex and the next thing I know, there's this cold running through my body. It was so cold, it was burning. I passed out and the next minute I'm looking up at Lilith. I never wanted this, Damien. He just did it to me."

"Who, Chels?" Damien's fangs elongated at how angry he was.

It didn't matter that Chelsea hadn't understood what was going on. She was still one of the only ones who stood by him after everyone else labeled him a freak. "Who did this to you?"

Chelsea choked, brushing a strand of golden hair away from her face. "Stoker. It was Stoker."

A growl, more wolf than man rose from Damien's throat. He'd already owed Stoker for all he'd done. He probably did what he did only to get back at Damien.

"He'll pay for this. I promise you, Chels. He'll pay for what he's done." Damien's fist clenched at his side. His nails drawing blood from his palm.

"It doesn't matter, Damien. Stoker isn't the one who drove me to this madness," Chelsea's eyes glowed a ruby red. Her eyes staring lustfully at his dripping hand. "This is all your fault, Damien Pierce. If you would have only given me a chance. If I can't have you, there's no way in hell I'm letting that mangy slut keep what should be mine!"

Damien barely had time to move when Chelsea ran at him, hitting him in the chest. The force was hard enough to knock him into the pool. Coughing up water, he rose to his feet, shaking off the dizziness.

Before Chelsea could hit him again, she froze in the shadows.

Damien shook the water from his face to see Kain.

"It would appear I came just in time. I must admit, it is a surprise to see a vampire risk so much just to satisfy her own petty jealousy." Kain straightened from his leaning position against a nearby tree.

"Stay out of this, Kain! It has nothing to do with an outcast like you!"

"An outcast? Really? I can see Stoker has been telling lies again. Be that as it may, I am not below silencing a newborn who has yet to even break in her new fangs. Leave or I will make sure you will despise the day you were turned." Kain began stepping slowly towards her, giving Damien time to get out of the water.

"Calen, come back here!" A mother's call to her pup grabbed the attention of both lycans. A small pup ran towards Damien only to be snagged by Chelsea and raised as a shield.

"Chelsea, no! Don't!" Damien tried to reason with his friend. "Please, don't do this!"

The pup began whimpering as the vampire's hold grew tighter. "Let me go or I'll kill it. I mean it Kain. Back the fuck off or I'll kill this mangy dog." Smirking she squeezed tighter, making the pup begin to gasp for air.

"Calen!" The mother tried to push by Kain only to be stopped. "No! My baby!"

Something inside Damien snapped. The pup's whimpers of pain combined with his mother's pleas for his life sent waves of pure rage through him.

Without thinking he threw his full weight into the air, shifting mid-jump to land on Chelsea. The pup went flying as she tried to stop him only to find her neck pierced by his fangs. Her blood flowing from her jugular vein in pools of black tar.

Kain picked up the pup, handing him back to his mom.

"Thank you. Thank you, Kain." She held Calen close, kissing his furry cheek.

"It's not me you should be thanking." Kain's expression turned sullen as he focused on the sight in front of him.

Damien knelt on the ground holding his friend as she lay dying. Her head resting in his lap.

"Damien? Where am I?"

Damien's surprised eyes met Chelsea's own crystal blue. She was once again the friend he remembered. Not the dark, jealous vampire she had become. "I'm here, Chels. You're with me."

A tired smile fell across her face as she reached up to touch Damien's face. "Did I...get the ball we lost in old man Jamison's yard?"

Damien's heart sank. Chelsea had gone back to a memory when they were kids. They had been playing with a soccer ball in the front yard of his parents' house and accidentally kicked it into the grumpy neighbor's yard. Chelsea had gone to get it since she was the only one that could fit through the broken fence posts.

"Yes, Chels. You did." Damien replied, trying not to break.

She smiled, tears falling down her face. "I'm glad. I know...it was...your favorite ball." Her eyes closed. The sun peeking through the clouds fell on her body, rendering it into nothing but ash.

Damien didn't move, his lap was covered in the remains of one of his dearest friends. His heart torn to pieces that things had gotten so out of control. *If only I hadn't...come back...*

"Kain, have you seen Damien?" Jill's worried voice alerted the alpha who seemed deep in thought. He was still trying to make dinner for the begging, hungry pups.

"I'm sorry Jillian, I haven't seen him since this morning. I will go look for him if you want to take this over," Kain handed her the ladle he had been using to make his homemade chili. "Be careful. Some of them are so hungry they're biting."

Jill shook her head, taking the spoon. A concerned expression on her face. "I will. Thank you, Kain."

When Kain found him, Damien had isolated himself in the Circle of Stones. His back leaned against them. The look in his amethyst eyes fierce as he stared at the ground.

"There you are. I have been looking for you. May I join you?" Damien didn't say anything so Kain sat down next to him. "Jillian is worried about you. Perhaps you should at least send her a howl so she knows you are alright?"

Damien continued to ignore him, clasping Chelsea's blue bird necklace her mom had given her for Christmas in his hand. She'd worn it almost every day in her life. It had been hidden among her ashes.

"Damien, I understand how you feel. It grieves me to see you go through such pain."

"Does it, Kain?" Damien's voice was full of anger and sadness as he cut Kain off. "Does it grieve you?"

"Damien, calm down. I had to kill a friend too, remember? She became a werewolf so I had to hunt her down and kill her with my own fangs. We have all lost loved ones in this war."

"I didn't have to! I wasn't a part of this! I should never have come back to this place!" Damien threw his fist into the stone behind him so hard his knuckle cracked against the pressure.

"What about Jillian? You love her, do you not? Our world is not for the weak of heart, Damien. We lose loved ones. We bury our pups and have to hide to avoid being killed. Still, we find reasons and people to keep living for," Kain rose from his seat.

As he prepared to leave, he turned around. "What are your reasons to keep living? Who are the people that would grieve if they lost you?"

Damien felt his heart grow lighter as Kain's words began to sink in. He had lost some friends but gained a family. "You're right, Kain. I'm sorry I lost my temper with you. Things have just gotten so insane."

"It is alright. I have been through it a few times. You are allowed to hurt, to grieve. However, in the wake of war is not the time to mourn those you have lost," A howl in the distance made Kain's ears perk towards the town. "That was Vincent. We need to go back."

Kain began running back towards the camp, shifting mid-run into his wolf form. Damien joined him, tripping as he went from two legs to four.

Kain has got to teach me how to change like that.

Holt stood with Gabriel, Lune, Jill and Clint when the two lycans returned. Both shifting into their human forms.

"There you two are. Where in sun's hell have you been?" Holt greeted Kain with a hard pat on his shoulder.

"Learning a lesson." Kain looked over his shoulder at Jill. She was kissing Damien smack on the lips, passionately.

Gabriel handed him a pair of jeans and his favorite plaid jacket. "Glad you found him. Vincent told us that Lilith is on the move. Apparently, she's heading this way. We better stop her from getting too far into the forest. We can't risk being found," Gabriel shook his friend's hand. "Damien, we have to be heading out. You two can pillow talk later."

Jill flipped him off, kissing Damien on the lips again before nudging him away, smirking as she walked back into her tent.

"Woman is still a total badass." Gabriel snickered as he ran his hand through his dark hair.

"I'm ready. Where're we going?"

"A rather undesired meeting." Kain's gaze intensified as he followed the other alphas out of the camp towards Holt's truck.

Damien followed closely. His gut churning at the idea that he would have to see the vampires again so soon.

CHAPTER TWENTY-EIGHT

Holt stood next to his truck, the only one in his human form. Damien, Kain, Gabriel and Lune all flanked him, ready to defend him if needed.

Lilith stepped out of the black limousine after her guard, as big as a bouncer, opened the door for her.

Rayes stayed sitting on his black Harley motorcycle. His leg propped up on the saddle with a rather smug look on his face despite the cigarette he smoked. Stoker got out of the other side of the limo.

The glare of utter hate and vengeance met Damien's eyes. Damien growled, his muscles tensed as he tried to stay in place.

"We come under the flag of parlay, dog. We give our words to keep the peace as long as you do the same. Got it?" Lilith said, disgusted.

Holt uncrossed his legs and arms, stepping forward. "Fine with me, bloodsucker. So, what's this little soiree about?"

Lilith looked at the new white wolf. Smirking, she addressed Holt. "Shut your trap, mutt. I refuse to talk to you. However," Lilith seductively walked forward, her eyes locked hungrily on Damien. "I will talk to him. I missed you, precious."

"He's not your concern, parasite." Holt spat angrily at Lilith's disrespect. A low growl escaping his throat.

"Either Damien talks to me or we slaughter more humans in a fortnight than the rotten deer you pathetic beasts hunt in an hour. The beauty of it is, we can make sure the humans think it's rabid wolves." Lilith smirked a wicked grin, kicking her hip out.

Damien gritted his teeth. He didn't want to shift in front of Lilith and give her the satisfaction of seeing him in his full glory. After glancing at Kain, he dropped his head. If he refused, the pack would be in even more danger.

"Fine, Lilith. You want to talk, I'll talk." Damien walked forward, his body guarded by Kain.

Ignoring Kain, Lilith walked towards him, getting uncomfortably close to Damien. The proximity crushing Kain's head between the two of them. The alpha let out a whimper.

"So gorgeous. Your body remains a masterpiece despite the smell of wet dog." Damien winced as Lilith ran her nails down his pectoral muscle. "I'll still take you, precious. I'll forgive your rotten bitch for scarring my face if you would but come with me."

Kain snapped. He began growling and snapping at Lilith, forcing her to step back.

Damien dropped to his knees, his arms wrapping around his friend's neck. "Easy, easy, Kain. I'm not going anywhere. Thank you for your concern but I promise I'm not leaving."

Damien patted Kain's sandy fur, the alpha still snarling and growling.

"Fine, dog. You want to end this peacefully? I would be willing to but I want something in exchange. How about it?" Lilith watched Kain and Holt intently.

Gabriel cocked his head to the side. The look in his eyes suspicious while Lune tightened his brow to a thin line.

"You would end this peacefully? What is it you would want for such a steep offer?" Holt replied. His eyes flashed a look of caution. His body posture stiff and rigid.

"Damien comes with me. He's the price I'll accept for a peaceful ending to this. Otherwise, we shed the blood of your females, your wounded, your elderly, and those pathetic pups."

"Fuck that!" Holt stepped in front of Damien who was still trying to calm his alpha.

Kain jerked against his hold, nailing him in the jaw with his head.

Stoker stepped forward, his eyes locked on Damien's. "I have an idea, Lilith. Since they refuse to end things amicably, why not choose a decent battleground? I have one in mind."

"And where is that Stoker?" Lilith replied, rolling her eyes.

"The Circle of Stones. It lies in a clearing deep in the mountains. Five nights from now. If they refuse, we go through with slaughtering the humans and offering these dogs up as scapegoats. How does that sound?" Stoker grinned a wicked grin at the look in Damien's eyes.

Lilith actually laughed. "It's perfect!"

The lycans' eyes all grew as big as plates. It was the ultimate disrespect. The Circle of Stones was once a sacred place. The very ground holy to the lycans of the mountains.

"Well? Accept the terms or lose your freedom to hunt without being hunted yourselves." Lilith placed one hand on her hip, the other running through her platinum blonde hair.

Damien's body went stiff with rage. His mind battled itself. If he gave up, agreed to be Lilith's, then the Circle of Stones wouldn't be defiled. If he didn't, the most sacred place to the lycans would be soiled.

As if he understood the turmoil Damien's mind was in, Kain nuzzled his face, whimpering.

"Fine. We agree. Five days." Holt's voice sounded defeated.

Damien looked up at Holt. The alpha was willing to sacrifice his sacred site to protect him.

Holt looked down at him, smiling. "What? There was no way I was going to let a friend, let alone, Kain's beta to be turned into some slave for a bloodsucker. He'd never let me hear the end of it."

Kain groaned, dropping his head.

Lilith jeered at the lycans. "Glad that's settled. Now if you don't mind, I don't wish to be in your company anymore. Damien, if you change your mind, you are welcome to come alone to the coven. I'll welcome you any time." Lilith blew an air kiss to Damien, getting into the limo.

Rayes chuckled as he revved his engine, tearing the tire of his bike across the ground.

Stoker scowled at Damien mouthing to him "I will see you on the battlefield, Pierce," before joining Lilith in the car.

When the alphas returned to the camp, Yuna and Galeck met them.

"Your spirits are low. Did something happen in your meeting with the vampires, my lord?" Yuna walked next to Damien, the look in her eyes troubled.

"They want to have the fight in the Circle of Stones." Kain stayed near Damien, obviously worried. Damien felt connected to the alpha. His chest felt burdened as if he could feel his friend's need for his comfort.

Jill walked up to them, her hand running down Kain's sandy fur. He turned nuzzling her hand.

"That is the ultimate dishonor. Centuries have gone by and still they have no respect. We will have to devise a clever strategy to end this quickly." Yuna replied, her anger apparent.

Damien had been thinking about that on the ride back in Holt's truck. "I think I may have one, Yuna. We need to get everyone to Holt's tent. I'll meet you there shortly."

Damien took Jill by the hand, leading her to their tent and zipping the door closed.

"I don't like this. What you're proposing is dangerous." Jill handed Damien some clothes.

"I know, Jill. But what choice do we have? My dad sent me a text telling me people are starting to panic. He says he can't keep covering for much longer. If we don't end this soon, then we won't be able to provide for our families. We'll have to leave and lycans like Rayna and Betsy who are just trying to live in peace will be killed during some crazed witch hunt."

Damien took his lover in his arms, his hand petting her lower belly. "You're not fighting Jill. You can't. If my plan works, we'll be able to end most of the coven if not all of them."

"I understand, but..." Damien stopped Jill with a deep kiss.

"I will come back. I promise you. Both of you. This is no longer about us Jill. It's about our packs. If we do nothing, they'll die. Trust me."

"I do." Jill placed her hand on Damien's on her cheek. "Come back to me, I beg you. I've already almost lost you so many times. I would die without you."

Damien kissed Jill one last time and left the tent.

Jill followed him, watching his back as he walked away. Her eyes filled with tears she had been holding back. The thought that she could lose him tore at her heart and ravaged her mind. *Please Tenebris. He is your son. He doesn't have to but, he's chosen to fight for those he considers his family. I beg you, Night Father, please protect him.*

Holt, Yuna, Galeck, Kain, and Gabriel all sat around a small fire in Holt's tent. Channon, Harou, Dolph, Damien and Cade all sat next to their alphas, the room silent until Galeck spoke up.

"So, we all know we need to cover the major players. Jill was set to handle Lilith, yet she isn't here. Damien, is she still alright to fight?"

Damien closed his eyes, sighing. He hadn't told anyone about the baby yet. "No. She isn't." Every eye in the room fell on him, Kain's the most intense. "She's pregnant. I told her she wasn't fighting."

Kain's expression went from curiosity to shock. The room echoed the look in his eyes.

"Congratulations, my lord. A new life is indeed precious. However, now Lilith is left uncontended with on the battlefield. Do we have an alternate plan?" Yuna bowed to Damien as she congratulated him.

"I'll handle Lilith." Damien volunteered, earning the immediate protest of the leaders. All except Kain who closed his eyes, clenching his teeth.

"No offense, Damien but Lilith is a vampire noble...there's something..."

"Enough, Holt," Kain's voice silenced the room. "None of you understand the power Damien has. His determination alone is enough to defy every leader in here, even me. If he chooses to face Lilith, I will back his decision,

"Holt, you have a score to settle with Rayes so handle him. Gabriel, take Stoker. Damien and I will take Lilith and allow the rest of the pack to handle the others. The first plan hasn't changed. As long as we can remove Lilith, the others will fall by the wayside."

"We may not have to take the others." Damien took out a piece of paper he'd gotten out of Holt's truck. Crudely drawing the meadow's layout, he put the map in view of the leaders. "Look, I know this place. I've stood in it, trained in it. I know what to do."

Damien drew a compass rose. "Look, the meadow is a wide open field. They'll be risking way too much by staying so exposed. They'll arrive just as the sun is setting so they can retreat into the woods as the sun rises."

He closed his eyes, remembering the vision of Tenebris and Barghast. The battle they were in. It all fell perfectly as a battle plan in his mind. "Galeck, Yuna, the secret is to make them think we have fewer of us than we really do. Galeck, you keep your pack on the west side. Yuna, you keep your pack in the east ring of the forest. Stay hidden and quiet. The rest of us will focus our attention in the center. We'll meet them in the evening and hold them until the sun rises the following morning. Whichever way they go, they'll meet our fangs waiting for them."

Kain began seeing Damien's plan fall into place. "Astounding. They'll run right into Galeck as they try to flee to the west following the night towards the mountains, cut off from the coven."

"Impressive. A trap. We just have to manage to hold them." Galeck smiled in awe at the young lycan's plan. "What's the plan to hold them?"

"Stamina. We don't directly engage and avoid direct contact unless needed. They may be strong but we hunt every night and have to outlast the stamina of our prey. We'll outlast them. We know the layout of the land in the mountains and woods better than they do," Lune chimed in from the back of the room. "The vampires focus on luxury and rarely ever fight unless they need to. A fatal flaw we can exploit."

"Exactly. We outlast them. We don't have the handicap they do. Even Lilith will fall if exposed to the sun's light directly. We simply use the sun to our advantage." Damien ended his speech with a deep breath of relief.

"Amazing. Truly amazing. Fight without fighting. Well done." Kain patted Damien's shoulder.

"Well alright. We have a plan and it should work even if we do have lower numbers. I'm impressed, Damien. That's really well thought out." Holt shook Damien's hand, grabbing him in a headlock and ruffling his hair with his knuckles.

It was so uncomfortable it made Damien feel bad for every time he'd done it to Rob.

Damien stepped out of the tent with Kain to see Nathaniel walking up to them. His fists rolled into balls at his sides. His brow crinkled.

"Hey Damien."

"Nathaniel."

Nathaniel scratched the back of his head, his face turned towards the ground as though he were embarrassed at what he was about to say. "Look, uh. I've been talking to Lune and I wanted to apologize. To you too, Kain."

Kain and Damien both looked at each other and back at Nathaniel.

"I know. I've been a real jerk. I'd like to help in any way I can. I know Holt doesn't have many soldiers so I'd like to offer what remains of my pack or, my former pack to try to help out in the fight. We aren't much but..."

"You are more than enough. Thank you." Damien placed his hands on Nathaniel's shoulders, relieved they were getting more help.

Nathaniel softly smiled, nodding. "You're welcome, my alpha."

It took a moment for Damien to register what he'd just been called. A feeling of nervousness settled in his gut. He walked off from both lycans to try and do some final mental preparation for what was fixing to transpire.

CHAPTER TWENTY-NINE

"S omething bothering you?" Kain sat next to Damien on the log next to the main campfire. "You just gave us an amazing plan. It was based on the vision you had, wasn't it?"

"Yeah. You told me to be mindful of signs. When Jill could no longer fight and Lilith named the battleground, it just clicked in my mind. I'm still not sure about so many things, Kain."

"Like what?"

"Like whether or not I can actually handle Lilith? If I can even fight well despite all the training."

"You will do just fine, Damien. You have heart, guts and spirit. Besides, you won't be alone. You have allies ready to back you," Damien glanced at Kain, swearing he saw him wincing in pain. "I have to go for now but I will see you in the morning."

Damien watched as the alpha walked away, his spirit bothered to the suddenness of his departure. Kain never left with such short advice.

He decided that in the morning he would go see his dad, just in case something did happen to him during the fight with the vampires.

Standing in front of his house, Damien took a deep breath and exhaled. His dad's cruiser was in the driveway. As soon as Damien felt ready, he unlocked the door and walked in.

"Dad?"

"In the living room, come on in."

Damien walked into the living room to find his dad sitting in his lounge chair.

Charlie looked tired. He'd kept in contact with Damien via text message, working late nights to try and keep the panic from taking hold.

"How have you been, Dame?"

"Busy." Damien hadn't thought about how he was going to tell his dad about Chelsea's death or how he was going to be a grandpa. "Dad, how would you feel about being a grandpa?"

Charlie's eyes grew as wide as quarters. "Are you kidding me? Damien, that's amazing! Yes! I'm ecstatic! I was beginning to think I'd never get grandkids!"

Damien smiled, sighing since the next bit of news he'd had wasn't that great. " Look uh, about Chelsea, " Damien clenched his teeth, the words still felt so unreal to him.

"What?"

"Chelsea...moved." Damien cursed under his breath at the lie but he couldn't bring himself to say it out loud.

"Ah, well that's too bad. She was a good kid. Hopefully she finds a new love interest considering the one she had here just randomly brought his girlfriend home." Charlie chuckled at his joke.

Damien gagged on the coffee he was drinking. " Yeah, I bet that was odd. It was good to see you again."

"Dame, I hope you and Alex have a plan. I've been working my fingers to the bone to keep folks calm but I can't lie much longer. They're starting to panic."

"I know. We have a plan. It'll all be okay soon. I have to be getting back though."

"Okay. Come back soon, son. I miss having you around. Let me know when the baby is due, I'll get you some diapers." Charlie chuckled, getting up out of his chair to follow Damien to the door.

He placed his hand firmly on his son's shoulder. "Damien, kids can change a man. Make sure you are more than you ever were as a father. They need you to be at one-hundred-eighty percent."

Damien swallowed hard at the weight of his father's words. He nodded, revving up the engine up his motorcycle.

"D! Hey, D!"

A familiar voice had Damien nearly dropping the hot tea in his hands. He'd stopped by Rayna and Betsy's coffee shop to get a drink to help him against the cold air and a sense of normalcy.

Rob sat down across from him at the metal table.

"Rob? I thought you couldn't be involved with me anymore." Damien looked away, thinking about Chelsea.

"I was wrong, D. I've missed you, man. We were like bros. I was wrong to bail when you needed me most. If you can forgive me, I'd like to try and help in whatever way I can."

Damien couldn't believe what he was hearing. "I don't understand, Rob. Why the sudden change of heart?"

"Charlie's been talking to me. Says things are really bad for...you guys," he looked around trying not to mention the lycans. "Look, I can't stay long or Langston will hang me for being late but I wanted you to know, I have your back, bro. Whatever it is. By the way, have you seen Chels? Her folks hadn't seen her either. They moved to England of all places."

Damien sighed. There was no way he could lie to Rob knowing he'd spoken to Chelsea's parents. "She's dead, Rob."

The look on his friend's face was a mix of pure terror and sadness. "What? When? How? Was it them?"

Setting his tea on the table, Damien took the blue bird necklace out of his pocket, showing it to Rob. He'd carried it as a reminder of how badly he was going to maim Stoker when they met.

"Christ, D. I... I almost don't..."

"I know. Me neither. I'll make them pay. For myself, Jill and Chelsea. I promise." Damien stood up from the chair, patting Rob's shoulder.

"Be careful man. There've been more disappearances going on. Folks are starting to blame the wolves around here. Something's gotten into them."

Damien winced. Things were getting out of control just as his dad said. The lycans were running out of time. If they were to survive the winter, something had to be done.

"Thanks. I'll be careful. You do the same. It's not the wolves, you know this. Try to keep people from blaming them. Just a few more days."

Rob started to talk but Damien didn't hear him. He'd become too concerned with getting the information Rob and his dad gave him to Holt and Kain. He was just glad that Rob came back. No way did Damien want to lose him like he'd lost Chelsea.

Damien parked and got off his motorcycle to start walking back to the camp, the cool of the night kissing his cheeks. It was nice to have some time to himself to think and enjoy his favorite tea again. It gave him space to destress despite the looming war with the vampires.

He'd reached a small clearing when his chest started burning so badly it forced him to his knees in the snow. Try as he might, he couldn't seem to catch a breath, his lungs seizing with each attempt.

Damien abruptly found himself on his side as though he'd been hit by something. The intense heat inside of him kept him from moving as he got hit again and again by something solid. Something colder than even the winter air around him.

What's going on? It feels like I'm getting hit but I can't see anything. Damien attempted to get on his feet only to have his legs taken back out from underneath him. With each hit, he felt a piece of his strength sucked out of him.

Barely able to move, Damien lay on his stomach. His eyes blurry as he made out a dark shape. *The hell is that? A giant, black claw?*

A giant claw dangled in front of Damien. Its twisted, blackened shape hung in such a way it was if it dangled from a lamp post. It started speeding towards Damien, kicking up waves of cold snow.

"Damien!" Just as it was about to hit him, he heard a familiar voice call his name prior to sinking into unconsciousness.

"He's waking up! Oh, thank Luna!" Leah, Holt's mate's voice came through the hazy blur of Damien's mind.

"What? What happened?" Damien saw Kyle next to him, putting something into his doctor's bag and closing it.

Jill hugged her mate close, careful not to hurt his ribs. "You were attacked by something in the forest. We don't know what happened but Lune brought you back here."

Damien rubbed his head. His ribs bandaged from his mid-torso down. He barely remembered what happened and still wasn't sure he believed what he'd seen. Looking around there was one lycan he didn't see.

"Kain. Oh God, Kain!" Damien suddenly remembered the voice that called his name. "Jill, where's Kain?"

Jill looked away from him. "He's not doing so well. He was hurt really bad."

Despite Jill and Kyle's protest, Damien got to his feet, pushing past Gabriel to go find Kain.

The lycan alpha was in his tent, lying on the floor on his side. His breath was heavy against the deep wound now laying across his flesh. It had been bandaged. Blood stained the white padding.

Damien knelt beside him, looking at the still-bleeding wound. "Kain, what was that? What happened?"

Kain clenched his teeth against the pain wracking his body, opening his eyes. "Don't worry...about it. You aren't ready, Damien. Please...just trust me." Exhausted, Kain closed his eyes.

"Don't tell me not to worry about it when you have a gaping gash in your side, you asshole." Damien stayed next to Kain trying to think of a way he could help.

A thought struck him about something Jill had once done. *Would that even work? I mean, I can heal myself from wounds like this.* "Kain, if you can hear me. Would you lay on your back? I may be able to help."

Struggling, Kain rolled over onto his back. "Don't do anything insane. Not so close to the battle."

"You aren't anyone to order me not to do anything insane. I'm not the one homing crocodiles in the Nile of my own blood." Damien took the knife he'd used to puncture the line of his truck during his fight with Stoker, out of his pocket. *God, I hope this works.* He cut his finger, flinching at the sting.

If his healing ability transferred through blood, maybe he could heal Kain. He would also be able to talk to him on the battlefield. From what Jill told him, blood was their way of speaking when they were apart.

"Here."

Kain opened his eyes to see Damien holding his hand out to him, his finger bleeding from a fresh cut. "I was right, you are insane."

"Shut up and take it. Don't make this weirder than it already is."

Hesitantly, Kain sat up. Taking Damien's wrist, he lapped up the blood on his finger. "It feels like pure sunlight in my body. There's definitely more to you than any of us can understand." Kain rose to his feet. "It has been so long since I've felt this strong."

"Great. As if you couldn't kick my ass before. Do me a favor and don't tell anyone. The whole blood thing is still so strange to me." Damien got up with Kain, putting his knife back in his pocket.

"Why?"

"Because where I came from, we don't exactly share blood to talk to each other. As a matter of fact, it's seen as unsanitary."

A "tsk" sound came from between Kain's teeth. "Blood is a bond. Families are bonded by the blood they share. Children connected to their mothers get their blood in the womb. Blood is given to patients of severe trauma to save their lives. It is a powerful life giver. To a lycan there is nothing strange about what happened. I may not have been able to get up if you hadn't thought to act as you did."

Once again, Kain made Damien second guess what he thought was reality. He was right, blood was powerful. Maybe that was why the lycans valued it as much as they did.

CHAPTER THIRTY

Two days remained until the final battle at the Circle of Stones. Damien spent most of his time at Kain's side preparing both the soldiers and the lycans that would be left behind. Each one looked more uneasy than the last.

"Kain, they look scared. Do you think they have faith in the plan we have?" Damien watched each face as they walked passed him. Hopelessness and despair seemed to loom in each eye.

"That is normal, Damien. For many of them this is the first time they have seen battle in centuries. For others, they have never experienced one since arriving in the new world. That is why they came here in the first place. Take some time to rest and be with Jillian." Kain replied, holding his signature confidence in times of turmoil.

Damien couldn't help his own inner feeling of discord at the upcoming war. He had nightmares almost every night after the meeting with Lilith. Even going as far as to entertain the idea of surrendering himself to end things peacefully.

Calen made his way beside Damien after he sat on the log in front of the main campfire. His mother sat on the log next to him.

"My lord, I wanted to thank you personally for saving Calen's life. If there is anything I can do to return the favor, please don't hesitate to ask."

Damien looked at her, smiling. She always had such a soft face despite the fact he never saw her with a mate. "Where's Calen's father?"

She lowered her head, her hands clasped in her lap. She grimaced, her eyes squeezing shut. "My mate is dead, my lord. He fought in a battle much like this one many moons ago."

"Oh. I'm sorry. I shouldn't have asked. It was none of my business." Damien picked Calen up, holding him in his arms. The pup hugged Damien with his paws on his shoulder.

She smiled. "He loves you. Please don't apologize, my lord. It's been a while since someone has asked. You bring us hope. Thank you for coming. I had begun to think we had been forsaken."

"I'm..." Damien paused. He still held doubts that he could do what everyone expected of him. Calen looked up at him, his tail wagging. Damien pet his head, smiling. "I'm glad I could help."

The mother smiled, taking Calen. "Alright you rascal, it's your nap time. Leave Lord Damien alone for once, will you?"

Gabriel took her seat after she left. He had a piece of straw sticking out of his mouth. "Have to hand it to you, that's the first time I've seen Zasha smile in a while. I have to thank you for that."

"You're welcome but what does that mean?" Damien asked, puzzled.

"Zasha was my brother's mate. He lost his life just before we moved to the States in a vampire attack. She always had such a bright smile until he died. Then she rarely ever smiled."

A small gasp escaped Damien's throat. "Gabriel, I didn't know you had a brother. I'm sorry about your loss."

"It's okay. Azazel never was one to crumble under too much pressure. If it weren't for him and a few others staying behind, we probably wouldn't have been able to get out alive," Gabriel took the straw out of his mouth. "Look, as much as I hate to admit it, you have brought light back to the packs around here. It was dark and hopeless until you came. I'm sorry I was such a jerk."

"It's okay. I keep telling everyone I'm no one special. I'm still not sure how to take all of the 'my lord' and 'my alpha' comments."

Gabriel burst out laughing. "Don't sweat it. Just take the compliments. Kain told me what you did for him. From the bottom of my heart, Damien, thank you. You may have saved my life too."

Before Damien could inquire about what Gabriel meant by yet another cryptic comment, Jill wrapped her arms around his shoulders.

"You seem deep in thought. I saw you talking to Zasha. Do you know who she is?"

Damien nodded, reaching up behind him to touch Jill's face. "I'm nervous, Jill."

Jill made her way around the log. Standing above her mate, she held her hands out. "Come. You need comfort. You won't find it out here with everyone staring."

Damien got up, letting Jill lead him to their tent.

Once inside, Jill led Damien to the bed. "Wait here. I have something Leah wanted me to give you when the time was right. I think now might be the time."

Jill walked behind the separating curtain Yuna got her as a welcome present to the pack. Her silken body nothing but a solid shape as she got undressed.

"Jill, do you ever wonder what things would have been like if I never came back here? Maybe you all would be able to still be at peace if I didn't show up." Damien still couldn't shake the feeling that he could have been a key factor in all of the death and chaos.

Resting his elbows on his knees, he leaned forward, his hands clenched together in front of him. *What if all of this is because of me? If I hadn't come back, maybe Gabriel would still have his gym. Kain wouldn't have been hurt and Chase would probably still be alive. What if all of this is my fault?*

The shadow above him brought his attention to Jill. She wore a silken blue dress so light it almost looked white. The thin material did little to hide her slender form, hugging the curves of her body.

Damien's mouth about fell open. "Jill. You look so beautiful. This is the first time I've seen you in a dress."

Jill blushed, playing with her dark hair, pulling it to one side. "Yeah, I know. Leah said the same thing. She made it herself."

"I'll have to remember to thank her." Damien pulled Jill close to him, his hands savoring her porcelain skin.

"Damien, may I come in?" Kain's voice echoed on the other side of the door.

Damien cursed under his breath. "Yeah, just a sec." He kissed Jill. "We'll continue this later. I'm going to need it."

Jill smiled, petting his face. "As am I."

Kain led Damien to his tent. "Forgive my intrusion on your time with Jillian. I wanted to tell you one last thing before the fight. Holt nearly mentioned it in the meeting but I stopped him because it wasn't the time or the place."

"What is it?" Damien replied, curious.

"The dark secret of the vampire noble. As it is with us, the vampire nobles and high class have the ability to change into more powerful forms. Unlike lycans however, they only have a single transformation. I have only seen it once in my many years but it is very formidable."

Kain pulled a box out from under a pile of old books and blankets. It was covered in dust as though Kain had been trying to bury the memory.

Laying it down before Damien, he opened it, revealing what looked like a talon.

"Kain, what is this?" Damien took it in his hands, carefully examining the detail.

"It was pulled out of my father's side. When he returned, his body was dripping blood, his side ripped open," Kain lowered his head. "Damien, he was in his full lycan form. Whatever left this has power. I want you to be very, very careful. Lilith most likely has the power to become the monster much like the one that left this talon."

Damien's breath stalled in his lungs. From what he learned about their history, Pentacost Kain was one of the strongest lycan soldiers in the war.

To hear he was torn apart so badly in full lycan form by something that Lilith could possibly become sucked any hope Damien had of having a chance against her out of him.

"Kain, I can't fight her. What if I'm not strong enough?" Damien raced in his chest as fear fought to take hold of him.

Kain took the talon, placing it back in the box. "Damien, you are more than strong enough. Lilith is inexperienced and most likely whatever it was that took down my father was much more powerful. I just wanted you to be aware of her ability. I will be by your side against her. Gabriel and I have already talked about it. Holt, Yuna, Galeck and Lune agree it's the best course of action. Just be ready."

Damien nodded, his words freezing in his throat.

"Good. The moon rises. I must hunt with Gabriel and Lune. Damien, if you need to, you may stay here tonight. I know Jillian does not yet understand how strong your bond with the gods is. It may help to be in the company of someone that does. For now, though, I believe I interrupted something between the two of you. Hell hath no fury and all that." Kain walked out chuckling.

Jill rested her cheek against the warmth of Damien's shoulder blade, her hips fitting comfortably in the grooves of his lower back.

"Damien, you've been silent since you came back from your visit with Kain. Is something bothering you?"

Damien couldn't respond. His mind was plagued with doubt and chaos as he tried to find peace.

Even Jill's warm, silken body against his back hadn't helped ease the strain he was under.

He thought about much pain Pentacost must have been in from his wounds. How Kain must have felt seeing his father so torn apart. It must have devastated him.

"Damien. Please, let me in. What's troubling you?" Jill ran her hand up her mate's shoulder blade, down his arm. The tension in his muscles both concerned and stirred a sense of desire in her.

"I'm not sure what I'm doing anymore. Kain told me the nobles can transform too. I still can't become my full lycan form. I've tried but I can't seem to figure it out."

Jill moved to sit beside him, rubbing the tense muscles of his back. "Damien, you have to let go of doubt. Remember? In order to become a true lycan, you must banish regret. Its power cannot be used for revenge, even against vampires."

"I thought that was to prevent someone from becoming a werewolf."

"It carries into the change. If your heart's intention is to take revenge or you have doubt or regret, you can never become a true lycan."

Damien got up from the bed. He needed some time to spend with a certain god and he knew exactly where to go. The Circle of Stones.

The following morning was the eve of the final battle. Holt was speaking with Kain, Gabriel, Galeck and Yuna when Damien came out of his tent, his muscles sore.

"Damien." Kain bowed his head as Damien walked over to them.

"Morning Kain. What'd I miss?"

Kain's eyes narrowed, almost appearing to study him. "Nothing. We were just going over the strategy one more time."

"It looks like we're going to have to try and push things a bit. Luckily for us, the vampires won't be able to appear until sundown. We just have to make sure to keep morale up until we're able to actually meet the bloodsuckers." Holt said as he went over the rough map again with the other leaders.

"My lord, perhaps if you spoke to them. They may be inclined to keep their spirits high if they heard you encourage them." Yuna addressed Damien who focused intently on the map in front of him.

Kain's gaze never left Damien's eyes.

"I will but for now, let them spend time with their families." Damien replied, his voice devoid of the fear and uncertainty of the day before.

The leaders all nodded their agreement, dispersing to spend some time with their family and friends.

"Damien, a minute?" Kain's voice had Damien stopping in his tracks.

"What's up?"

"Not here. Come with me, please." Kain led Damien to his tent. "Have a seat. I'll make us some coffee."

Damien sat down, puzzled as to why Kain was acting more strange than usual. When the alpha returned he sat down across from his friend.

"Damien, your eyes. I can see the change in them. Did something happen?"

"I had a word with Tenebris, Kain. I asked him for some help."

"Regarding what?"

"Peace. I've been so full of doubt and confusion recently. Jill told me I would never know what it was like to be a true lycan if I didn't clear my heart and soul of regret, revenge and doubt. I asked for help with that." Damien focused on the floor in front of him. He'd begun to feel lighter after the god took the negative feelings from him.

"That would explain your eyes. I take it that your mind feels clearer, now?" Kain smiled.

"Yeah. It feels nice. I feel lighter. Tenebris wasn't thrilled, but he did what I asked of him."

"That's understandable. He doesn't usually like to influence the feelings of his children but he has been known to do things for us he otherwise wouldn't want to."

The pain on Kain's face made Damien tilt his head in question.

Kain grinned. "It's nothing. Go be with Jillian. We start packing to leave in the morning. It will be at least a half a day's travel with supplies on our backs."

"Alright. Thanks, Kain. Look, I don't know what's going on with you but the offer for help extends both ways. If you ever need anything, ask." Damien reached out his hand which Kain took with a warm smile.

"I will. Thank you, my friend."

CHAPTER THIRTY-ONE

Jill held onto Damien's waist, her face buried into his chest. "I don't like this. I don't like you going somewhere I can't watch over you."

"Jill, I have to. They're all counting on me. If we don't end this now, we're all going to die." Damien guided her face to look up at him. "Trust me. I promised you last night while we were making love, remember?"

He dropped to his haunches, kissing Jill's stomach. His hand rubbed soft, reassuring circles over her womb. "I am coming back. To both of you. Stay here, wait for me."

Hesitantly, Jill let her lover's hand go, watching him as he walked away.

"Damien!" Gabriel came running up to Damien, panting. "He won't listen. I've tried and tried."

"Whoa, whoa. Gabriel, who won't listen? About what?"

"Kain, he's not doing well. He's not fit to fight but he won't listen to me. Please, I need you to talk some sense into him."

Damien set his bag down, walking with Gabriel to where Kain stood using a tree to support his weight. His breath was labored, his body covered with the fresh gashes Damien hadn't seen in a while. They were angry, as if whatever made them tried to keep Kain from fighting.

"You can save your breath. I am fighting. No one is going to tell me otherwise." Kain snapped at Damien before he even had a chance to speak.

"Good, I wasn't going to. Can you even walk, Kain?"

"Hell yes, I can still walk."

Damien threw a bag at the alpha. "Then carry that. Whatever you do, asshole, don't die on the field or I'll kick your ass myself. Deal?"

For the first time in their history together, Kain actually burst out laughing. "Alright. Deal. Same goes for you by the way."

They shook hands in agreement.

"This was not what I hoped you would do!" Gabriel spat at Damien who just shrugged.

"What? Did you actually think I could stop him from going? If you did, you're more insane than he is." Damien replied, chuckling.

Gabriel stood visually dumbfounded as Damien turned on his heel.

Holt, Kain and even Lune all fought back laughs at their fellow alpha's embarrassment.

Upon arriving at the Circle of Stones, the lycans started setting up fires to prepare the food for an early dinner before the sun started setting just inside the ridges of the forest.

Yuna and Galeck positioned their packs as planned.

"Damien, talk to them. They need some encouragement." Holt pleaded.

"Holt, I'm not much of a public speaker. I wouldn't know what to say. They need to have faith for their families and friends who need them. Not for a single person. Besides, I have a friend in need of help. He's not doing well and I can't be both places at once." Damien walked off, leaving Holt who seemed satisfied with his answer.

Kain lay on his side, his body hot to the touch from a fever trying to manifest itself from his wounds. "I'm sorry. I feel like I'm failing you. Like I'm failing Jillian."

Damien rung out the towel he'd been using to try and get Kain's wounds to stop bleeding. "You aren't, Kain. Besides, you're so stubborn, I know you'll be back on your feet and ready to fight when the vampires arrive."

Kain chuckled weakly. "You know me well. Almost feels like I'm at a disadvantage."

Damien rolled his eyes at Kain's stubbornness. "I swear if I had a brother in another life, it would be your stupid ass. Now shut up and get some sleep. The sun will set in another hour."

A howl from Clint proved Damien right, the vampires had followed the waning light to the center of the clearing and were demanding a meeting.

Kain forced himself to his feet. "Looks like I won't be getting any sleep."

"Our deal still holds, Alex. You die, I kick your ass."

Lilith stood in front of Stoker on her left, Rayes on her right. Jack Nantucket stood behind her, his eyes full of bloodlust.

The rest of the vampires appeared as though they'd rather have been anywhere else. They stared off into the distance, almost appearing to ignore the wolves in front of them.

Lilith was dressed completely in black leather, her stiletto heel boots matching the dominatrix look she was trying to put on.

Damien stood behind Kain. Holt in the forefront with Gabriel.

"Same deal as last time, mutt. I speak to no one but Damien." Lilith spat, sashaying herself forward, throwing her nose in the air.

Rolling his eyes, Damien went to meet her with Kain and Gabriel close on his flanks. "Lilith, this doesn't have to be this way. We can still walk away and live in peace with one another." Damien spoke with resolve despite the unease he felt inside.

He'd come to love the lycans as his family. Seeing them so unsure, scared and shaking strengthened his determination. He was no longer fighting for himself. He thought of Calen, of Zasha, of Kain and Jill. His child.

"Disgusting. I can see they've softened you. There is no way to end this except what I offered to you not five days ago. I'm hurt you didn't accept my offer by the way." Lilith's words were laced with toxic jealousy.

Silence took over the field. The whistling of the winter snow stung Damien's eyes as he focused on the vampires. The tension in his own body combined with the calm aura he could feel radiating from Kain. His only shield against the cold. *How? How am I able to feel Kain? It's like I'm inside of him and he in me. Is this the connection he spoke of?*

Lilith's shrill voice forced Damien from his thoughts. "Let's get things started shall we? I will take you by force if need be, Damien."

Damien jeered at her. "So be it then. It's your loss Lilith and it sickens me that you're willing to throw the lives of your own people away so easily. The lycans aren't the monsters, you are and it's pathetic you three are so blind to follow her."

Stoker flipped Damien off while Rayes lit a cigarette as though he didn't really care either way. Jack just hissed through his teeth.

"Please. You sound like the weak Purifier rotting inside you. 'My people' as you call them are nothing but tools and they're content to be so for their nobles. That's what makes us so much stronger than you. We aren't afraid to make more if we need them and lay them down when we don't. Like your sad excuse for a friend, Chelsea."

Damien growled at the disrespect Lilith was showing. He could see clearly there was no reasoning with the cold bitch. He slowed his breathing, letting Tenebris' peace take over his burning soul.

He turned to the lycans behind him.

Taking a deep breath for courage, he spoke up. "I've been asked to speak to all of you for almost five days. I know you're scared, you're unsure, you're shaking. It's not me you should be looking to but the desire inside of each of you to protect those you love and who are in danger. Those that can't defend themselves who just want to live in peace. Those are the ones you should look to for encouragement. They are why you're here fighting. Not me. I'm broken, I'm imperfect and have long looked towards the leaders here for mentoring and guidance. So, fight for those that can't do it for themselves."

The wolves stood silent for a while only to erupt with howls in agreement and renewed determination.

"Well said, my lord." Kain said, bowing.

"Kain, don't. You know how I feel about that title."

Kain shrugged. "I know but it's still fun to haze you. Technically you are still a newborn."

Damien heard Lilith as she commanded Stoker and Rayes to bring him to her beaten and broken.

"Let's end this." Gabriel was the first to break out of the starting line, shifting mid-run as he made straight for Stoker.

Kain shifted followed closely by Damien who sprinted before the alpha towards Lilith.

Holt ran at Rayes while Lune kept close to Gabriel to aid him in case he needed help with Stoker.

Lilith's claws struck Damien across the face sending him skidding on all fours across the ground. He barely had time to react before she slammed his skull into the ground. Her hand caressed his side. Her fingers gripped his fur with such force it made him whimper.

"You can still be mine. I'm willing to forgive you if you become my personal slave." Her words were like poison in his veins, the heat of her breath sickening to him.

Damien growled, snapping as he struggled against Lilith's strength.

Kain slammed his full body into the vampire sending her tumbling and rolling across the grass.

"Alexander Kain!" Lilith's voice was almost a high pitch scream as her hate for Kain manifested itself.

The alpha panted against his wounds, shaking his body to try and keep going. Kain rose up in his full lycan form. The shift smooth in its transition.

Lilith glared at him. "You know what I'm capable of, Alexander. From the looks of you, I can tell you won't last long. The last of your nauseatingly annoying line dies today!"

Damien watched as Lilith took off her leather jacket revealing a backless leather shirt. Thin leathery wings tore from her flesh of her back. Her shoulders rippled into broad muscles. Her arms bulked up to support her wings.

Lilith bent over at her waist as her legs warped and distorted into those resembling a lycan. Her ears rose stiff towards the sky, her teeth elongating to fit into a squatty muzzle.

She looked like a female version of the dark god. Her warm breath met the cold wind forming thick steam flowing from her bat-like nostrils. Her chest puffed out as she showed off her full glory.

"Now Kain, you die."

Damien was surprised, she could actually still talk. Her voice held two tones. One the vampire she was, the other a darkened echo of the beast she became.

Damien wondered if lycans could do the same.

Angry, Kain roared at her only to be answered with her own just like in Damien's vision.

Lilith launched towards the sky, diving to slam her full weight into Kain. The ground below him shattered around him as he struggled to hold her back.

Damien got up to try to help Kain only to be kicked so hard by Lilith he whimpered and was sent flying. He shook his head against the dizziness.

God, it felt like getting hit by a train. Kain's words suddenly made sense.

As soon as his vision cleared, Damien's eyes widened in horror at what he saw. Lilith had Kain pinned down and was hitting him over and over again.

The alpha howled in agony as his flesh was slashed repeatedly, struggling against the weakness of his wounds to try to recover from his present position.

Something inside shattered when Damien's eyes met Kain's as though he were telling him goodbye. He grew still, only soft whimpers could be heard as he lay in the cold bleeding.

Damien let out a piercing howl, gaining the attention of everyone on the field. They froze as Lilith walked over to him. The two leaders circled each other in preparation for their conflict.

"Finally. That wretched line will never bother me again."

Realization hit Damien as to who he was staring down. The same dark god that had challenged him stood in Lilith's form. Damien's heart inside his chest burned as he thought about Kain and all he'd done for him. *Jill. Dad...Rob...Gabriel...Holt...Chelsea.*

"Looks like it's just you and me, Damien. You can surrender and die in peace or you can fight and die anyway. Your choice."

Save him. Luna's voice inside of Damien's mind drew his attention. *Save him. I beg of you. Please.*

Damien's body became surrounded with a radiant light so bright it forced Lilith step back. Her wing covered her face. He braced himself on his front legs, roaring at the monster in front of him responsible for taking so much.

The light became so intense not even the lycans could stare at it.

When it finally faded, Damien stood in his true lycan form. His white fur blew in the wind like mist at the tip of his stiffened ears to the end of his tail. The dark markings of his wolf form only seen on the tips of his ears, feet and tail. The fur on the back of his neck was thicker, almost resembling a mane.

"By the gods, he looks like..." Lune stood in awe.

"Tenebris." Gabriel's finished, his voice nothing but a whisper.

265

Stoker used the opportunity to sneak off, nursing the wound on his arm inflicted by Gabriel when he shifted into his full lycan form.

The vampires hissed at the light rising from the east, trying to flee towards the waning night. They had fallen right into Damien's plan and were intercepted. Howls and snarls joined dying screams as the vampires were overwhelmed.

"What trickery is this?!" Lilith's fangs spat as she tried to speak.

Damien ignored her, seeing the fear in her eyes as he made his way over to Kain on the ground.

The alpha was so weak he couldn't retain his shifted form.

"Kain." Damien's voice was a comfortable echo. Warm and reassuring. "Alex. Can you hear me?"

Kain opened his eyes, slightly jumping. "Tenebris?"

Damien shook his head. "No. It's me."

"Damien. How?"

Damien took Kain's jacket he was always wearing around his waist and covered his friend with it. "Stay here. Don't move and don't die."

He stood back up and went to face Lilith. The lycans in his way stepped aside, their heads bowed. "This ends here, Lilith. You won't hurt anyone else."

Lilith laughed, slightly shaking. "You think you can defeat me? Take the form of your weak god, I don't care. You're nowhere close to my skills in your full form."

"Pathetic."

Lilith stopped laughing, her glare intense as her eyes began glowing an angry red. "What did you just dare to call me?"

"You heard me." Damien braced himself as the vampire took to the sky. He closed his eyes as he focused on each of her wing beats in the darkness.

The soft voices of the fallen; vampire and lycan alike, filled his ears as they begged him to help them.

Damien whipped around, taking the defensive stance Kain taught him.

Lilith reached out her talons ready to slash them across his face to blind him. He weaved effortlessly through her talons, his own silver nails raking across her throat, tearing it open. The black blood splattered across his muzzle.

Lilith fell to the ground shrieking and thrashing as she shifted back to her more human form. She choked on her own black blood, trying to catch a breath. "I...don't understand. You're...a newborn. How?"

With ease, Damien shifted from lycan form to human form and knelt beside the dying noble.

He answered her, his voice gentle and saddened. "I didn't fight for myself, Lilith. I had others who needed me more. Your people aren't tools for you to throw their lives away. Vampire or lycan, we are both living beings in one way or another. That's something I think you learned too late."

The sun peaked over the mountains, piercing through the dark clouds, warming the clearing. Lilith's body joined the countless others, turning to ash in the rising light.

Gabriel limped over to Kain with Lune. They helped him to his feet as Gabriel bent down for Kain to get on his back. Lune nuzzled Damien's hand, softly whimpering. Damien patted his dark grey fur.

Cade walked up to them, his head lowered. "Holt..."

The alphas looked at each other, then at Damien.

They made their way across the battlefield where Holt lay in the snow, his stomach torn open almost deep enough to empty it. Damien closed the fallen alpha's eyes while the lycans all howled a sorrowful cry at the loss of their leader.

Rayes' knife lay in the snow not far from Holt's body covered in ash. From the looks of it they wound up killing each other in their fight.

The rest of the morning was spent burying the fallen lycans. There hadn't been many but, each life was still a loss.

Kain had been put on Damien's back at his request for the journey back to the campsite.

When they arrived, the females, pups and lycans unable to fight all crowded around them.

Leah ran up to Cade. When he lowered his head, she started sobbing into his chest. He held her in such a loving way, Damien couldn't believe it was still Cade. He hadn't seen him show any affection or heard him speak until the battle.

Damien took Kain to his tent where Kyle waited. He dropped to his belly to let Kyle take Kain off of him. His white fur stained with blood. He left to let Kyle work.

There was a beautiful, pregnant woman he wanted to see more than anything.

Jill was lying on the floor of their tent in her wolf skin. From the looks of the wet fur on her cheeks she'd been crying.

"Jill."

Jill's ears perked up when she heard his voice. Shifting quickly, she threw herself into her lover's chest. "Damien! Oh, thank Luna!"

"Ow. Easy on the ribs." Damien lowered his eyes, his heart aching at the loss of Holt. "Holt's dead."

"Oh, dear Luna," Jill's voice was saddened. She remembered Holt's broad smile, his boisterous laugh and how drunk he would get during the lycan festivals. "Does Leah know?"

"Cade's with her. He went down taking out Rayes. From the looks of it, they killed each other."

Jill hugged Damien close to her, taking his mouth in a deep, passionate kiss, her tongue tasting him as if it were their first kiss. "I want you later, my love. I won't take no for an answer."

"You won't have to. Just let me check on Kain." Damien chuckled, kissing her again.

Kyle had Kain's body wrapped up from his shoulder all the way down to his stomach.

"He was lucky you got to him when you did, Damien. He was torn up worse than I've ever seen him. One of these days his luck's going to run out."

"Thanks Kyle. I'll take care of him from here." Damien shook Kyle's hand, shocked when the lycan bowed to him and walked out.

Don't think I'm ever going to get used to that. Damien thought, making his way over to Kain's side.

"Well you didn't die but, you got damn close." Damien chuckled at the look on Kain's face.

"Fang off, Damien. I've had a long last two nights," Kain rested his arm over his eyes, appearing annoyed at his friend's mocking. "What was that, by the way? I saw a blaring light and then you were in your true form."

"I'm not sure. I just thought about how I didn't want to fail you, Jill, Gabriel and the others. The next thing I knew I was standing on two legs and killing a vampire that looked like a bat-wolf," Damien still couldn't grasp what happened but he was glad it was over. At least for now. "So, what now?"

"Now? I'm thinking about taking a long ass break. Get fat on pheasants and catch up on some football."

Damien chuckled, fighting the urge to burst out laughing. "Somehow Kain, I don't think you would let yourself get fat first of all and second, I had no idea you even liked football."

"What guy doesn't? But seriously though, I'm probably going to be taking a long break from everything. Too many close calls since you showed up," Kain chuckled at the look of disbelief on Damien's face. "What about you? What are your plans?"

Jill walked into Kain's tent, her hand resting on her stomach. She'd developed a small bump over the past few weeks. She knelt beside her mate, resting her head on his shoulder.

"Me? Think I might just settle down with my mate and when the time comes, be the proud father of some rowdy pups." Damien kissed Jill.

"Sounds like a plan. Now go get a room you two, I'm catching some sleep." Kain rolled over on his side to get some well-deserved rest.

Damien didn't wait long to take Jill to their bed after stripping them both down. "Thank you, Jill."

"For what?" Jill replied, petting his face.

"For staying with me as long as you did. You saved my life."

Jill smiled, kissing Damien's lips. "You're welcome. Do you think it's over? Can we finally have peace?"

"For now, I think we can." Damien curled up with his lover under the blankets, his heart filled with more peace than he'd ever felt since his mother died.

The rage of the dark god was finally purged from his body. The fear and loneliness replaced with the comfortable light of the moon...

And You Probably thought it was over!
Don't miss the Exciting Sequel in the *Wolfgods* series:

BANE
OF
TENEBRIS

A lexander Kain had grown weary of the constant threat of war. After the battle at the Circle of Stones, he decides it's time to take a break.

Unknown but to a certain few of those close to him, Alexander comes from a long line of "shadow" sacrifices for the royal line of lycans. It has brought him to the brink of death which leads him to seek out isolation.

When Kain does the unthinkable, the gods decide it's time to intervene on his behalf.

Things change further with the arrival of the beautiful and mysterious hybrid, Tala whom Kain is led to by the gods, beaten and left for dead in the woods.

With the growing threat of a new and more powerful enemy, Kain must not only have to come face to face with a past he's long tried to hide but also cope with the looming desires he's developing for Tala. Feelings that carry an internal struggle against the Bane on his family.

ACKNOWLEDGEMENTS

I would like to start by thanking God for the gifts I've been blessed with. A family that loves me, friends who are there to help me.

My husband, John, for his continued support even though I know this really wasn't his kind of thing. Damien wouldn't be who is without you. You are an inspiration for his quarks and his damage but also his strength in times of trial.

My kids: Amberrose and Grant for putting up with the overtime and sudden deadlines. I know there were tons of hours you wanted my attention but thank you for understanding, even if you are both so young.

My mom, Shannon and dad, Long who are proud of this achievement and for keeping the kids when I needed to pull an all-nighter. Even though you may not like the genre. Lol.

I want to thank Alisha Fisher for being such an inspiration to me and the support system I needed when I wanted to give up.

To Darci Steele for editing the tar out of the manuscript and offering feedback. My beta readers who served as the eyes and ears of the *Wolfgods*, thank you all. I will definitely be reaching out to all of you.

Kristin Martin and Kim Chance, we may not know each other personally but you two wonderful women have been inspirations and leaders in my life. The positive outlook you have, the passion you show for your books and the world of authors and literature and the overwhelmingly constructive advice you continue to give lit a fire under my rump I have needed for a long time. Thank you for doing what you do.

I want to thank the beta readers who devoted your time to help me get this book finished. Your feedback helped *Blessing of Luna* become something it would have taken me a long time to do on my own. You guys are my front lines, without you, I don't think this book would have become what it is.

Finally to my followers and friends on social media. You are more valued than you know.

Thank you all for your support. I hope you will return for part two: *Bane of Tenebris*.

ABOUT THE AUTHOR

FyreSyde Publishing owner and founder Blaise Ramsay worked over fifteen years in the graphic design industry, with some experience in indie gaming. Recently she shifted her attention to the world of literature with her debut paranormal romance series, *Wolfgods*. The debut title, *Blessing of Luna* is set to release in 2018. She currently lives in North Texas with her two children, her husband and pets. A UTD graduate with a Bachelor's in History with an intention on teaching, Blaise decided that the world of teaching just wasn't for her. A stay at home mother of two, business owner and self-publisher, Blaise loves to meet new people and encourage others to follow their dreams . When she's not writing, she spends her time baking, cooking, cleaning and reading. Always reading.

For more information please feel free to visit FyreSyde's website:
www.fyresydepublishing.com

NOTE FROM THE AUTHOR

Word-of-mouth is crucial for any author to succeed. If you enjoyed *Blessing of Luna*, please leave a review online—anywhere you are able. Even if it's just a sentence or two. It would make all the difference and would be very much appreciated.

Thanks!
Blaise

Thank you so much for reading one of Blaise Ramsay's novels.

If you enjoyed the experience, please check out
the next book in the *Wolfgods* series!

Bane of Tenebris by Blaise Ramsay

"A fast-moving story of love, war, and curses."
-Cranky TBC

View other Black Rose Writing titles at
www.blackrosewriting.com/books and use promo code
PRINT to receive a **20% discount** when purchasing.